The
Main
Corpse

Also by
Diane Mott Davidson

Catering to Nobody
Dying for Chocolate
The Cereal Murders
The Last Suppers
Killer Pancake

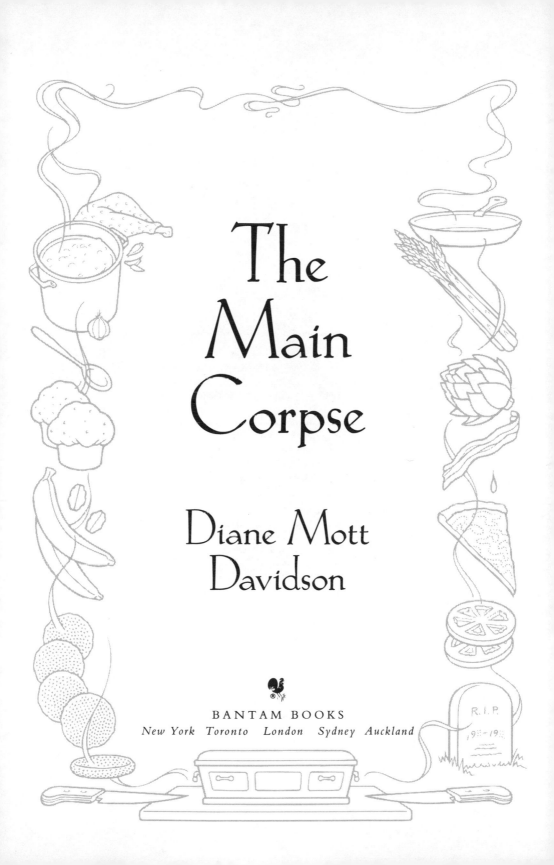

The
Main
Corpse

Diane Mott Davidson

BANTAM BOOKS
New York   Toronto   London   Sydney   Auckland

THE MAIN CORPSE

A Bantam Book / October 1996

Book design by Donna Sinisgalli

Library of Congress Cataloging-in-Publication Data
Davidson, Diane Mott.
The main corpse / Diane Mott Davidson.
p.   cm.
ISBN 0-553-09999-X
I. Title.
PS3554.A925M35   1996
813'.54—dc20   96-23042
                                                    CIP
                                                    AC

Published simultaneously in the United States and Canada

Bantam Books are published by Bantam Books, a division of Bantam
Doubleday Dell Publishing Group, Inc. Its trademark, consisting of the
words "Bantam Books" and the portrayal of a rooster, is Registered in U.S.
Patent and Trademark Office and in other countries. Marca Registrada.
Bantam Books, 1540 Broadway, New York, New York 10036.

PRINTED IN THE UNITED STATES OF AMERICA

BVG   0 9 8 7 6 5 4 3 2 1

To our dear children,
Jeffrey, J.Z., and Joe

The author wishes to acknowledge the help of the following people: Jim, Jeff, J.Z., and Joe Davidson; Kate Miciak, a brilliant editor; Sandra Dijkstra, an extraordinary agent; Lee Karr and the group that assembles at her home; John Schenk and Karen Johnson, J. William's Catering, Bergen Park, Colorado; Deidre Elliott and Kathcrine Goodwin Saideman, for their careful reading of the manuscript; Janet Alexander, a friend who gave support as well as the title; Lucy Mott Faison, Sally Mott Lawrence, and Bill Mott, Jr., for loaning their kitchens for recipe-testing; Mark D. Wittry, M.D., Assistant Professor of Internal Medicine, St. Louis University Health Sciences Center; Carmen Laronn, M.D.; Richard L. Staller, D.D.; Emyl Jenkins; Carol Devine Rusley; Joanne P. Smith; Spike Christensen; Sandra Dallas; Mr. and Mrs. James Hartley; Mark A. Bowron, Vice-President and General Manager, Alma American Mining Corporation; Jack Hiatt, Office of the Attorney General, Santa Fe, New Mexico; Robert T. Ammann, C.F.A., Equity Analyst, Founders Asset Management, Inc.; Susan Conant, for dog food research; Bob Springsteel, Theatrics, Inc.; David Harris, Colorado School of Mines; Martha Poley, Carl Mount, and William York-Fiern, Office of Active and Inactive Mines, Colorado Division of Minerals and Geology; David M. Abbott, Jr., Senior Associate, Behre Dolbear and Company,

Inc., formerly regional geologist, U.S. Securities and Exchange Commission; William Butler, Butler Research and Investigations; Paula Millsapps, Bookkeeping Supervisor, FirstBank; and as always, Investigator Richard Millsapps, Jefferson County Sheriff's Department, Golden, Colorado, for patiently providing invaluable assistance and insights.

"The service a man renders his friend is trivial and selfish compared with the service he knows his friend stood in readiness to yield him. . . ."

—RALPH WALDO EMERSON, "Gifts"

The
Main
Corpse

Prospect Financial Partners
Luxury Beer and Hors D'Oeuvre Party

◆

EURYDICE GOLD MINE, IDAHO SPRINGS, COLORADO

SATURDAY, JUNE 5

◆

Chinese Shrimp Dumplings

Tomato-Brie Pie

Crab Quesadillas

Giant Mushrooms Stuffed with Chicken Sausage

Bacon-Wrapped Artichokes with Dijon Cream Sauce

Assorted Beers, Ales, Wheats, and Stouts

White Chocolate Truffles, Gold Foil-Wrapped Fudge Bars

French Roast Coffee

Chapter 1

Sometimes you'd kill for a booking. I was ready—I'd had a rotten spring. The lack of business meant I spent afternoons frantically scrolling through my client files. Wasn't the Hard-castles' daughter supposed to get married? Didn't they want me to do the reception? And what about the Garden Club brunch, Newcomers' picnic, and Kiwanians' First-of-Summer barbe-cue? In terms of scheduled events, these last two months were the worst in the five years since I'd become a professional ca-terer. It wasn't just a rotten spring: It was disastrous.

The problem, everyone said, was the weather. From the middle of March until now, the beginning of June, maddening, endless rain and snow had assaulted the Colorado high country. The Audubon Society announced that birds migrating north had overflown the state completely. Drownings were up, land-slides were up, catered events were way, way down. The clubs had all canceled their outdoor events, and the Hardcastles' daughter was on Prozac.

I set aside the dumpling dough I was kneading and looked out my kitchen window. Morning fog shrouded the mountains of the Aspen Meadow Wildlife Preserve. In a recent empty moment—I was having lots of those lately—I'd read an article in which a psychiatrist claimed people actually eat *more* during long bouts of depressing weather. But if folks dig into whole grilled swordfish and soup bowls of chocolate mousse during gray-day melancholy, then caterers should hit the jackpot when it pours, right? Reading the article, I'd known in my heart the shrink's argument was wrong. Now, I finally had the bank statement to prove it.

I rolled the dough to razor-thinness. It wasn't the lack of income that bothered me so much. After all, I'd been married to a man with a regular paycheck for just over a year. But second-time-around connubial bliss was one thing. Financial independence was another. Since I'd had five years of being on my own, to have my business fail would be *mortifying*. I whacked the next batch of dough with my rolling pin. To lose Goldilocks' Catering would be *unthinkable*.

Thank goodness my best friend had come to the rescue— bless her large, recovering-from-cardiac-arrest heart. In her midforties and ultrawealthy, Marla Korman was the other ex-wife of my ex-husband—known to both of us as the Jerk. When my business began to falter, Marla wanted to extend me a business loan. Very firmly, I'd said thank you, but no. Next she offered to have a venture capital firm—Prospect Financial Partners, in which she had more than a passing interest—analyze Goldilocks' Catering as an investment prospect. To this I'd also given a polite no thanks. If too many cooks spoiled the broth, there was no telling what a venture capital firm could do to a catering business. But then Marla had the devious but brilliant idea of booking me to do a celebratory event for Prospect Financial Partners. How could I say no? So this afternoon, I was catering a heartwarmingly profitable luxury beer-and-hors d'oeuvre affair for the venture capitalists—at an extremely unusual site.

I eased up on the rolling pin and pictured the venue for the party: the portal opening to the Eurydice Gold Mine. Of course, the party wasn't being held *in* the old mine, but under a tent erected at its entrance. And I was grateful for the last-minute booking, even if the firm had called on me in a state of panic. No question about it, Prospect Financial Partners needed a social bash. In the worst way.

The firm had been in an uproar the last few weeks over the unexpected death of their chief investment officer. In what I viewed as peculiar hard-heartedness, clients had flooded the firm with unsympathetic calls to find out how Victoria Lear's dying would affect their *portfolios*. In particular, the clients demanded, would the fact that CIO Lear was gone to that great securities exchange in the sky postpone the scheduled reopening of the Eurydice? The partners had assured their nervous investors that plans to capitalize the reopening of the gold mine were absolutely on track, despite the unscheduled demise of Victoria Lear. But chaos and uncertainty are not easily quelled, especially when money is involved. Prospect's clients were close to rebellion, otherwise known as *pulling out*.

Finally, Marla had convinced the Prospect partners that it would be marvelous fun—not to mention a break from the crisis atmosphere at the firm—to do a catered affair next to the Eurydice portal. Wine and dine 'em, she'd said, and they'll forget their uneasiness about Victoria's death. And she, Marla, had the perfect caterer for the occasion. . . . With the temperature hovering in the low fifties and rain and hail threatening, it wasn't a place *I* would have chosen for a party. But I assured the Prospect firm of my ability to adapt. When the rain arrived, I told them, we could make like rich Arabs and huddle under our tent.

Marla had a large portfolio with Prospect. More significantly, she was in the fifteenth month of a rocky romantic involvement with Prospect's financial whiz, Tony Royce, one of the two partner-owners of the venture capital firm. Clever, intense, and perpetually well-dressed, Tony had been with Marla constantly through the darkest days of her illness almost a year ago. But rumors abounded of how handsome, dark-haired Tony had dated other women before and after Marla's hospitalization. The gossip mill even worked overtime spreading a kinky tale concerning Tony's relationship with a certain Vegas stripper. A couple of months ago, Marla had heard of Tony's wanderings. She'd told him she'd remain a Prospect client, but her heart couldn't take him seeing other women. She'd ended their relationship. Secretly, I was glad. I didn't want my best friend with *another* jerk.

In May, however, Tony had repented. He swore a very public, ceaseless devotion to Marla. Even I was impressed. I'd desperately hoped they'd celebrate their new togetherness with lovely, intimate dinners catered by yours truly. But no.

Ever one to combine business with pleasure, this last month Tony had taken Marla to every restaurant where the Prospect Partners were thinking of putting their money. Marla regaled me with stories about this panorama of eatery outings, where she would muse over the food—delicious, unusual, or just plain weird. Tony assessed each restaurant's ability to attract diners. After the mine venture, Tony told her, Prospect was going to diversify by putting capital into a restaurant with regional expansion plans. But when Marla's cardiologist had heard she was taste-testing hollandaise sauce and deep-dish pizza all over the state, he'd put an immediate stop to this particular type of financial analysis.

"Tony and I are in love," Marla had confided to me when she made the booking. "It's the real thing, Goldy."

"Is he going to find someone else to do his taste-testing?"

"He says so," she'd dreamily replied. "But he needs me now more than ever. For moral support. He's so distraught over the firm's loss of Victoria."

I said nothing. I didn't want to be reminded. I couldn't think of Victoria Lear's death without shuddering.

An avid off-roader, Chief Investment Officer Lear had lost control of her car while negotiating narrow, precarious Orpheus Canyon Road. Orpheus Canyon, two miles east of the Eurydice Mine, snaked through the mountains between Idaho Springs and Central City, another old mining town that now featured legalized gambling. The dirt road's precipitous drop-offs frequently claimed drivers who made the smallest miscalculation of the road's lethal curves. No one had seen Victoria Lear's Toyota Land Cruiser dive off the mud-slick road. It had been a week before her body had been discovered within the gnarled wreckage. There had been little forensic evidence to recover. The constant rain on the dirt road had obliterated the Toyota's tracks. Three days ago, the Clear Creek County coroner had ruled her death accidental.

"Prospect Financial needs to make everything appear normal," Marla claimed over the phone. "That's why they loved my idea of having the party up at the mine. To show the investors they're in control."

Pondering all this, I sighed and cut the delicate dumpling dough into squares. I sautéed morsels of fresh shrimp with scallion, water chestnut, and soy sauce. *In control of what,* I had wanted to ask, but had not. The mouth-watering odors of Chinese food filled the kitchen. When the shrimp had cooked to a succulent pink, I turned the mixture out to cool and started slicing thick slabs of tomato for the tomato-Brie pie.

Really, I reminded myself, I had enough problems of my own without worrying about Marla's romantic and financial interests. With the Jerk leaving his medical practice to his colleagues so he could take a sabbatical—otherwise known as *can't-stand-the-Colorado-weather-need-lengthy-vacation-in-Hawaii*— Marla and I had lost the person we loved to complain about most. And then there was my dear husband Tom, who had a whole plateful of problems all to himself, in which the death of Victoria Lear played a significant part.

I cut wedges of creamy Brie and alternated them with the tomato slices. Tom called this particular dish heart-attack-on-a-plate, so I would never serve it to Marla. I grated pungent Fontinella to sprinkle over the Brie. I wouldn't give it to Tom either, as I was extremely worried that his current job situation might lead to heart-attack-at-the-office.

Tom had been an investigator at the Furman County Sheriff's Department for more than a decade. His problem was his new boss. Five years from retirement, Captain Augustus Shockley was so paranoid he stayed locked in his office most of the day. Tom had taken to slipping his notes and reports under Shockley's door. In his two months as chief honcho, the only thing Shockley had seemed able to do was to move totally incompetent people into positions where they swiftly managed to drive Tom insane. Shockley had also, as it turned out, placed his retirement savings with Prospect Financial Partners, and he'd become obsessed with Victoria Lear's car accident. *Check it out, Schulz! Go investigate the site!* Shockley's frantic memos to Tom had ignored the fact that the steep, rain-soaked crash site was virtually unreachable. The memos also ignored the fact that Idaho Springs was in Clear Creek County and outside of Furman County jurisdiction—thus, not Tom's problem. Nevertheless, Tom had been in contact with his counterpart, the Homicide Investigator at the Clear Creek Sheriff's Department. As a result, Tom had been one of the first people the coroner had called with his report. *This isn't very helpful,* Shockley had scrawled across Tom's summary of the fatal wreck. I often thought my handsome husband resembled a bear. Now, with Augustus Shockley to deal with, he was beginning to act like one.

But, I thought as I whisked eggs with whipping cream, I was looking forward to tonight, after the party. Tom and I would toast the financial turnaround Goldilocks' Catering was making with the Prospect event. The party by the mine was going to be marvelous, I told myself confidently. I'd worked hard on recipes, I'd gathered mountains of fresh ingredients. Since my former in-house assistant, Julian Teller, had moved to upstate New York to attend Cornell, I'd hired another helper. Macguire Perkins had been one of Julian's classmates at Elk Park Preparatory School. For the party at the gold mine, Macguire had ordered beers, ales, stouts, and wheats—brewed beverages for aficionados. And I'd begun to cook with gusto.

A rental company was setting up the tent early this morning. The electricity wired to the mine would provide power for a compact disc player and rented portable ovens, which the same workers would place behind a makeshift counter at the back tent flap, all ready to use when I arrived this afternoon. Getting up the narrow dirt road to the mine, which was situated five miles above Idaho Springs, wouldn't be quite as convenient. High Creek Avenue did not wind and dip as dangerously as Orpheus Canyon Road, but first-time visitors to the mine were bound to be spooked. The invitations warned the guests to come in four-wheel-drive vehicles and to maneuver their vehicles with care. I prayed that the rental company folks had made it. The specter of Victoria Lear's car catapulting off a cliff had propelled me to do a very slow dry-run trek in my van the previous day. Yesterday's run, of course, had been anything but dry. To get from my house in Aspen Meadow to the mine—fifteen miles away—took Marla and me nearly an hour. We bumped across wooden bridges spanning rain-swollen creeks and rocked through deep mud on mountain roads. If the catering didn't work out, I'd told Marla on our way back home, I could always become a Sherpa.

I wrapped spoonfuls of the shrimp filling in dough packets and set them aside. Then I quartered artichoke bottoms and skewered them with the bacon slices. These would sizzle and bubble in one of the portable ovens until Macguire and I served them with Dijon mustard judiciously thinned with whipping cream. I took a greedy whiff of fresh cilantro, then sliced a pile of it to go into the salsa for the crab quesadillas.

As I began to fold the quesadillas, I wished for the hundredth time that I, too, had been able to invest with Prospect Financial Partners. Marla swore she'd made a nest egg fit for a hen of any size. To prove it she'd bought, in addition to her Jaguar, a Mercedes that boasted four-wheel drive. When I doubted Tony would accept a client with so little money, Marla laughingly replied that I could always approach the *other* partner, Albert Lipscomb. Albert would take on anyone, as long as he or she listened to his reasons for investing in a company. *All* his reasons. Albert, she laughed, made life-insurance salesmen look like stand-up comics. I envisioned a public reading of the Dead Sea Scrolls, and said no thanks.

I smiled and topped the Fontinella with glossy dark leaves of aromatic basil, then poured on a lake of cream beaten with eggs. Prospect was struggling with its image, Marla was trying to cope, Tom had a horrid boss, and my business was faltering. But I was cooking. *Big-time.* As always, working with food soothed my nerves and made all mundane problems appear faraway, or at least on the other side of the Continental Divide. When I brought the spicy chicken sausage to sizzling and gently stuffed it into giant mushroom caps, I felt a rush of joy. I was so happy I whistled, which brought our new dog, Jake, loping into the room. At Jake's heels was my son Arch, who had turned fourteen on the snowiest, coldest day of April. The dog skidded to a stop and bumped into my leg. I begged Arch to take Jake—a tawny, ungainly, oversized bloodhound—away. Jake's claws scrabbled across the kitchen floor as he recovered his balance, raised his deeply furrowed brow, and gazed at me with droopy, bloodshot eyes that appeared deeply, deeply hurt.

I shook my head. "Teach him to play dead, or something, while I finish the food for the Prospect shindig. *Please.*"

Arch straightened his tortoiseshell glasses on his freckled nose. His eyes were reproachful. "If you don't want Jake to come, Mom, then you *shouldn't whistle.*"

I hugged him and apologized. When Julian Teller had been boarding with us, he had been like a big brother to my son. Now, Arch missed Julian more than any of us. The new dog, I told myself, was a welcome substitute for the much-admired friend. Despite my warnings about the weather, Arch and Jake took off on a long hike. Arch told me not to worry. He thought the sky was clearing.

By early afternoon, however, icy raindrops fell in a chilling,

Tomato-Brie Pie

Crust:

1¾ cups all-purpose flour
¾ teaspoon sugar
¼ teaspoon salt
¼ cup chilled lard, cut into pieces
6 tablespoons chilled unsalted butter,
    cut into pieces
1–3 tablespoons ice water

Preheat the oven to 350°. Place the flour, sugar, and salt into the bowl of a food processor fitted with the steel blade. Process 5 seconds, then add the lard, process until the mixture is like cornmeal (10 seconds), then add the butter and process until the mixture resembles large crumbs (10 seconds). Add the water one tablespoon at a time, pulsing quickly just until the mixture holds together. Roll the dough out between sheets of wax paper to fit into a buttered 9-inch pie pan. Prick the dough and flute the edges. Bake the crust for 5 to 7 minutes, or until it is an even, pale gold. Set aside on a rack while preparing the filling.

Filling:

1½ pounds (5 medium-size) ripe tomatoes, trimmed but not peeled, cut into eighths, seed pockets removed

5 ounces Brie cheese, rind scraped off, cut into small cubes

2 ounces best-quality fresh mozzarella cheese, cut into small cubes

1 ounce Fontinella cheese, cut into small cubes

⅓ cup chopped fresh basil

3 large eggs

⅓ cup heavy cream

⅓ cup milk

Preheat the oven to 350°. Drain the tomatoes thoroughly on paper towels. Place the cheese cubes evenly around the prepared crust. Place the tomatoes on top of the cheese, and top with the basil. Beat the eggs, cream, and milk, and pour this mixture over the tomatoes, basil, and cheese. Place in the oven and bake 35 to 50 minutes, until center is set. Allow pie to cool 10 minutes before serving.

Serves 6.

slashing curtain. To arrive early enough for the Prospect party, I allowed an extra half-hour of travel time and secured pan after pan of the expensive appetizers into a Cambro, a heavy plastic stacking device that locks into place on my van floor. When I inched my vehicle onto Aspen Meadow's Main Street, I winced at the sight and sound of Cottonwood Creek. Our normally placid, usually picturesque tributary of the South Platte River had developed into a roaring, turgid beast. In fact, the rain had turned our whole town into a mud pit. The shoulders of all the mountain roads oozed mire. Streamfront properties, usually highly prized, became disaster areas when the creeks had crested their banks. As the van rocked forward behind a line of cars, I fretted about the appetizers tilting inside the Cambro, not to mention the trays on the overhead racks. Cleaning up six dozen meticulously layered quesadillas from the floor of my van was not my idea of a good time.

Unsurprisingly, traffic in Idaho Springs was detoured. I prayed the bungee cords would hold the trays in place as I piloted my trusty vehicle over rocks and through silt to avoid a road crew. Sporting fluorescent life vests and calf-deep in mud, workmen pulled debris from a plugged culvert. I inched forward and tried not to imagine my platters of savory hors d'oeuvre skimming down the rapids.

At last, I pulled up to the sheds in front of the Eurydice Mine. No one else had arrived, so I parked the van and rushed through the rain with the first plastic-wrapped platters. Once under the tent, I scanned the dark interior until I turned on the tent lamps and spotted the portable ovens. I heaved the trays onto the makeshift counter, checked the ovens, then switched them on. I paused to look around. A string of light bulbs that went back as far as the eye could see illuminated the railroad track that led into the depths of the old mine. The light bulbs had been strung beside the track for the Prospect investors' tour of the Eurydice in May. I fought off a shiver.

"There's a superstition about women in mines," Marla had told me after she returned from the tour. "We're supposed to be bad luck. 'Women prohibited for decades!' they told us before we went in. Poor Edna Hardcastle showed why by promptly having a claustrophobia attack. Got fifty feet inside and threw up."

Maybe I was better off with savings bonds.

I pulled my eyes away from the dark portal of the mine, which seemed to leak cold, dank air, and nipped back and forth through the downpour to unload more trays. Ten minutes later, Macguire roared up in his Subaru. Lanky, acne-scarred, and endearingly unambitious, Macguire was the son of the headmaster of Elk Park Prep. Macguire was taking what was euphemistically called a "year off," while he lifted weights, did odd jobs, and occasionally attempted to decide what to do with the rest of his life. He wasn't too adept at the food biz. But he could carry heavy trays. And he liked people. From my point of view, that was half the battle.

"Hey, Goldy." His tall body curled out of the Subaru and he smiled crookedly, squinting against the rain. He wore an unbuttoned, too-large, yellow plastic slicker he'd probably scrounged from the Elk Park Prep lost-and-found. But the gaping slicker revealed that he had remembered to wear black pants and a white shirt, a good sign. "The beers are gonna be late," he informed me. He shook his short, wiry red hair. Droplets skittered through the damp air. "It was all the truck driver could do to get up Marla's driveway. When she told him he needed to come up a dirt road leading out of Idaho Springs, he said, Forget that! So she bribed him to put a few cases into the trunk of her Mercedes. Tony could only get a couple into his

Miata, and Albert's going over to get the rest in his Explorer. Marla is not happy. But I told her, hey! You know, it's like the bumper sticker, sh—"

"No," I interrupted him. I put the covered platter of quesadillas I was holding down on the van floor and held up one hand. "Need to change your thinking, Macguire. Clients cuss. Caterers don't."

He grinned good-naturedly, released the lock, and heaved up the Cambro. "Your clients are going to cuss *a lot* if they get up here and don't have anything to drink. Anyway, I really need to talk to Marla before the festivities get started. She here yet?"

Even as he spoke, we heard the distinctive growl of the Mercedes. Marla emerged from her shiny new car in a cloud of dark green silk dotted with gold. She shook her fist dramatically at the weeping clouds and struggled to open her new Louis Vuitton umbrella. Although she'd only lost about ten pounds since the heart attack, she swore she was exercising regularly, eating virtuously, and not losing her temper more than once a month. As she merrily trundled toward us through the downpour, I doubted all three.

"Darlings," she exclaimed extravagantly once she was under the tent. She closed the umbrella with a flourish and shook it. The bright gold barrettes holding her unruly brown curls in place twinkled in the light of the rented tent lamps. She sniffed at the delicious aromas seeping from the ovens. "Let's indulge! Correction: Let's unload this designer beer, and *then* indulge. Ah, Macguire," she trilled, "you left a message saying you had something for me?"

"I do," he muttered. His face darkened with uncertainty. "But I don't think you're going to like it."

"You don't think she's going to like what?" I asked as I whisked the mustard and cream for the bacon appetizers.

But Marla reopened the umbrella, walked with Macguire to his car, and ignored me. The rain continued to pelt down, so I couldn't hear what the two of them were saying as they huddled next to the Subaru and spoke in confidential tones. Then Macguire ducked into his car and brought out a manila envelope. Marla tore into it and yanked out a sheet of paper. Under the shelter of the umbrella, she pored over it while he talked quietly, pointing here and there on the sheet. Marla scowled. Macguire appeared to be trying to calm her.

"Brau-au-au-gh!" she yelled, as the first of the guest cars crested the dirt road. I couldn't help wondering what the problem was. Marla continued to stare at the paper in her hands. "I don't believe this!" I heard her yell.

"What are you going to do?" Macguire said loudly, crossing his arms and frowning down at her. "Confront him?"

"Are you kidding?" my best friend shrieked. She crushed the paper and stuffed it into a silk pocket. "I'm going to *kill* him!"

Chapter 2

Try as I might, I couldn't discover what Marla was so angry about. When Macguire unpacked the crystal glasses—not real, of course, for an outdoor event—he mumbled that I'd learn soon enough. And then I became so busy loading the quesadillas and tomato-Brie pies into the ovens that I didn't have time to ask again. I didn't even notice when Prospect partner Albert Lipscomb arrived with the last of the cases of brew. The boxes of gleaming brown bottles just seemed to appear magically in the tent. I was briefly aware of tall, athletic Tony with an equally tall, but bald, man moving confidently in the direction of the large storage shed abutting the side tent flap. From their assured manner together, I figured the balding man had to be Prospect partner Albert Lipscomb, the most tedious man on earth, as Marla had called him. After a moment the two men emerged from the shed wearing miner's hard hats complete with cap lamps. Without stopping to talk to the few clients who'd already arrived, they walked briskly into the mine.

I watched curiously as the two men disappeared down the dark-hewn throat into the earth. But I was even more interested in their mission. Before leaving they'd spoken with Macguire briefly, pointing at the middle of the tent. Macguire had in turn disappeared and returned with another man, whom I could see only from the back. With great effort, Macguire and his helper hauled a glass display case the size of a large coffee table back to the spot in the center of the tent that the partners had indicated.

"What's going on?" I asked Macguire when I was by his side. He was dusting off his hands and muttering about having to wash them again before serving the food.

The man with him, whom I belatedly (and with a sinking heart) recognized as Captain Shockley of the Furman County Sheriff's Department, spoke first.

"Well, now. If it isn't Mrs. Schulz." Shockley, in his late fifties, towered over me. I took in his formidable paunch and green polyester suit. He had thin, ruffled black hair above an ominous, horsey face. Within a mass of crepey wrinkles, his bulging brown eyes glared at me. He looked like a boss. I just wished he wasn't *Tom's* boss. He said, "I wonder why Prospect happened to hire *you* to cater this event?"

Anxiety gnawed at my stomach as Shockley tilted toward me. His oversized teeth were set in a joyless grin as he waited grimly for my reply.

"Um, because my best friend is dating one of the partners?"

He turned back to the display case. "I figured as much." He stared glumly into the empty glass compartments.

"What are you two doing?" I asked brightly. "I mean, I

guess this table isn't a place where we can put trays of dumplings."

Shockley ignored me, and Macguire gave a barely perceptible shake of the head. *Don't ask.* But I didn't need to inquire
again, because within a minute Tony and his partner reappeared
at the mine opening, each with a knapsack slung over his back.
When they approached the display table, Macguire tugged me
aside.

"It's supposed to be a surprise for the clients," Macguire
said in a low voice. "They made it a surprise mainly for security reasons," he added. "The partners didn't want anyone to
know in advance about a display of samples from the mine
safe." I watched Shockley open the top of the glass case. Tony
and Albert Lipscomb began to place chunks of streaked rock
inside. "That police captain? Shockley? He said they're doing a,
like, before-and-after exhibit. You know—samples of ore on
one side, ingots of refined metal on the other. The partners are
giving Shockley the key to the case. You know—for safekeep-
ing during the party."

The partners opened the second knapsack and carefully
lifted out thick, gleaming bars of gold. For a moment, Macguire and I did not speak. We were transfixed by the sight of
the precious yellow metal glimmering seductively in the light
of the tent lamps. I was sure the bars were worth a fortune.

"But," I said finally, "I thought they already gave the investors chunks of ore. Marla said she got one when they came up
for their tour."

When Macguire didn't answer right away, I looked at him.
The same uncertainty I'd seen earlier again clouded his face.
"Maybe I just shouldn't talk about it." He gestured to the
makeshift parking area that was bathed in icy rain. "Anyway,
here come some more guests."

And indeed, car after car was pulling into the parking lot. Macguire and I hustled off to the serving area and loaded up our trays with bottles, glasses, and napkins. *Have a good time,* I warned myself. *Guests can always read your mood! So forget the weather and buck up!* Unfortunately, a caterer's worries are as contagious as measles.

But my apprehensions proved groundless. Despite the rain, despite the recent loss of the firm's investment officer, the atmosphere among the partygoers soon vibrated with joviality. Wave after wave of guests extricated themselves from muddy Range Rovers and Jeep Grand Cherokees and greeted each other with loud cheers and high fives. *We made it through the Red Sea, doggone it, and now we're going to party!* Just as heartily, they hailed Macguire and me with demands for drinks. We were happy to oblige.

Once the first batch of thirty-five-dollar-a-bottle Belgian ales was gone, the party became more like a bash at the end of exams than a dignified gathering of wealthy investors. Fine with me. I am ecstatic when rich people celebrate *anything,* as long as I supply the food. With these folks in such excellent humor, maybe I'd even be able to wangle a couple of July Fourth bookings.

Then again, I reasoned as I served another round of ales, these guests certainly had reason to whoop it up. Tony Royce and Albert Lipscomb had made them a bundle. Tony's job was to come up with investment ideas and bring in clients. Albert analyzed the companies' balance sheets and managed the money. The investment officer ran—or rather, used to run—interference between the clients and the partners. And they'd all done spectacularly. Year before last, Prospect had infused money into Medigen, a regional biotech company. This year, Medigen had gone public and made the Prospect clients a widely reported packet. Now they were trying something new. Contrary to their usual pattern, Albert Lipscomb had been the one who'd pushed the idea of investing in the Eurydice Gold Mine. A lifelong Coloradan, Albert had inherited the mine from his grandfather, who'd vehemently insisted up to his death that the mine contained untapped gold ore. Prospect had hired a geologist who agreed with the grandfather, and the high-rolling clients had piled in. Coloradans can't resist gold. When they climb the peaks, they kick over rocks to search for untapped veins. When they picnic, they scan the creeks for shiny nuggets. Mention *gold,* and people go wild. Let them, I say, especially if it means they'll need catered functions to celebrate their strikes.

Once everyone was flourishing a third or fourth crystal glass full of brew, I brought out the crab quesadillas with chili cilantro salsa. Macguire offered the hot mushroom caps stuffed with savory chicken sausage. Guests were all too happy to drool and consume. *Fantastic! Scrumptious! Who cares about calories? We're all going to get rich!* It was great.

For a while after the display case was set up, I didn't spot Mr. Magnetic, Tony Royce. Marla took time from her chatter with friends about her upcoming travel plans with Tony to wave me in the direction of bald Albert Lipscomb. With the miner's hat and heavy jacket off, Albert appeared unexpectedly lithe and well-built. His slender chest was covered with a pale blue monogrammed shirt. His madras tie, seersucker jacket, yellow pants, and hand-sewn loafers couldn't have screamed *preppy* more loudly if he'd been wearing a sign. While Macguire stopped to talk to Marla, I scooted toward Albert to offer the tray of quesadillas on the first pass. *Suck up to the high rollers,* my cooking instructor had advised, *or you're going to have a brief career in catering.*

"Marla tells me you're recently married?" Albert said slowly after I'd introduced myself. His light brown eyes regarded me seriously. "To a police officer? Is this true?"

I felt myself frowning. Was this a trick question? "Ah, yes. My husband works for Captain Shockley over there."

Albert smiled painfully, showing small, even white teeth. "And will your husband be happy when Captain Shockley gets enough money in his Prospect account to retire?"

"Well. . . ."

"Never mind." Again the pained grin. Lipscomb was trying, unsuccessfully, to find some common ground where we could banter. "So." He took a deep breath. "Do you find yourself catering a lot of policemen's picnics?"

"In this weather," I replied sincerely, "I'd be happy to cater *any* picnics."

"In that case . . . we'll certainly keep you in mind," he drawled, chuckling and giving me that same agonized smile. *Kip yew ian mahnd.* Although he was from Colorado and not the South, he apparently had picked up a southern accent during his years at the Citadel, where Marla mentioned Albert and Tony both had gone to school. Albert rubbed his free hand over his bald pate and droned on: "We're always needing wonderful food like this. My grandfather was particularly fond of smoked meat. Is that Smithfield ham I smell?"

I mumbled something along the lines of "Not exactly," and wondered if Macguire was listening to his Walkman instead of taking the bacon-wrapped artichokes out of the oven.

Albert Lipscomb moved past me to talk to Eileen Tobey, the new president of Aspen Meadow Bank and a loyal client of mine. Eileen winked at me and held up a glassful of raspberry-flavored beer in a silent toast. I smiled, nodded, and gave her a thumbs-up, even though I'd drink liver-flavored lemonade before indulging in raspberry beer. But I did treasure Eileen's business. In the midst of my current downturn, she'd booked me for a small, regular catering job at her bank. If this Prospect party was a success, perhaps Eileen would want me to do a businesswomen's luncheon event later in June . . . *inside,* that is. . . .

"Oh, Goldy!" gushed a nearby female voice. I turned from Albert and Eileen in time to see a gnarled hand reach out to stop me. "These Mexican pizza things are out of this world! Did you make them? For someone with no formal chef training, you *amaze* me." My heart sank. It was Edna Hardcastle.

Under the current slender-bookings circumstances, I decided to be eager to please. I turned a blinding smile toward Mrs. Hardcastle, a willowy, sixtyish woman whose swept-up henna hair and bright yellow polka-dotted suit with matching pumps were a vision of scarlet and yellow. Both the suit skirt and the pumps had become muddy en route to the tent. Her white-haired husband Whit—short for Whitaker, I'd learned when I catered at their cabin by Bride's Creek last fall—shuffled uncomfortably and craned his long neck inside a knotted tie that appeared to be decorated with spackling compound. On the other side of Edna stood a short, blond man I recognized as restaurateur Sam Perdue, the proprietor of Sam's Soups in Aspen Meadow.

Sam's Soups, a year-old eatery by the lake that I had not yet visited, must be doing awfully well, I thought. Sam had prepared the soup for the Hardcastles' party in the fall, while the bulk of the preparation had fallen to me. But if Sam Perdue could afford to park his cash with Prospect Financial Partners, that meant he'd anted up the minimum investment of a hundred-thousand-dollars. Digging out my soup recipe file seemed suddenly appealing. "Sam?" I tried not to sound envious, merely curious. "Are you getting lots of orders for soup these days? I mean, because of the bad weather?"

"No," he said softly. He didn't appear to be eating anything, and his slender fingers held an iceless glass of water.

Mrs. Hardcastle, undeterred, raised her voice. "Usually the Prospect Partners have Cherry Creek Caterers. But . . . I understand CCC couldn't make it all the way up here, so the partners called you, instead, Goldy." Her tone made it clear who *her* first choice would have been.

"Oh, ah, well," I started to reply apologetically, "actually it was Marla Korman . . ."

"On the other hand, you and Sam did *such* a lovely job last fall, catering the land preservation fund-raiser at our cabin. People are still talking about that roast pork with . . . whatever it was."

"Cumberland sauce. I'm so pleased to hear this." I tried to sound gracious, humble, and deserving of more bookings.

Mrs. Hardcastle went on wistfully, "The weather's so dreadful this spring, I don't know when we'll get up to the cabin. . . ."

Here it comes, I thought. *You did a great job last year, but this year we can't use you.*

"It's a lovely setting, Mrs. Hardcastle." I wanted to say, *Do the words* Bride's Creek *make your daughter think of anything relating to her future?* Instead, I assumed a concerned tone. "How is your daughter?"

"Let's not talk about it, shall we?" Edna Hardcastle's face twisted. "Let's talk about . . ." Her pained gaze shifted to the mine opening, and she shuddered. She didn't want to talk about investing in the Eurydice, either. Perhaps it was those nauseating memories of claustrophobia. She sniffed. "Oh, dear . . ."

"I'm sorry, I was just hoping that—"

"Goldy?" Edna Hardcastle's voice was once again drenched with false cheer. "Are you an investor? I mean, do you invest in food concepts?" She paused, and her face became solemn. "Do you even *understand* food concepts?"

"Er, well, sort of." I glanced at the gaggle of Prospect clients *ooh*ing and *ah*ing over the gold bars in the display case. Maybe they hungered for some concept hors d'oeuvre. "It looks as if I might need to check the chafing dish and portable ovens—"

Edna dismissed my protest by waving a quesadilla in my face. "Tony Royce said you were going to taste the soups at Sam's place. It's a concept restaurant," she said, with a knowing look at Sam Perdue. "And Tony's thinking of bringing Prospect in. Have you done it yet?"

"Concept restaurant?" Sweat trickled down the inside of my caterer's uniform. I knew the restaurant Sam managed was one in a chain. A very short chain, as in two. What was Edna talking about? This was not the time to figure it out, for the bacon smell was getting stronger. "Ah, no. Tony hasn't mentioned my doing any tasting. Marla does his testing, anyway, or she used to—"

I looked at Sam for help. He was obviously miserable. "I'm hoping the Prospect partners will take my chain public," he murmured. "If Albert and Tony like my restaurant, it'll mean I can stay in business."

I nodded. So soups weren't doing so well, either. I didn't hold out much hope for Sam. Marla said people were always approaching Tony and Albert *looking for investors*. Which usually meant *needing a quick cash bailout*.

Edna quirked hennaed eyebrows that matched her hair. "*I*

told Tony that food was a better investment than an abandoned mine!"

"Well, perhaps you should tell him again," I murmured sympathetically as I scanned the tent for Macguire.

"I did! *I* told him—"

"Excuse me," I interrupted, "Mrs. Hardcastle? Thanks for the kind words and your . . . confidence in . . . food." It was lame, but it was the best I could do. "I do need to be off now because I've really, *really* got something burning back here."

With another sniff that didn't speak well for my getting future bookings, Edna Hardcastle grasped one of Sam's elbows, turned on the heel of one of her splattered yellow shoes, and strode away with Sam in tow. Whit Hardcastle patted his white hair, straightened his spackled tie, and waddled after her. Some rich people can't abide it when a servant terminates a conversation, I'd found. They want the honor of doing that themselves. If I snubbed Mrs. Hardcastle, it would become town news. And I could not afford any bad news with my business in peril.

At the back of the tent, Macguire was cautiously removing the sheet of bubbling bacon hors d'oeuvre from the oven and muttering, "Uh-oh. I couldn't tell how long they'd been in. There's no timer on these ovens."

"They're okay," I said as I eyed the glistening appetizers. I held up a paper-towel-covered platter. "Just use a spatula to scoop them out to drain."

This Macguire did. I held a silver platter over the hors d'oeuvre, flipped the two trays, then handed the platter of wrapped artichokes back to him. He placed a bowl of the Dijon cream sauce in the center of the tray and lumbered off to the group gathered around the display case.

Bacon-Wrapped Artichokes with Dijon Cream Sauce

5 artichoke bottoms (one 14-ounce can, drained)
10 slices center-cut bacon
3 tablespoons Dijon mustard
¼ cup half-and-half or heavy cream

Preheat oven to 400°. Cut each artichoke bottom into 8 equal pie-shaped wedges. Cut each bacon slice into fourths. Wrap a piece of bacon around each artichoke wedge and secure with a toothpick. Place on a rimmed cookie sheet and bake for 20 to 30 minutes, or until the bacon is crisp. Drain thoroughly. Combine the Dijon mustard with the cream and serve as a dipping sauce.

Makes 40.

Note: Occasionally cans of artichoke bottoms will contain 6, rather than 5 pieces. In that case, use 12 slices of bacon to make 48 appetizers.

I visually searched the clutter behind the counter for the chafer I was going to use to reheat the shrimp dumplings. I had managed to sully the space with heaps of trays, pans of appetizers, and row upon row of beer bottles. To my surprise, I caught sight of Tony Royce. He was rummaging through the Cambro.

"Tony! Why aren't you mingling with your guests?"

Tony uncoiled his athletic body and frowned at me. He gnawed on his perfectly trimmed bottle-brush mustache, brushed unseen lint from his khaki pants and khaki shirt, and smoothed his pouffed hair, which had not been flattened by the miner's hard hat. He looked like Hitler with a blow-dry.

"Well, Goldy, they're not all here, for one thing. For another, I don't want to have to listen to Edna Hardcastle tell me how great Sam's soups are. We're going to look at the place, the clients know that. But Victoria tried them and she didn't . . ." His voice trailed off, and his eyes darted back to the Cambro.

I wanted to be polite to Tony, since he was my employer for this particular shindig. I was also keenly interested to know what the late Victoria Lear's involvement in food concepts might have been. But I had cooking to do and we were in the middle of a party. Besides, I didn't want to argue with Tony— yet—about his appointing me to be Prospect's taste tester to succeed Marla and the deceased financial officer.

"Look, can you help me?" His voice grew desperate. "I need a vodka martini to clear the mine dampness out of my head. I hate that god-awful place. Do you have a freezer back here with some Stoly? Am I looking in the wrong place?"

I smiled. The new test for machismo, I'd learned, was to take long draughts from an icy bottle of Stolichnaya vodka. Even more macho was to slug down the vodka while gobbling a plateful of jalapeño peppers. "Sorry, Tony. We've just got beer and coffee." I finally spotted the chafer and hurried over to it. "What guests aren't here?"

Tony frowned, popped the top off a bottle of stout, and took a long swig. *Hey! I'm a guy, I don't need a glass!* "Who's not here? Marla's brother-in-law, for one thing. I've never even met the guy, but I sure have heard a lot about him."

"General Farquhar?" I tried to conceal my surprise by opening the chafer cover in front of my face.

Tony paused with the stout bottle halfway to his lips and eyed me curiously. "Yeah, after the Medigen IPO got so much publicity, we had all kinds of people wanting to get into the Eurydice venture. Farquhar sent us a check and said he was too busy to come in."

Too busy. Right. Too busy in jail. I pretended to be absorbed with the contents of the chafer. Thank heavens Macguire had already filled the bottom pan—the *bain-marie*—with hot water. Tiny bubbles floated promisingly upward. I heaved up the hotel pan with the shrimp dumplings and lowered it into place.

"Hey, Tony," I said. "I need to borrow a watch. There's no timer on the oven, and we almost burned the bacon appetizers."

Tony glanced at his gleaming Rolex. He said solemnly, "You're not borrowing my watch."

Okay, so his watch probably cost more than my van. I kept my voice courteous. "Well, could you tell me when ten minutes is up?"

He nodded, swallowed the last of his stout, and popped the top off another. Albert Lipscomb's bald head shone like an approaching beacon under the tent lights as he strode toward us. He put down a plate with a half-eaten quesadilla and leaned toward his partner.

"Tony, Captain Shockley wants to talk to us about Victoria," Albert said in a low voice. Tony groaned and took a swig of stout from the new bottle. Albert persisted glumly: "He's very upset. We need to talk to him."

"My head's full of damp air. He's your friend. You talk to him."

Albert sighed and rubbed his scalp. "Oh, all right."

But he didn't have a chance. Marla strode up, pinched a wad of Albert's madras jacket, and yanked him in the direction of the shed.

"I don't want you to leave before we have a talk," she announced. "About assay reports. Let's go in here with the cap lamps and have a chat."

Albert, dumbfounded, looked at Tony for help. Then his mournful eyes turned back to Marla. "I don't understand what . . . what is so important—"

"Don't *pretend* you don't know what I'm talking about," Marla snapped. She let go of his jacket and put one hand on an ample hip. She shook her other hand in a furious fist under Albert Lipscomb's nose.

"Wait, wait," I implored, with a harried glance out at the center of the tent. "Don't talk about this now. Don't ruin the party. . . ."

Tony was suddenly between the two of them. He lifted his dark eyebrows and bit his mustache. He murmured, "For heaven's sake, guys, this is not the time . . ." He put his hands on Marla's shoulders. "Please, sweetheart, you know you shouldn't distress yourself. You could get sick—"

Marla shot him a withering glance and slapped his hands away. "I'll talk to you later, Tony. This whole thing was his idea, not yours, and you're being duped, too. So move back."

Tony, aghast, took two steps away from them. Marla and

Albert advanced in the direction of the corrugated metal shed. Or rather, that was as far as Marla could back Albert up. With a hasty glance at the guests, Tony followed them. I used tongs to move the dumplings around, keeping an eye on the confrontation. What had gotten into Marla? Couldn't whatever it was wait?

"Absolutely not." Albert's voice rose in answer to something Marla had said. He laughed. The chuckle I'd heard earlier from him had been an awkward, uncomfortable one. The new one was derisive, as if Marla had told a particularly absurd joke. "You're completely mistaken. The Kepler lab is well known, and totally reliable. It—"

"Oh, I don't *think* I'm mistaken," Marla sniped right back. "My source says the only reliable process is a *fire* assay—"

Tony once more tried to intervene. "Marla, please. We can all sit down together—"

Albert snarled at Marla, "You *bitch*. What are you trying to do?"

She cried, "It is *my* money and *my* investment!"

Macguire timidly knocked on the top of the dumpling chafer, as if that could gain him admittance to our uncomfortable little scene at the back of the tent. "Uh, that Captain Shockley guy doesn't want to come back here and leave the display case out of his sight. But he just asked if there was some kind of problem—"

Tony must have seen Macguire and guessed his mission, for he hurried back over to the two of us. "No, no," he said with a desperate wave to dismiss my assistant. "Nothing's wrong. Tell anybody who asks that it's about corn futures. Or something. Go pass around some more food. Please," he added belatedly. Then he darted back to Marla and Albert.

I didn't know if ten minutes had gone by, but I used the

tongs to arrange a platter of hot dumplings for Macguire to distribute. At that moment, Albert adjusted the lapels of his madras jacket, lifted his chin, and shrugged mightily.

"And today I got the *paper*work to *prove* it," Marla shrilled. "But I had to have three glasses of that vile beer before I had the courage to come over here and *confront* you—!" Perhaps to make certain he was paying attention, she thumped his chest. Caught off guard, Albert dropped his glass, which shattered. Ale foamed across the tent floor. *No, no, no,* I thought uncharitably, *I haven't been paid yet.*

"Look, guys," Tony began again. "We need to postpone whatever discussion—"

"Shut *up,* Tony," Marla snarled. I'd never seen her so enraged.

Albert Lipscomb turned away from Marla. Marla held up her index finger and continued to scold. A blare of sound erupted from the far side of the tent. The chink of glasses and babble of guest voices—not to mention the noise of this fracas—were suddenly drowned under the flood of violin music cascading from the portable speakers. Poor Macguire must have turned the volume way, way up. Over Vivaldi, I heard Marla yell, "And *another* thing!"

But Albert didn't want to hear about the other thing. He stumbled past us, out into the rain. Marla stomped after him. Her crimped brown hair had shaken loose from the twinkling barrettes. Her green-and-gold silk dress drooped off one shoulder, and her bejeweled fingers were clenched. I rushed over to Tony's side.

"Doggone it, do something," I demanded.

"Like what? You saw how I tried," he said sourly. "They won't listen to me."

The rain was changing to hail. With her recent medical

history, Marla had no business being out in a hailstorm. I wiped my hands, now damp with fear, on my chef's jacket. Surprised by the unexpected downpour of icy pebbles outside the tent, Albert Lipscomb wobbled on his pale loafers. Perhaps his sudden loss of equilibrium was owing to the beat of hailstones on his bald pate. He extended his long arms to get some balance, but the muddy road proved too slippery and he faltered. To my horror, Marla flew forward to try to catch him. He slipped from her grasp and careened sideways onto a car. Before he could stand up, Marla started yelling at him. The only word I could pick out was *creep.*

Tony smoothed his mustache and looked around to see if any guests were watching. He tried to appear nonchalant as he walked along the shed wall to the edge of the tent. With another cautious glance at the guests, he loped after his partner and his girlfriend. I doused the flame on the chafer and scooted around the counter. As inconspicuously as possible, I kicked the broken glass under the shed and headed for the edge of the tent. I needed this job: I was not about to let this party fall apart.

Out in the parking area, Marla reached into a pocket and flourished a sheet of paper at Albert and Tony. Tony talked rapidly while Albert stood with his arms crossed, his long, pale face a study in disgust. The three seemed impervious to the thickening wash of hail. *Why, why, why?* I wondered wildly, studying their furious faces. Albert snatched the paper from Marla's hand and tossed it into the air. Hail thudded hard on the car roofs and the tent overhead. Oblivious, Marla and Albert continued to yell at each other.

Since Tony didn't seem able to pry Marla and Albert apart, I thought I should try, but out of view of the guests. I yanked on the rope that would let down the tent flap. It wouldn't budge. I signaled to Macguire to take over serving the food. A few guests were straining to get a glimpse of the contretemps outside, but thankfully, most were still looking at the gold, eating, drinking, and chatting.

I pulled again on the rope: no luck. I had to convince Marla and the partners to stop bickering, because it was *not good* for Marla to argue. Her excitable temper frequently got her into trouble, although she'd been doing better lately. One of her most notable fights, I recalled as I strode across the tent floor, had been with our violent ex-husband. When the Jerk had come at her with a rolling pin, she'd swung a hanging plant at him and dislocated his shoulder. But post-heart attack, she'd promised to stay cool no matter what the circumstances. I had to stay cool, too. No brawls, I promised myself.

I opened the storage shed's flimsy door and peered into the dark interior space, as if I needed to search out more supplies. My footsteps gritted over the dirty floor as I rushed past rows of hard hats, wide belts, and what looked like cloth-covered flasks. When I opened the outer door, I gasped as hail hit my cheeks. I blinked and trotted through the jumble of parked four-wheel-drive vehicles. Attempting a shortcut, I headed through a mass of shrubbery and promptly got caught in a web of branches. Breathing hard and shivering, I untangled my damp skirt from several sandcherry bushes and considered dashing back to the tent. But the raised voices spurred me on.

"Don't try to tell me what I don't understand! You're this mine's promoter, Albert!" Marla's normally husky voice cracked with rage. "I *trusted* you!"

Marla and Albert stood inches apart. Like boxers in the thirteenth round, both swayed slightly. Whatever their argument was about, it had exhausted them both. Tony stood off to one side, his head in his hands.

Marla's wet dress was plastered to her body and her damp hair had slipped askew in weedlike clumps. Lean-built Albert Lipscomb staggered uncertainly. I suddenly wished I'd had the means to call 911 while I was under the tent. But Arch is always scolding me for overreacting. Marla and Albert hadn't hit each other. They'd only been arguing. At least, I hoped they were only arguing.

"I swear . . . I swear . . ." Albert's voice had hardened. *Ah sweah, ah sweah . . .* Without warning, he straightened. "The Eurydice is going to produce!" he yelled. *The Yer-ih-dahsey.* "You don't understand, this mine was closed by the government during the height of its gold production! The assays show an average of two troy ounces of gold per ton of ore! Do you have any idea how good that is? When are you going to listen to me?"

Tony dropped his hands from his face and groaned. He said, "Could we please, *please* discuss this down at the office?"

Marla ignored Tony, ducked, and scooped up the sodden paper Albert had thrown into the mud. "But . . . but . . . look at this report!" she shouted. "The only way to test ore reliably for gold is to do a *fire* assay. This guy at the Colorado School of Mines says—"

"Oh, dear God," Tony grumbled. "I do not believe this. Do not, do not. If you just would have let me—"

"What the *hell* is this?" Marla screeched, undeterred. She thrust the sodden, muddy sheet under Albert's nose. "What *difference* does it make if you have the best geologist in the universe? You have to have a good assay! I want my hundred thousand dollars back, you scum! Tony says you've got it!"

"Do something!" I begged Tony.

Tony's mouth hung open beneath his bedraggled mustache. His eyes were on Marla. He didn't seem to hear me.

"Marla, will you listen to me?" Albert protested angrily. "That might be from the wrong—"

I'd had enough. "Okay, look," I told Tony. "I'll get Marla. You get *him*."

Tony snapped to attention and nodded. Tall and thin as a whippet, he strode obediently in his partner's direction. I approached Marla, shaking my head. I couldn't imagine what they'd say down at her cardiac rehab program Monday morning. Of course, it was unlikely that she would tell them she'd engaged in an ear-splitting dispute with her financial adviser. In a hailstorm, no less.

"Look, just go home," Tony shouted to Albert through the spatter of hail. He glanced nervously toward the tent. He seemed suddenly frantic that this collection of guests—their best clients—not end in disaster. A few partygoers had gathered by the unbudgeable flap to watch the sideshow. Tony lowered his voice. "For heaven's sake, look at you, Albert. You're going to get pneumonia. So will Marla if I don't take care of her. *Please* go home. We'll talk later, okay?"

Albert yanked away from him and wiped hail off his bald head. "You've got a problem, Tony! And your problem is that lying woman! I am leaving this party, you bet! I will be delighted to leave!" *De-lahted.* And with that he tucked his wet blue shirt into his yellow trousers, straightened his tie, and slogged through the mud in the direction of his car. Tony shot after him.

I put my arms around Marla and murmured what I hoped were calming words. Her skin was cold and wet and she was shivering. Still, she wrenched herself away from my grasp and hollered after Albert's retreating form. "I want to see you, you creep! Monday morning, nine A.M.! Do you hear me? And have a *reliable* assay report ready for me! Or else!"

Albert Lipscomb did not acknowledge her challenge. I looked back at the curious partygoers gaping at the quarrel. *A huge argument, caterer in the middle,* I imagined them thinking. *Must be something Goldilocks' Catering did wrong, don't you think?*

Marla screeched: "Nine sharp, Albert, at your office! With the paperwork! Have you got that? *Nobody* steals from me!"

"Some crummy idea this party was, Marla!" Albert flung over his shoulder. He was drenched and mud-spattered. Beside him, even handsome Tony didn't look much better. Albert added with vicious gusto, "You! Your friend! Weird beer! And who ever heard of a *crab* quesadilla?"

The partygoers all burst out laughing. *Hello, failure.*

Chapter 3

Pain descended on my head. Until Albert hollered his criticism, I tried to convince myself as I watched him stumble off, the party had been going well. No matter what he claimed, the guests had seemed to be *enjoying* the crab quesadillas, the tomato-Brie pie, even the raspberry-flavored beer. But when the clients' attention became riveted to the parking lot, the festive atmosphere underwent a sea change. The Vivaldi ended and the pleasant chattering stopped. The only noise was the sifting sound of hail changing back to rain.

I gritted my teeth as Albert's car engine caught and growled away. Tony hustled over to Marla and hoarsely commanded me to take care of the guests. Marla was gasping.

"I can't seem to catch my breath," she said. "I can't . . ."

"All right," I told Tony, "see if you can find some towels and warm her up in the large shed. You have a cell phone on you?" He mumbled something unintelligible as he held onto

Marla with one hand and groped in one of the khaki pockets with the other.

When he finally handed me the flip phone, I tucked it into my apron and returned to the tent. The clients parted to let me through. Without Tony or Marla to query, they watched my every movement with narrowed, suspicious eyes. Whispers rose all around. *What happened?* they asked each other. *What's going on? What was the fight about?* And chief among their questions: *Is there a problem with the mine?* To each person who tried to corner me, I replied cheerfully, "Oh, just a little disagreement. Something about corn futures, I think." Ha. Serious and somewhat sullen, the clients reluctantly turned their attention to Macguire. He had assumed a blank expression and was dutifully serving ales to go with the dumplings.

I made a clandestine call to Marla's cardiologist. The answering service replied that Dr. Lyle Gordon was in surgery but should be able to call back within half an hour.

Tony Royce reappeared in the tent and murmured to me that Marla was resting. His thin face was tight with strain. Marla's breathing, he reported, was back to normal. Tony then moved through the crowd—touching arms, patting backs—like a politician visiting the site of a tornado. I could just hear his reassurances: *Everything is fine, fine, there's only a silly dispute about a stray piece of ore. Yes, that beer might muddle people's thinking!* And then, sadly, *Oh, undoubtedly. Everyone's on edge since we lost poor Victoria.*

I heaped freshly ground coffee into the filter for the large pot, plugged it in, and set out paper cups. When I could slip away, I visited Marla. Wrapped in frayed, mismatched towels, she was sitting in front of a space heater in a tin-lined bathroom. Her limp green silk dress hung on a bent nail close to the heater. Near tears, she said in a thick voice that she didn't want to talk about *that damn Albert. That slime-ball! That bald buzzard! How dare he——!* But no, she wasn't going to talk about it. She gasped and plunged right back into talking about it. *Me, Tony, everybody—we're just being swindled! But Tony won't listen! He and Albert have been friends since they went to that damn military school!* I begged her to calm down. She took a deep breath and vowed that she would. She was going to leave as soon as the clients had departed and her accursed dress was somewhere close to dry.

When the appetizers were gone, Macguire trundled through the tent collecting debris. I poured the first cups of coffee and busied myself arranging a tray of white chocolate truffles and fudge wrapped in gold foil. Finally, Dr. Gordon beeped the cellular. I handed the desserts to Macguire.

The good doc seemed not in the least surprised to hear that Marla Korman, the most irascible cardiac patient in the history of Southwest Hospital, had become involved in a blistering debate with a party guest. Didn't I remember, he asked mildly, what had happened after the atherectomy? Marla, citing her generosity to the hospital, had demanded a private room, a private nurse, and meals sent in from a delicatessen fifteen miles away. Yes, I told her doctor as I watched Macguire circulate with the truffle tray, I remembered. And didn't I recall that Marla had threatened to whack him, Dr. Lyle Gordon, with her IV if he didn't let her out of the hospital earlier than he felt was advisable? Ah, no, I wasn't there for that part. I merely had a vivid memory of the time she'd threatened from her hospital bed to cut off Southwest Hospital from future gifts. That warning had produced both the services and the discharge her damaged heart desired.

Was Marla having chest pains or any trouble breathing now, Dr. Gordon wanted to know? I asked her; she was not. *Make sure she gets rest,* Gordon ordered crisply, *especially since she's taking this cockamamie trip to Rome with her art appreciation group next week.* Right, right, I replied, I was taking her home to lie down. *And make sure she's taken today's dose of Inderal. Inderal,* I repeated. A beta-blocker, Dr. Gordon elaborated. She needed to have it every day. *And make sure she has a little something to eat, but no artificial food colorings in any form.* She had a food allergy, he reminded me. We didn't want her heart revving up. I replied that I was well acquainted with the food allergy. Would she be in for her regular rehab appointment on Monday? Yes, yes, I said meekly, wondering whether that would be before or after the scheduled office confrontation with Albert Lipscomb. *Make sure Marla doesn't get into any more quarrels,* Dr. Gordon concluded ominously. *Fat chance,* I said with a laugh that probably didn't jibe with the cardiologist's idea of comedy.

When the guests finally departed, Macguire and I worked rapidly to clean up the trash and pack up the soiled pans and platters. Marla reported that she felt better and that her dress was almost wearable. After some discussion, Captain Shockley and Tony Royce began to dismantle the display of gold ore and bars. Since I'd been too busy to examine the brilliant samples at close range, I brought my garbage bag over to the case.

"Come on and take a look," Tony invited me. His brown eyes were merry. He looked as dapper as ever, and his anguish over the Marla–Albert conflict had evaporated. Maybe Prospect clients violently disagreed with the partners all the time, and he was used to handling confrontations. Smiling, he held a chunk of ore out to me. I put down the garbage bag and took it.

Thick gold streaks ran through the gray rock. I turned the lump over. The glittering bands widened on the stone's other side. In grade school, Arch had learned about the history of mining in our state. When the Cub Scouts had visited the nearby Edgar Mine, Arch had been in heaven. Until the moment that I held that deliciously shiny chunk of gold ore in my hands, I had never felt even the slightest interest in Colorado gold mining. Suddenly, I was captivated.

"Nice, isn't it?" asked Tony pleasantly. "Now take a look at a bar of unpolished *doré* gold. This is how gold ore looks when it's been refined."

He handed me a heavy, grainy-textured gold bar with a crusty, rippled underside. I found myself wondering how much it was worth.

"Hoohoo!" called Marla. Wearing the much-rumpled green dress, she waved to me from behind the counter with the portable ovens. "I'm leaving!"

"Want me to follow you?" Tony called.

"No, no," she cried back. "Goldy will!"

"It's nice," I said to Tony, and handed the pebble-surfaced bar back to him. "Do you mind if my assistant oversees this last bit of the cleanup? The rental company will be by within the hour to pick up the ovens, the tent, and the rest of the equipment. I know *I'd* feel better following Marla home in my van. To make sure she gets there safely, you know."

"No problem," Tony said as he loaded the last of the samples and bars into the second oversize backpack. He smiled. "You're a good friend, Goldy. Tell Marla I'll call her later."

Captain Shockley grunted, "What kind of car does that woman own, that you have to follow her? Isn't she a good driver?"

"She has a four-wheel-drive Mercedes," I replied crisply. "But she's had a heart attack, so—" Wait a minute. Why did I feel I had to explain myself to this man?

"Four-wheel-drive Mercedes, huh?" said Shockley as he hefted one of the packs onto his back. His bulging eyes peered in the direction of the parking lot. "Where'd she get the money for that?"

I walked away. Let Tony explain Marla's financial situation to Shockley. I'd had enough for one day.

Macguire promised to finish up. He'd be coming over in the morning, he said, to discuss a new job not related to catering. What new job, I asked. But he only put a finger to his lips. A secret. Great.

I guided Marla to her car, ignoring her fierce protests that she didn't want to be babied. The van sputtered and coughed as I followed my friend's taillights to her home in the Aspen Meadow Country Club area. At least the rain had finally let up. I fixed Marla some crackers and herb tea while she got ready for bed. When I went up to her bedroom with the tray, she was under the covers, looking remorseful and sorting a bright pile of cosmetics and jewelry. But I knew better than to get her riled up again by asking what had started the altercation with Albert in the first place.

"Did you take your Inderal?" I asked. When she nodded, I said, "Hey, I'm pooped. But it was a super party," I added with false conviction. "Those folks drank a *lot* of beer. And you really looked gorgeous in the silk. Besides, I don't think anybody's really going to remember—"

"Oh yeah, it was just a marvelous party," she interrupted, avoiding my eyes. "I didn't have a thing to eat, and my new dress is ruined." Pink plastic bottles and gold lipstick containers cascaded from her hands. "This pile is for the fishing trip I'm taking with Tony," she said lightly. "We decided to move it up, to get a break, just the two of us." She fingered a smoky white plastic bottle of cream. "But this large pile is for Rome, where I am going *without* Tony." She exhaled in exasperation. "He gave me your check for the party, Goldy, because I told him you needed it right away. It's on the bureau."

"Look, Marla, you didn't have to—"

She stopped dividing containers and finally looked up at me with doleful, red-rimmed eyes. I felt a pang. She looked years older than she had when she arrived at the Prospect Financial party that afternoon. "Don't start. Some people don't honor their financial commitments. Tony's not one of them, you'll be happy to know. Neither am I."

"I'm already aware of that fact. But—"

Her dark eyes flashed. "That Lipscomb moron thinks I'm stupid. That's the problem. Partner's girlfriend? Got a lot of money? She's ripe."

"Can't Tony—"

"No, Tony can't anything. I tried to convince him that Albert's up to something. He wanted to know who'd called the assay into doubt. 'What makes you think there's no gold in the mine?' he asked me. 'Our geologist is the most highly respected in the state.' Now he wants to have *all* of the ore they've brought out analyzed by a different lab, in case the Kepler lab down in Henderson, Nevada, is some kind of fraud joint."

"Whoa," I said. "I know an assay is an analysis of ore that tells you what metals are in it, and what the concentrations are. So what's the problem?"

"Gold is an element, my friend," she replied. "You have to heat up the ore to separate out the good stuff. It's what's called a fire assay. Any lab that tells you they can figure out what's in your ore without a *fire* assay is lying."

I sighed. "But all these Prospect clients have put up a ton of money. I mean, they're not dumb, are they?"

Marla went on: "I don't know. I didn't tell Tony I'd paid

good old nineteen-year-old Macguire to get the copy of the assay analyzed by a student down at the Colorado School of Mines. Maybe Macguire's friend doesn't know enough about assaying yet." Her forehead wrinkled. "I guess I shouldn't have looked at the report before the party began."

"Tony probably wouldn't believe Macguire was your source. And you're right, Tony and Albert will put even less stock in what a student says. I mean, over their fancy geologist."

Marla deposited the jewelry and cosmetics into two plastic bags and fluffed her coverlet. "You think? Well, Tony promised me everything would be fine. They'd get it all sorted out. That mine was producing gold during the Second World War, and FDR had it closed down with that order of his, what was it, L-two-oh-eight?"

"I'm sorry, the Roosevelt administration is not my area of expertise, although I understand Harry Truman liked buttermilk pie."

She sighed at my ignorance. "All nonessential mineral mines were closed. FDR wanted only copper, zinc, and lead. For bullets, isn't that depressing? Albert's grandfather swore the place was, well, a gold mine. So now *Albert* swears that with the discoveries they've made, by putting capital into the place to bring the mine back into production, we're all going to be rich as blazes."

I decided not to say, *But you already are rich as blazes.* . . . In any event I didn't resent her inherited wealth. She was generous, even carefree, about giving it away. Besides, to me, Marla's riches were a very clear object lesson that money didn't buy happiness.

"Anyway," she went on, "if the gold thing pans out, ha ha, I may become Midas yet." She frowned. "Except the student at the School of Mines says it's a red flag when you get an assay that's not a fire assay. Tony promised me that Albert will get it all worked out. Maybe the early ore samples weren't as promising as Albert claims, or maybe the assay is from the wrong place. . . . Do you believe that?"

I didn't know what to think, but I didn't say so. It was getting late. I made sympathetic clucking noises and promised to call soon. Then I revved up the van and tried to put the party out of my mind. As I drove out of the country club, I turned on my wipers. The rain had turned to large flakes of snow that splatted on my windshield. Welcome to June fifth in the high country.

At home, my dear, wonderful husband Tom looked delighted to see me. His greeting was the first good thing to happen to yours truly all day. He grinned widely, opened the back door, and relieved me of the first box of dirty pans. I felt the anxiety of the afternoon slide away. Tom's large body was encased in a sea green terry-cloth robe I had bought him for our first anniversary. It matched his green eyes, which twinkled in his handsome face. I scooted back to the van and brought the second box of pans through the softly falling snow. Tom was cooking, and I couldn't wait to see what delicacy he'd put together. It is a truism of the culinary world that the caterer never has a chance to eat until all the food is cold, picked over, or gone. When I came back into the kitchen, Tom had set out two fluted champagne glasses and a large bottle of bubbly.

"Uh-oh," he said. "The caterer doesn't have that successful event look on her face." He took the last load from my arms, set the carton on the counter, and wrapped me in one of his warm, tight hugs.

"Gosh, I need this," I murmured into his warm shoulder

that smelled of soap. "It was not only unsuccessful. It was hor-
rible."

He drew back, and I wanted to say, *Lord, but you're gorgeous,*
but decided to save it. He gave me a look of deep sympathy.
"Weather ruin things?"

"No. Marla nearly got into a fistfight with the host."

"Gee," he said with jovial sarcasm. He let me go and
squeezed my hand. "What else is new? Hold on a minute."

I eyed the counter while Tom worked to open the champagne. He appeared to be making cookies. But what kind of
treat contained whole wheat flour, nonfat dry milk, and liver
powder? Something that went with champagne? I said, "I'm
afraid to ask what you're making. Health cookies?"

He popped the cork. "Not cookies. Homemade dog biscuits. For Jake." He smiled.

"Oh, Tom, you have *got* to be kidding."

He put down the champagne bottle and brandished a large
cookie cutter in the shape of a dog bone. He wasn't kidding.
As he poured, I glanced at the kitchen clock—it was almost
one—and sank into one of our kitchen chairs. Tom had put out
a crusty loaf of sourdough bread and a large wedge of Bel Paese
cheese. He handed me a glass full of spritzy bubbles.

"Here's to good work situations," he said seriously, raising
his glass.

I clinked my glass against his and sipped. "Speaking of
which. I saw Shockley."

"Please don't ruin my cooking experience," he said with
the same jolly sarcasm. He turned enthusiastically back to the
dog biscuit dough. "And before you say one word, I'll tell you
why I'm doing this. Jake needs to trust us. So we've got to
pamper him. Show him that we care."

Jake's Dog Biscuits

2¹/₂ cups whole wheat flour
¹/₂ cup powdered milk
¹/₂ teaspoon garlic powder
¹/₂ teaspoon salt
1 teaspoon brown sugar
6 tablespoons margarine or shortening
1 egg, beaten
3 tablespoons liver powder
¹/₂ cup ice water

Preheat oven to 350°. In a large bowl, combine flour, powdered milk, garlic powder, salt, and sugar. Cut in shortening. Mix in egg, then add liver powder. Add ice water until mixture forms a ball. Pat out dough ¹/₂ inch thick on a lightly oiled cookie sheet. Cut with any size cutter and remove scraps. Bake 30 minutes. Cool before serving.

"I certainly hope making homemade dog biscuits at one o'clock in the morning does the trick."

Undiscouraged, Tom grinned again. "Besides that, Shockley made me so damn mad yesterday, I'm thinking of having his secretary give him some of these with his coffee Monday morning."

I groaned. Would that idiot police chief never stop bothering my husband? "Now what?"

"First tell me about your party. The food turned out all right, didn't it? Did the tent and ovens get there on time? How about Macguire?"

I briefly recapped the evening's events, concluding with my worry that Marla's erratic behavior might lead to another bout with heart disease.

"Trouble with an assay?" Tom frowned. "Why didn't she ask Tony about it before confronting Albert?"

I sipped the champagne. "Discretion and tact have never been Marla's long suits, Tom. Besides, the mine is Albert's baby, not Tony's. Anyway, I'm sure that now she wishes she *had* had a tête-à-tête with Tony instead of bawling out his partner in front of everybody."

"This is going to put the captain in a foul mood," Tom mused. "Glad he'll have the rest of the weekend to think about it."

"You mentioned that he had upset you."

"Upset me? Upset me? You mean, after I've worked two months on the case against David Calvin, the fact that Shockley has ruined it for me has *upset* me? Nah."

David Calvin had shot and killed his ex-wife not five miles from our home. Calvin hadn't liked the fact that his ex was going out with somebody, so he'd shot the boyfriend, too. The boyfriend had been in a coma for two months. I knew that

Tom had recovered Calvin's murder weapon and vehicle, and had been confident about getting a conviction.

"Oh, Tom, don't tell me. What did Shockley do now?"

Tom heaved a huge sigh and fingered his glass. "We have investigative keys. What that means is, say we know a guy was wearing a black shirt, that he used a thirty-two, that he shot the victim four times. Those facts are the keys. They are secret. Very, very secret. The reason we don't divulge the keys is that we use them in questioning the suspect. Say we ask about the weapon, without being specific. The guy says, 'But I don't even own a thirty-two!' Then we know we've got our guy."

The kitchen began to fill with a savory, homemade-bread aroma. Lucky Jake. I cut myself a slice of sourdough, smeared it with the creamy cheese, and waited for Tom to continue.

"Shockley was so proud of all the work we've—no, wait— the work *I've* done, that he blabbed about it to a lawyer friend of his. The captain needs to impress people. Anyway, that attorney just became the court-appointed defense lawyer for David Calvin." He took a last swig of champagne. "Good-bye, case."

"No, no," I protested. "You've got other evidence, you've got—"

"Trust me," he said as he brought the sheet of warm bone-shaped biscuits out of the oven. "You lose the keys, you've lost the case."

I rinsed our glasses while he set the biscuits on racks to cool.

"I'm going to take a shower," I murmured in his ear. "And then I want to have some fun."

"Oh, woman," he said with a chuckle. "You better make that a *quick* shower."

The snow turned back to rain that pattered on the roof as

we made love. Afterward, I snuggled into Tom's arms, my hair still damp from the fast shower. As I felt his warmth surround me, I pondered what kind of wonderful man would take the time to make biscuits for my son's new dog after two months of work had been ruined and a killer might go free.

Chapter 4

Sunday morning I was startled awake by an ungodly canine howl. At first I thought the sound was a dream. Maybe it was the Hound of Heaven's wail, promising divine retribution. Or perhaps it was the bellow of the Hound of the Baskervilles, on the trail of a hapless victim.

It was neither. It was good old Jake, the hound of Arch. Our much-desired-although-not-by-me canine pet had a problem with allowing people to sleep. Apparently Tom had already succumbed; I could hear the familiar clinking of dishes as he worked in the kitchen. I rolled over and covered my head with a pillow so I didn't have to see the still-falling rain. I didn't resent Jake, I told myself, because Arch loved him. And Tom was working hard with Arch to rehabilitate the dog. I knew I shouldn't feel like Scrooge, but I did.

The sheriff's department had branded Jake an unreliable bloodhound. When the dog's handler of many years retired, the

new handler insisted Jake had lost the scent on three consecu-
tive trails. Jake fell into disrepute, was released from his Furman
County K-9 unit, and ended up in a kennel. When the hound
lost weight and became despondent, an activist group of dog-
lovers obtained his release from the department and put him up
for adoption. Seizing an opportunity, Tom had brought Jake
home last month. Brought him home *gleefully. Unrepentantly.*
As if to mock me, Jake raised his howl an octave and several
decibels.

I burrowed under the handmade king-size quilt Tom had
presented to me on our first anniversary. Yes, I loved Tom, I
loved him to pieces. I just didn't love Jake, even if my good-
hearted husband had brought him home because my son had
been pleading for a pet from time immemorial. Now the two
males in my life seemed to have found new meaning in nursing
the wretched animal back to mental and physical health. Unfortunately, despite a layer of batting over my ears, I could still
hear unreliable, untrustworthy, unhappy Jake. Perhaps he
needed to share his misery.

He wasn't the only one who wasn't happy this morning.
Depression surfaced. I wished Tom were back in our warm
bed, so I could forget the feeling of defeat that inevitably comes
on the morning after a bad catered event. Disrupted party, no
bookings, sullied reputation looming. Not to mention the possibility of going out of business. I groaned. Even a bloodhound's plaintive wail couldn't drown out the memory of
Marla screeching. Now, six too-short hours later, I was in no
mood to order Jake-reincarnated-from-the-Baskervilles to be
quiet. Not that the The Howler would pay the slightest attention to me, anyway.

As I hauled myself out of bed, I remembered I had a solitary
booking for the day—an anniversary dinner for the Kirby-

Joneses, buyers for a local gift store who had just returned from Kenya. Weddings and anniversaries were usually my bread and butter in June. This June, however, it seemed as if people either were not getting married, were getting divorced, or were celebrating their anniversaries in Fiji. Today's job would be the perfect antidote for worry. I had been thankful for it, even though it had posed a few problems.

I stretched through my yoga routine and recalled all the fun Macguire and I had had planning the menu for the Kirby-Joneses. Twenty-five years ago, well-wishers at their wedding reception had so besieged the newlywed K-Js that the bride and groom had left Washington's Congressional Country Club ravenous. *So we drove and drove, and then we stopped and had this wonderful Italian food,* Mrs. Kirby-Jones had wistfully informed me at our planning meeting. *It was at a marvelous place called Guido's on Rockville Pike. I wore my pink dress with the double-orchid corsage.*

As it turned out, the Kirby-Joneses desired a menu offering Italian items that *exactly* matched the dinner they'd had right after their wedding reception. I'd promptly acquiesced. After all, most food orders are emotionally based.

I moved from the yoga *asana* known as the Sun Greeting to some leg stretches. I recalled poor Macguire's unhappy face when he'd reported back to me. His painstaking investigations had revealed that Guido's-on-the-Pike in Rockville, Maryland, had gone out of business over a decade ago. Guido, now deceased, hadn't bequeathed any menus to his heirs. Of course, I had not revealed these details to Mrs. Kirby-Jones. As I said, I was frantic for work. *I just need to know what you ordered,* I'd said confidently to my new client. *Don't give it a second thought,* I'd maintained, *we'll ask the restaurant for their recipes and it'll taste just like Guido's.* With what I considered promising resourcefulness,

Macguire had located a single back issue of *Gourmet* that contained Guido's-on-the-Pike recipe for Bolognese sauce. So now I was committed to serving pizza with goat cheese, ravioli in white wine cream sauce, lasagne *verde* with Bolognese sauce, tossed salad, Italian bread, and *tiramisù* to twenty people. But in April, when I'd booked the event, hoping we could serve dinner on the Kirby-Joneses' expansive deck, I hadn't figured on an incessant downpour on June 6. Maybe that was why Jake was howling. Somebody had left him out in the rain. I wanted to howl, too.

Coffee, I thought. *I need coffee.* I finished dressing for church and went in search of caffeine and the rest of the household. The only family member I could find was Scout the cat, a stray I'd adopted two years ago. He was crouched in a window well watching Jake bark. I would have sworn the cat was delighted to observe the dog's misery. To date, Scout had made no sign of forgiving us for adopting the hound.

"I'm sorry," I muttered, and stroked his back. "I know you would have preferred a gerbil."

Scout's response was the scathing feline equivalent of *hrumph.*

"Mom?" came Arch's voice from behind me. "Why are you talking to the cat about rodents?"

My son's appearance this morning was a jumble of tortoiseshell glasses magnifying brown eyes, freckles, tousled brown hair topped with a baseball cap worn backwards, sweatpants, and a too-long, crookedly hanging orange poncho. "Well, Mom?" he said in the reproachful tone he often took with me these days. He straightened his glasses on his freckled nose and waited.

"I feel sorry for Scout. Why is that dog howling, anyway?"

Arch peered out the window and adjusted his cap. "He's not *that dog*. Jake's just excited."

"About what?"

"About going out with Tom and me."

"Out where? Aren't you coming with me to church?"

Arch frowned. "We're going on a mission, actually. Tom took me to the five o'clock church service yesterday. Jake is feeling a lot better, and not acting so . . . you know, nervous. We wanted to see if he could get his trust level back." He paused. When I didn't protest his attempt to rehabilitate Jake, he plowed on. "Listen, General Farquhar called while you were gone last night. I told him about getting Jake. He wants us to come visit."

"Who's 'us'?" I asked. I hated sounding like an interrogator, but when it came to General Bo Farquhar, there wasn't much choice. *The only guest who isn't here is General Farquhar,* Tony Royce had said. *Says he's too busy.* Really. General Bo, who also happened to be Marla's brother-in-law, had recently finished his prison sentence for possessing rocket-propelled grenades, a large quantity of C-4, Kalashnikovs, Uzis, and all kinds of other contraband. Until he became settled, the general was staying on the estate of some friends who were adapting military technology for law enforcement. I'd heard their thousand-acre spread west of Aspen Meadow was surrounded by closed-circuit cameras and a nine-foot electrical fence. Not the place you wanted to send your son with his untrustworthy dog for a pleasant afternoon romp in the pouring rain.

"Listen, Mom, General Bo says he's *real* depressed. He was hoping you could bring him something made with chocolate, since the people who're taking care of him don't like it or don't have it or something. His phone number's down in the kitchen. Anyway. Gotta fly." His high-topped black sneakers made squishing noises as he fled before I could raise any more objections.

"Arch, please tell me where you're going. I won't veto it. Even though it's raining, in case you hadn't noticed."

The orange poncho rustled as Arch's short legs hastened down the hallway. "Better ask Tom," he threw back over his shoulder. "I have to go make sure we have everything. Jake's getting impatient."

No kidding. I glanced at my reflection in one of Tom's antique mirrors, and wondered if what folks said about owners looking like their pets would come to pass. I was still a short, slightly chunky thirty-three-year-old with unfashionably curly blond hair and brown eyes. Jake, on the other hand, boasted a sleek brown body, a long nose, droopy eyes and ears, and a perpetually slobbery mouth. All these attributes, my son had enthusiastically reported, helped him smell better. I pressed my lips together. I wished I liked Jake more, since he made Arch so happy. When I'd divorced his father six years ago, Arch had started begging for a pet. But I was freshly single, financially shaky, and struggling to launch a new catering business, not to mention a new emotional life, and I couldn't face the idea of tending an animal. I couldn't picture tearing up endless heads of lettuce for guinea pigs or listening to hamsters race all night on their little wheels. Back then, it was all I could do to maintain myself and Arch and handle the food preparation for nervous clients.

I remembered the rainy day last month when Tom had arrived with Jake. The prospect of caring for an emotionally distraught and out-of-work *bloodhound* in addition to running my not-so-healthy catering business had been too much. I'd threatened to stick my head into the proofing oven with the cinnamon rolls. I was prevented from doing so by Jake's enthusiastic scrabbling up the cabinet door. Then his not-always-reliable olfactory gland directed him toward the oven, and his powerful legs and body shoved me out of the way as he moved in closer to the rolls. Apparently, Jake loved the smell of cinnamon.

I sighed and entered the kitchen. The delectable smell of lemon and cherries mingled. Outside, Jake yowled away from his doghouse. Rain spat against the windows. My kitchen was warm and snug and smelled terrific. Still, my mood failed to improve.

Tom was setting a single place with a flowered Limoges plate. Hearing my sigh, he shot me an appraising look. Like Arch, he wore a tentlike fluorescent orange poncho. I couldn't imagine what they were planning to do in the rain to restore Jake's shattered ability to trust humans. Clearly, homemade dog biscuits were not enough. Tom gave me his usual jaunty smile. His sand-colored hair was damp. Perhaps he'd already tried to quiet the dog outside, to no avail. Seeing my forlorn look, his handsome face and green eyes softened.

"Morning, Miss G." He pressed the button on the espresso machine while his other big hand reached for a diminutive cup. "Not feeling too happy? How about some coffee cake? Be out in five minutes."

I sighed again. "Sure."

"Now, sit down and have some caffeine. We're going to be going out pretty quick here. Marla called. She wants you to go down to the Prospect office with her tomorrow morning."

"Oh, great." I gratefully sipped the dark, *crema*-laden espresso he handed me. "I'll be the referee between Marla and Albert Lipscomb. Sounds like loads of fun, huh?"

"You know, I've been thinking. I know I've heard of Albert Lipscomb," Tom said pensively as he removed the golden brown, cherry-studded cake from the oven. The fruity, buttery-rich scent was indescribable. "I mean, you told me he's Royce's partner, but there was some other context. It's been a while, though."

"What other context?"

He frowned. "Did he invest in goats? Or goat cheese?"

I laughed. "Not to my knowledge."

He sniffed the cake. "Listen, I just realized Arch and I won't be able to help you pack up for your event this afternoon. I know it's a big deal for you—"

"My dear, it's the *only* deal for me until I take muffins to the bank on Friday."

"No, no, you had two other calls besides the one from Marla."

I sighed once more. "Arch already told me about General Farquhar."

He slapped the cake onto a cooling rack and rummaged in his back pocket for his trusty spiral notebook. "People named Trotfield, they're Prospect Financial investors who say they loved your food at the mine yesterday. They're friends of Tony's or Albert's, I think. They need you for a dinner party this week. The husband is flying to Rio for five days, and they want to give him a big sendoff. They need you because their chef, an illegal alien from Sri Lanka, skipped." He gave me a wide grin. "I didn't tell Mrs. Trotfield I was from the sheriff's department. Didn't want to jeopardize your booking. Here's their number."

I took the sheet from him. "Yeah, I know them. He used to be a pilot for Braniff, wife has the money, now he flies charters. Thanks loads. What else?"

"Aspen Meadow Women's Club. Dinner meeting on home improvement, tomorrow. The club president, Janelle Watkins, called. She wanted your cheapest chicken dinner, keep it under twenty bucks a head. I said I thought you had a standard menu and Ms. Watkins begged me to fax it to her with a contract. Seize the day and all that. Didn't want her calling some caterer in Denver." He handed me two slick pages from the fax machine, one with my chicken dinner menu, the set prices, and contract stipulations—all signed by Janelle Watkins—the other a photocopy of Janelle Watkins's Visa.

I said admiringly, "Very good, Tom. But why the short notice?"

"Well, the club vice president was going to make the food, but seems she had a tiff with President Janelle yesterday. Veep huffs off saying the *only* way her home could be improved was if *Janelle* resigned from their club. I should have offered her a job working for Captain Shockley. Anyway, Madame President Janelle is paying for the dinner herself, says it's worth the price to be rid of that bossy veep who drove everybody nuts anyway."

I grinned. "Fix me another espresso, lawman. I think my luck is changing."

He laughed and ground more Italian roast beans. "Okay, look. We're doing a trail with Jake this morning. Arch is out getting a piece of scented clothing from the trail-setter right now."

"You're *what*?" I said, incredulous. "Doing a trail? With a bloodhound who was fired because he couldn't smell his own dinner if his life depended on it? And in this rain?" I wailed.

"Best time. Scent's stronger when it's damp. Arch's friend Todd has already hiked up to a spot we agreed on, behind a big rock in the Aspen Meadow Wildlife Preserve. He's waiting for us. We'll start at the beginning of that four-wheel vehicle path. It's not more than three miles."

"You and my son are going to hike a trail with Jake the retired hound dog for three miles, *in the pouring rain*? Do you know how much more chance you have of being caught in a rock slide with all the moisture we've been having?"

The second espresso hissed into the flowered Limoges cup. Tom clicked the tiny cup down in front of me and stooped to kiss my cheek. "Come on, don't ruin our fun, Miss G. Arch is dying to do this."

"Just listen, okay? Think of a cake with frosting. The frosting is the soil and loose rock we have in the mountains. Underneath is fractured rock—the cake. All this rain has added extra weight to the soil-frosting and could make it slide right off the underlying rock-cake. Got it? The land is especially unstable where streams have undercut banks. That's how you get major rock slides. And then—" I caught sight of his bemused expression and said, "Would you at least promise to be very careful?"

"Yes, Miss G. And would that be butter cream or meringue frosting?"

"With this weather, Arch is going to come home sick."

Tom grinned. "Oh, so first he wasn't going to come home at all because of the frosted-cake rock slide, and now he's going to come home with a cold. We're doing better. Anything else?"

Well, great. Tom had never had children and was not burdened with the worry that accompanied every foray into mountainous terrain. Nor did he know that taking a child out in wet, cold weather led to countless hours spent poring over old magazines in a pediatrician's office. These hours would be followed by countless pink teaspoons of Amoxicillin. Strep throat, ear infections, bronchitis, sinusitis . . . the man had a lot to learn. On the other hand, he did have a kid's own enthusiasm for going on adventures, and Arch treasured the time they spent together. I could just hear Arch if I vetoed their expedition. *C'mon, Mom, I'm not going to get pneumonia!* Sure. I sighed for the fourth time, sipped the espresso, then took a bite of Tom's coffee cake to keep from saying more. The delectable taste of lemon and the richness of cherry preserves infused the moist sour-cream cake. I narrowed my eyes at Tom, but he laughed.

"Delicious, huh? Be nice to your favorite cop and you can have the recipe."

There was a pounding at the back door and Arch traipsed through. "Here I am!" he announced as he joined us. His poncho and face were slick with rain. I suppressed a groan. "I've got Todd's T-shirt!" He held up a plastic bag containing a crumpled piece of grayish-white cloth.

Tom appraised the bag. "Not in the laundry? Not contaminated with other scents? Nobody else in the family touched it?"

Arch shook his head vigorously; the wet baseball cap slipped down over his forehead. He straightened it. "Can we leave? Please? I'm getting worried about Todd. You know, out in the rain. He has a poncho to keep him dry, but he *is* my friend."

"We're ready." Tom picked up a thermos and backpack bulging with what I guessed to be sandwiches, trail mix, and (of course) homemade dog biscuits. He pointed to a tangled piece of leather on the counter. "Hey, buddy, can you hold on to your plastic bag and bring the working harness out to the car? You're going to be amazed at Jake, Arch. Bloodhounds are renowned for their intelligence." Tom held up one hand in farewell, winked at me, and opened the back door. The rain beat down. Jake's howling increased in volume. "You know the word we don't use prematurely? Remember, Arch? Don't even use it in conversation?"

"F-i-n-d," my son spelled knowingly, then dashed out after him.

"Don't get near the creek edge!" I yelled after them, but I doubted they heard me.

Moments later, Jake fell abruptly silent. The blessed absence of barking was followed by the dull roar of Tom's Chrysler. I looked out the dining room window and saw the dark blue car move slowly past. In the backseat, Arch and Jake pressed their noses against the rain-smeared window. Both looked gleeful.

Chapter 5

When I returned from the first service at St. Luke's Episcopal Church and a quick visit to the grocery store to pick up supplies for the Aspen Meadow Women's Club dinner, I found Macguire Perkins sitting on my doorstep. Rain still washed across my waterlogged front yard and ran in rivulets down the sidewalk. Yet Macguire wore no rain gear, and his hair was as sopping as his sweatshirt and torn blue jeans.

"Macguire," I said impatiently, "why don't you put on . . ." Oh, forget it, I thought. It was hard enough trying to be mom to one kid who did his best to ignore me. I unlocked the door and disarmed the security system—needed protection against the Jerk's periodic rampages—and shooed him into the house.

Macguire snuffled, tilted his head backward, and shook his hair. Raindrops sprinkled across the room. Taking lessons from Jake, apparently. "I'm okay." He snuffled again. "The rain's not too bad, you don't really need a coat." His long strides propelled him, camel-like, toward the kitchen. "Besides, I brought my uniform stuff in the car. It's not wet. In the car, I mean. I'll be all right."

Well, fine. We had work to do. I put vats of thick, tomato-rich Bolognese sauce on for a last simmering. Macguire washed his hands, grated hillocks of gold-threaded Parmesan and creamy fresh mozzarella cheeses, then looked around for more work. The pizza dough I'd taken out to rise before church had come to room temperature. He carefully punched it down. As the Bolognese sauce began to bubble, the phone rang. Mrs. Kirby-Jones, no doubt. Clients invariably feel duty-bound to call on Sunday morning. They want to make sure you're not sleeping in. They expect you to be slaving away in the kitchen for their evening shindig. In fact, they expect you to have been working there since dawn.

"Goldilocks' Catering," I said with agonizing sprightliness as I reached for a package of the frozen green lasagne noodles I'd made the week before. "Where everything is just right!"

"It's me," Marla said morosely. "I'm in hell. I feel so damned guilty. Tony just phoned, and he's on his way over. I am about the farthest thing from *just right* that you could possibly imagine. Matter of fact, I'm sitting here thinking about what I'm going to say when I get a call from Albert Lipscomb's lawyer."

I cradled the phone against my ear and tried to unwrap the noodles. Whenever Marla plunged into precipitate action, she ended up in exaggerated remorse. "For heaven's sake," I soothed, "why do you feel so bad? Didn't Tony talk to Albert?"

"Oh, I doubt it. Tony went straight to the Aspen Branch Bar after the party and got plastered. Now he's nursing a hangover. He has a conference tomorrow morning, so he can't be in on our meeting." I heard her bite into something. I hoped it was one of the lowfat lemon muffins I'd given her. I also prayed her use of the term *our meeting* didn't mean she was counting on me for tomorrow's confrontation with Lipscomb. She went on: "Okay, I'll tell you what I'm worried about with Albert. He throws around those terms like *year-over-year* and *same-store sales* and *technical support.* Now he's all ticked off, so he'll probably treat me like a dummy."

"But how can year-over-year data or same-store sales have anything to do with a mine being reopened?"

"Ooh, Goldy," she whined, "I don't know. I guess I should have just hashed it out with Tony, or called my lawyer or the state consumer fraud people, or *somebody,* instead of going after Albert like that yesterday. It's just Episcopal guilt. You know, you worry about how you're handling your money."

"Wait, wait," I said with a glance at the clock. By the time we got through a litany of her worries, hours could pass, and I only had ninety minutes to finish the preparations for the Kirby-Joneses. Much as I loved Marla, I didn't have time for a party postmortem now. "Can we talk about this later?"

"Please, please tell me that it's going to be later, as in to-morrow morning later," she pleaded between bites. "As in, when you come down to the Prospect office with me?" I tried to block out the vision of Marla and Albert squabbling vi-ciously in one of Prospect Financial Partners' plush Cherry Creek offices. "Please, Goldy? Don't say no."

I opened a plastic container of fresh basil leaves and inhaled their flowery scent. "Oh, Marla, I've got this new booking for a dinner to do tomorrow night—"

"Come on, you can help me stay calm. It's bad for my

health to get upset. We won't be there for an hour, even. We'll go have brunch afterwards—my treat."

"But why do you want *me* there?" I measured out olive oil, Parmesan, and pine nuts and prayed that I could do my pesto recipe from memory. "The only thing I know about business is that I don't have much at the moment."

"I've invested a hundred thousand dollars just in the mine venture, Goldy. With that money, I could have put my dear nephew Julian through Cornell. Twice." Her husky voice cracked.

"You're already putting him through," I reminded her gently, and started the food processor whirling.

"Yes, but still, a *hundred K!*" she fumed. "I could have . . . well, let's see, I could have . . . put in a few new windows at the cardiac rehab center. Then I'd have a nice view of the hospital grounds while I'm on that damn treadmill."

And wouldn't Lyle Gordon, M.D., have loved that, I thought. The pesto ingredients had turned into a brilliant green, fragrant paste. "Marla, please. I need to cook. Are you feeling okay?"

Ignoring my question, she demanded, "Remember what I did to John Richard's shoulder? Think Albert knew about that? Maybe I *intimidated* him."

I groaned. My assertiveness was a behavior I'd learned only after my disastrous marriage to Dr. John Richard Korman ended. But Marla had stood up to him, and consequently had managed to be married a lot fewer years, and with much less grief, than I.

I said truthfully, "You didn't actually *hit* Albert yesterday. You just yelled at him and called him names. There's a differ- ence," I added, sneaking another look at the clock. Macguire was almost done punching all the air pockets from the dough.

"Okay, look," she said reluctantly, "I know you're busy. In addition to crying on your shoulder and begging you to come with me tomorrow, I just wanted to tell you that Tony and I are leaving for our fishing trip on Friday night, and we were hoping you could do that other favor for us before we go."

I began to slice fat vine-ripened tomatoes thinly, removing the seed pockets as I went along. "What other favor?"

"Oh, didn't he tell you? Tony was really hoping you'd do a taste-test for Prospect. Could you manage it? I think he'd pay for your time . . ."

I barely avoided slicing my index finger. "You're not serious, are you? I don't want to be paid to taste someone else's food. Besides, I thought you got out of analyzing restaurants. How does Tony think I can possibly help?"

"Don't ask me, I'm the dumb broad who can't even read an assay report," Marla said blithely. "And as for tasting—well, Tony just doesn't trust his own taste buds. What he'll do is watch the traffic in and out of Sam's Soups there by the lake. He'll talk to people, maybe conduct exit interviews, like that. Albert will crunch the numbers. All you have to do is sample Sam's menu and tell Tony if there's any way that *soup* will be the next food craze. You know he'll appreciate it, he'll have you cater Prospect's next big do. Please?"

"Friday lunch," I agreed reluctantly. Whether Tony would have me cater Prospect's next big affair was something I doubted very much, given yesterday's fiasco at the mine. But Marla was my closest friend, and I couldn't bear to disappoint her. Besides, it was the only way to get her off the phone. "I've made a couple of unexpected bookings, and Friday's the first time I can manage. Now please, I have to—"

"What, go feed the dog? How come I can't hear the mighty canine? Usually he's in the background singing away."

"He's out with Tom and Arch."

"In this weather?"

"Don't remind me." I removed the wrappings from several packages of milky-white *chèvre* and started to cut it into small cubes.

"No, I'll let you go if you'll just promise you'll come to Cherry Creek with me tomorrow morning. Be the buffer at the Prospect office."

I inhaled deeply, turned away from the *chèvre,* and stirred the dark Bolognese sauce. "If I come with you, promise you won't lose your temper again with Albert Lipscomb."

"I'll be like Mr. Rogers. On Librium," she added, and signed off. As the former wives of a doctor, Marla and I always laced our similes with drugs.

"Okay, look," I said to Macguire, but stopped. "Macguire, what are you doing?" I cringed as a large chunk of dough just missed the ceiling. "Macguire!"

Macguire held his hands out for the dough, but it landed on the counter. "Oops." He gave me a sheepish look. "You know how you see those pizza guys . . ." He scooped up the dough and began to press it into a jelly roll pan. "Never mind. How's Marla? Has she recovered from that big argument? Did that guy explain what he was up to?"

"No, he's doing that tomorrow morning." I let water gush into my pasta pentola and set it on the stove. "I'm going down to the Prospect office with her and try to keep things sane."

He stopped reading the pizza recipe and gave me a look. "The two of you are going down there together? Alone? Are you taking a referee's uniform and a whistle? Can I come?" He was hoping for fisticuffs, apparently.

The phone rang again and I begged Macguire to answer it so I could start on the salad. Instead of giving my customary greeting, however, my ever-helpful assistant barked, "Yeah, this is Goldilocks' Catering! What do you want?"

Even across the room I could hear Mrs. Kirby-Jones' hysterical voice over the wire. I gestured desperately for the phone.

Macguire cupped his palm over the receiver and opened his eyes wide. "I'm never going to learn how to *handle* people if you don't *let* me *handle* them. Go make salad. If she hangs up on me, you can call her back and say some weird teenager just broke into your kitchen— Ex-*cuse* me? *What?*" he said into the phone.

I held my hands up in mock surrender and returned to the counter to tear radicchio to shreds. Just when you think you're getting a handle on things in your personal life, your business life intrudes with a crisis. Or vice versa.

"Oh, my. Mm-hmm," Macguire said with unsettling empathy. "No. How many people, again? What? Oh, yes, we're *completely* mobile." I felt my heart lurch. What was he promising? Macguire furrowed his brow and watched me rip into a head of arugula. "We can move around the African decorations in your dining room, that's absolutely no problem at all. Oh, no, you don't know who you're talking to. This is Goldilocks' Catering—"

His blithe assurances were interrupted by more hysterical objections that threatened to rise to a shriek.

"What?" he demanded, cradling the phone under his ear and reaching for the pizza dough again. I cringed, envisioning another attempt at spinning it through the air. "Oh, *pull-leeze!* What did he say?" I waved the sauce spoon, trying desperately to get Macguire's attention. But he was staring at my shelves of cookbooks. Knowing him, he wasn't reading any of the titles. "Vegetarian burritos? For twenty people? In the next two

Provençal Pizza

1¼-ounce envelope active dry yeast
1 cup warm water
½ teaspoon sugar
½ teaspoon salt
2 teaspoons olive oil
2½ to 3 cups all-purpose flour
½ cup prepared pesto
12 ounces ripe tomatoes, thinly sliced and
    seed pockets removed
3½ ounces *chèvre*
4 ounces best-quality fresh mozzarella, grated

In a large mixing bowl, sprinkle the yeast over the warm water. Add the sugar, stir, and set aside 10 minutes, until the mixture is bubbly. Stir in the salt and olive oil. Beat in 2½ cups of the flour, then add as much extra flour as needed to make a dough that is not too sticky to knead. Knead on a floured surface until the dough is smooth and satiny. (Or place the dough in the bowl of an electric mixer and knead with a dough hook until the dough cleans the sides of the bowl, approximately

5 minutes.) Place the dough in an oiled bowl, turn to oil the top, cover with a kitchen towel, and let rise in a warm place until doubled in bulk, about 1 hour.

Preheat the oven to 425°. Brush a little olive oil over the bottom and sides of a 10- by 15-inch pan. Punch the dough down and press it into the bottom of the pan. Spread the pesto over the dough. Lay the tomato slices in even rows over the pesto. Dot the surface evenly with the *chèvre,* and sprinkle the mozzarella over the entire surface. Bake for 15 to 25 minutes, or until mozzarella is bubbly and dough has cooked through.

Serves 6.

hours?" He hesitated. "Oh, no. No way. We're having green lasagne the way Guido used to make it, lady! I mean, uh, Mrs. Kirby-Jones."

The voice on the telephone rose precipitously.

"Please listen to me, Mrs. . . . er . . ." Macguire faltered. He clutched his throat with his free hand, and stuck out his tongue. *I'm being strangled by Mrs. Kirby-Jones!* The shrill protests had changed to pleading. "Please," he repeated. "Will you listen? I did the research myself. I called Guido's-on-the-Pike. I don't care what your husband says he remembers. . . . You didn't eat at Taco Tita's. They even *remember* you at Guido's. You were wearing that gorgeous pink dress with that wonderful corsage. . . . Nope, you were at Guido's, not Taco Tita's, that's for sure. The whole staff gets teary-eyed every time they think of it. You were the most beautiful bride they'd—" I signaled violently. Macguire turned to me, finally. And winked.

Oh, Lord, I prayed, *please get us out of this mess.*

"Yes, ma'am. Talked to them my*self.* Talked to Guido, as a matter of fact. Who, me? Who am I? Why, I'm Goldilocks' researcher. Macguire Perkins. Yes, the same Perkins." Macguire smiled and rolled his eyes. "Yes, my father is the headmaster of Elk Park Preparatory School. What, me? I've already graduated. Oh, Harvard. Next year."

I pictured Macguire's father in his large, airy office with his gilt-framed degrees and his large, airy ego. I didn't want to imagine how he would react to this string of lies that was growing more fanciful by the minute.

But Macguire was all smiles. "Oh yes, we can be there early to set up. Are you going to wear pink again? Wonderful. Pink is *definitely* your color. Yes, your husband is wrong. There's no way you ate at Taco Tita's that day. But don't make a big deal out of it," Macguire advised solemnly, the world's sagest marital counselor. "It *is* your anniversary." He hung up.

"I don't believe this." I dotted the pesto-slathered pizza dough with the bright red tomato slices and creamy cubes of goat cheese. "What if she finds out Guido's been dead all these years?"

"Hey," said Macguire. He reached over to preheat the oven for the pizzas and then pulled out a kitchen chair. He missed the rungs and the chair fell on its side. "Oh, sorry, sorry . . . listen, everything's going to be okay!"

"What if she learns that restaurant went out of business ten years ago?"

Macguire widened his eyes in mock astonishment. "Oh, Mrs. Kirby-Jones," he shrilled in uncanny imitation of our client's neurotic tones, "you must be thinking of the Guido's on Connecticut Avenue!" He grinned. "Y'see, I knew that junior-year trip to the nation's capital would pay off some time. It sounds like I actually *know* something about Washington."

I sprinkled mozzarella over the pizza. Give up, I thought. It seemed Macguire could be perceptive or deceptive, as the occasion demanded. Still, the kid did have a way of leasing a place in your heart. Aloud, I said mildly, "I don't know why I ever thought you wouldn't be able to handle Mrs. Kirby-Jones."

"Yeah, most people think I'm pretty stupid if they meet me," he agreed cheerfully. "Just barely graduated, no college. But if I talk to them over the phone, then they think I must be like my supereducated, golf-groupie father, the prep school headmaster—"

"Macguire! I didn't mean—"

"Oh, it's okay." He set the chair upright and flopped into it. "Hey, listen. I felt real good doing that investigation into that ore for Marla. It was like a head trip—I mean, there they are at this big financial party having a big, loud fight over something I'd researched! Man!" He hopped up to slide the pizzas into the oven. Then he crossed his arms, leaned against the oven, and gave me a look of triumph. "I finally found something I'm really good at. I'm a great investigator." He paused. "So I'm thinking about going into law enforcement. Tell Tom Schulz I want to talk to him. I want to be a cop."

"Oh, come on. I'm not sure this is something you want to consider seriously. . . ."

"Chill, Goldy! Who do you think would miss *me* if I got shot by a bad guy?"

"Macguire!"

"I'm kidding, kidding." He sat back down and stretched out his legs. His sneakers looked sopping wet. "It's just that I don't think I'll ever go to like, some university. So I'm thinking of my future. I really do think I'd be good at cop work. Everybody figures I'm dumb, so they'd trust me and like, tell me stuff."

I finished tearing up the lettuce and stirred the Bolognese again, then tasted it. The dark, spicy sauce exploded with flavor. I tried to think of how to say what I thought I needed to. "If you decided to be a cop, you know your father would have a fit."

Macguire's grin split his face. "Hey, that's the best part," he said heartily.

Chapter 6

The Kirby-Joneses' house was a massive log-and-glass building that reminded me of a ski lodge. The architect had tucked a kitchen on one end of the first floor as an afterthought. Lucky for us we found the back entrance right away. As we hauled in our boxes, all I could see beyond the kitchen counter was a forest of tropical trees crowding the interior space. A banner announced the decorative theme of the party: "Marriage is a Safari." Italian food for an African motif. Well, I'd had weirder assignments.

In the great room, Macguire and I bustled between fake palm trees and huge containers of ornamental grasses to set up the bar. I was thankful we hadn't been asked to wear safari hats or explain how to make lasagne in the outback. Macguire, thank heaven, didn't broach the topic of a career in law enforcement again. Which was merciful, because within half an hour we were very preoccupied with guests. Macguire tossed salad, passed pizza, stirred ravioli, and served perfect cheese-glazed wedges of lasagne with an enthusiastic smile. I rejoiced that none of the guests were dieters. Everyone dug into the dishes with relish. At the end of the meal, Macguire and I moved smoothly around large ceramic elephants hung with ornamental lights to offer trays of gold-lined coffee cups. While we were finishing the dishes, Macguire shyly complimented Mrs. Kirby-Jones on the radiance of her skin. She handed him a fifty-dollar tip. He volunteered to split it with me, but I told him to keep it.

The rain had finally eased when Macguire and I parted around eleven that night. Tired, but happy with the successful evening, we decided to meet at four the next afternoon to prep the easy-to-cook Women's Club dinner. With any luck, I told myself as I luxuriated in a very hot shower at home, I could spend the morning helping Marla resolve her business problems, get her over to her cardiac rehab for a late appointment, and cook for the Women's Club without a hitch. Tom welcomed me into bed with a warm hug.

"You seem pretty pleased with yourself, Miss G.," he whispered.

"Well, I am. If I can get through tomorrow, I'll be in good shape." I nestled my head into his shoulder. "Man, how come you always smell so good?"

"Maybe it's because this woman I'm married to keeps buying expensive guy soap they don't stock down at the sheriff's department." He stroked my hair.

"How did you and Arch do with Jake? Did those home-made dog biscuits improve his accuracy?"

He groaned. "Not exactly. Todd climbed up a tree. His pool scent was at the bottom of the trunk, of course, but they don't teach dogs to look up. So Jake couldn't find him."

"Great."

"At least we found the kid before he got bronchitis."

"I won't say what I think about your idea of a fun-filled outing."

He grunted noncommittally. "Speaking of which, I suppose you're going down to Prospect Financial Partners tomorrow with Marla."

I pulled the covers over his shoulder. "Tom, listen. If they really have a problem with that investment, her heart could go ballistic. There's an awful lot of money at stake."

"Yeah, well. Try not to get into trouble."

I nestled into his arms and murmured, "If marriage is a safari, would you say you're a hunter, a guide, or a lion?"

"What?"

I found his ear and whispered into it. "Never mind. Just let me get a whiff of that high-class soap."

"You are asking for it, caterer. You know that, don't you?"

"Well, now, I guess I do." I suppressed a giggle as his large hands reached out for my body. If marriage was a safari, I didn't ever want to come back.

✦

The next morning, fog like gray wool pressed down on the peaks of the Continental Divide. For the moment the rain had ceased. But a steamroller of dark mist churning toward Aspen Meadow promised to change that. I saved drinking my double espresso until I was following Marla's Jaguar down Interstate 70. That way, the caffeine couldn't fire up my brain until it was too late to turn back. I remembered Tom's words: *Try not to get into trouble.* No problem. I took a sip of coffee. There was no way I was getting into trouble this morning. Except for Marla and Tony, I didn't even know the folks at Prospect Financial

Partners. Or care about them, for that matter. I was just there to referee.

The fog swallowed Marla's Jaguar just below the Genesee exit. I slowed my van, slugged down a little more espresso, and reconsidered. Actually, I did care. The sudden death of Victoria Lear in Idaho Springs, the problem Marla had presented at the party, the vehemence of Albert's denials—all these had piqued my interest. But Tom would not be pleased if I angered Albert Lipscomb or anybody else in Prospect management. I'd already backed into involvement—Captain Shockley would have called it *interference*—in several of Tom's investigations. The last thing I wanted was to upset Shockley by raising hackles at the venture capital firm where the captain had his retirement account. Still, with Marla's temper so volatile and so much money at stake, I certainly didn't want my best friend blowing a fuse at the Prospect office without me there to calm her down, did I? Of course not. I smiled, finished the last drop of the rich black espresso, and pressed the accelerator. Within moments the van was paralleling sudsy, swollen Cherry Creek.

We turned on Third Avenue and passed designer boutiques, supertrendy cafés, experimental restaurants, and a host of offices dedicated to making money to support the folks who patronized the expensive shops and eateries. After several blocks I parked in front of an elegant two-story building with square gold letters announcing the offices of *Prospect Financial Partners*. The modern façade of polished bloodred granite was threaded with veins of black and gold that glimmered in the clouded light.

Marla met me on the wet sidewalk. The last time I'd seen her wearing her subdued navy blue suit and double strand of pearls had been at my wedding. I felt out of place in my black pants, sweater, and old raincoat. Marla waved a dismissive hand

and quickly briefed me on how she was going to handle the encounter with Albert.

"Okay," she said, "say Albert says assays are too complicated for women to understand. Then you say he needs to explain it or I'm going to have a heart attack. Then he says he's too busy to take time for us, so I clutch my chest—"

"No," I advised sternly as I stepped over a mud puddle. "We wouldn't want to precipitate the real thing."

She defiantly shook her higgledy-piggledy hair, glanced up the street, and reluctantly reshaped her strategy. "Okay . . . if I ask him to show me the Kepler—" She gripped my arm. "That car looks familiar. Isn't that Macguire's Subaru?"

I glanced down the packed row of parked cars. "I sure hope not."

But it was. Even as I spoke, Macguire Perkins unfurled himself from the battered blue wagon and gave us a shy grin. "Look," he called before we could utter a word, "I'm here to help you." In three long strides, he was suddenly at our side. He wore a collarless, button-up black shirt and black pants, the kind of outfit rock stars wear when they're being interviewed. "You and Marla really shouldn't try to do this alone," he said earnestly. "I mean, I'm the one who got that assay report analyzed, and I even know somebody who works here. You know—a *contact*." He ran his fingers through his perpetually damp hair. "She went to Elk Park Prep a couple of years ago. She used to be a snob, but somebody said she's turned out kind of nice—"

I shook my head. "No, no, no. Go back to Aspen Meadow, Macguire. Please. What are we going to do, invade Albert's office and say, 'Hey, here we are, one client and two bodyguards!'? We just can't—"

"Oh, sure we can," Marla announced with another toss of

her head. She linked one arm through mine and another through Macguire's. "You can help us storm Albert's office. And Macguire, introduce me to your friend if you see her. I love reformed snobs. There are so few of us."

Dread filled me as we pushed through the first of two sets of heavy glass doors. *I want to get this straight,* I could imagine Tom saying with one sandy-colored eyebrow lifted. *Without an appointment, the three of you breezed into a multimillion-dollar financial firm, one of you faked a heart attack, and then the other two crashed into the partner's office?* And I'd reply, *Something like that.* And he'd say, *And you were* surprised *when they kicked you out?*

"I'm here to see Albert Lipscomb," Marla proclaimed to the receptionist. "He's expecting me!" I assessed the dark-suited woman behind her tall rosewood desk. She seemed to be the first obstacle in a succession of battlements.

"Well, Ms. Korman, it's good to see you," the receptionist replied pleasantly. Her black hair was cut severely around a face painted with ultrapale makeup. After giving Marla a hundred-watt, brown-lipsticked smile, she cast a disdainful glance at Macguire and me.

"They're with me," Marla told her. "Friends of Albert."

The receptionist glowed again. "Well, then. Why don't the three of you just go on back?" I guess caterers weren't the only ones taught to suck up to the high rollers.

We followed a muted purple, green, and coral tweed carpet down a coral-painted hallway bisected with rosewood wainscoting. Phones rang; noises burbled out of open-doored offices; harried, well-dressed assistants rushed to and fro. One strikingly quiet spot was the closed door to an office with the metal panel removed from the orangey-pink wall. The door's gold lettering still read *Victoria Lear, C.F.A., Chief Investment*

Officer. She'd died in Orpheus Canyon, near the mine that Marla was now questioning. I couldn't help myself: I surreptitiously grasped the handle. As I turned the knob, I imagined Tom shaking his head. But the door was locked.

Albert Lipscomb's secretary, a gorgeous platinum blonde who informed us her name was Lena Pescadero, wore a low-cut red dress that made Macguire's mouth fall open. Personally, I was transfixed by her hair, which was stylishly teased into a voluminous, tangled cloud. Lena turned away from greeting us to announce matter-of-factly into the phone that Albert was in conference and would return the call at his earliest convenience.

"Albert's expecting me," Marla said chummily when the secretary had hung up the phone. "We made a nine o'clock appointment over the weekend."

Lena Pescadero raised a thread-thin eyebrow. "You did?" She made a note on a pad and tapped the computer keys to bring up Albert Lipscomb's schedule.

"Hmm," said Lena as she stared at the screen. "I wish someone would tell me what's going on."

Marla rolled her eyes at us, then turned back to Lena. "Albert's not in conference?"

"No."

"Well, where is he?"

"I don't know, but he's had a lot of calls," Lena replied. She chewed on her lip and considered Marla thoughtfully. "What's going on with the clients? Did Medigen's antiviral drug get rejected by the FDA over the weekend, and nobody told me?"

Taken aback, the three of us were silent until Macguire piped up with, "Uh, I don't think the FDA works over the weekend."

Marla sighed. The phone on Lena's desk buzzed again and she answered it.

"No, no, not yet, Mr. Royce," she said. "Print out what?" She turned to the computer screen. "Okay, one moment, please." She tapped a few keys and lowered her voice. "Excuse me, but are you all getting a lot of . . . No, no, I'm sorry, sir. Charts for Sam's Soups, yes, certainly. Opportunity for margin expansion, and what was the other . . . oh, recurring revenue base. Yes. Right away. No, I don't know if she was the only other one who had it in her database before she . . . before the . . . yes, sir. Just as soon as he gets here."

I murmured to Macguire, "Let's go look for your friend." To Marla, I said, "We'll be back." Once Macguire and I were out in the hall, I said, "What's your friend's name? How long has she worked here at Prospect?"

Macguire blushed. "Bitsy Roosevelt." His acne-scarred forehead wrinkled in thought. "She's been here a year or so. I think."

"Would you be willing to ask Bitsy if she knew this Victoria Lear person? See if Victoria was doing anything with the Eurydice Gold Mine?"

Macguire began, "Sure, but why do you—" but I grasped his arm and shook my head.

Brightly, I said, "Looks like we're not the only food folks here today."

Shifting his weight nervously next to the massive reception desk, Sam Perdue seemed to have utterly lost the serene composure he'd exhibited at the mine party. There, his blond hair had been neatly combed over what I now saw was a bald spot, and his pale face had been unemotional, almost ethereal. This morning his thin hair splayed out from what looked like a monk's tonsure. His flushed face appeared miserable. His tie stuck out at a cockeyed angle, and one of his shirttails hung from his pants like a dishrag. Not surprisingly, the receptionist was resisting admitting him.

"I want to see Tony Royce right now!" I heard him demand. "It's about unit expansion. He knows all about it."

"You'll have to wait, please," the receptionist chanted as she pressed buttons on a telephone.

I greeted Sam with, "Hi, there. Are you doing all right?" I gave him a sympathetic look. "You seem upset."

He looked at me with disbelief. "Goldy? Goldy Schulz? Are you catering another party for them already?"

"No, no, we're just down here . . . with a friend." Behind me, in his sweetest voice, I heard Macguire ask the receptionist about Bitsy Roosevelt.

Sam sucked in his thin stomach and nudged the shirttail into his pants. "Are they going to invest in your catering business? You can tell me the truth, Goldy. Maybe I'm just wasting my time here."

"I *promise* they're not investing in me," I replied heartily. The receptionist had hung up the phone. Carrying a load of papers, Albert Lipscomb's secretary whisked down the hall to our right. A short, pear-shaped young woman in a beige suit entered the lobby and squealed with delight on seeing Macguire. Bitsy Roosevelt, no doubt.

"You're married to a policeman, aren't you?" Sam asked me uncomfortably. Albert Lipscomb's question. Sam straightened his tie, but his face was still pinker than the walls.

I nodded and said cautiously, "Sam, are you *sure* you're all right?"

He cleared his throat. "A woman fell on the steps going up to my restaurant at eight o'clock this morning and broke her ankle. We weren't even open. It's a bad break, and she was supposed to go by ambulance to Lutheran Hospital. I wanted to follow the ambulance, of course, to see if she was all right. But . . ." He paused and gazed at the massive rosewood desk. He seemed to have lost the thread of his story.

"And was she?" I prompted him. "All right?"

His face wrinkled with pain. "I don't know, because there's a picnic area that was washed out . . . you know the one just as you're coming into Aspen Meadow?" When I nodded, he continued, "A child fell into the water this morning and nearly drowned. The parents flagged down the ambulance, and the ambulance stopped. The EMT gave the kid mouth-to-mouth and CPR."

"What?"

"The ambulance . . . they have to do that, I guess, when's it's a matter of life and death, but the broken-ankle lady wasn't very happy. . . . The kid's okay, but they had to take him to the hospital, too . . . and I knew I was going to be late getting here. . . ." He blushed even more deeply and groped for words. "And then I couldn't find a place on this street to park—"

He was prevented from telling me more of his sorrowful saga by the receptionist's announcement that he could go back to Mr. Royce's office. Sam excused himself and rushed away.

Bitsy told us she had to go take the minutes of a meeting, "like right now," so Macguire and I started back toward Marla.

"Bitsy says she didn't work with Lear," Macguire told me under his breath. "But she has a few people she can talk to. Says she has to be discreet, though."

"Great."

"I told you I'd make a good investigator."

I sighed when we walked back into Albert's reception area. There, Marla sat nonchalantly at the secretary's desk copying words from the computer screen. Make that *two* good investigators.

"For heaven's sake," I exclaimed without thinking, "what in the world—"

"Fantastic, you're back." She scribbled intently. "Keep a lookout for Lena, will you?"

Macguire squinted at the corridor, clearly delighted at an opportunity to conduct surveillance. I felt surrounded by lunatics. "Let's leave," I said, hoping to persuade them of the folly of their ways. "It's quarter after nine. Albert's not coming."

Marla tore the top paper off the pad. "No way. I wanted to see who phoned our friend Albert this morning. Guess what other clients are worried besides me? He's had twelve calls including the Hardcastles once and Sandy Trotfield twice." Anger spiked her husky voice. "*All* Eurydice Mine investors. I scared a few folks, wouldn't you say? Maybe Albert had more to hide with that assay report than he let on. So he's playing sick to avoid everybody."

"She's coming," Macguire reported, in a low growl that I suspected was heavily influenced by Humphrey Bogart. Marla tapped a few keys to bring up another screen.

"Everybody get on the couch," I begged.

Lena entered looking as if she'd seen the proverbial ghost. "Who just talked?" she demanded. "Who said to get on the couch?"

"I did," I replied. Heat flamed up my neck.

Lena recovered and stared at me. "You have no idea how much you sound like . . . oh, never mind."

I didn't question her, just settled onto the couch by Macguire and Marla, who were earnestly flipping through investment magazines. Lena phoned Albert's house and left a message on his tape. Fifteen minutes later, she dialed his cellu-

lar. No answer. Calls from Eurydice investors continued to
pour in; I recognized their names from the Saturday night guest
list. At ten o'clock I tried to convince Marla to go to her
cardiac rehab. Instead, she got on the phone with Southwest
Hospital and rescheduled.

At eleven, Tony Royce, looking as handsome as ever,
rushed into Albert's waiting room. Today he wore a camel
blazer and dark brown pants that matched his perfectly
groomed mustache. "He's not *here* yet?" He addressed Lena.
"What the hell is going on?"

"He's had twenty-two calls," she snapped. "And, no—he
has not called, written, or E-mailed his whereabouts."

"Yeah, tell me about the calls." Tony lowered his voice.
"Marla, everybody seems to want to know about your little
problem with the assay report."

Marla exhaled loudly but did not reply. Tony's energetically
roving dark eyes took in our morose group. He asked if anybody wanted lunch and we all said we were staying put. When
he returned an hour later, he bore bags containing two cold
grilled cheese sandwiches for Macguire and grilled tuna and
polenta, along with a raspberry-custard tart, for Marla, Lena,
and me.

"I probably shouldn't eat this tart, but I really am very
upset," Marla grumbled as she forked up a bite dripping with
berries and cream. "It's all Albert's fault."

Lena said sympathetically, "If he's not here in a couple of
hours, I'll drive up to his house to see if he's hiding out."

"I'm coming with you," Marla said firmly.

Unfortunately, we were all still there at three o'clock. In a
convoy of four vehicles, Marla, Lena, Macguire, and I headed
back up the mountain toward Eagle Mountain Estates, a swank

development west of Genesee and east of Aspen Meadow.
Once we were off the interstate, the large houses loomed in the
mist. I felt a stab of worry about the Women's Club dinner. I
would give this expedition another forty-five minutes, and no
more. We meandered along neighborhood streets until Lena
pulled her Toyota up in front of an oversize A-frame of the
genus *mountain contemporary*.

We rang. We knocked. We called. The front door was
locked, as was the back. Marla traipsed around to a wall lined
with windows.

"Albert! Albert Lipscomb!" she shouted. The more Marla
called, the sicker Lena looked.

"Isn't there something else we can do?" Macguire asked
me. "The neighbors are going to call the cops if Marla keeps
hollering like that."

"I have a key, just wait a minute," said Lena. She pawed
through her purse and pulled out a key hanging on a chain
decorated with a red plastic heart.

Within two minutes, we were all through the front door.
Macguire loped up the stairs as if he owned the place. After a
moment, he returned, smiling uncertainly.

"I don't think there's anybody here," he reported to us.

As we walked through the first-floor rooms, I tried to calm
Tom's voice in my inner ear, something along the lines of *not
getting into trouble*.

"Albert!" Lena called. "Al! It's me!"

There was no answer.

"Everybody wait here," said Lena. "I know this place and I
. . . know where Al keeps his things. If anyone's going to pry,
it should be me."

Marla and I settled in the living room, which was decorated

in brown, black, and beige. Along one wall were shelves full of books with fancy names like *Driving Venture Capital on the Information Highway*.

"Don't touch anything," Marla warned.

"We're already in trouble, just for being here," I informed her sourly. After the stunts she had pulled in the past few days, this hardly seemed the time for her to advise caution.

Macguire gazed out one of the floor-length windows. "The neighbors came out, anyway. They're all gathered around like there's been some kind of accident. Man, people are so nosy," he said without a trace of irony.

Lena returned, looking even more anxious and ashen-faced than she had outside. Her blond cloud of hair appeared deflated. "He's gone." Her voice was vacant. "His suitcase, his clothes . . ." Her voice cracked. "His passport. We . . . he and I . . . He's gone."

"What?" Marla shrilled.

Wordlessly, Lena sank into a chair. I walked out to the kitchen, retrieved a Waterford glass from a cabinet, and filled it with water. Maybe I should have filled it with whiskey. Upon my return, Lena looked closer to fainting than when I'd left. She took an absentminded sip of the water, then said: "His closets are empty. His suits are all gone. Ditto his suitcases."

Macguire interjected with, "Oh, man. I mean, can you believe this?"

"Wait," I said. "What do you mean, *gone*? How do you even know where he kept his suitcases?"

"We . . . used to go to Estes Park together. . . ." Lena's voice trailed off.

Marla addressed me tersely. "Call Tom."

I gave her a helpless look and tried to think. Albert's clothes *and passport* were gone? Where was he? "I will call Tom," I said, "but I can tell you what he's going to say. The cops won't take an official missing person's report yet. They have to wait forty-eight hours." It was just shy of four o'clock. If Macguire and I didn't hustle back to my kitchen right now, the Aspen Meadow Women's Club would be out of luck.

A car honked out front and Macguire leapt to check the window.

"It's Mr. Royce."

Marla greeted Tony at the door and gave him the bad news. He choked and then he howled and insisted we were being ridiculous. Albert had to be somewhere around, he said firmly. Lena managed to struggle to her feet and confirm that Albert had absconded.

Tony looked wildly around the room. "There has to be a reason!" he cried. "This is absurd! He must have left a note or *something!*"

"You and I should go," I said to Macguire. "We have an appointment to do food."

"Well," my ever-committed assistant protested, "who's going to call the sheriff's department? They should jump right on this."

I exhaled patiently. No question about it, Macguire was romanticizing police work. Once he spent a couple of months trying to track down drivers' licenses and reports of missing persons' vehicles, he'd change his tune.

When we came out to the stone foyer, Marla was slumped on the floor next to Tony. Both faces were studies in misery. Lena kept murmuring into a cellular phone about Albert being gone.

"I'll call you," Marla promised me.

But she did not. At least, not for the rest of that day, Monday. Macguire and I were so busy with the chicken dinner for the Women's Club, I didn't have time to talk anyway. On Tuesday Marla did phone and say Lena had gone through Albert's files at the office and the house. His datebook revealed nothing unusual planned, except for the partner meeting with Sam Perdue, which Albert missed. Tony confirmed that Albert's passport and all his best clothes were indeed gone. Albert appeared to have packed and departed in haste. His Explorer was gone. None of the neighbors saw him leave. They hadn't heard anything either, but of course it had been raining. Probably nobody even wanted to look outside.

Marla didn't call again on Tuesday. I hoped her silence meant she'd spent most of the day at the hospital doing her rehab, the way she was supposed to. In any event, on Tuesday I was tied up preparing a last-minute vegetarian picnic for the board of the Audubon Society—under porch eaves, because of the rain—and came home so totally wiped out I slept for twelve hours straight. On Wednesday morning, Jake got loose. Arch and I spent several pleasant hours traipsing through damp pines and over soggy grass locating him. On our return, I pondered grinding up his dog biscuits in the disposal.

Marla showed up on my doorstep late Wednesday afternoon. Her frizzy hair was unkempt, and she was not wearing makeup. She was wearing a denim skirt and flowered T-shirt. Both her outfit and her appearance were totally atypical. Her skin, usually peaches and cream, was pale. I was afraid to ask if she was again short of breath.

"May I come in?" Instead of her usual bounciness, she sounded frighteningly subdued.

I invited her to sit down and gave her a glass of Dry Sack. The hand she took it with was trembling. For once it was good to have no jobs. I asked her to stay for dinner. She declined and drank her sherry in silence.

"Let's go for a walk," she said finally.

Arch was in the next room. I told him we were leaving. Even though the sun was finally shining intermittently through towers of white cumulus clouds, I put on a slicker, tossed Tom's raincoat over Marla's shoulders, and picked up two umbrellas. It would be good for Marla to walk. We emerged into the cool, wet-scented air.

I waved to a few neighbors as we moved down the sidewalk. Now that the rain had momentarily let up, the entire neighborhood, it seemed, was either out in their gardens putting in flowers, or out on their decks trying to soak up a little sun, dermatologists be damned.

"I feel totally depressed," Marla offered glumly as we rounded the corner and started up a graveled footpath put in by some earnest Boy Scouts about ten years previously. The path was lined with pine trees and white-barked aspens, their buds still tightly closed because of the late spring. A sudden burst of sunshine made raindrops glisten sharply on each pine needle.

"What's going on?" I asked. "Did Albert Lipscomb ever show up?"

"No." She chuckled bitterly. Her fingers brushed pine needles and sent a shower of drops onto the gravel. "No indeedy. Tony filed the missing person report this morning. The cops started looking for credit card usage, the usual. The Denver police department is mobilized now, too." She took a deep breath, then moaned, "Oh, God."

I tried to think. Had Tom mentioned anything unusual going on at the department? He had been tied up testifying in a forgery case he'd been working on for over a year. But I hadn't heard a thing about what was going on at the department except for the usual complaints about Captain Shockley.

"The Denver department?" I asked. "Why?"

We came to a wooden bench, also placed by the Scouts. Marla said, "Goldy, will you sit down?"

I brushed raindrops off the cedar boards and obeyed. The sun slipped behind a billowing cloud; the sky darkened ominously. Next to me, Marla shivered as a raindrop fell. She said, "Before he left, Albert Lipscomb cleaned out the partnership account. Three and a half million dollars."

"Judas priest. . . . How did he do that?"

"Well, he went to the central bank location. First of the Rockies, downtown Denver. Ordered the cash out of the account on Monday, picked it up on Tuesday. Apparently he charmed the teller, too."

"Some charm job."

"Must have been," Marla said with eerie calm, "because she disappeared with him."

Chapter 7

Marla did not elaborate on Albert's and the bank teller's disappearance, as no details were known. She did report that Tony was in a state of shock. He kept saying, "We have to make everything look normal. This is just a glitch. The work got to him. He's just holed up in a motel with the girl. Maybe they're in the Caymans." The partnership would not immediately go under; they had a small escrow account as well as modest equity positions in Medigen and other companies. "It's going to be okay," Marla said Tony kept repeating like a mantra. "We just have to believe it's going to *be okay*."

This was not the case at the Furman County Sheriff's Department.

"I don't know how the cops reacted to the 1929 crash," Tom told me as he patted an appreciative Jake that night. Tom shook his head. "But it couldn't have been much worse than the way Shockley is handling this. He calls Prospect every hour on the hour. He calls the Denver P.D. every hour on the half, to see if they've found that teller yet. He's handling the Missing Persons on Lipscomb himself."

I looked up from my recipe file. I'd promised to take a chocolate care package to General Farquhar the next day. "The captain is handling the Lipscomb search personally? What happens to all those rapists and murderers out there while Shockley searches for *his* missing money?"

Tom chuckled. "Not much. Law enforcement in this county has been put on hold, you can bet that." When I made incredulous noises, Tom wagged a finger at me. "You gotta keep the distance in this job, Goldy, it's the only way to stay sane. Besides, I want Prospect to get straightened out. If Shockley doesn't have enough money to retire, I'm going to have a heart attack myself."

"Has he found anything?"

Tom shook his head. "First place he sent his team was to Orpheus Canyon Road, to see if Lipscomb had pulled a Victoria Lear—you know, maybe had a car crash. He hadn't. Why would you risk escaping across Orpheus Canyon Road, with all that money and a cute bank teller? Then he sent guys to that damn mine, where, if you'll excuse my saying so, he didn't exactly strike pay dirt either. The place was totally deserted and all locked up. It's not in his jurisdiction anyway. This Lipscomb? If he changes license plates, doesn't use his credit card, and doesn't get stopped for anything, it could take forever to find him." He rumpled Jake's ears and gave me a serious look. "I gotta tell you, Shockley called me in and asked about Marla."

"Marla? Why?"

"I don't know," Tom replied slowly. "Shockley's secretive and paranoid as hell. He asked how long I'd known Marla, did she seem entirely stable, did I know how much she stood to lose if Prospect went under. He implied her little argument with Lipscomb at the party might have turned sinister at a later point."

"Good God. That's ridiculous. Marla couldn't hurt a soul." If you didn't count the Jerk, that is. And he had deserved it.

"I was very offhand, said Marla's bark was worse than her bite, a wonderful friend to you for many years, all that." He sighed. "But I have to tell you, Miss G., I didn't feel good about the conversation. At all."

Neither, of course, did I.

◆

The next morning, I suggested Arch take his dog far from the sounds and smells of my kitchen while I prepared General Farquhar's chocolate treat. If Jake loved cinnamon, there was no telling how he'd flip for products made from the cocoa bean. Arch was only too delighted to lead Jake up to his room. Gleefully, he vowed he was going to teach the hound the difference between fake blood and the real thing. Although I was not eager to know the details of this lesson, Arch assured me he had a whole bottle of fake blood left over from his Halloween disguise, and he'd just use a pinprick of his own blood for contrast. How comforting.

So, while Arch and Jake played with blood upstairs, I sifted dark European cocoa with flour, and thought back to when I'd worked for General Bo Farquhar. Two years ago he'd been married, strong, utterly confident. A battalion commander in his 1960 class at West Point, he had distinguished himself in the Special Forces in Vietnam and been promoted early to the rank of general. He'd become the army's ranking man in the study of terrorists. To his superiors' eventual chagrin, however, Bo developed his own idea of who deserved to share his military know-how. A group of Afghans—facing Russians who refused to retreat—had found a friend in General Bo Farquhar. While the Carter administration insisted the Russians withdraw, the Afghans scored a few hits with suddenly acquired state-of-the-art weapons, smuggled to them by none other than General Bo. When the story broke, the general had been forced to retire. Undeterred, he'd settled with his wife Adele, Marla's sister, in a huge house on Sam Snead Lane in the Meadowview area of Aspen Meadow Country Club. There he'd experimented with his cache of goodies, with the unfortunate conclusion that while I was working for him, things and people had blown up, including Adele. Although he had not been charged with killing anyone, the general had ended up at the Colorado state penitentiary at Cañon City for illegal possession of explosives.

I beat unsalted butter with brown sugar and remembered bringing Bo brownies while he was in prison. I'd visited him there twice. Each time he had asked about Arch; he'd wanted to hear all the details of my son's checkered school life at Elk Park Prep. Bo had wanted to know about Julian, too. But most insistently, the imprisoned general had questioned me about Marla. I'd always replied she was fine. He'd looked at me expectantly: Would Marla ever come to visit?

There was no chance of that, unfortunately. Illogical as it was, Marla still blamed Bo for the death of her sister, despite the fact that he'd had nothing to do with Adele's demise. Marla had said as much to me last fall, when we'd visited Bride's Creek, the spot where Adele Farquhar's ashes were scattered. General Bo, ever heroic, still loved the deceased Adele himself. The fact that Marla refused to see him pained the general deeply.

As I scooped out dark balls of the rich, chocolate-chip-dotted cookie batter, I tried to imagine the general's new hosts. What kind of deal had Bo Farquhar hatched with these guys to get free room and board at a luxurious, privately owned ranch? Mind you, these former military-industrial-complex honchos didn't call it a ranch, Bo had told Arch when he'd called to let us know he was back. They called it a *compound*. And I had no clue what Bo was doing out there that kept him so busy. I melted luscious, creamy white chocolate over the stove and resolved not to worry. General Bo was astonishingly good at survival. At least, he had been before he'd been sent away.

I tasted one of the triple-rich chocolate cookies and shivered with pleasure. The warm chips were seductively gooey inside the dark chocolate dough that was robed in white chocolate. If these didn't give General Bo his desired chocolate fix, nothing would.

Oddly enough, I was looking forward to seeing General Bo again. I didn't have any catering to do until this evening, when I visited the Trotfields, formerly served by their Sri Lankan chef. The food for that sumptuous dinner in Meadowview was mostly prepared. I smiled; the Trotfields did not live far from the Farquhars' old estate. But our family had no emotional link to the Trotfields—nothing like our connection to General Bo. Not only had I worked for General Farquhar at a time when I'd desperately needed a job to support Arch, but he had wormed his way into our hearts: Arch's, Julian's, mine, even Tom's. Of course, Tom had not been enthusiastic about my visits to the general when he was behind bars. Still, I reflected as I greedily licked my chocolate-smeared fingertips, eccentric as he was, General Bo was a friend.

Tom, however, had been skeptical when we'd discussed my plans.

Chocoholic Cookies

2 cups rolled oats
2 cups (1 12-ounce package) semisweet
  chocolate chips
1 cup (2 sticks) unsalted butter, softened to
  room temperature
1 cup firmly packed dark brown sugar
1/2 cup granulated sugar
1 1/2 cups all-purpose flour
1/2 teaspoon baking soda
1/2 teaspoon salt
1/4 cup unsweetened cocoa, preferably
  Hershey's Premium European-Style
2 large eggs, slightly beaten
1 tablespoon milk
1 1/2 teaspoons pure vanilla extract
9 ounces (3 3-ounce bars) "white
  chocolate," preferably Lindt Swiss White
  Confectionery Bar
1 1/2 tablespoons solid vegetable shortening
  such as Crisco

Preheat oven to 350°. Butter 2 cookie sheets.
*Do not alter the order in which the ingredients are
combined.* In a large bowl, combine the oats and

chocolate chips; set aside. In another large bowl, beat together the butter and sugars until creamy. Sift together the flour, baking soda, salt, and cocoa, then add to the butter mixture, stirring until thoroughly combined. The batter will be very stiff. Stir the milk and vanilla into the eggs, then stir this mixture into the butter mixture until thoroughly combined. Add the chips and oats; stir until well mixed.

Using a two-tablespoon scoop, drop batter 2 inches apart on cookie sheets. Bake 9 to 12 minutes, until cooked through. Cool on pan 1 minute; transfer to wire racks to cool completely.

Melt the white chocolate with the solid vegetable shortening in the top of a double boiler over simmering water. Holding a cooled cookie between your thumb and forefinger, dip the edge into the warm white chocolate to cover the top third of the cookie. Place on a rack over wax paper to dry completely. Store between layers of wax paper in an airtight container in a cool place.

Makes 5 dozen.

"There's nothing unusual about the general not having to serve his whole sentence," Tom announced that morning, before leaving for his sixth straight day in court. "I checked with his parole officer. Bo doesn't need to work because he has an income. From the army and the sale of what was left of his property, because the land underneath the house that blew up was valuable. I guess he invested the proceeds of the sale." He frowned. "But the guy's a nut case, Goldy, you know that."

"He's just . . . odd," I'd replied cheerfully. "He doesn't think things through the way most folks do. He gets all passionate, demands to be in charge, and that's what gets him into trouble. But I promised I'd go see him and I'm going. Anyway, with his wife dead and Marla refusing to see him, who knows how many friends he has left?"

"Oh, he has plenty of friends. I checked on that, too." Tom chuckled. "Friends who managed his financial affairs while he was in jail. Friends who have oddball radio programs. Friends who would plan the invasion of Saturn if they thought there'd be a payoff in it."

"Please, no cop paranoia, all right? I'm just taking the man some cookies. That's all he wants. Okay?"

Tom shot me a skeptical look. "I'd feel better if Macguire or somebody went with you. I'm not sure I like the idea of you paying a house call on a convicted felon *and* surrounded by those paramilitary wackos."

I'd sighed, but said nothing. Who was there to go with me? Not Marla. And if I asked Macguire, the would-be law enforcer, to be my bodyguard at an army-type compound, he would probably show up in battle gear juggling a brace of hand grenades. No gasoline needed on *that* particular fire, thank you very much.

I took the second batch of chocolate cookies out of the oven, set the cookie sheets aside to cool, and reflected on what I hadn't told Tom: that the general had instructed me to come alone. Sometimes you just had to act on your gut instinct. I was keeping my mouth shut and going unaccompanied. Like most caterers, the gut is the only organ I trust, anyway.

Arch pelted down the stairs to report that he was taking Jake over to his friend Todd's. I didn't ask about the blood test. Fifteen minutes later, I'd packed the cookies and revved up the van. Time to see just what was going on out at that thousand-acre nonranch.

Despite the fact that it was the tenth of June, fat snowflakes mixed with rain splattered softly on my windshield as I drove along the wet streets of Aspen Meadow. The water in Cotton-wood Creek was so high that it no longer flowed under the main bridge in town, but instead hit the concrete at midpoint and created a turbid backwash the length of the cross street. I turned and headed toward the small mountain town of Blue Spruce, five hundred feet above and fifteen miles west of Aspen Meadow. Actually, it was fifteen miles on the main road, General Bo had said, then ten miles meandering on dirt roads that were sure to be treacherous with snow and mud. I couldn't wait.

Just west of town, traffic had been diverted because of yet another washed-out bridge. Sam Perdue's dishevelment and frustration at the same type of crisis earlier this week made me resolve to go slow. The van bumped precariously over the makeshift bridge. Here the creek was particularly tumultuous, like dirty laundry water in a wild washing machine. But also dangerous. It made me nervous to look at the culverts, which had obviously not been designed to swallow so much liquid. Each concrete cylinder I passed was clogged with stones and brush. Above the culverts' rims, thick, wet sticks protruded like skeletons.

The van wheezed and climbed, topped a hill, and descended into a deep valley. I passed Carl's You-Snag-'Em, We-Bag-'Em Trout Fishing Pond, High Country Auto Repair, which looked abandoned, the equally decrepit Aspen Grove restaurant, and finally the minuscule Blue Spruce fire department and even tinier Blue Spruce post office. I wheeled the van right on what I hoped was the first dirt road Bo had described. Another road and then another deteriorated into rutted pathways, where it was all I could do to avoid stony fissures and puddles the size of small ponds. The muddy pathway with its central ice-crusted grass strip did not appear promising. Just when I became convinced I had gone the wrong way, the bumpy road abruptly ended at a gate and a high chain-link fence that extended in both directions through thick pine trees. There was a freshly painted white guard shack at the gate. Within moments of my approach, a tall man in a hooded green slicker came out to the van. He held a clipboard covered with plastic.

"Yes?" He was light-skinned and dark-haired, with sparkling espresso-colored eyes.

I told him who I was visiting and why. The guard politely demanded that I open the back doors of the van so he could inspect it. Moving methodically, he used a flashlight to peer along all the racks, under the seats, into the glove compartment. He even asked that I uncover the platters of chocolate cookies. He tapped the bottom of each platter and eyed the enticing contents dispassionately. So much for everyone being a chocoholic at heart.

He motioned for me to re-cover the plates, then squeaked the gate open and impassively waved me through. The van rocked upward as the rutted dirt road became smooth pavement without warning. Five minutes later, I pulled up in front of a massive, styleless stucco house that looked more like a barracks than a dwelling. Parked outside were three camouflage-painted trucks. Two camo-suited men greeted me at the heavy wooden entrance. Just inside, a closed-circuit camera monitored my movements. One of the men wordlessly took the keys to my van. The other ushered me into a room decorated with a long mahogany conference table and another surveillance camera.

A short, white-haired man in a beige suit soundlessly entered the room. He had pale skin and white hair, and a quiet, assured air. I couldn't decide if he was a CEO or a yogi.

"Mrs. Schulz," he said serenely, as if he were greeting me after a church service instead of here in paramilitary purgatory. He extended his hand and I shook it. He did not introduce himself. "You have brought food for our friend. The kind of food he craves, he tells me."

"Yes. I . . . used to work for him, and . . . he loves chocolate. We . . . have been friends for several years," I added carefully, as if to explain that I usually didn't meet the general's buddies under circumstances like these.

"I see." He gestured and we both sat down. He steepled his short fingers. "We are extremely worried about General Farquhar. He is being treated for depression by one of our doctors. He is also finishing an important project for us here. We do not think it wise for him to leave the compound."

"I'm sorry to hear that."

His colorless eyes regarded me somberly. "We would be very happy if you could help him in any way he asks."

I was feeling increasingly uncomfortable, but merely mumbled, "Well, sure." What I thought but didn't add was, *We're not talking about illegal or immoral help here, are we?* The pale man stood: I was dismissed. I was led by Greeter Number One down a joyless, undecorated corridor to a long, windowed room that resembled the day room of a hospital. The guard opened the door and waited for me to pass through, then stationed himself by a window, sentrylike.

In the far right corner, General Bo Farquhar was slumped in a turquoise plastic chair. When he heard us come into the room, he moved slowly to get up. He turned to face me, then held out his arms. I walked forward and hugged him. He smelled of fresh detergent and starch.

He pulled back and assessed me. "I'm so happy to see you, Goldy." His voice seemed gravelly with disuse. Tears filled his eyes. "It has just been too long."

In the months since my last visit to the correctional facility at Cañon City, General Bo's hawklike features had gone distressingly slack. His skin had grayed and his expression was distracted. After he had dabbed them with a handkerchief, his blue eyes—eyes that had always reminded me of equal parts of ice and sky—were cloudy. When I'd first met him, his hair had been so close-cropped that it was hard to determine its color—ash blond or white. In prison it had looked like an unevenly mowed hay meadow. Now the general's hair had grown out in loose, pale yellow waves. I found myself wondering how this compound could have a shrink but no barber. Bo's muscle-hard constitution had registered at least a fifteen-pound gain since the last time I'd seen him. He still looked fit, but the olive green uniform he wore hugged the new folds on his stomach and splayed out over his hips like pajamas.

"Let's go for a walk." Again the dulled voice surprised me. In fact, everything about him—his painstaking movements, perplexed expression, lack of focus—made him look twenty years older than the fifty-five I knew he was.

"Will they let us?" I whispered. "We could just stay here and have cookies." His expression immediately turned crestfallen, and I was sorry I had suggested hanging around. To tell the truth, this place gave me the creeps after just ten minutes. It was no wonder Bo was depressed. "Why *don't* we go for a walk," I said cheerfully. "I'm dying to see the sights at this place."

He managed a pinched laugh. "Let me get us an escort, then," he said. He ambled over to the man who had brought me into the room and murmured to him. The guard disappeared. When he came back, he brusquely nodded and gestured to a side door.

One thing about hiking up a Colorado mountain: Unless you know the trail very well, it's hard to talk while you're doing it. I huffed up the dirt path at the general's side. If you're not as surefooted as a mountain goat—and it was questionable that I possessed any such balance—all you focus on is getting to where the hiking stops. Conversing is out of the question. With clouds still threatening overhead, and our guard close on our heels, we veered to a narrower, steeper path and entered dark woods. I was very glad I hadn't brought along Arch and Jake.

The general took long strides over the rocks ahead of me. For all his extra weight and unhealthy look, Bo was hiking without effort. Behind us, our dark-haired guard, who clearly could have won a speed-walking race to Vail, easily kept pace with us. After about a quarter mile of this torture, the general decided to ask, "So, how is everybody, Goldy? Arch? Julian? Tom? You didn't invite me to your wedding," he said accusingly.

"Yes," I panted. "I got . . . married." What was I supposed to do, send him an invitation in jail? "Arch is fine. Has a new dog." Another mile of this, and I'd be dead.

"I heard. And Marla, how is she? I sent her flowers when she had the heart attack. . . ."

"Fine." My own heart was pounding. Would he send *me* flowers if I collapsed? "Everybody's great. Marla's got a boyfriend. He's with that firm you've invested in—"

"I know, I know, that's why I invested in it, so I could see her sometime. I would love to get together with her, Goldy, if you could arrange it," the general interrupted, his tone very serious. "When I was in prison all I could think about was reconnecting with Marla. She's my only connection to my dear Adele. . . ."

My shins were on fire. Ahead, the trees thinned to reveal a grassy area. To the left, a sudden view of overcast sky indicated that we were on the edge of an overlook. In the distance, I could hear roaring water.

"Please," I panted, "let's . . . stop."

"Keep going," was the barely audible command from our dark-haired companion.

Oh, marvelous. I fastened my eyes on the ground, put one foot in front of the other, up, up, up, and tried to think about energy, white light, and running the bases in softball when I was ten. These did not help.

"Look, let's take a break," the general said finally. He stopped and put his hands on his hips. "It'll be okay," he told the guard. "Let's go to where we can see the creek. It's across from the spot where we've been doing some testing—"

"Not a good idea, sir," countered the guard. "There's a full moon . . ."

Bo gave him the ice-blue gaze I knew of old. "I don't think

we're in any danger." The guard looked away. I guess Bo got whatever he wanted from everybody. And why should a full moon matter, anyway?

We threaded through the trees until we reached the rocky overlook. Water roared close by. Where were we? I held out both arms to keep my balance as I teetered between granite boulders the size of elephants. I inadvertently stepped into a mud puddle and quickly hopped out. The ridge lay ten yards ahead.

Thunder cracked overhead. Or was it an explosion nearby? To my astonishment, the earth seemed to be moving, crumbling under my feet. The enormous rocks on either side of us skewed sideways.

"Rock slide!" the guard cried as he vaulted back.

I swerved instinctively and caught a glimpse of General Farquhar's grim face. I grabbed his large hand and we leapt. I cried out to him, but my voice was lost in the clamor of exploding earth.

Together we somehow scrambled in the direction we'd come. The deafening noise of snapping trees filled the air. Behind us, rocks thundered on their way downhill. *Move, move fast,* I commanded my feet. Instead, I slid in deep mud. Mud, mud, everywhere. And rocks. My hand held tight to General Bo's. We both bounded up, up over rocks and cracking earth. A final fast hurdle brought us onto solid, but still shaking ground. We fell down, gasping. Miraculously, we had been on the very edge of the slide. Thank God. Another five feet forward, and we could have been killed.

How much time had gone by? Ten seconds? I shivered uncontrollably. Beside me, the general winced and cursed softly. I glanced back. Where we had been standing was air.

"General Farquhar, sir!" our guard shouted.

The general croaked a response. The guard appeared from within a stand of pine trees. There was mud on his face and uniform. He pulled out a radio and began hollering into it. There was another reverberating *ka-boom:* A last boulder tumbled into the stream. The same stream that had so treacherously undercut the bank we'd been climbing, no doubt. Again I cursed my own idiocy. After all my warnings to Tom about being careful on the trail! I shuddered. The radio crackled and a high, excited voice showered the brand-new silence with coded questions that sounded like *Alpha Bravo Charlie, et cetera, ten four.*

The guard spoke into his radio, then told us to stay still, HQ would be bringing a stretcher. Very, very carefully, I touched Bo's left leg. He cried out with pain.

"It's just a sprain," he insisted. He looked appreciatively at the guard. "I should have listened to you."

The guard turned his glittering dark eyes on me. "During a full moon," he explained to me in a curt tone which indicated that every moron already knew what I didn't, "the lunar gravitational pull acts on rocks in the continental crust the way it does on the ocean. Rocks rise in a tide, up to a foot. Plus we've had all this rain, and we're working with explosives nearby, which makes the entire area, especially above a stream, unstable." He shrugged.

I was soggy with rain and slick with mud. What I needed was a long hot bath—and this guy was giving me a geology lesson. I murmured, "Good Lord."

"The full moon adds to the earth's instability," our guide concluded knowledgeably.

So does explosives testing, I added silently.

A four-wheel-drive vehicle cracked through the undergrowth. The two camo-suited men I'd seen earlier hauled out a stretcher and loaded a protesting General Bo onto it. Then we all climbed into the all-terrain makeshift ambulance.

When we got back to the compound, Bo didn't ask me to stay, which was fine with me. He was in a great deal of pain and needed attention. And as I said, I needed a bath.

"Call us," I urged. "Let us know how you are."

"The ankle will be fine," said Bo with a rueful smile. His voice turned pleading. "But Goldy, could *you* please have Marla call *me*? I want to talk to her about the Eurydice Gold Mine, about any old environmental studies that have been done of that area. Also, I'm wondering about this guy who did the geological study that their ore projections are based on. I'm too tied up to look into these details myself. Would you get her to call?"

"I'll try."

He studied my anxious, filthy face. Chocolate cookies, a military compound, weird people, explosives nearby, and a rock slide. Normal excitement for him, maybe, but not for me. His look became indulgent. "Poor Goldy. Ready to go back to Aspen Meadow and your kitchen?"

I decided not to reply.

Chapter 8

As my van splashed home, I had a hard time blocking out the memory of the ground giving way abruptly under my feet, or the din created by the fall of boulders and trees. I tried instead to concentrate on the swish of the windshield wipers. When I'd left the compound, the dark, low-lying clouds had delivered a furious downpour of icy rain. At least it wasn't snow. I ran from the van to our porch steps and pushed inside, my heart thumping.

Arch was in the kitchen heating pizza. I was so happy to see him I rushed over and gave him a hug. Jake's tail whacked the floor happily in greeting. His red-rimmed eyes, furrowed brow, and long, floppy ears made even an old cat-lover like me smile. Jake panted excitedly, and, it seemed to me, smiled back. Maybe we were bonding after all.

"Gosh, Mom, where have you been?" Arch eyed my filthy jeans and jacket. "I thought you hated hiking. Is that where you went with the general, that you wouldn't let me come because you wanted to check it out first? Hiking? I swear, Mom, you look like you fell into a mud pit."

"I did, sort of. And you're right," I replied, "I do hate hiking. Unfortunately, that's what I had to do with Bo Farquhar. Sort of hiking and sort of climbing." *And sort of scrambling for our lives.*

"In this weather?" It was hard to ignore his friendly mimic of my voice, but I did. Upstairs, I quickly stripped out of the muddy clothes and ran the bathwater. And to treat myself, I poured in double the amount of perfumed bath salts.

Soon I was back in the kitchen, sipping piping hot Formosa Oolong, snugly wrapped in Tom's green terry-cloth robe. I tried to think. After a few minutes, I put down my teacup and dialed Tom, only to get his voice mail. I left a message. Somehow I couldn't imagine going out on my evening catering assignment alone. Not right after I'd survived a natural disaster that had very nearly deprived my son (and his dog) of a mother. Which gave me an idea.

"Arch," I said. "Macguire can't help me tonight—"

Arch swallowed his last mouthful of pizza. "Why not?"

This was no time to get into a discussion of why Macguire had chosen this evening to watch all the *Die Hard* movies so he could learn how to be a policeman. I rushed on with: "Would you please shower and get into a black-and-white outfit so you can come help me tonight? I'll pay you."

After we'd negotiated a suitable salary and fed Jake, we quickly packed up the ingredients for the shrimp pilaf I was preparing for the dinner at the Trotfields' mammoth house on Arnold Palmer Avenue in the Meadowview area of Aspen Meadow Country Club. The rain had turned back to mist by the time we set out. On the way over, I asked Arch if anyone had called while I was gone. He said no and wondered suspiciously why I was asking. Of course I wasn't about to tell him that I wondered how the general was recovering from his rock slide injury.

"Jake wasn't outside barking, if that's what you're getting at. The neighbors weren't complaining. He's a good dog, Mom. After what he's been through, he just needs a lot of affection."

"I know, I know. That's why I let him stay on your bed while we're gone."

"He probably misses me already."

"We're only going to be away a few hours."

"With Meadowview clients?" Arch huffed. "You've got to be kidding. Cook this, clean up that. Call so-and-so and get more chardonnay delivered. Oh, better make that six cases, looks like we're running out. Then go take Mrs. Smith some aspirin, because she's got a terrible headache and is upstairs lying down. And you just want to say, 'Well, if she hadn't drunk all that chardonnay—' "

"Arch! That has never happened."

"Just about." We swung through the elegant stone entryway to Meadowview. Large, pale houses sailed past in the dusk. "These people have *too* much money," Arch said. "They are *too* stuck-up."

"The Farquhars used to live over here," I reminded him.

"They were different. The general was doing cool bomb experiments and he had all that nifty security. And he wasn't stuck-up."

Crazy, maybe, but not stuck-up. Thank goodness for small blessings. I wheeled the van onto Arnold Palmer Avenue. "The place where we're going has good security."

Arch shot me a fierce look. "I bet they're not guarding a batch of state-of-the-art explosives."

"No, they have paintings. You know, art. The husband flies all over the world, but the wife's the one with the money. She uses it to buy paintings by famous artists."

He snorted. "See, I told you. They'll have a teensy-weensy yard that their kids can't even play in. And then they'll have a great big house filled with gross *paintings*. There'll be pictures of people with horses, people with dogs, horses with dogs, dogs with—"

"Arch, *please*. You're acting *prejudiced* against these people, and you don't even know them. Besides, with the money you earn tonight, you can buy some rawhide for Jake. And if you want a portrait of him, you can paint it yourself."

He *hrumph*ed. But he was right about the area where we were catering. Less than twenty years old, Meadowview is a posh development that features enormous houses that resemble yachts anchored to small grass lots. The lots might boast one or perhaps two pine trees. But the heavy demand for the residences in this expensive mansionhood had come from East Coasters and Californians fleeing high crime rates and even higher living costs. These new Coloradans could now look forty feet across their property and find themselves peering into their neighbor's bedroom. Would that make them feel perfectly secure, I wondered? Probably not.

"Gosh, *this* is valuable?" Arch asked half an hour later, when we were setting up the buffet. "*This* is what they have all that security for? Do you suppose somebody *meant* to paint this way?" He was staring at a large Motherwell canvas on the Trotfields' foyer wall. In the dining room, Amanda Trotfield had hung Giacometti and Henry Moore sketches. A Franz

Kline and a de Kooning graced the living room. The Mother-well that Arch was regarding so skeptically featured a large section of blue, with a fragment of a cigarette painted in one corner. Not a painting I would have chosen for the entryway to a smoke-free house.

"I don't know, honey, but yes, I think the artist probably meant to paint that way. At least it's not people on horses. Let's serve the appetizers and then we'll be able to take a break."

While Arch passed trays of filo-wrapped spinach triangles, I tossed fat, juicy strawberries with chilled, steamed sugar-snap peas in a light vinaigrette. It was a delicate, unusual salad that would contrast well with the Plantation Pilaf—a rich-tasting lowfat dish featuring succulent shrimp bathed in sherry and tomato juice. Marla had told me she was invited tonight, and I was eager to see her again. She had looked so bad when she'd told me the news about Albert absconding with the money that I was deeply worried about her. I hoped she'd have some news about either the teller or the missing money tonight. Then again, maybe someone else would have news. The Trotfields were Prospect Financial investors; Sandy Trotfield had called Albert Lipscomb's office the morning the infamous partner hadn't shown up for work. According to Tom, the Trotfields were friends of Tony, Albert, or both. Tony Royce himself, as well as the Hardcastles, would be in attendance tonight, too. One of the guests ought to know *something*.

I loaded a tray with ice and liquor bottles. Perhaps I could ask a few questions that would help Marla find out what was going on with that mine. Then again, maybe I was just being nosy.

As soon as the hors d'oeuvre and drinks were well in hand, I advised Arch to take a break. He had just poured himself a soft drink when Marla popped into the kitchen.

Sugar-Snap Pea and Strawberry Salad

1 tablespoon extra-virgin olive oil
2 teaspoons raspberry vinegar
1/4 teaspoon Dijon mustard
1/4 pound (1 cup) sugar-snap peas, including
    pods, strings removed
1 pound (4 cups) ripe strawberries, thickly
    sliced

Combine the oil, vinegar, and mustard in a small bowl; whisk thoroughly and set aside. Steam the sugar-snap peapods for 30 seconds or until bright green but still crunchy. Remove them from the heat, drain, then quickly run cold water over them to stop the cooking, and drain again. Combine the sugar-snaps with the sliced strawberries. Whisk the dressing again and drizzle over the peapods and strawberries. Serve immediately or chill for no more than one hour.

Serves 4.

Plantation Pilaf

3 tablespoons olive oil

8 ounces (1¼ cups) onion, halved and very
    thinly sliced

3 garlic cloves, pressed

1¼ cups rice

2 cups homemade low-fat chicken stock
    (recipe is in *KILLER PANCAKE,*) or
    use 2 cups canned chicken broth

¾ cup tomato juice

¼ cup dry sherry

¾ teaspoon paprika

½ teaspoon salt

1 quart water

1 tablespoon Old Bay seasoning

24 medium or large raw "Easy-Peel" shrimp
    (8 to 10 ounces of frozen raw shrimp)

1 cup canned pineapple chunks, thoroughly
    drained and patted dry on paper towels

1 cup frozen baby peas

In a nonstick skillet, heat 1 tablespoon olive oil
over medium heat. Add onions and cook until
they are translucent. Add garlic, stir, and lower

heat. Cook very briefly, only until garlic is also translucent. Do not brown the onions or the garlic.

In another wide skillet, heat the remaining 2 tablespoons olive oil over medium heat. Add rice and sauté until golden brown. Add cooked onions and garlic, stock, tomato juice, sherry, paprika, and salt. Cover the pan and cook 20 to 30 minutes, or until juices are absorbed.

While the rice is cooking, bring the quart of water to a boil. Add the Old Bay seasoning and the shrimp. Cook just until the shrimp has turned pink. Drain immediately and discard seasoned water. *Do not overcook the shrimp.* Peel, devein, and set the shrimp aside until the rice is cooked. Remove the cover from the rice and add the shrimp, pincapple, and peas. Raise the heat to medium and cook, stirring, until the peas are just cooked and the mixture is heated through. Serve immediately.

Serves 4.

"Hey, guys!" Her cheeriness seemed forced, and her complexion was splotched. She was wearing a shiny royal blue Princess Di sort of dress, only she looked more like a young Queen Mother. "These abstract paintings destroy my appetite," she grumped. "Why can't the Trotfields at least buy a few Warhol soup cans?"

"Oh, stop it," I said. "Go have fun with the guests."

She made a face. "Oh, sure. The cops have been around questioning all the Prospect clients, and nearly everyone here tonight has invested with Prospect, as you probably know. Did we know this about Albert Lipscomb, do we know that? Tonight we'll hear everyone's theories on what *really* happened to Albert. Sort of a replay of last month, when I had to endure everybody's theories on what happened to *Victoria*. Was she depressed, was she a bad driver, was she forced off the road, did she have car problems?" She lowered her voice. "Tony says the clients don't know about the missing three and a half mil yet, so mum's the word, Goldy. The clients *suspect* Albert took a wad of dough, though. And not a *word* tonight about the mine. Tony's in his act-normal mode. It's boring as hell." I muttered a silent curse. So much for sneakily questioning the guests. Marla winked at Arch and said, "Hey, guy, got any chocolate? I'm desperate."

Arch laughed. "You haven't even had dinner yet."

I poured tiny amounts of glistening olive oil into two wide frying pans. "What's the act-normal mode?"

Marla scowled. "Oh, don't get me started on Tony and how he's repressing his hysteria. I used to think he needed me. Now I think he needs an IV full of Demerol, a straitjacket, *and* a padded cell. Make that an IV full of Thorazine. I'm so tired of the man I could spit."

"Well, don't do that," I said as I shook the pan of sautéing onions. They sizzled invitingly. "Listen, Marla. There's something I need to ask you . . ." But what was it the general had said? I inhaled the rich scent of caramelizing onions and tried to remember.

"When am I getting rid of Tony? The sooner the better."

"Marla, please." I showered grains of rice into the remaining pans. On the other side of the kitchen, Arch was banging cupboard doors open and shut. "Oh, yes. General Farquhar was wondering if you knew the fellow who did the geology for the Eurydice. He also said to ask you about environmental statements. You know, like inspections of the mine."

Marla's face wrinkled in puzzlement. "Why does *he* want to know? He's a right-winger, he doesn't give a damn about the environment." When I shrugged, she exhaled impatiently. "Tell him they don't do an environmental impact statement when they're reopening a mine. And ask him why he cares, anyway, okay?"

"Chocolate-covered jelly beans," Arch announced triumphantly. He held up a glass candy jar that he'd somehow uncovered in one of the Trotfields' cabinets. "Want some? Wait, let me check the ingredients."

"You've trained your son well," Marla remarked with a wink.

"Marla," I said, "don't eat candy. Please. What in the world am I fixing a lowfat pilaf for if you're going to snack before dinner?"

Arch frowned as he read from the jar's label of contents. "Uh-oh. Artificial food coloring. Just a second, there it is. Yellow No. 5."

Marla raised her eyebrows. "Maybe Tony would be more willing to break up with me if I broke out in hives."

I sighed. Tony called Marla from the other room, and she

disappeared. The rice sputtered with the garlic and onions as I drizzled dry sherry, tomato juice, and homemade chicken stock over it. I gently swirled the ingredients and put on the cover. Cocktail refill time. For the guests, that is.

While I poured drinks in the living room, Edna Hardcastle declared to the other guests that Albert Lipscomb must be in Argentina. That's where all criminals ended up, she maintained. Whit Hardcastle overruled his wife. She must be thinking of *Colombia*. Tony Royce somberly told them that the police thought Albert was in California. This prompted Sandy Trotfield, a slender, strawberry-blond fellow who wore a collarless cotton shirt and designer pedal pushers, to observe loudly that he thought *California* was where all criminals ended up. He guffawed while the guests laughed uneasily. Marla rolled her eyes at me.

I joined Arch in the kitchen. Friendship notwithstanding, Sandy Trotfield had called Albert's office not once but *twice* this past Monday morning, presumably over possible problems with the mine assays. Now that Albert had absconded, though, Sandy appeared oddly blustery. Why would you be in a panic one day, and be making forced jokes about your money manager's disappearance four days later? It didn't make a whole lot of sense. Then again, maybe Sandy Trotfield was just a jerk.

The Trotfields' calendar was posted on the side of the refrigerator, and I surreptitiously looked it over while drinking a glass of bubbly water. Sandy had flown to Johannesburg a month ago, stayed five days, and come back. Three weeks ago he'd flown to Puerto Vallarta and stayed for another five days before returning. He was off for Rio tomorrow and would be back next week. Apparently pilots with rich wives managed to worry about their money, recover, laugh about it over spinach hors d'oeuvre, and then take off for extensive globe-trotting without a blink.

The doorbell pealed softly. Mrs. Trotfield had greeted her guests herself, so I felt no compunction to answer it. Arch didn't even hear the bell. He was listening to the Walkman he'd borrowed from Macguire while rocking unrhythmically but enthusiastically in front of the cookbook shelves. Suddenly he tore the earphones off his head.

"Receipts?" he cried as he reached for one of the books. "What's a book of receipts doing in with Julia Child and all that?"

I said, "Let me have a look," as the doorbell rang again. Why, indeed, would the Trotfields have a money book inserted between the food volumes? My heart sank, though, when Arch handed me a green publication entitled *Charleston Receipts*. "Oh, honey," I said as I flipped through the famous Junior League cookbook, "this kind of receipt *means* recipe—" I stopped talking as the book fell open to the title page. A hand-written inscription read: *"For my new friends Sandy and Amanda Trotfield, from an adopted Charlestonian! Best regards, Albert Lipscomb."*

Hmm. The Citadel, I remembered, was in Charleston, South Carolina. More significant, though, was the fact that the *Trotfields* and *Albert* were not just friends, but *new* friends. How new; and what would they do for a new friend?

The doorbell rang again. I flipped the cookbook closed and peered out the window over the sink. It had started to rain again. All I could see through the curtain of wetness was a line of fancy cars and four other Arnold Palmer Avenue houses. When the bell chimed the third time, I had come out to refill the platters on the buffet. The glistening, ruby-colored pilaf steamed invitingly and the guests *ooh*-ed.

Ding-dong, a fourth impatient ring through the loud riffs of Dave Brubeck's *Take Five.* The rat-a-tat-tat of precipitation on the fashionable blue tin roof was so loud, Mrs. Trotfield had turned up her stereo.

I retrieved the smooth, pink raspberry mousse pies from the refrigerator. When I started to whip the cream, I tapped my electric mixer against the side of the steel bowl in time with Gene Krupa's Maori-inspired drumbeat, which filtered through speakers the Trotfields had installed above the custom-made maple cabinets. Unfortunately, the doorbell rang again as I was starting to spoon heaping mounds of cream on each pie. Whoever was at the door was not going away. Amanda Trotfield, a slender, fortyish woman with translucent skin and black hair spiked outward in a fashionable punk, appeared in the kitchen. She announced that everyone was here who was supposed to be here, that the ice was just getting broken, meta-phorically speaking, and would I please get rid of whoever was at the door? She wanted her guests to enjoy their expensive food.

"It's probably FedEx," she hissed in my ear, "with some more stuff from Jeppesen for my husband." When I looked confused, she explained, "Maps. But he's also ordered a load of information on diamond mining in South Africa. If the guy rings again, would you get it? The security's off." So when the chime tolled for the umpteenth time, I marched out to answer it.

It wasn't FedEx. It was the police. One cop was a towering, muscled redhead. The other was slimmer, with an acne-scarred face and jet-black hair above a receding hairline. They wore plain clothes, but their sheriff's department vehicle, invisible from the kitchen window, was pulled conspicuously perpen-dicular to the Trotfields' crowded driveway. No one from this party was getting on Arnold Palmer Avenue without these cops' say-so.

"Mrs. Schulz?"

A familiar, chilly trickle of fear shot through me. "Tom. It's Tom, isn't it? Something's wrong. What's happened?" I cursed myself for not answering the insistent ringing earlier.

The short fellow, whose wiry black hair had been severely pomaded down to conform to his missile-shaped head, frowned. "No, nothing's wrong, we're just here to talk. Ask a few questions about—"

"About *what?*"

"Mrs. Schulz, please," said the big redhead, looking uncomfortable. I laughed as relief swept over me. Of course! This had something to do with the Trotfields. Maybe one of the neighbors had complained about all the cars.

"Yes," I said to the two policemen. "I'm sorry. Let me go get Mrs. Trotfield." Then I hesitated. After all, I was the caterer: I had a professional obligation to protect this party. "Her guests are almost through their entrée . . . any chance you could come back later?"

"We're here to see you," rasped the redhead. His eyes bulged. "Just to ask a few questions, Mrs. Schulz. Would it be possible for us to see you someplace private? For maybe ten minutes? Someplace where it *isn't* raining?" The downpour had soaked through his dark windbreaker.

My concern about Tom turned to disbelief. The last thing I needed at this moment was another disrupted party and a disgruntled client.

"Are you *serious?* Can't this *wait?*" I hissed indignantly. "Please? Do you know who my husband is? I can come down to the department tomorrow. I'll answer all the questions you want then."

"We know who you are and it can't wait," replied the black-haired man grimly. "It's about Albert Lipscomb."

Tom's words: *Shockley's put himself personally in charge of the investigation.* I took a steadying breath. "Let's get into the kitchen, then." I opened the door. "Please come quickly before any of the guests see you."

They followed me into the foyer, where to my annoyance, they stopped to take in their surroundings. I felt a prickle of impatience. Before I met Tom, I'd heartily disliked the police. Perhaps my misgivings about the sheriff's department had developed from the fact that when I was deeply bruised and even more deeply depressed, the cops had been unwilling or unable to lock up the Jerk and toss the key to his cell over the Continental Divide. After the divorce, I'd realized that law enforcement folks, unfortunately, don't have a whole lot of power in domestic disputes unless someone is killed. Marrying Tom and going through the harrowing experience of having him kidnapped by a would-be killer, I'd also come to realize how dangerous his work with the department could be, and how steadfastly most cops carried out their responsibilities. So my attitude had done a complete turnaround. Nevertheless, in the presence of these two men who now stood brushing raindrops off their clothes in the Trotfields' art-filled foyer, I couldn't shake my old feeling of discomfort.

"Excuse me, but before we go any further, could I see some ID? Quickly?" I asked. I glanced into the living room. No one looked my way.

The portly redhead with the bulging eyes, I learned, was Investigator Hersey. The black-haired fellow with the missile-shaped head was named De Groot. Neither gave any indication that they knew Tom, which for some reason I didn't take as a good sign. I handed them back their identification cards, then motioned toward the kitchen.

Hersey puffed himself up as if to follow, but De Groot kept his muddy boots planted on the Trotfields' Oriental runner. He patted his greasy black hair and stared intently at the deep blue canvas that had so puzzled Arch. After a few moments he leaned over and brought his face up close to the painted cigarette image.

"It's by Robert Motherwell," I said, still impatient. "It's—"

"One of his *Gauloise* paintings," De Groot said without looking away from the painting. Then he straightened and gave me a deadpan look. "The series he started after *The Elegies to the Spanish republic.*"

"Do you mind, sir?" I whispered. "Could we please go out to the kitchen? I'm trying to do a job here." De Groot raised his shaggy black eyebrows. When he didn't move, I rushed on with: "The Trotfields are very wealthy art collectors. I'll tell you *all about it* if you'll come out to the kitchen and ask your ten minutes worth of questions *there.*"

De Groot stared straight into my eyes as he said, "Very wealthy like your friend Marla Korman?"

I could feel the color rise in my cheeks. What was going on here? Hersey walked past me into the kitchen. De Groot lifted his pointy chin and swaggered after him. I peeked into the living room. Sandy Trotfield wrinkled his forehead at me and scowled. Doggone it. *Caterer caught with cops.* I smiled and gave him a thumbs-up, but he looked past me into the foyer, puzzled. If this inopportune visit from the sheriff's department ruined this party the way Marla's fight had wrecked the mine party, I would have Captain Shockley's head on a platter.

Arch had removed his headphones and was saying, ". . . Well, she's my mother," when I banged through the kitchen door. My son gave me a bewildered look. I asked him to tend to the buffet platters and told him I would be talking to these men for ten minutes *or less*.

"You know you can't question a minor without a parent present. What's the matter with you two?" I demanded angrily once Arch had made a wordless exit. "And what's so important it can't wait for me to get home?" Next to the counter where the raspberry pies sat partially decorated and unsliced, De Groot stood at attention. I guessed he wasn't going to have a go at the Rothko above the kitchen table. Hersey leaned his muscled body against a convection oven. There was a small notebook in one of his meaty hands. For guys who had been in some kind of hurry, they now seemed to have reverted to a designed-to-be-infuriating interrogation technique. Or maybe they were waiting for me to offer them food. *It's not going to happen, guys.*

Finally Hersey hauled himself up. "Nothing to worry about, Mrs. Schulz. We just need to ask about an event you catered this past Saturday at the Eurydice Mine. Did you know that was one of the last times anyone saw Albert Lipscomb before his disappearance?"

"No, I guess I didn't know that," I replied. I glared at the cops. Maybe *I* could get information from *them*. "What do you mean, *one* of the last times?"

They ignored this. De Groot said, "And your function at the party was what?"

"I'm sure you're aware I was just the caterer, not a guest. I'd never met most of those people before." I paused, because I knew they'd want me to clarify that. "Excuse me. The people I knew at the party were Marla Korman, Tony Royce, ah . . .

Eileen Tobey from the bank and . . . let's see, the Hardcastles I've known for a while and . . . the Trotfields. Oh yes, and I know Sam Perdue."

"Did you talk to Albert Lipscomb during the party?" De Groot's pitted face was inscrutable.

I shrugged. "Not much. He asked about the food I was serving. He said Prospect Financial would consider having me cater a picnic. He was just being polite, I think. Why do you want to know if I talked to him?"

"Please, Mrs. Schulz. Let us ask the questions. So you're saying . . . he was enjoying the party," De Groot concluded. "For a while, anyway. Until he got into a fight with your friend Marla."

"An argument, I'd call it. Not a *fight*," I said firmly.

"Argument about what?" asked De Groot. His eye finally caught the Rothko, but this time, apparently, I was going to be spared further enlightenment on the history of abstract expressionism.

"Who sent you?" I demanded. "Why didn't Tom come ask me these questions himself?"

Hersey said, "Investigator Schulz isn't on this case."

"That's not normal, is it?" I asked mildly. "Tom does more than homicide, and he usually heads cases like this. He does forgery, mail theft. And missing persons," I added after a pause.

Hersey retorted, "It's normal for an investigator to be removed from a case when he knows some of the people in the investigation. We're under direct orders from our captain. Now, please, Mrs. Schulz. Just tell us about this fight on Saturday between Mr. Lipscomb and Ms. Korman. Did you hear them?"

I paused a beat before saying, "Not really. They were outside of the tent where I was catering, and hail was coming down rather hard."

"Whose idea was that?" asked De Groot. "To go out in the hail? Your friend Marla's? How did Albert Lipscomb react to a client dragging him out into the hail to fight?"

"Did Captain *Shockley* say Marla *dragged* Albert out into the hail?" I retorted. Neither cop replied. "There was no *dragging*. Albert went outside first, then Marla followed him." I *tsk*ed. What was their game plan here? Whatever it was, I had to get the raspberry tarts ready. I glared at De Groot. "I need to work, if you don't mind."

De Groot moved away from the counter. I quickly spooned the rest of the whipped cream on all the pies, then sprinkled them with fresh, plump raspberries. I cut each tart into eight equal pieces, then levered the thick slices out and put them on individual plates.

Hersey asked, "What were Albert and Marla fighting *about*?"

Marla had told me the cops had been around her home asking questions, so these guys surely already knew the answer to that one. "The lab doing the assays for Eurydice ore," I said impatiently. "You know Marla is a Prospect client. I think she was upset about how Albert was handling an investment. I can't believe you haven't been able to learn all you need to know about this from other people who were at the party. Everyone was listening."

At that moment, Sandy Trotfield pushed into the kitchen. When he saw the two policemen, he recoiled.

"What are you two doing here again? Wasn't one investigative visit enough?" he demanded. "We're trying to have a party. First you bother *us,* now you're bothering our caterer. Why can't you keep normal hours?"

"We'll be done in a few minutes," De Groot said with a curt nod.

"Some people are asking about coffee and dessert," Sandy Trotfield announced to me, as if the two policemen weren't there.

"Coming right up," I replied. Sandy stormed out of the kitchen. So the two policemen had already visited the Trotfields. Maybe that was when De Groot had gotten his art lesson. To Hersey, I said, "So you've talked to everyone who was at the party?"

"Just about."

I switched on the coffeepot. "Then do me a favor and don't belabor this. If you're working directly for Captain Shockley, he ought to be able to tell you what happened." Emphasis on the *ought,* I added mentally. "After all, he was there, too."

Hersey said, "Shockley said you helped break up the fight. You were right next to Albert Lipscomb. How did he seem to you? Like a guy whose scam had been discovered? Like, now that something had come out about the mine, he had to get out of Dodge?"

"Why is Captain Shockley so interested in Marla's argument with Albert Lipscomb?" I demanded.

Hersey repeated blandly, "How did Albert Lipscomb seem to you?"

I closed my eyes and again saw Albert Lipscomb's furious thin lips and shining wet pate. "Hard to tell." I opened my eyes and concentrated on Hersey. "Marla told Albert she wanted to see him Monday morning at the Prospect offices. There was nothing in the way he acted to indicate to *me* that he was going to run away. He was just . . . ticked off. It happens at parties. People drink too much. They argue. They sleep it off and call me the next morning with a hangover and ask if they did anything really stupid. If I want repeat business, I always say no."

"But Albert didn't say he'd meet Marla Monday morning?" Hersey persisted. De Groot crossed his arms and waited his turn. The coffeepot burbled and hissed, and the wake-up smell of java filled the room.

"No," I replied evenly. "He didn't say he'd be there."

"What about Tony Royce?" asked De Groot. "What was he doing while they were fighting?"

I gave De Groot a half-smile. "Tony Royce helped to break up the *disagreement.* He was as upset as I was, and was worried about Marla, as I was. But twenty minutes later he seemed to have recovered. I don't think he'd had as much to drink as Albert."

Watching Hersey's bulging eyes, I wondered vaguely about thyroid medication. Six years the ex-wife of a doctor, and I was still jumping in to diagnose.

"Did you know Lipscomb before the party?" Hersey asked.

"Not at all." Although at this point I was desperately wishing that I *had,* since he'd successfully absconded with millions of dollars that included some of my best friend's money. From the tone of their questions, I tried to assess how much these cops knew about Lipscomb. Not a whole lot, it seemed to me.

I asked them, "What do you know about the bank teller who disappeared?"

Before either had a chance to answer, Amanda Trotfield chose that moment to bolt into the kitchen. Fast on her heels was her husband.

"Enough!" Amanda's voice was fierce. "I've had as much as I'll stand of you two policemen invading our lives! Get *out!* If you want to talk to the cook, go to *her* almighty house, not ours!" She stabbed an auburn-painted fingernail in my direction. Her eyes blazed. "And you. Get those pies and coffees out there, or there will be no check."

I gestured helplessly in the direction of the pie slices and the coffeepot with its glowing red light. I certainly didn't appreciate her threatening me in front of these cops.

Hersey looked at Mrs. Trotfield, who was quivering with indignation, then jotted in his notebook. He pressed his lips together. "Okay, Mrs. Schulz, go back to your cooking. We appreciate your taking some time for us." He nodded at De Groot.

I didn't see the policemen to the door. Neither, I was sure, did the Trotfields.

Chapter 9

When Arch and I got home, Tom was sitting in the living room talking to Jake. Actually, he was *murmuring* to Jake. *Cajoling* him. The man never gives up. Easily distracted by our arrival, Jake thumped his tail supportively as he drooled long skeins of saliva on our living room rug.

Tom appraised me. "Uh-oh. Looks like she had another unhappy evening. Come on and have something to eat. You probably haven't had a bite all day." He gestured to his offerings: English crackers, a cheddar spread veined with port, a soft drink for Arch, and a bottle of dry sherry. "Which is worse, not having jobs, or having bad jobs?"

"Can't decide." I dropped onto the couch beside him and spread a hillock of the rich, smooth cheese onto a thick cracker. I bit into it: divine. "Thanks for all this."

"Yeah, this is great!" Arch exclaimed after swigging the

pop. He patted Jake enthusiastically. "What have you guys been up to?" Jake was now a guy, I noted.

Tom's green eyes shone. "We have a trick to show you. Arch, remember we were talking about a game to resocialize Jake? So that he could deal with new situations?"

Arch nodded vigorously.

Tom said, "Let's let your mom do this one." He turned to me. "Here's what we do. I'll hide. You say the word f-i-n-d."

I asked demurely, "Do you have a dog biscuit in your pocket, or will he be glad to see you?"

Arch said, "Mom? What are you talking about?"

Tom's handsome face remained unperturbed. "Joke, joke, Miss G., go ahead. Before you give him the command, allow me a few minutes."

He walked out of the room. Jake's mournful eyes followed him anxiously.

I called after Tom: "Two of the morons who work for Shockley came to interrogate me during the dinner. Maybe you could resocialize them next."

When Tom didn't answer, I turned to Jake and said dubiously, "Find?"

Jake scrambled off, nose to the carpet. Arch watched him, transfixed. Within fifteen seconds, Tom strolled triumphantly back into the room. Jake pranced and whined alongside. Tom told Jake what a great job he'd done, and the hound enthusiastically climbed Tom's chest. After the obligatory biscuit-gift, the dog and Arch took off for his room, and Tom sat down next to me.

"Which two morons? Now that Shockley makes the assignments, the morons are everywhere."

"De Groot and Hersey."

He groaned and poured himself a glass of sherry. "The Odd Squad. Shockley's right-hand goons. Those two guys so completely botched a robbery case of mine that I avoid working with them whenever possible."

"Yeah, well, I wish I could have avoided them. Oh," I toasted him and added matter-of-factly, "something else. I saw the general today, and you'll never guess what the two of us experienced together."

Tom smiled mischievously. "Don't tell me. An explosion. Wait, let me guess. C-four, his favorite. It was a very *big* explosion, and you were safely far away."

"It might've been an explosion some distance away that precipitated a very big *landslide,* and I was on the *edge* of it." I sipped sherry, related the events of the afternoon, and, remembering Bo's queries, asked if Tom had ever heard of environmental statements being done for a mine.

"You mean the claims?" When I shrugged, he said, "I think those are recorded with the county clerk, as well as down in Denver with some state agency. And I'm pretty sure operating mines have to be inspected periodically for safety. And hey, speaking of safety?" He gave me a searching look. "A landslide? What on earth were you doing?"

"Nothing," I protested. "Not a thing. It's not like an avalanche, where you can plan to trigger it. I mean, unless you have the right weather conditions and use an explosive. In this case, all we had was a full moon, and the fact that they were working with explosives in the area," I added as I reached for another cracker. Tom was right: I was ravenous.

He shook his head. "I swear, Goldy, you get into more trouble in a *day* than I do in a *year.*"

"I don't go *looking* for trouble," I protested, mouth full.

"Oh, please. You know how many crooks have said that to me?"

"Thanks loads." I wagged a finger at him. "I'm going to find out what's going on with this financial firm. Prospect's chief investment officer dies in Idaho Springs, one of the partners disappears, my friend's money gets stolen." I paused to lick creamy cheese from my fingers, then continued with my litany: "A problem with assay reports. Idiot cops hovering to insult and intimidate people."

Tom's look was somber. "It's a missing persons case, Miss G. That's it. It's not even a needle in a haystack. It's a caraway seed."

I scooted over on the couch and gave him an affectionate squeeze. I do love a man who makes culinary metaphors.

✦

The next morning, Friday, the phone rang early. Marla.

"Okay, listen," she began without preamble, "I'm sorry to be calling you so early, or so late as it turns out, but Tony thought that *I* ordered the food for this weekend, and of course I thought that *he* had, and we need nonperishables, if you can imagine. So I was thinking—"

"I'm sorry, ma'am, but you have the wrong number. And why didn't you warn me about those idiot cops?"

"I *tried*." She groaned. "Awful, aren't they? They offended the Hardcastles by implying they were nitwits for investing in an abandoned mine. And listen to this. First thing that happened at the Trotfields' place? You'll never guess. As soon as the two cops came into the house, De Groot sneezed on the Motherwell. But listen, I do need to talk to you about the food for our fishing trip—"

"I thought you and Tony weren't getting along."

"We're not, but it's temporary. And contrary to the prevailing opinion in Colorado, *I* don't think schlepping into the cold, wet mountains is going to transform us into a healed couple. But Tony's desperate to get away for a couple of days, and he's told everybody he's going, so if he comes back without any fish, he'll lose face."

We said in unison, *"Machismo."*

"But," I protested, "aren't you leaving soon? As in this afternoon? I may be able to cook fast, but I'm not superhuman—"

"Oh Goldy, please don't say no, you have such a knack with food, and Tony really is a wreck—"

I sighed. "Hold on." I tied a robe around my waist and scanned the bedroom. Tom was not under the covers. Oh, yes. I'd sleepily registered his predawn departure. What was it he'd said? Something about female soccer players getting into a brawl at an indoor game last night. Apparently the referee failed to whistle penalties for lots of rough play, and the game ended in a free-for-all. The cops arrested one of the goalkeepers, and Tom's presence was needed this morning to deal with the mess. One thing I'd learned in the last year: Policemen work a lot harder than doctors. And at odder hours. I stared at the clock: seven-thirty. I had to get cracking on my weekly muffins-and-coffee cake assignment for the Bank of Aspen Meadow. But guilt cut between these considerations. Marla had given me so many business referrals that I felt duty-bound to squeeze her in. And of course, she *was* my best friend. Besides, if I didn't intervene, she would eat fat-loaded junk food.

"Look, Marla, I have a job this morning, and then I'm meeting you and Tony for lunch at Sam's Soups. Why don't I bring you some food then?"

"Oh gosh, could you?"

I glanced out the window and thought my eyes must be deceiving me, because it *wasn't* raining. It was just very, very cloudy and dark. "What I'm trying to tell you," I said patiently, "is that I'm *not* going to be packing a fresh whole stuffed turkey for you. You'd get ptomaine. I'll fix one cozy campfire dinner, and you can do the freeze-dried routine for the rest of the time. Okay? By the way, what are you going to do about fresh water? And firewood? The ground is soaked."

She said that fuel, water, and beverages were Tony's department, that they'd need enough food and snacks to get through the weekend, and she'd see me at Sam's at noon for my taste-test. I threw open the upstairs window and took a deep breath of moist mountain air. Fog was moving, ghostlike, through the sodden branches of the pine trees. *I* wouldn't want to be out fishing this weekend.

I stretched through a yoga routine, got dressed, then answered a call from Todd Druckman's mother, Kathleen. Some vacationing neighbors had given her Rockies tickets for the weekend. She wanted to invite Arch to Coors Field for a doubleheader against the Dodgers. I was profusely thankful that Arch would have something to do during the day besides retrain Jake.

I awakened Arch, who was none too happy to be brought to consciousness before eleven on a summer morning. But the promise of spending even a foggy day watching the Blake Street Bombers—a quartet of the Rockies' best players—and the rest of the beloved baseball team brightened his spirits considerably. I promised I'd bring Jake inside if it started to rain, and yes, the dear hound could stay in Arch's room while I was out. Then I gave my son breakfast and managed to convince him to wear a waterproof jacket before he slipped out the back door.

I checked the computer for my morning assignment at the bank. It was one of my favorite regular jobs, as I usually heard enough gossip from Eileen Tobey, the bank manager, to last a full month. Eileen infused all of her stories with great drama, which might explain why in her spare time she was the diva of the Aspen Meadow theater group. When she wasn't playing Blanche DuBois or Lady Macbeth, she was on the phone tracking down the town's latest rumors. Eileen was the kind of person who became your closest friend when a misfortune—cancer diagnosis, contested divorce, suicide of a relative—befell you. Unfortunately, the intimacy did not last a week past her learning every grisly detail of your crisis. And since she found out *everyone's* details, she was the most remarkably informed gossip I knew. She'd been talking to Albert at the Eurydice Mine party. Given her personality, I knew I could pump her for information today and she'd never even speculate about the reasons for my nosiness.

I ground Italian roast coffee beans and watched twin spurts of dark liquid hiss out of my machine. Then I sipped the espresso and tried to remember what I'd heard lately about Eileen herself. This past January, Eileen's ex-husband had filed for bankruptcy within a week of Eileen being named the new branch manager of the Bank of Aspen Meadow. I seemed to recall a rumor that she had celebrated both events with none other than Tony Royce. Was she one of the girlfriends who'd been jilted when Tony swore undying loyalty to Marla this spring? I wondered.

For the lavish employee coffee break Eileen had me cater every Friday, I usually served an assortment of fresh fruit and baked goods. Eileen set aside an hour when she was available to talk to her employees during this time about any problems they were having. I was always surprised by how many problems could be recounted, and how much food could be consumed, in sixty minutes. This Friday I'd decided on fresh Strawberry-Pineapple-Kiwi Skewers, Scones with Lemon Curd, Banana-Pecan Muffins, and Almond-Poppy Seed Muffins. At the end of the computer menu, Tom had typed me a note: *Why don't you treat the bank employees to my Sour Cream Cherry Coffee Cake? Love you, T.* His recipe followed the note. Honestly, this guy.

I beat butter with sugar and put in a call to the sheriff's department. Once again, Tom wasn't at his desk. I said to his voice mail, "This is your wife, who's making your scrumptious coffee cake. How about a date? This weekend?"

I hung up and smoothly blended cool, fat-free sour cream into the golden batter, then stirred in a spill of inky cherry preserves. The mixture was buttery-rich and fragrant with lemon and vanilla, and it occurred to me that I could eat the batter without even cooking it. I rid myself of such a devilish idea, slid the pan into the oven, and phoned Elk Park Prep.

"Yeah, this is Elk Park Prep, we're closed now," said Macguire's voice.

"Macguire? Is that you or a recording?"

"Hi, Goldy, yeah, you're speaking to me live. I don't like answering the phone here." He sighed extravagantly. "But . . . I guess even a private eye has to do his own phone work."

I let this pass. "I just wanted to let you know I can do the bank gig this morning myself, and then I'm doing that doggone taste-test at Sam's Soups, for Tony Royce, before he and Marla go on their fishing trip. I just didn't know what your plans were—"

"Oh, I have lots of plans. But don't you even want to know what I've turned up? In my investigations?" Before I could answer, he rushed on with: "Victoria Lear was starting

Sour Cream Cherry Coffee Cake

¼ pound (1 stick) unsalted butter
1 cup granulated sugar
2 large eggs
1 cup fat-free sour cream
2 cups all-purpose flour (High altitude: add
    2 tablespoons)
1 teaspoon baking powder
1 teaspoon baking soda
¼ teaspoon salt
1 teaspoon pure vanilla extract
1 tablespoon finely chopped lemon zest
½ cup best quality cherry preserves

Preheat oven to 350°. Butter 2 8-inch-square cake pans. In a large mixer bowl, beat butter with sugar until well combined. Add eggs one at a time and beat well. Add sour cream and mix thoroughly. In a small bowl, mix together the flour, baking powder, baking soda, and salt. Add the dry ingredients to the butter mixture. Batter will be stiff. Stir in the vanilla, zest, and cherry preserves. Spread batter in pans. Bake 20 to 30 minutes, or until a toothpick inserted in the center comes out clean.

Makes 2 cakes.

Banana-Pecan Muffins

4$\frac{1}{2}$ cups all-purpose flour

1$\frac{3}{4}$ cups sugar

5 teaspoons baking powder (High altitude: 4$\frac{1}{2}$ teaspoons)

1$\frac{3}{4}$ teaspoons salt

1$\frac{3}{4}$ cups mashed ripe banana

$\frac{1}{4}$ cup canola oil

2 large eggs

1$\frac{1}{3}$ cups nonfat milk

1$\frac{3}{4}$ cups pecan halves (do not chop)

Preheat the oven to 350°. Line 2 12-cup muffin tins with paper liners.

In a large bowl, mix together the flour, sugar, baking powder, and salt. Set aside. In another large bowl, mix together the banana, canola oil, and eggs. Gradually add dry ingredients to banana mixture, alternating with the milk, adding dry ingredients last. Stir in the nuts.

Measure out batter evenly into lined muffin cups, filling cups $\frac{7}{8}$ full. Bake 25 minutes, until muffins are puffed and golden brown.

Check with toothpick for doneness. Serve warm, or cool muffins on racks. Freeze for longer storage.

Makes 2 dozen.

Note: Muffins are about fifteen percent fat; to make them even lower in fat, omit the pecans.

paperwork for the Securities and Exchange Commission, stuff you have to do before you have an initial public offering of stock. They call that an IPO. You see, for the Eurydice Mine, the three and a half million Prospect raised was called a *private placement*. Thirty-five investors had put up a hundred thou each. Over the next year, the Prospect partners were going to hire a mining company to bring the mine into production, at the same time they worked on the IPO. But the SEC demands all kinds of stuff for an IPO, and that's where Victoria hit a snag. Right before she croaked. Anyway, that's all Bitsy could get out of the secretary, who hasn't worked there very long. The secretary even said that Mr. Lipscomb had come in and taken all of Victoria's files on the Eurydice Mine out of her office right after the accident."

"Good Lord."

"Hey, do I do my job, or what? The secretary got nervous talking about Lear there in the office. She said she and Bitsy should go out for lunch. Should I tell Bitsy to keep poking around? Go have lunch with this woman?"

Jake began barking furiously at the garbage man, even though he was at least six houses away. I told Macguire yes, he was fabulous and yes, Bitsy should go out for lunch with Lear's secretary, and continue to poke around as much as possible without arousing suspicion. I signed off and called Jake inside. As the hound trotted toward me with a distinctly guilty air, I hugged myself against the chill wind and considered. So Victoria Lear was working on assembling paperwork for the SEC. Not that that was related to her death, but one had to wonder. What kind of paperwork was required for an IPO? I settled Jake in Arch's room, where he no doubt jumped on the bed the instant I closed the door, then returned to the kitchen to finish the cooking for the bank affair. For the muffins, I whirled blackened bananas in my blender until they were dense and smooth, measured whole pecan halves into the flour mixture, and began to spoon the thick batter into paper cups.

The fragrant hot cherry cake emerged from my oven puffed, golden brown, and speckled with the dark berries. I slipped the tin of banana muffins in, closed the oven door, and took two dozen poppy seed muffins out of the freezer. Then I sliced and skewered the fruit, made a batch of Scottish scones on Tom's oversize griddle, and donned a fresh chef's jacket. Within forty-five minutes I had the fruit, muffins, scones, and cake packed, and I headed purposefully toward the bank.

"Oh, *Goldy!*" cried Eileen with her usual melodrama when I carried my lusciously scented goodies past her office. She jumped up to greet me. Eileen engaged in an aerobic and muscle-conditioning program that would put Arnold Schwarzenegger to shame. She also visited with bank clients while working with big free weights; she claimed to be a living symbol of the bank's strength. Whatever works. "I'm so glad you're here!" she exclaimed. Her blue eyes shone beneath black lashes, and her long black hair was tightly woven in a French braid. She wore a pink silk shirt that slid flatteringly over her sinewy shoulders. A short black skirt hugged powerful hips. I didn't know how strong the bank was, but I'd lay money on Eileen. "We're in some kind of mess, I can tell you that," she continued. "Thanks in no small part to Prospect Financial Partners. Creeps!"

"Well, let's hear all about it," I said as we headed into the empty conference room. I uncovered the first tray and offered it to her. "Have something to eat. Food heals all messes."

Eileen plucked a banana muffin from the platter. "Lowfat?"

I nodded. "Even lower if you don't count the pecans."

She shrugged and bit greedily into the muffin. "Mm-mm, yum. First thing I've had to eat today."

"What's the problem with Prospect Financial Partners?" I asked casually. "They don't use Bank of Aspen Meadow, do they?"

"No, but *our* merger with First of the Rockies becomes final today. A whole bunch of our account numbers are being changed to avoid duplication. Customers who didn't order checks are coming in *totally* irate. Not to mention the confusion with the doggone ATM cards. And of course I'm on the phone every other minute about this Lipscomb disappearance." She put the muffin down and looked wistfully out the window. "I knew Dottie Quentin, the teller Albert Lipscomb ran off with. She's probably on her way to Cozumel right now." She sighed and nibbled more muffin. "Dottie was looking for a guy like Albert. She even had a copy of that infernal book, *How to Meet and Marry a Millionaire*. In this case, he's worth a tad more than a million," she concluded darkly.

"I know, I heard," I said sympathetically. "A three-and-a-half million-aire. Does the bank stand to lose money?"

"Oh, you heard about the amount. It's supposed to be so hush-hush. No, the bank didn't do anything wrong. We followed standard procedures. How were we to know the guy was stealing money? Besides, Prospect had the cash in the account, for a change. But I am worried about Dottie." To console herself she sliced a thick wedge of coffee cake.

Prospect had the money, *for a change?* Hmm. Two employees came in and started to moan to Eileen about the new ATM cards; I busied myself slicing the rest of the cherry cake.

When the employees left and Eileen again assumed a morose expression, I ventured over with the muffin tray. "How old was that bank teller—did you say her name was Dottie Quentin?"

"Twenty-four. Dottie was my protégé during an exchange program between the branches. That dumb girl, I swear. I just wish I could talk to her."

I nodded sympathetically. "Albert wasn't *that* attractive, and he certainly didn't impress me as the kind of guy who could make love to you with words. Did he impress you that way?"

"Oh, no." She may have been in the middle of a bank merger crisis, and her protégé may have run off with a rich embezzler, but Eileen's dark-lashed blue eyes, which she tried to keep downcast, gleamed with triumph. Maybe she wasn't such a good actress after all.

"There's nobody here," I ventured, always one to take advantage of an opportunity for further sleuthing. "Want to sit down and visit for a little bit?" She nodded, and I poured two cups of coffee. "What I wonder," I said carefully, "is *why* he did it. Lipscomb, I mean. Three and a half million shouldn't be that much to a big money guy, should it?"

"It is if it's all you've got in the account," Eileen replied slyly. "Besides, maybe Albert wasn't motivated so much by money. Maybe what he really wanted was to get back at Tony Royce for something."

"Revenge? But get back at him for what?" I asked innocently.

She shrugged. "What few people know is that that mine was *Tony's* baby as much as it was Albert's. Albert usually analyzed their investments, while Tony brought in the clients. That's how they cleaned up on Medigen. But Albert inherited the mine, so he was the official promoter looking for cash investors. Tony was desperate to analyze his own project. He told me so himself. First he was going to score with Albert's mine, then he'd move on to regional restaurants." She waved her hand dismissively. "But first, Prospect would have to prove Eurydice still had gold; second, go public with their little enterprise; and third, make a bundle. Maybe things went sour. Maybe Albert decided to clean out their partnership account and leave Tony . . ."—she smiled—"high and dry."

"But . . . what could possibly have gone sour, Eileen? I mean, Marla just lost her temper over something she didn't understand in the assay report. My understanding is that you do lots and lots of assays to be sure a mine has gold or silver or whatever it is you're looking for. Surely one bad assay wouldn't be enough to ruin the whole project?"

She shrugged again. "Who knows? Because they're not going to be doing any more exploration up there for a while. Not without money. Albert Lipscomb certainly saw to that," she added maliciously.

I smiled at her and sipped coffee. "Clearly that doesn't cause you any pain. You must not be a Prospect client."

"*I* would never invest in one of their ventures." Her voice had turned back to vinegar. "God for*bid*."

"How come?"

Three employees appeared at the door. "It's not something I can talk about," Eileen replied curtly, and moved off to greet her workers. I got to my feet and offered fruit, coffee, and baked goods to the new arrivals. They dug in happily. When they left twenty minutes later, fed and content, Eileen lingered to pour herself some more coffee. She still looked hungry for conversation, so this time I decided to try a new tack.

"You know what *I* wonder about," I said conspiratorially, "is how, in this day and age of bank security, a guy like Albert Lipscomb could talk his way into a big wad of cash and a compliant teller."

Eileen glanced nervously at the conference door, blew on her coffee, and gestured with the muffin she held in her hand. "Oh, we know that part. Lipscomb went into the downtown branch of First of the Rockies Monday morning, June the seventh. He had a big check written out to himself, three and a half mil. He wanted *cash*. What did they teach him about banking in business school, I'd like to know? You can't expect to get same-day service with that size transaction. So the teller—my idiot friend Dottie—said, 'You have to order that kind of cash, we can't get it for you right away.' She alerted the officer, but the officer was drowning in this merger. So the officer told her, 'Order the cash, and convince the guy to come back tomorrow for it.' The officer told Dottie he'd join her in a minute to do the Large Currency Transaction Report. Required by the federal government, thank you very much, because of all the drug traffic," she said to forestall my question. She took a big bite of muffin, spilling crumbs over the conference table. She didn't seem to notice them. "Anytime you're doing cash over ten thousand deposited or withdrawn, you have to fill out a Large Currency Transaction Report."

I dumped my cold coffee and poured myself a new cup. "And what did Albert say to all this? I mean, it sounds as if he expected to leave that day with a couple of briefcases full of cash."

"Apparently he had all the right identification for the Transaction Report." Eileen sighed. "Albert left, then came back the next morning all smiles and charm, with a glitter in his eyes and a shine on his bald head. He loaded that three and a half mil into a large backpack, said thank you very much, and walked out. After the transaction, Dottie bubbled over telling all her co-workers how cute her rich customer was, and how nifty it was that he seemed so interested in *her*! She gushed about how she was going out to lunch with him. Which she did. And didn't come back. Wednesday morning, Tony Royce called the bank about overdraft protection for some large checks to his mine exploration people. You'd better believe the salami hit the fan. There wasn't enough money in the account to pay the exploration people, forget overdraft. Royce screamed and yelled and had a fit. He would never cosign on a withdrawal of that amount! Albert Lipscomb must have forged his signature on that check! Tony swore to decapitate the bank manager! And if one word of this got out, he said, he'd firebomb the damn bank!"

"What did the bank manager say?"

"Oh, my dear, that's the problem. The bank manager says they need to question Dottie, but she's drinking piña coladas in parts unknown. Now they're saying Dottie might have been in on the deal with Albert from the beginning." She rolled her eyes. "I'm just waiting for someone to call me in and say, 'You *trained* this woman? What in heaven's name did you teach her?'"

I swirled my coffee, hardly able to conceal my curiosity. "I wonder what makes people think they were in on it together?"

Blithely, Eileen waved a hand, scattering still more crumbs. "Because she didn't call Prospect that day to confirm the check was valid. Still, I do believe the conspiracy theory is a rumor perpetuated by the *bank* so the teller won't look quite so *stupid*. People will excuse crime before they *dream* of acquitting *imbecility*. My tellers, of course, are all spooked. They're playing *What would you do with a rich stranger* until I am sick to death of it." She frowned. Then she finished off the muffin.

"I wonder if Tony had insurance," I said idly.

"For that type of account? No way. I mean, he'd be insured up to a hundred thousand if the bank collapsed, but that's not what we're talking about here. We're talking about loss of cash, period. Maybe forgery. Serves Prospect Financial right, I say."

Once again I found myself wondering about the precise origin of Eileen's bitterness. Was she so triumphant *because* Prospect had lost the private placement money? Or because Tony had jilted her? We were interrupted by the arrival of the second gaggle of excited employees. I picked up our coffee cups while Eileen chatted with her people. After a few minutes, she wandered back to me to say she had to check her messages. I asked if she'd return to clarify Friday's upcoming assignment. Of course, I didn't give a hoot about next week's gig; I wanted to know what else she knew about Albert and the missing millions. But as I served coffee and delicacies to first the tellers, then the loan officers, I became intrigued with their conversations. Nobody ever thinks a caterer is listening. And you don't mean to be eavesdropping, you're just the invisible servant who hears people talk.

——*Well, I'd go out to lunch with a stranger if he'd picked up three and a half million in cash. Even if he did go to the Citadel.*

——*Not me! Don't forget, she refused to give him the cash the first day, and you know they keep lots more than that in the downtown branch.*

——*Maybe he was pissed off.*

——*Maybe he was asking her how he could get his three and a half million without his partner knowing.*

While I was cleaning up, Eileen came back in. She looked even more harried than she had when I arrived. "They're going to have a big meeting in an hour about this missing-Lipscomb-and-Dottie predicament. Big meeting means *long* meeting, and I'm starving just thinking about it. Would you fix me a plate?" When I nodded, she went on: "The regional managers from all over are getting antsy for an internal investigation. And damage control is out of the question now. So many people know how much money was taken, it's just a matter of time before investors start trying to bail out of Prospect, and the whole enterprise goes belly-up." I expected her to frown again, but she snickered.

I handed her the covered plate. "Sounds as if you're not too brokenhearted."

Her reply was defiant. "Well, I'm not." She paused, wormed her fingers under the wrapping of the plate, and pulled out a piece of cherry cake. She bit into it and made *mm-mm* noises.

I said, "You're not brokenhearted because Tony had already broken your heart, maybe?"

She shrugged. "Tony and I dated, yes. Off and on. He always acted as if he owned three-fourths of Denver. Plus, he seemed to know everybody. And I wanted to *get* to know everybody." She finished her cake, licked her fingers, and put down the dish. Then she pulled a mirror out of her handbag, looked at herself, grimaced, and pulled out a silver lipstick container.

"You do know everybody," I observed.

"Not in the Denver business community I don't. Albert and Tony and I were in a network, very professional, called WorkNet. Costs a mint, as in a thousand a year to belong. But it's for business leads. You scratch my back, *et cetera*. Very well organized. Very productive. You should join."

"A thousand a year for business leads? They'd have to be pretty incredible leads."

"But Goldy, they are. Say one guy in WorkNet does commercial leases. He knows months before anybody else that a company is coming into town. Now, the company coming *in* needs everything from telecommunications to decorating to a two-million-dollar pad for their CEO. So in WorkNet, we'll have, of course, decorators, telecommunications executives, real estate agents, even caterers. The deal is that we all help each other. Say the real estate agent who sells the CEO the mansion finds out that the CEO's daughter is getting married next summer. Our agent comments, 'I know this great caterer, absolutely the perfect person to do your daughter's reception.' And of course, it's going to be a twenty-five-thousand-dollar gig."

"Tony and Albert were in WorkNet?"

"Oh, Tony and Albert were in it to the max, darling. This was about five years ago," she said dreamily. "I simply loved going to those meetings with those guys. They were looking for rich investors right and left, and I basked in all that power, I must say. They wanted me to find wealthy people for them. You're Marla's friend. Doesn't Tony do that with you?"

I nodded. "He does, all the time. He used to ask if I catered for any rich widows. Last month he wanted to know if I knew any rich doctors."

Eileen reached back under the plastic wrapping to pull out another muffin. "Oh, jeez. Does he know your history? I mean, about your ex? I hope you told him off."

"No," I replied matter-of-factly, "I told him I tried to stay away from rich doctors as much as possible. So he asked me if I knew any rich *dentists*. I said no. Lawyers? Pilots? Plumbers? He said rich folks *needed* him."

"Did you help him?"

I smiled broadly. "I gave him a few names, but I'm not sure anybody had the kind of net worth he was looking for."

Eileen took another bite of muffin and nodded appreciatively. "I didn't bring Albert or Tony anybody, either. And no alarm bells went off when they wanted to invest my entire divorce settlement of two hundred thousand dollars. Make you a million in two years, they promised. I gave them forty thousand." She paused. "Tell me, as a food person, would you have invested your divorce settlement in goats?"

"What? Goats? As in farm animals?"

She licked her pinky. "As in farm animals. Tony and Albert didn't get caught, so maybe it was a genuine deal. Anyway, they said they only needed about five hundred thousand to get started. After they took my forty thou, they went out to meet people in churches. I'll bet you Tony and Albert spent my money on Sunday clothes. Those guys went to more churches, I swear, they were like apostles of the ecumenical movement. The two of them convinced numerous devout folks that the climate in Morrison, Colorado, was the same as that of Kashmir, Pakistan. That's where they raise the goats that provide the hair for cashmere yarn, in case you're interested. Mountainous region, sound familiar?"

"Vaguely."

"Well, I haven't gotten to the food part." She relipsticked her mouth and opened her eyes wide. "Goat cheese. Or *chèvre,* if you prefer. The Morrison cashmere goats were going to provide goat cheese *and* yarn. A double-barreled investment. Plus Albert said slaughtered goats would go to feed Denver's hungry, and the skins would be sold to raise money to build shelters for the homeless. That's how they got the churchpeople. As I recall," she stared at the ceiling, "they raised about four hundred thousand dollars on that one. Without so much as a single strand of goat hair or plate of cheese to show for it."

"So what happened?"

"Oh my dear, so painful. The two of them actually bought some land, bought a few goats, brought investors out and had them try on cashmere sweaters, taste a little Montrachet. But the samples were from a delicatessen, and the cashmere sweaters were from Scotland. *Their* goats all died. They unloaded the land. The investors, including yours truly, got back less than ten cents on the dollar."

No wonder she was so pleased with Prospect's recent run of disastrous luck. "Sounds like maybe it was just a bad investment," I murmured.

She gave me an incredulous look. "I looked up the deed for that land this year, although I wasn't smart enough to do it back then. Prospect *doubled* its money on it. Maybe they were sincere, maybe it was all a mistake, who was I to judge? Either way, this winter, I alerted the state consumer fraud people."

I held my breath. "What did they find?"

"Nothing. They said there was a statute of limitations problem and their staff had just been cut back to the bone. Plus, I was the only one who'd made any noise."

I straightened out the last of the fruit skewers and tried to think what to ask next. "Did you keep . . . seeing Tony during that time?"

"What was I supposed to do when all his damn goats were dying? I'd never seen a man so sad. He chalked it up as a loss, and he and Albert quietly got out of the goat business. I didn't get suspicious until the following year, when the two of them were yakking away in WorkNet about selling ostrich eggs to all the would-be ostrich farmers. One day, I got up my courage and cornered Albert. I told him in no uncertain terms that if he and his partner didn't get out of animal husbandry, I'd write up the goat fiasco for the WorkNet newsletter. Albert told Tony I was upset. Tony said, Oh, sweetheart, can't we go out for dinner? So I went, but I wouldn't give them a dime for ostriches. Now what I don't know is when the two of them started investing in regional companies. Prospect Financial Partners did great when Medigen went public. And might have done great with mining gold, who knows?"

"Sheesh. But," and I tried to sound thoughtful, "didn't you start dating Tony again? As in this year?"

Her cheeks colored. "A couple of times, why? Why shouldn't I try to stay friends with Tony? He's a part of the business community, whether I like it or not."

"I'm just saying it doesn't *sound* as if you're friends."

"Well, I . . . I mean I guess Marla is the jealous type, or something." She pressed the plastic wrap tightly over her plate. "Tony and I haven't seen each other in ages."

"You saw him at the mine party, didn't you? Of course, I was busy, but I thought I saw you talking to Albert—"

Eileen glanced out the window, and I had the sudden feeling that she didn't wish to discuss that particular conversation. "Just casual, I assure you, Goldy. Trying to bury the hatchet. I'm not an investor in the mine—they just invited me for . . . social reasons, I think." She turned her gaze from the window and winked at me. The wicked gleam was back in her eyes. "I certainly hope Marla didn't loan either of them any money. I'd never entrust either of those guys with my money again. Never. But listen, I have to go. You can just call me about next week."

I felt a headache looming, and groaned. "Okay. But . . . what worries me is that I think Marla wants to make the relationship with Tony permanent. I mean, they have tiffs, but—"

"Well, maybe she'll reconsider now that Tony's three and a half mil lighter. I promise, Goldy. Those Prospect Financial guys are bad karma. I never take a bite of goat cheese without thinking of them."

Chapter 10

I raced home to prepare a dish for Marla and Tony's evening meals out on the range. Or rather, by the trout-swollen brook. In the spirit of the taste testing I'd be doing later, and also because it could be such a comfort in rainy weather, I decided on homemade chicken soup. I chopped mountains of leeks, onions, carrots, and celery, then gently stirred them into a golden pool of olive oil along with the chicken breasts. If I hadn't been making the soup for cardiac patient Marla, of course, I would have used unsalted butter instead of oil. Small sacrifice.

I removed the chicken breasts when they were tender and milky white, then whisked in flour, white wine, and lowfat chicken broth. The homey scent of cooked vegetables wafted upward. My mind churned. As I sliced the chicken, I wondered how much of Tony's character Marla really knew. Or wanted to know. But then again, as a former girlfriend, especially one who'd been jilted, Eileen Tobey was *not* the most reliable of sources. And besides, my own Tom had remembered *Albert* in connection with the goats and goat cheese, not Tony and Albert together. Maybe Eileen was indulging in some reputation-destroying back-stabbing, by exchanging the names and the players.

When the soup had cooled, I packed it into zipped plastic bags and wedged frozen ice packs between the bags in a large cardboard box. I also loaded in fruit, granola, yogurt, raw vegetables, nonfat sour cream dip, and homemade bread. As I revved up the van, I wondered if I should be the one to confront Tony about the goat story. Then again, Eileen had left out a few significant facts in her tale, including that she'd resumed dating Tony several years after the goat swindle. Nor, she said, had she alerted the consumer fraud people until after she and Tony broke up *this year.* Maybe Albert was the real swindler; that certainly seemed to be in line with the way he was acting now. No matter what, I thought as I pulled up in front of Sam's Soups, I doubted this afternoon's scheduled taste testing would give me an opportunity for a business-oriented heart-to-heart with Tony.

"Here you are, finally," he said, as he guided me through the tables by the bank of windows facing Aspen Meadow Lake. The bright navy-and-white interior of Sam's Soups was meant to conjure up culinary memories of New England, I guessed, as I watched waiters and waitresses clad in sailor's outfits zip between tables. A long fisherman's net hung along one wall, while another festooned the ceiling. Framed posters depicting cross sections of seashells graced the other wall. And what did I hear? I moved close to a wall-mounted speaker. Yes: It was the piped-in sound of seagulls. Tony grinned proudly as I took all this in. He was his usual dapper self: white monogrammed

Rainy Season Chicken Soup

2 dried porcini mushrooms
2 tablespoons butter
2 leeks, white part only, split, rinsed, and
    diced
1 medium-size carrot, diced
1 medium-size onion, diced
1 large celery rib, diced
2 boneless, skinless chicken breast halves
2 tablespoons all-purpose flour
2 tablespoons dry white wine
4 cups chicken stock, divided (preferably the
    homemade lowfat chicken stock made
    from the recipe in *Killer Pancake*)
1 cup fat-free sour cream
1 cup fideo (fine-cut egg noodles)
salt and pepper

Using a small pan, bring a cup of water to boiling and drop in the porcini mushrooms. Cook uncovered over medium-high heat for 10 minutes, then drain the mushrooms, pat them dry, and slice thinly. Set aside. In a large sauté pan, melt the butter over low heat. Put in the leeks, carrot, onion, celery, and chicken, stir gently, and cover to cook over low heat for 5 minutes. Take off the cover, stir the vegetables, turn the chicken, and check for doneness. (The chicken should be about half done.) Cover and cook another 5 minutes, or until chicken is just done—not overdone. Remove the chicken from the pan and set aside to cool. Sprinkle the flour over the melted butter, vegetables, and pan juices, and stir to cook over low heat for 2 minutes. Slowly add the white wine and 2 cups of the chicken broth. Stir and cook until bubbly and thickened. Add the sour cream very slowly, and allow to cook gently while you slice the chicken into thin, bite-size pieces.

In a large frying pan, bring the remaining 2 cups of stock to boiling, and add fideo. Cook 4 minutes, or until almost done. Do not drain. Slowly add the noodle mixture to the hot vegetables and sour cream mixture. Add the chicken and bring back to boiling. Serve immediately.

Serves 4.

shirt, navy pants, mustache freshly clipped, hair blown dry into a soft wave. "We've been waiting for you, Goldy. Sam's chef has prepared a whole smorgasbord of soups just for you."

I glanced around the crowded restaurant. As the only caterer in a small town, I'd learned that it's not a good idea to frequent the local eateries. Then all the people who see you say, "Why do you suppose she's eating here? Think it's better than her own stuff? Is she here to spy? Or to be critical?" Experience made me doubt Sam Perdue would join us for the taste test. Why submit your own wares for judgment from a rival? And how could I honestly evaluate his soups in his presence? Alas, he waved at Tony and me from his seat next to Marla. They were at the table in the middle of the restaurant that I guessed was our destination. At least Sam looked more composed than he had at the Prospect office four days ago. His baby-fine blond hair was neatly combed over his bald spot. His slight frame made him look much younger than the thirty-two years of age someone had once told me he was. If I criticized his food, I'd feel as if I were hurting a child. My heart sank.

Edna Hardcastle fluttered up to the table just as I was sitting down next to Marla, who greeted me with a grateful smile. "Oh, you're here, you're here," Edna gushed. She wore a two-piece beige herringbone knit. Her henna hair was swirled up in an intricate twist. "Now don't worry about a thing, Goldy," she admonished before I could say a word. "I know you're probably thinking, Oh, what can I do? I'm just a *local* person. In fact, we're all putting a great *deal* of faith in you, dear, and *much* is riding on your opinion. Of course, if we had only invested in food from the beginning . . ." Her voice trailed off. "But never mind, here you are, and we're all going to be *so* interested in your opinion, it'll give us a chance to get in on the ground floor. . . ."

As she blathered on, Tony sidled over to his seat and gestured for me to pick up a spoon and dig into one of the blue porcelain bowls in the center of the table. Helpful sticky notes on the platter containing the soup bowls said: *Terrapin Tom's Tomato, Moby Dick's Chicken, Cocoa Beach Chocolate, Cranky Crab, Big Cheese Chowder.* Hold on. *Cocoa Beach Chocolate* soup? I didn't think I could get even the chocoholic General Farquhar to sample that. Mrs. Hardcastle was chattering about the cook she'd had in Wisconsin. You could just get the *best* cheese there, and had Tony ever tasted *upstate* cheddar?

Sam murmured placating noises to Mrs. Hardcastle, while Marla and Tony talked about soups they'd tasted at French restaurants. I suddenly recalled the late Victoria Lear, who had not liked Sam's Soups, despite the cute names. I should have been smiling and paying attention to Mrs. Hardcastle, or getting off a gentle barb that the only cheese Tony knew was from goats, but unfortunately, what went through my mind as I contemplated the blue bowl was, *You can die doing a taste test.* I scooped up a spoonful of Cranky Crab soup. Flaunting risk, I lifted the spoon toward my lips. Suddenly all eyes in the restaurant seemed focused on my open mouth. I hesitated. Images of medieval poison tasters came to mind. One bite, and it might be my last.

"For crying out loud, Goldy," Marla admonished as the spoon holding the crab mixture trembled in my fingers. She waggled her head in reproof. "When *I* taste test, it's *fun*. It's just seafood. Don't think *soup*. Think *casserole*. It's not going to kill you." Could Marla possibly still want to invest in a chain of soup-only restaurants, after all that had been happening with Prospect Financial? Apparently so. But not until I gave a thumbs-up to the Cranky Crab concoction. I noticed *she* wasn't having any soup-casserole, however. Trying to be careful about her diet. Mm-hmm.

"Let Goldy try the stuff, will you?" Tony Royce advised as he shifted in his chair and glanced around at the other tables. "We have to make things appear normal," he added. He sounded nervous. *Normal*, his favorite word. "We're carrying on with business as usual. We're tasting. We're investing. Big crowd here, likes soup. Okay, let's go, Goldy. Eat."

There was no soup bowl in front of Tony, either, I noticed. Not a good sign. Sam Perdue ran his fingers through his thin blond hair. His eyes crinkled with anxiety.

Over my shoulder, Mrs. Hardcastle gabbed without a break. ". . . This is no ordinary soup, you know. Sam's is about to expand from its Denver and Aspen Meadow locations because this is really a *singular* creation, don't you think so, Tony?"

Tony waved his hands expansively. "They use all the freshest ingredients. All the restaurant critics are raving about this . . . what, Mrs. Hardcastle?"

"Light-tasting magic," she responded rapturously, with a hand on her throat. "Oh, how I do wish that Victoria had felt . . . oh, but never mind. And that awful Albert! Oh, Tony, Tony, I knew he duped you back with that *goat* cheese—"

I faltered and set the spoon down on the platter.

"Maybe I should go back to my table," Mrs. Hardcastle murmured.

"Perhaps that really would be best," said Marla, with a frosty smile.

I gazed down into the soup bowl. Across the table, Sam Perdue squirmed in his chair.

"Listen, Goldy," Tony soothed. "This could be a marvelous opportunity for you. We could bring this place public and make a killing. They've got a recurring revenue base, which means people come back for the experience of eating soup here. Plus people order breads, salads, and cookies. Comfort on a grand scale. The concept has done extremely well in other locations, except Wyoming. My exit interviews at Sam's in Denver were fantastic. Am I making sense to you?"

I looked at him and said evenly, "Tony, I would be a much more amenable taster if you would not treat me like a complete idiot."

"Oh, honey, I'm so sorry," he said, with a huge phony smile beneath his manicured mustache. "Okay, listen. Sam's has plans for new restaurants in more cosmopolitan markets—Colorado Springs and Boulder. You know what an initial public offering is?" He regarded me patiently.

"Why don't you just give me a dunce cap, Tony?"

Marla gargled with laughter.

But Tony, undaunted, continued sharing his financial expertise. "The company is expanding management to try new markets. Isn't that right, Sam?"

Sam, who appeared increasingly catatonic, nodded apprehensively.

Tony went on: "After opening locations in the Springs and Boulder, Sam wants to look northward, open a place in Fort Collins, but skip over Wyoming altogether. Try his luck selling soups in Montana—Missoula first, then Bozeman. I want to tell you, Goldy, I expect this is going to make us all *rich*."

Or at least recoup a million or two, I reflected.

I picked up the spoon, with its load of Cranky Crab. I sniffed it; the aroma was bland—like a canned clam chowder. I assumed a studious expression. Tony and Marla exchanged an eager glance and leaned forward. Would I pronounce the Cranky indescribable? Luscious? One of a kind? Fortunately, the chef was sequestered in the kitchen. One of the things Mrs.

Hardcastle had been at pains to inform me was that the poor chef couldn't stand the tension. Reportedly, he was anxious to learn my findings. I rolled the soup over my tongue. Sam, Tony, and Marla cocked their heads. What would I say? *Its texture is divine! Its taste unequalled! I'll take two—no—three bowls full!*

"Hmm," I said. *You guys are in serious trouble.*

Outside of Sam's, another relentless rain had swept down upon us. Raindrops pelted Aspen Meadow Lake. I swallowed the tasteless, thin concoction, tried to think of how to phrase my assessment, and looked out at the inlet abutting the lake. A group of hardy members of the Audubon Society stood in the downpour peering through their binoculars. According to the *Mountain Journal,* rotten weather or no, the birders were making daily walks around the lake in hopes of a second sighting of a long-billed curlew.

Sam cleared his throat with a frightened squeak and twisted in his modified Adirondack-style chair. Tony consulted his sculptured nails, gnawed his bottom lip, brushed more imaginary dust off his white shirt, then shot me another questioning look. Clearly, Marla hadn't been as persnickety a taste tester as I was turning out to be.

"Goldy?" said Tony. "I like to involve the common folk. A little nine-year-old kid next door told me to buy Clearly Canadian. I did, and made a mint on flavored water. Got another tip from Zane Smythe. Know who he is?"

I nodded. Zane is a local fisherman who teaches fly tying and writes articles on fishing for the *Mountain Journal.*

"Zane tipped me onto Timberland. I've done real well going long on backpacks and water." Tony lowered his voice. "Things aren't going so great now, as you know. And in addition to everything else, my taste buds are shot."

Sam murmured, "Yours and everyone else's in that firm." They were the first words he'd spoken.

Marla put a friendly hand on Tony's elbow. "Honey, if I'd put jalapeño jelly on English muffins every morning for the last ten years, my taste buds would be gone, too. It's one of the laws of food."

Tony removed Marla's hand from his elbow. "Will you stop?" Now he gave me the full benefit of his dark brown eyes. "I need you to be *honest,* Goldy. If you approve of Sam's offerings, I'll round up the cash so he can open two more locations." He paused. "Actually, you need to do more than approve. . . ."

Marla flapped a hand in my direction. "You need to *love* it, Goldy. You need to say it's going to be the next nationwide rage. Like Mrs. Field's, right, Tone?" Tony shrugged. "Like Starbucks," she whispered.

I didn't dare look at Sam. Outside, rain fell. The birders gingerly trod through the soggy wetlands. I lifted the spoon and took another bite. No better. I tried the Big Cheese Chowder; it was lumpy and if there was cheddar in the soup, it was barely discernible. I moved on to Terrapin Tom's Tomato. My own homemade tomato soup boasts the rich, sweet smell of fresh tomatoes, combined with a thick, smooth texture. Sam's tomato soup was thin and indeterminately spicy. Well, I had my integrity. I'd finally tasted, and I'd found the soups wanting. I felt Tony's glare but said nothing. And Marla's best friend or no, I wasn't going to taste the chocolate.

I glanced back toward the kitchen, but the chef was nowhere in sight. At this very moment he might be concentrating on his commercial-sized Hobart as it beat ponds of cream sauce with broth into soups that he fervently hoped would make him a multimillionaire. Maybe he believed money would bail him out of being stuck in the kitchen. I doubted both.

Tony impatiently spread his fingers on the rim of the empty dish in front of him. "Look, Goldy. Just tell me. Everybody says these soups are great. Gonna be the next craze. Lowfat, rib-sticking, but . . ." He chewed the inside of his cheek to find the right word, then brightened. "Lowfat, rib-sticking, but *delish*. There've been articles in local papers. Pretty soon all kinds of venture capital folks will be itching to get in here. Once this thing takes off, it'll be too late. I want to get in on the ground floor. Know what I mean? Understand? *Comprende?*"

"I guess I don't," I said honestly. Sam Perdue pressed his thin lips together. His terrified expression had turned resentful.

"I may have missed Boston Chicken," Tony continued insistently, as if I had not spoken. He picked up a three-pronged fork and tapped the table in time with his next words. "And I may have missed Outback Steakhouse. But I am *not* going to miss Sam's Soups. So tell me. Tell me that these journalists are right." He scrutinized my face, the dark mustache aquiver. I took another spoonful of the cheese chowder and closed my eyes. I rolled my tongue over the lukewarm mélange of ingredients. There was a hint of cheese, yes, but the mixture was not smooth, creamy, or light, not to mention redolent of cheese, whether it was fine Swiss or sharp cheddar. Even *I* had a better recipe for cheese soup than this. I swallowed and sighed. Every muscle in Tony's taut, expectant face rolled, tightened, and rolled again, like cables on a high-speed ski lift. Should I take another sip of the tomato, I wondered, smile, close my eyes, swallow? Venture a fourth bite? What happened if I frowned and delicately set the spoon aside? Would he really holler at me?

"Well—" I began.

"She doesn't like it," Marla interrupted with a fluttering of bejeweled fingers. She put one chubby hand on Tony's forearm. He jerked away. "Give it a rest, Tony. Come on."

Sam Perdue, his face a mottled study of anger, scraped his chair back, stood, and silently marched away. Marla's efforts to mollify Tony were unsuccessful. When he made one short, fierce shake of his head, she sent a hopeful gaze around the restaurant.

"I want to lose money," she said brightly. "I know how to throw away more than we've already allowed to slip past. Hey, Tony! All we have to do is invest in a restaurant producing food that Goldy thinks is garbage."

"Damn it, Marla!" Tony snapped. Then he relented and rubbed her hand. "Don't get in the middle of this, sweetie. If it's no good, we're not going to invest in it. Okay?"

I could practically hear her purr at his saccharine attentions. *Fool!* I wanted to shout, but did not. Tony sighed gustily and dipped a clean spoon into the chocolate soup. He didn't look at me as he put the spoon loaded with dark stuff on my plate.

"Hey Tony, what am I, a kid?" I demanded. "Don't you think I can feed myself?"

"No, you're not a kid," he said quietly, still not meeting my gaze. "In fact, I hear you're the right-hand woman to the county's number one investigator."

"Yeah, too bad he doesn't investigate soups, right?" I parried. I eyed the chocolate, which was dark and velvety-looking. When the Aztecs had named chocolate "food of the gods," they'd been onto something. I didn't want to imagine, much less experience, how Sam's chef had wrecked it.

"Eat the damn soup, Goldy, and tell me if it's any good. It's

the last one." He scanned the restaurant again, and spoke con-
fidingly. "Sam's had a hard time with Prospect, and he's ready
to go to the newspapers with his tale of how cruel we've been
to him. The last thing I want is more bad publicity, okay?
Victoria didn't like the soups, Albert got away with a bundle,
and Sam's going to hate the hell out of me if we veto his plans.
I do want to try to help this guy expand, if I can." He gestured
at the chocolate soup. "Tell me if anything here has potential."
He exhaled, then spoke with clenched teeth. "I need a successful investment at this time, because of what's going on at the
firm."

"You're be-ing a jerk, To-ny," Marla singsonged, winking
at some friends and holding up an index finger to indicate
she'd be right over.

Tony's voice was corrosive. "Oh, *I'm* a jerk? I thought you
two saved the term *jerk* for your mutual ex-husband."

Marla *tsk*ed, rose, and flounced off. She wriggled through
some tables, poured herself some forbidden coffee, and carried
it off to greet her buddies.

Tony smoothed his mustache with his index finger and gave
me a blank look. "Eat your chocolate soup, Goldy," he said
coldly.

I watched Marla's back as she sipped from her coffee cup
and chatted with her acquaintances, women who from their
expensive clothing looked as if they, too, like Marla, belonged
to the nonworking segment of the populace. Maybe they were
also signed up for the art appreciation adventure to Italy. The
excursion was supposed to be all-female, but maybe the *Botti-
celli and Bernini* would be supplanted by *marinara and men*. Actually, that would have been good for Marla, I mused. Much as I
worried about Marla's health, I worried more about her social
life. Not the country club variety, but the intense kind you

have with guys. Guys like Tony. Tony who was now giving me the soup-sipping evil eye.

I took a dainty spoonful of the chocolate concoction. It was too thin. And too sweet. "No more," I said.

"Oh, for heaven's sake!" Tony cried. "Can't you at least give me more information than that?" he demanded in a nasty tone I tried to think of as *concerned*. He wanted to hear sensory analysis, or at least reasons for culinary rejection, straight from the caterer's mouth. "You realize we're talking about a lot of money to be made here?" he added in a lower, patronizing voice.

Well. That did it. If the man wanted a bona fide taste assessment, the man was going to get one.

"They're *all* boring. They lack creamy texture and depth of taste. They're too thin. Worse, the seafood and cheese selections are not spicy enough for the American palate. They're not terrible," I said wistfully. "Just not . . . unusual. And I should tell you, Tony, good soups can be extraordinarily labor-intensive. Labor-intensive means *lots* of money. Plus, soup is volatile. Cook it too long, and it gets like library paste. Cook it too little and it tastes like puddle water."

He exhaled loudly and put his head in his hands.

Outside the restaurant, the soaking wet Audubon group was breaking up. A tall fellow tentatively raised his head, spylike, and trained his binoculars on Sam's. No long-billed curlew here, I wanted to call to him, just a few odd ducks. The man watched the restaurant just a moment too long to be credibly involved with the birders. I stared until he folded his body down next to a beat-up Subaru. Oh, Lord: Macguire. Trying to be an investigator. What did he think he was doing? Was he tailing somebody? And who? The teenager was going to give new meaning to the term *loose cannon*.

Tony caught Sam Perdue's eye and gave him a sympathetic, sorrowful look. Sam lifted his chin and turned his back. *He* sure didn't want to hear analysis of his soup samples from a local caterer.

"This was a mistake," I said, and meant it. Poor Sam.

"Oh, well." Tony was already on the rebound, just as he'd been after the scene at the mine party. Apparently things went badly in the venture capital world quite often. "You brought the food for our camping trip?"

"Yes, I did. It's in the van."

He smiled mischievously. "Marla says your husband is a big fisherman. Is he jealous of what we're doing?"

"If you actually catch any trout, he'll be jealous after the fact."

Again Tony leaned over and addressed me in an oddly confiding tone. "Has he found my partner yet? Has he gotten any leads?"

"I wouldn't know. Tom's off the case."

He wrinkled his brow and continued to whisper. "Why?"

I shrugged. "Shockley's the captain, and as you undoubtedly know, his retirement funds are with Prospect. He wants his own people out looking for Albert Lipscomb."

"But . . . but . . . I thought your husband was the best. That's what Marla says. 'Tom Schulz is the best.' " Tony's face contorted with alarm. "Jesus. They'll never find Albert if Schulz isn't working the case. What's the matter with that Shockley? Doesn't he *want* to find Albert? What about *my* money?"

Taken aback, I couldn't think of a word to say. This possibility had never occurred to me. Tony looked apprehensively in Marla's direction and said: "Listen, Goldy, speaking of husbands, there's something more important that I need to talk to you about." He hesitated. "I'm going to ask Marla to marry me this weekend, when we're up at Grizzly Creek. Think she'll have me?"

My heart plummeted. *I certainly hope not.* "You're going to ask her to marry you on a fishing trip? Why don't you just go to the Brown Palace and skip the rod-and-reel routine? I think she'd be more likely to say yes. You'd certainly get less wet."

"No, no, no," he said desperately. "This is important, Goldy. I told Marla this fishing trip was going to be a big deal. She thinks we're trying to catch enormous cutthroat trout. Being by the water is very romantic." He snorted. "So," he said as if he were discussing a merger he'd just read about in *Forbes,* "do you think she wants to get married or not?"

"I don't know," I said truthfully, but was prevented from saying more by Marla's approach. I suddenly had a vision of myself standing up and screaming, *Marla, get an ironclad prenuptial agreement!* But of course, I didn't.

"I'll talk to you when we get back," Tony whispered hastily. "Save the first weekend in August for us. You can cater the reception."

I grunted and was stopped from saying *Why, thank you, Your Highness,* by Marla's arrival.

"I see you all got your differences straightened out," she said impatiently. "I just saw Nan and Liz and . . . uh-oh, there's Sam!" she hissed. "Did you tell him you didn't like the soups, Goldy? He certainly doesn't look very happy."

That was an understatement. The man looked ready to drown me in his precious soup.

"We need to go," Tony said curtly. "We still have to pack up all the gear. Is your van locked, Goldy?"

"Come on, guys," I begged them, "can't you go fishing another weekend?"

Tony stared at the ceiling. Over the sound of seagull calls, he said, "We need to get moving. Is the food really in your van, or did you forget it?"

"I remembered the food, chill out. Oh, and speaking of which, refrigerate the"—I lowered my voice—"*soup* until you leave." I directed my plea at Marla. "It's raining. You're going to get drenched even if it stops—"

"You don't seem to know who you're talking to." Tony's voice had gone from insulting back to its normal arrogance. "All my stuff is waterproof, Goldy. State-of-the-art. And we'll get up there when all the other fishermen are too wimpy. We'll catch a lot."

"That I doubt," said Marla with a perfumed shrug.

"You won't say that when I fix you my pan-fried trout," chided Tony, as he helped her into her shiny white raincoat. "Maybe we won't even need Goldy's soup."

As we left, Edna Hardcastle was condoling with Sam Perdue, who refused to acknowledge our departure.

Outside, Macguire was nowhere to be seen. I hoped, rather than believed, that he'd given up his investigative fantasies.

I turned to Marla. But she was making a joke with Tony, something about being smart like fish, something about schools. The old joke.

I didn't say what was on my mind. *Stay home, Marla,* I wanted to beg, but I couldn't say the words. She looked over, wanting me to share in her laughter. Again I tried to speak, but the warning remained in my throat, unspoken.

Don't say yes.

Chapter 11

It was another slow weekend with no bookings and intermittent rain. Friday and Saturday, I experimented with shrimp
curry and grilled tuna with Japanese noodles. After marination
in lemon juice and crushed bay leaves, the tuna was delectable.
But the curry was so hot even Jake turned his nose up at it. An
unusually fierce, windy rainstorm late Saturday night took out
our telephones as well as our electric power. We drove through
thick fog to get to church, then decided to take Arch and Todd
Druckman to a Rockies game, tickets courtesy of the Druck-
mans' vacationing neighbors.

The Rockies were playing the Mets. By the eighth inning,
the Rockies were ahead by one. In the top of the ninth, with
two out and a runner on second, the Mets' catcher hit a line
drive down the left field line. Ellis Burks backhanded the ball
on the first bounce and flung it with such force to home that I
thought Jayhawk Owens was going to spin a cartwheel when

he reached for it. Owens managed to catch the ball, pivot, and tag the runner out to end the game. The crowd went wild.

The memory of that play flickered in my mind Monday morning, when an event came out of left field that shocked me no less than if I'd tried to catch Burks' throw with my bare hands.

The phone's ringing pierced the silence when the clock's digits glowed exactly 7:30. Apparently, both our electric power and telephone service had been restored. I figured that Tom had reset the clocks before he left. Arch, I was fairly sure, was still asleep. Since I didn't have any bookings, I thought it must be my mother calling from New Jersey to do a postmortem on the game. She's a big Mets fan.

It was not my mother. It was Macguire Perkins. He rasped and wheezed so badly into the receiver that at first I barely recognized his voice.

"Oh, Goldy, I'm so sorry. I'm in Lutheran Hospital. In Denver. I've got such bad news. I really screwed up."

I threw off the sheets, shot up in bed, and dragged my mind from baseball to Macguire. Macguire *in the hospital?* "Macguire, what's wrong?"

"I was tailing them. But I lost them. Marla and her boyfriend. Something happened. Somebody . . . somebody hit me over the head—" he wheezed. "—and I guess I struggled, but then the perp must have hit me again, because I just like, passed out or whatever."

"Someone hit you? When? Where? Macguire, start over, please. Are you okay?"

"Out in the woods, near Grizzly Creek. It was at night. And there was that big storm, you know? When I came to, there was a ton of blood coming out of this gross cut on my scalp. I mean, the blood's all over my shirt, pants, everything. It was *nasty*." More wheezing. "I thought I was dying. I figured I'd been hit by a rock, or a rock slide, or jeez, I don't know, because I can't remember *hearing* anything. But sometimes you don't, you know, remember hearing a rock slide. Your mind blanks it out. At least that's what this guy at school told me." His voice shredded into coughing. "Anyway, I tied my shirt around my scalp and tried to drive my car out, but the front tires were flat. I thought, that's weird, how could they *both* be flat? And I couldn't see any big rocks or boulders nearby, so I was like, totally confused. And scared. Even though there was nobody around and all I could hear was the rain." There was murmuring in the background. "Yeah, okay," I heard Macguire say. "I'll be off in a minute." He sighed, which led to more coughing. "That was the nurse. I had to have six stitches, and the covering of my skull is torn. I didn't even know the skull *had* a covering. I mean, you know. Besides skin. And, of course, hair," he added dutifully.

"Macguire, I'm so sorry . . . but why . . . why did you do this? What were you thinking?"

He sighed gustily, with the world-weary air of Sam Spade. "I know it's dumb. But I was up at Albert Lipscomb's house with you guys, and it was all so weird when he skipped. So I just thought if I followed Tony it would lead to Albert. I mean, eventually. Then I'd be the hero. I should have known better, I know. Don't tell me, I already feel totally stupid."

I was out of bed and pulling on a sweat suit, the phone tucked under my ear. "For heaven's sake, Macguire, how did you get back to town? Couldn't Marla and Tony help you? Did you call the police?"

"I couldn't *find* Marla and Tony," he whined helplessly, and I was painfully reminded of how young he was. "That's what I called to tell you. After I came to, I went over to where I'd watched them fixing dinner. I had to wait for flashes of lightning to see anything. You wouldn't believe how dark it was. And it was really raining—Anyway, I called, but they weren't at the campsite any more. Marla's car was there, that new Mercedes, all locked up. I don't know where they went, I swear. But it was real dark, you know. The wind was blowing like crazy, it was raining so hard. . . . And it was really cold."

He hacked again, then spoke to someone, probably the nurse. I prayed that he had some idea of where Tony and Marla were, some idea that they were okay.

"Did you ever see Marla and Tony? I mean after you were hit?"

"No, I'm telling you, I couldn't find them. And I called and called. They must have left on foot, because they only had the one car up there. Goldy, it looked as if a bear or something had gone through their campsite, it was such a frigging—excuse me—mess. I stumbled back until I came to the dirt road, then I walked out to the state highway. A guy in a truck picked me up. He brought me here. And then I guess I like passed out again, or something, because my memory gets kind of blurry. Oh yeah, the guy in the truck said he would call the police. They operated on me, sewing up that cut, yesterday sometime. Gosh, I feel like hell. And the nurse says I have to get off the phone. I'm going to call the school secretary at home, in case my father phones and wonders where I am."

"Oh, Macguire, you poor—"

"Don't worry, I'm supposed to get out of here tomorrow. That's a good thing, because they've got me rooming with this guy who snores, and it's so loud he sounds like someone trying to start an airplane in a cave. I swear, I gotta get back home so I can sleep."

"I'll check with the police and call you later. I promise." I hung up and fumbled with my shoelaces. My fingers were like ice. *A bear or something.* What did I know about grizzlies in our area? Supposedly they didn't come this far south. But there had been reports of mountain lions in Idaho Springs, and there was no telling how the recent weird weather had affected migration and feeding patterns of Rocky Mountain wildlife. *Oh, Marla, where are you?*

I turned back to the phone. *Call Tom immediately,* a voice in my head commanded. But despite what I'd told Macguire, I was afraid to contact my husband. And I knew it was because, deep in my heart, I was certain he'd have bad news for me. As I debated, the phone rang again.

"Goldilocks' Catering, Where . . . everything . . ."

A young female voice hesitantly inquired, "Er, is this Goldy, the caterer?"

"It is." I ran my fingers through my hair. "I can't talk business, unfortunately, because I'm kind of tied up at the moment."

"This is Kiki Belknap, calling from Prospect Financial? I'm Tony Royce's secretary? Is he there? Because—"

"Of course he's not here, it's not even eight o'clock in the morning! Why on earth would Tony be *here*?"

"I'm sorry, because his calendar says so? I just don't know, are you like, meeting with him, or just talking to him on the phone? It says here, *Goldy, ask about menus for August reception, eight A.M.,* with your phone number—"

"Look, please let me call you back, Kiki, I have to check on my friend. Marla Korman—you know her, don't you? She was supposed to be with him—"

"But you see, our office has just had a call from the police—"

"What did they say?" I interrupted sharply.

"They wanted to know where Tony was! And I'm like, I mean, after *last* week with Mr. *Lips*comb, I'm like, what are you *talking* about, asking where Mr. *Royce* is—"

"I have to go," I said brusquely. "Tony's not here."

I tapped the button impatiently to get a dial tone, then punched in Marla's number. Her machine picked up; I slammed the phone down.

I tiptoed quickly to Arch's room. His bed was empty. Wherever he'd gone, he'd taken Jake. I rushed down to the kitchen. Where was Arch? There was a note crookedly taped onto the table:

Mom, I'm taking Jake for a walk around the lake. Don't worry, I'm wearing my rain jacket, just in case. I'll go out the back way. Love, Arch.

I was so upset I forgot Tom's number and had to look up the sheriff's department's main number in the phone book. The operator put me through to Tom's extension, where I again encountered a machine. I urged Tom to call me ASAP. I turned on the water without fitting grounds into the espresso machine. To make matters worse, when hot water spewed all over the counter, I picked up a dry sponge and managed to slosh the scalding liquid onto my hands and the floor. "Start over," I mumbled. I dropped a paper towel onto the steaming counter and fumbled for the coffee beans.

I sighed and looked out the window at fog so thick I couldn't even see my neighbor's house. Would this wretched weather never end? I ground a cupful of coffee beans, scrupulously remeasured the water, and then pressed the button for espresso. While the dark strands of liquid began to spurt out, I again punched the numbers for Marla's house. This time I got a busy signal. My heart leapt: I tried again and once more got a busy. The next time I punched in her number, I encountered her machine. I waited this time and said, "It's me, pick up! It's Goldy! If you're there, damn it, pick up!"

No response. Perhaps someone else had been calling the machine just at the moment I'd dialed and received the busy signals. I shook my head, then tried Tom again.

He answered on the first ring. "Schulz." His voice was guarded, as if someone were right there looking over his shoulder.

"Can you talk?"

"One sec." He put me on hold, then came back. "Go ahead."

"Macguire just called. He's in the hospital. Tom, have you heard of any accidents? Has something happened to Marla?"

"Wait, wait." He lowered his voice. "How do you get from Macguire Perkins in the hospital to something happening to Marla?"

"Let me back up," I blubbered. "I should have told you that Macguire had started to fancy himself an investigator. He's decided to become a cop instead of going to college. I didn't tell you because I was afraid you would think it was dumb. Anyway, I saw him Friday outside the soup restaurant, and I guess he was tailing them—Marla and Tony. I never thought that he'd follow them on their fishing trip this weekend." I gave him the substance of my conversation with Macguire in the hospital. He listened patiently, without interrupting once.

"First of all, Miss G., I don't think anybody's aspirations are dumb, okay? Marla is his friend. He was worried about her. Now, where's Headmaster Perkins? Has somebody let him know his son's in the hospital?"

"I don't know where Perkins is. Vermont, I think. For a month-long educational conference? I'm not sure. Macguire's calling the school secretary, and he's due to get out of the hospital tomorrow. But, Tom, where could Marla be? I mean, if Macguire was following them, and he got hurt, and then he couldn't find Marla and Tony in the storm . . . where are they? Have you heard anything about people hurt up at Grizzly Creek? Tony Royce's office just called—"

"Hold on a sec." He put me in telecommunications limbo for what seemed like an age. When he came back his voice was grim. "Okay, they got a call late yesterday morning, a trucker said he picked up a hitchhiker who claimed a bear had torn up a campsite where Tony Royce and Marla Korman were camping. We haven't heard from Marla or Tony, but you know the phones in Aspen Meadow were down most of yesterday."

"The hitchhiker was Macguire."

"A team's already gone up to Grizzly Creek. Because it was Tony and Marla, Captain Shockley's put himself personally in charge." His tone very clearly said, *And you know what that means.* "Goldy, you're going to have to let me get back to you."

"Are there any . . ." I couldn't say the rest.

"No reports of death, no bodies floating in the creek or washed up on the shore," he said curtly, and hung up.

I grabbed my mug of coffee and my keys and ran out the back door.

Once I was in the van, however, I sat, bewildered. What was I doing, exactly? I took a slug of espresso and thought, What's a logical explanation for this? Okay, Tony and Marla were miserable out there camping in that awful storm. There was some kind of problem with Marla's Mercedes, so they got a ride out. Macguire said they only had the one car, and he didn't see them leave. Then some animal got into their campsite while Macguire was asleep in his car. After that, a rock hit Macguire. . . . No.

I inhaled more caffeine and struggled to kick-start my brain. Okay. Say they came back early, for whatever reason— they could be at Tony's place right now, or Marla's, sleeping in, having fun, being naughty and missing Monday morning appointments. Maybe Marla's answering machine was on but the volume was off—she rigged her phone that way all the time. She could have called somebody this morning when I got the busy signal, but not heard me begging for her to pick up later. So . . . was I going to go hauling over to Marla's house, if that's where they were, and barge in?

Was I up to making a fool of myself? Well, it wouldn't be the first time. And anyway, what if Marla and Tony weren't even there, what if they were at a hotel somewhere? I turned the ignition on, then off.

What about Macguire? What was the worst-case scenario? I wondered about Albert Lipscomb. If what Eileen Tobey had said was true, then the Eurydice Mine venture was Tony's project as much as it was Albert's. If it was a bust, Prospect might not recover. Maybe, I wondered wildly, maybe Albert hadn't left town at all. Tony had told everyone he and Marla were going fishing at Grizzly Creek this weekend. Albert could easily have come back for revenge on his partner, after Marla had found problems in the assay reports. Revenge for what? For not analyzing the mine properly? For risking the assets of the entire firm? Huge *maybe* questions. Then, after doing something to Tony and Marla, Albert had whacked Macguire for good measure, and slashed his tires, so that he could make his getaway with all that money before anyone got back to Aspen Meadow. . . .

But then *where were Marla and Tony? With Albert Lipscomb? Dead in the rain near Grizzly Creek?* I suddenly knew what I had to do.

Fog pressed against my windshield as the van inched toward Main Street. Cottony mist wove through streetside aspen branches. The van crunched over rutted gravel left in the destructive wake of the heavy rain. Once again, I had to slow behind a line of traffic. Ten car-lengths ahead, a road crew with two bulldozers scooped up the remains of a rock slide. I drank the last of the tepid espresso and tapped the steering wheel in frustration. I didn't want to think about rock slides.

Where was Marla?

Twenty minutes later I pulled up in front of her house. A large pine branch, blown down in the storm, lay like a gnarled black bone in her groomed flower bed. The driveway was empty, the draperies pulled. There was no sign of movement on her street. I hopped up the stone steps. If Tony was here, I was going to recommend she break up with him. Immediately. Being involved with investment advisers, shady or otherwise, was getting to be burdensome on *my* cardiac health.

The doorbell dingdonged inside the silent house. I stared at my blurred reflection in the brass nameplate inscribed *Chez Marla* and waited. I rang again.

Decision time. She'd had a heart attack last summer. I'd gotten two busy signals and then nothing this morning. What if she was inside, and couldn't call out, because she was having another heart attack? What if she needed me to do CPR? *That's my mom,* I could hear Arch's mocking voice. *Always imagining the worst, and making you pay for her imagination.*

Lucky for me, Marla frequently locked herself out of her own home. I hurried to the lock box under the utility gauges where I knew she kept at least two spare keys. I wrenched the box open, grabbed the one spare that was there, and sprinted back around to the front of the house.

The cold key bit into my palm as I once again pressed the

doorbell and listened to it bong through the interior space. The key slipped from my hand and clanged onto the flagstone entryway. I picked it up and gently fit it into the lock. Unlike me, Marla had no sophisticated security system to protect against the Jerk or anyone else. She always claimed she had her ferocious personality to keep enemies at bay. The latch clicked, the knob turned, and I pushed the door open.

Stepping inside, I tried to prepare myself for the worst. If only I knew what the worst was, I reflected grimly. It was strangely heartening to sense a trace of Marla's perfume in the air. In fact, the air in the house, surprisingly, was not three-day-old stale. I moved cautiously along the light blue Kirman runner into the front hall and sniffed again. Marla's scent seemed to become stronger. So did the aroma of coffee.

Coffee? What the hell have I done? I wondered. She's here with Tony and just not answering the phone. I've crashed in on a romantic interlude. She'll never speak to me again, after this.

"Marla?" I ventured. "Hey, guys! Where are you? It's Goldy. I'm here making a fool of myself because somebody said a bear got into your campground! Are you here?"

I fully expected to hear Marla's familiar voice trill a sarcastic remark. Or perhaps her impish face and wild hair would appear and teasingly demand an explanation for my panicked behavior. Instead, I heard a tiny sound. Something hissed down the hall. I walked quickly toward it. Oddly, the kitchen floor was gritty with dried mud. The red light of the coffee machine blinked mockingly. Bubbles in the decanter bubbled and spat, producing both the scent and the sound I'd heard. I pulled the cord out of the wall and looked disconsolately around the room.

I suddenly remembered something my mother used to do when she came home, and my brother and I looked guilty, and things in the kitchen didn't look quite right. She would make a beeline for the trash bin. Whatever mischief we had made, whatever forbidden pizza or ice cream we had snitched, she figured, the telltale detritus was bound to be in the trash. I wrenched open the white cabinet and peered into the plastic garbage bag. It was filled with crumpled paper towels. I pulled one out. The towel was covered with dried blood.

"Marla!" I shouted. I threw down the towel and pawed through the trash. There was no meat tray or packaging to explain the bloodstained towels. I slammed out of the kitchen and ran up the back stairs, down the hall, and into her bedroom.

It was a disaster site. Clothes strewn on the beige carpeting. Towels draped over upholstered chairs. On her bed, the flowered bedcovers formed a mountainous tumble.

"Marla—" I croaked, fully expecting a corpse under the sheets.

The covers moved. If there were two people under there, I would never live down the mortification. That is, if Marla didn't murder me for being such a paranoid idiot. But it would serve them right for not answering the doorbell or my calls.

A half-full cup of coffee and opened container of pills sat on the dressing table. The bedside lamp was on. I stepped awkwardly toward the bed just as Marla's snarled mop of hair appeared from under a tousled sheet. I gasped.

"Marla? What's going on?"

An unearthly groan, full of shame and pain, issued from the rumpled bed. Then a batch of soiled towels emerged, then my best friend's face. I gasped again. One black eye, the other swollen shut. A bruised cheek. A dark, bloody gash down her forehead. She levered herself carefully to a sitting position. She wore a sweatshirt spotted with blood, which she tugged down self-consciously before raising her face to try to look at me.

"No," I moaned, dropping to my knees next to her. "Oh God, you need a doctor. What happened—"

"I wanted to call you, but the damn phone wasn't working." Her labored whisper squeezed my heart. "I'm sorry you have to . . . see me like this. I—"

I reached a hand out to her poor face but she pulled away. "Marla, please," I said firmly. "I'm calling your cardiologist. Won't you tell me what happened? We *must* call the police." The words tumbled out. Anger made my ears buzz.

She groaned. "I was going to call the police in a little bit, anyway, if I couldn't reach Tony. I don't know if he got out, too. I don't think he saw me . . . I've tried to reach him, but he's not answering his machine. He'll be *so* ticked off if we call the cops. More bad publicity for Prospect. Just give it half an hour," she begged. She stifled a sob and reached for a tissue.

"Marla, please tell me what happened."

"Somebody . . . I . . . I . . . think it might have been Albert. . . ." A sob shuddered through her. I put my hand on her forearm and waited for her to continue. She went on: "Actually, it started Friday night. Tony and I had a terrible fight."

"Oh, no."

She groaned again, peered uncertainly around the room, then fastened her gaze on the coffee and pills at her bedside. She groped for the brown pill bottle. I leaned close to see what it was. The label read: *Royce, Tony. Take one tablet orally every 4 hours as needed for pain. Acetaminophen with codeine.*

"Oh, Marla, don't take his prescription. What have you got it for, anyway?"

"He leaves his stuff here all the time. And he gets headaches. Actually, sometimes I think that guy *is* a headache."

"Marla—"

"Let me take some meds," she insisted, "and then I'll tell you what happened." To my horror, she shook out not one but three pills, popped them into her mouth, then washed them down with cold coffee. She grimaced. Then she groaned and sank back onto the pillow.

"Wait," I told her. "Let me get a washcloth for that eye." When I came back, she had pressed her face into the pillows and refused to look at me. "Marla," I implored, "don't talk. You *have* to let me call Dr. Gordon. He's going to want to see you right away. This is for your *health,* Marla. This is for your *life.*"

She moaned. Then she reached out and to my relief, took the cold washcloth I offered. When she had eased back upright, I found the bedroom phone, a gilt rotary contraption that was supposed to go with the French Provincial theme. My heart ached for her. She always tried to make everything beautiful. Miraculously, I remembered Dr. Gordon's number. The phone rang once, twice. It was an emergency, I told the answering service. Did I need an ambulance, the woman wanted to know. In the mountain area, I knew emergency medical services were handled by a private company called Front Range Ambulance. With only two vehicles available, and almost twenty-four hours without phone service in the mountains, ambulance service would be slow, misdirected, or worse, unavailable. I could get Marla to the hospital faster myself. No, I replied to the operator, I needed the doctor to call me. Dr. Gordon was in surgery, and a Dr. Yang would call me back, she informed me calmly. Within two minutes Dr. Yang phoned. I told him a cardiac patient of Dr. Gordon's had been badly beaten. He said to bring her to Southwest Hospital immediately.

"You're going to have to go in," I told Marla gently. "As soon as we get there, I'll call Tom to tell him you're all right and to ask him to put out an APB on Albert Lipscomb. Listen," I blurted out, "Macguire Perkins followed you because he wants to be a cop. . . ." No matter what Tom said, it still sounded dumb. "Anyway, Macguire's at Lutheran Hospital. Out at that campsite, somebody hit him, too. You, Macguire, probably Tony, too—all attacked. Marla, we *must* call the police as soon as we get you some medical attention."

"Oh, Tony, Tony." Marla groaned his name as she inched her way out of bed. Her legs were so bruised and badly cut that I bit back a cry of dismay. Without further protest, she let me help her into a large navy blue dress that buttoned up the front. I found her a pair of red sandals. She put them on, then slumped back on the bed, exhausted by the effort of dressing.

"Do you suppose Tony's at home, but not answering?" she asked. "What should we do, Goldy? I don't know if he'd like my pressing the panic button before we can at least connect—"

"Do you think you could tell me what happened?"

She sighed. But the painkiller must have been taking effect, because she began to talk, very softly. "It was too cold Friday night to camp, and I told Tony I couldn't sleep outside. I begged for us to drive up the next day. He got mad and we argued. But we came back here, cooked some of that soup you gave us, and then argued more about going up to the campsite that night. We went to bed—Tony in the guest room, mind you. But then he came in and woke me up, said he thought he heard an intruder. You know I sleep like a rock, I didn't hear a thing. But he was in a terrible state. He insisted on tiptoeing around the house, looking for some nonexistent burglar. Finally he calmed down. When I woke up the next morning, I lay here thinking, we're going out to share a tent in the wild, and he can't even get through one night without being a mass of nerves?" She managed a rusty laugh.

"But, why did you go out there at all? On Saturday, I mean? There was that terrible storm. . . ."

She sighed, touched one of the bruises on her cheek, then winced. "I didn't want to go, but he insisted. The weather was a little warmer, and the fog had cleared, it was just windy. By the time we got the car loaded up, though, rain threatened again. Tony was in a rotten mood. I was ready to tell him to go by himself. Except that we were going in my car, that Miata of his can't always do the rough-road stuff. I should have told him to rent a Range Rover. I *should* have told him a lot of things." She frowned. "Think it's too soon for me to have another pain pill?"

"Absolutely too soon. Wait and see what Yang says. At the campsite, did you see Macguire or his Subaru?"

Even shaking her head seemed to cause her pain. "No. We got up there to the site by Grizzly Creek, and Tony started acting jumpy as a rabid squirrel. He kept talking about Albert, saying this was their favorite fishing spot. We pitched the tent and of course it started to pour. We used Sterno and heated up some more of your soup. He kept saying, 'Did you hear something? Think somebody's out here with us?' I said no fifty times, and then told him his paranoia was making me nuts and I was going to sleep. I was so tired I could have slept through a hurricane. Or so I thought until somebody grabbed me and pulled me out of the tent."

"What? Who?"

"I don't know. Somebody just started hitting me. I screamed and called for Tony. I tried to get my footing but it was muddy, dark, thunder blasting overhead, rain coming down like crazy. . . . It was like a nightmare. And it all happened so fast. I'd been in a deep sleep and then all of a sudden I was screaming my lungs out. But whoever was hitting me didn't care. I finally managed to get out of the damn sleeping bag. I tried to hit back, grabbing at anything to use as a weapon. But this guy was strong. I thought it was a bear at first, but he grunted like a human. And what bear uses a piece of firewood to hit you? He hit me and hit me and hit me. Just as I was going down there was a flash of lightning, and I saw the guy moving away from me, and . . . he had no hair. It all went so fast. I thought, Where am I, where am I going, what am I supposed to do? I was sure I was going to die." Tears formed in her bruise-circled eyes.

"You fainted?"

"I was . . . I was . . . there was sand in my mouth and in my hair. The noise from the water was incredible . . . I finally figured I was on that sandy shoreline of the creek. With the rain coming down hard, and warm blood oozing over my face, I thought, *Finally, finally, I get to rest.* I was sure I was dead, or close to it. Later, in the night, I came to and the storm had become even more fierce, thunder, lightning, rain. I thought I heard someone calling me. 'Marla! Are you here? Marla!' "

"That was probably Macguire."

Her shoulders slumped. "I gasped, 'Here! Here!' But no one could have heard me over the creek and the storm. Besides, I thought I was hallucinating. My mind was so . . . mushy. Silly, even. My brain was laughing hysterically, saying, *Nobody's calling you, dummy, it's Rochester wanting Jane Eyre!* So there I was on the creek bank, every part of my body aching, wondering who would scream for me when I was about to kick the bucket. I knew I was dead."

"Oh, Marla, I'm so sorry—"

She held up a hand to stop me. "When I woke up it was just past dawn. I think. Anyway, our campsite was a mess. I limped to my car, but it was locked. I must have lost the keys when the guy—Albert—attacked me. I finally hobbled out to the main road. A family going to church brought me home. I tried to call Tony but my line was dead." The tears brimmed over. The painkillers were slurring her speech. "I was dying to *call* you . . . or come *over* . . . if we just had a *taxi* service in this hopeless *town* . . ."

"Don't," I said firmly. "Everything will be fine now. I'm here with you." I supported her as she stood shakily and walked, haltingly and with evident pain, toward the staircase. "My van's parked out front. Do you want me to bring it around back, or can you make it down the steps?"

"Let me try to walk to your car. It'll be good for me, I'm so cramped up."

We inched down the steps across the runner, then to the front door. I told Marla to hold on to a side table. I opened the door, and we both gasped.

Standing on the flagstone entry were two investigators dressed in plain clothes: Hersey and De Groot.

"Well!" said De Groot. He regarded the two of us with theatrical astonishment, his thick black eyebrows pulled upward. "Going someplace, ladies?"

Chapter 12

"What is it, what are you doing here?" I asked. It felt like such a stupid question. Nevertheless, these guys had already proven they could make me feel idiotic. The pair eyed us with an undisguised mixture of hostility and suspicion that made me squirm.

"Aren't you going to ask us about Schulz?" De Groot wanted to know. Before I could frame a response, he held up his hand and smirked. "He's fine. At least the last time we saw him he was." He quirked his eyebrows as if he were going to say more, but then seemed to think better of it. Blandly, he appraised Marla's battered face. "Ms. Korman?"

With an uncharacteristic lack of resolve that made me want to put my arms around her, Marla replied, "Yes? What is it?"

"Can we come in?"

I stepped between the cops and Marla. "No, I'm sorry, you can't," I replied curtly before she had a chance to respond. "As you can see, my friend's in pain. Her doctor wants me to bring her in right away. We'll talk to you later.''

Hersey ignored me. He stepped to one side and addressed Marla. "Got into another fight, did we, Ms. Korman?''

Marla said tonelessly, "It's a long story.''

I felt her embarrassment acutely. No woman likes to be seen covered with bruises and cuts: I knew that all too well from my personal experience with the Jerk. My tone to the two investigators was icy. "Would you please leave? We're under doctor's orders, on our way to the hospital. My friend is hurt.''

"I'm sorry,'' said De Groot. But he wasn't. Cold, moist air billowed into the foyer. De Groot ran his fingers through his slick black hair. "We're under time pressure, I'm afraid, Mrs. Schulz. If you take Ms. Korman here to the doctor, we'll just have to follow you down and talk to her there.''

"You're joking,'' I said. Again, he wasn't.

"It won't take long,'' said Hersey.

"Oh, let them in,'' said Marla dejectedly. "Let's get this over with, then I'll go see the doctor.'' She turned away from the door and started to limp toward the kitchen. Over her shoulder, she said, "I don't mind if you talk to me, as long as Goldy can stay with me.'' Her gait was pained and self-conscious, and I loathed Hersey and De Groot for their insensitive intrusion even as I jerked the front door open so they could enter.

They didn't remove their dripping raincoats, and I decided this must be some kind of psychological ploy: We don't want to be unprotected in this house. I didn't care. I just wanted them to ask their questions and leave. Hersey craned his thick neck upward to scrutinize the lushly carpeted staircase. Was he looking for someone? Hard to tell. De Groot peered at a framed painting. Executed in bold strokes, it showed a woman holding a cup of coffee.

"You won't know this one," I said defiantly. "It's by a woman, a Colorado artist whom Marla is patronizing."

De Groot said, "Yeah. I see she has plenty of money to pay people to do what she wants. Painting pictures. Driving her to the hospital. Sticking with her while she's questioned."

"You'd better cool it," I said.

De Groot looked down at the cherry buffet under the painting, which held a large Steuben vase filled with dried sweetheart roses. I was about to follow Marla when Hersey crooked a meaty finger in my direction.

"We know she wants you with her. But when we're talking to her?" His voice brimmed with menace. "If you say anything—you blink, you wink, you clear your throat—you're going outside. Understand?"

"Why are you here?" I shot back. "Does Captain Shockley know you're conducting this kind of interrogation, when a woman should be in the hospital?"

He grinned. "Shockley sent us."

"I *insist* you wait to question her until I call Tom."

Hersey scowled. "You want to talk to somebody? Go *home* and call Shockley. He's real interested in your friend Marla Korman."

Without a word I stalked into the kitchen. De Groot and Hersey sauntered in after me.

Evidently, De Groot had appointed himself in charge of this interrogation. And from the way the two policemen were acting—notebooks out, eyes noting each detail of the room, interrogation was precisely what they had in mind. I just hoped codeine-tranquilized Marla recognized the threat this posed.

De Groot smiled humorlessly at her. "We're here to ask you about Tony Royce."

Marla sank into one of the chairs and regarded De Groot

dolefully. "Is he all right?" she asked sadly. "Did you find him?"

"No, not exactly. When was the last time you saw him?"

Marla shook her head and looked away. Tears of embarrassment again welled in her eyes. "It would have been . . . Saturday night."

"And where was that?"

To my horror, Marla began to sob. She stumbled across the room to the cabinet where the paper towel rack was mounted. Balancing herself against the counter, she ripped a towel off and dabbed her bruised eyes. *Just don't throw the towel into the trash with all the bloody ones,* I implored her silently. She didn't.

Staring out at the swirling fog, she struggled to compose herself. Finally she murmured, "We were . . . up at a camping site. By Grizzly Creek."

De Groot asked, "And what were the circumstances of this last time you saw him?"

"There was a fight. Somebody dragged me out of our tent and beat me up. I think it was Albert Lipscomb."

"So there was a fight?" De Groot repeated, with a glance at his partner, who gave a barely perceptible nod. "Okay, then, Ms. Korman, I need to tell you that you have the right to remain silent." Goose bumps raced up my arms. "Also," De Groot went on in a friendly voice, as if he were reciting a recipe, "that anything you say can and will be held against you. You have the right to an attorney and to have that attorney present during questioning. If you cannot afford an attorney, one will be appointed for you."

"I can afford an *attorney*—" Marla spat. "What the hell do I need—"

"Hey!" I hollered. "Hey! Don't say another word, Marla!

What's going on here? What's she a suspect for? Are you arresting her? You just stop right there. I'm calling my husband."

Hersey stabbed his finger at me. "What did I say to you?
Now you just shut up, or you can drive your little caterer's van
right back to your kitchen, you got that? Tom Schulz is not
involved in this case."

I turned to Marla. "Don't talk. Let's just go to the doctor."

"She's not going to any doctor," Hersey interjected ominously. "She can either stay here and answer our questions or
she can come down to the *department* and answer our questions."

"Excuse me!" Marla yelled. Her bloodshot eyes were wild.
"I have nothing to hide! I didn't *do* anything except defend
myself against an attacker! Why aren't you out looking for
him?"

"That's what we're trying to ask you about, if Mrs. Schulz
here will be quiet," De Groot said gently.

Marla squeezed her eyes shut. Why had the cops
Mirandized her without an arrest? If she was a suspect, her state
of mind wasn't helping to clear her. Unfortunately, the codeine
was kicking in big-time. I cursed myself for letting her take
three pills. Finally she said, "Okay, look. I'll answer your questions, and *then* I'm going to the doctor, you got that? Now
exactly what do you want to know? I'm trying to tell you what
happened. I was attacked. One minute I was in my sleeping
bag, the next, somebody was whaling away at me."

De Groot thought for a moment, as if he wanted to be in
charge of the conversation, and resented having Marla wrest
control from him. "Can you describe your attacker?"

Marla said tentatively, "Well, there was so little time . . .
but it seemed to me . . . that it was a man, very strong. Me-

dium height, build. I saw the back of his bald scalp in a flash of lightning, as I was going down. . . ."

"Going down where?"

"At the side of the creek, after he hit me several times, I fell, and I guess I passed out. I came to in the morning, and got a ride back to town."

De Groot went on: "When you got back to town, did you report this assault?"

"No, I didn't, Officer, because our phones were dead. Is there something illegal about that?"

De Groot didn't answer her question. "You don't have a cellular phone?"

She sighed. "It's in the Mercedes."

"Where was Royce when this stranger was clobbering you?"

Marla clutched the paper towel and carefully eased herself back into the chair. "I don't know. I thought he was there at the campsite, but it was so dark, and I was just trying to fend off this person. . . ."

"How did the fight end?"

Marla faltered. "I told you, it happened so fast, bam, bam, bam, and then I passed out by the creek. That's how it ended. When I came to, I stumbled out of there and down a path to the paved road. I flagged down a passing car."

"Your Mercedes was there. Why didn't you just drive home?"

"Because I couldn't find my car keys, that's why! The key ring must have gotten lost during the fight. Anyway, when I woke up, Sunday morning I guess it was, I was dazed and terribly disoriented, and I couldn't find my keys. When I finally made it out to the road, this nice young family drove me home."

De Groot said, "Did you happen to get the nice young family's name?"

Marla huffed. "What was I going to do, write them a thank-you note? No, I didn't get their *name*. I wouldn't have remembered it anyway, the state I was in."

"Well . . . how old were they?"

"I don't know. Young."

"What did they look like?"

Marla searched her memory, but the painkillers were preventing access. She shook her head. "I truly can't remember."

"Do you remember what kind of car this nice young family drove?"

"I was in pain," Marla said through clamped teeth. "I don't know what kind of damn car it was. They drove me home, they were going to church."

"Did they offer to call us?"

Marla sighed. "Oh, yes. But I said I would do it." She shivered and wiped her face with the paper towel. "Then I got into my house, where the phone did not work." She looked angrily at De Groot. "I was dizzy, Officer! In pain. Bleeding. I wiped off the blood, showered, and took an indeterminate number of painkillers. When the phone came back on this morning, I tried to call Tony twice. You can check his machine if you want. I wouldn't even be going to the doctor if Goldy hadn't shown up this morning." She grimaced.

Neither policeman said anything for a moment. Then De Groot spoke.

"Before the car ride. Let's go back to that, shall we? You and Tony," he prompted, "Saturday night, had been doing . . . what?"

Marla replied, "We pitched the tent on a mound in case it

started to rain, which it did. So we used a camp stove to heat up some food Goldy had made for us. Now that I do remember," she said with a smile for me. "It was chicken soup and it was terrific. After we ate, we put our trash in the trunk of my car, you know, because of the threat of bears and other wild-life—"

Hersey interrupted with, "What else was in the trunk of your car?"

"What else?" Marla repeated blankly. "Well, let's see. Tony had a gun—"

"What kind?" De Groot demanded.

Marla's nose wrinkled. "Oh, I don't remember. I think it was a pistol. Anyway, it wasn't loaded, but he said you had to bring it because of wildlife. Mountain lions or whatever. What else . . . Tony and I put our backpacks in there, clothes and whatnot—"

"Two backpacks?"

"I think so, two or three. It was raining hard, and we brought the lantern inside the tent. We closed the flaps and zipped them up. Then we shared some wine, and eventually we decided to . . . go to sleep." She gave a small, embarrassed chuckle. "Anyway, we'd been asleep for a while, or at least I had, when something attacked us." A confused expression shadowed her face. "At least, I think whoever it was attacked both of us."

De Groot leaned forward intently. "And where was Royce? During this attack?" He still sounded skeptical that any attack had taken place.

"That's what I can't tell you. I couldn't *see* anything. I kept calling out for him, but he never said a word. And then I thought, it's Albert, he's come back and . . . he wants some-thing . . . or . . . he's angry with me, because we had that argument at the party, and now all the investors are suspicious. . . ."

"Albert Lipscomb," echoed De Groot, making a note. "That's who you thought was attacking you even before you saw his bald head when there was a flash of lightning. Lipscomb had come back to assault you and Tony Royce, only you don't have a clue where Royce was at the time."

"Well, I . . . no. Officers," Marla pleaded. "I really want to see my doctor."

"What time was this assault?" interjected Hersey.

Marla was startled, which was probably the effect Hersey desired. "I don't know. I took my watch off. Tony said you shouldn't keep track of time when you're camping."

Both detectives fastened their eyes on her wrist, where a gold watch twinkled between the cuts and bruises. "This is one I put on when I got home," she said with a defensive shake of her head. But even to me, it seemed the damage had been done. Was she lying or was she merely confused? Was there something she was concealing? "Anyway, I'd guess it was about two o'clock in the morning. Maybe later. Say four. It was dark, and the storm was unbelievable."

Hersey said, "And before the attack, before the camping trip, you'd say Royce was your boyfriend?"

She exhaled painfully. "Something like that."

Hersey persisted. "And how long had you known Royce before this little camping trip you took together?"

Marla slumped wearily. "I've been seeing Tony for about fifteen months. Give or take."

De Groot made another note on his pad. "Could you be a little more specific, Ms. Korman?"

"Well, I'd have to look it up in my calendar."

"You keep a calendar?" asked Hersey. "Like a diary?"

Marla nodded. "More or less. Upcoming events, stuff like that."

"Could we see this calendar?"

No, no, no, I screamed mentally. But Marla had already hauled herself up obediently and shuffled over to the shelf. Why was she being so compliant? It had to be the painkiller. I was dying to tell her that one rule applies equally to a criminal investigation and an IRS audit: *Never volunteer anything.* Marla frowned as she pulled first one thick notebook, then another off the shelf. "Okay, here we go, March, year before last. Let's see, *shopping, shopping, lunch,* okay . . . here it is. *Asti Spumanti and dessert at Eileen's house.*" My heart sank as she passed the notebook over to De Groot. "That's when I met Tony. At Eileen's house. He spent an hour trying to convince me to buy shares of Intel. I should have, as it turned out."

In an offhand tone, De Groot said, "And this year's? With the date of the camping trip?"

Marla groped along the shelf. She ignored my glare, brought out another fat notebook, and leafed through. "Oh, brother." Her voice sounded extremely tired. "Okay, here it is. Monday, June fourteen, that's today, that's almost exactly fifteen months, isn't it? What, are you checking my math?"

De Groot stared at the calendar, then made a note. His mouth twitched. He tapped the calendar. "Hmm. Going to Europe this week? You? Alone?"

"I'm going with a group, if I can ever get down to the hospital and have these cuts and bruises taken care of."

De Groot looked longingly in the direction of the coffeepot, then flashed a glance at me. I didn't budge. I wasn't about to indulge him.

"So, you have no idea where Tony Royce is now?" he asked Marla with surprising mildness.

"No, I don't," Marla replied. "I've been hoping he was going to call me, now that we have the phones back." I ached to warn her again to stop talking. Marla didn't know as much about interrogation as I did; that was why she wasn't challenging them. It was also why these two dolts were asking so many questions and getting away with it.

There was an awkward silence. Hersey broke it. "Ms. Korman, are you aware that Tony Royce is missing?"

She sighed. "No."

"And were you getting along with Tony Royce?"

"Yes, of course I was getting along with him," Marla snapped.

Hersey said, "Did you have a fight with him that night at the tent? Was it Royce who hit you?"

"I don't know!" cried Marla, furious. "I don't know who it was! I thought it was Albert Lipscomb! I told you that, except that it was all incredibly fast and . . . violent."

"Were you and Tony and Albert in on a scam with that mine? What went wrong? You and Tony had a falling out, Tony went off with Albert?"

"Don't be ridiculous." Beneath the bruises, Marla had gone pale.

"Did you find a weapon to use against your attacker?" Hersey persisted.

Marla sighed. "No. Although I wanted to get the gun out of the car—"

"Had Royce brought any other weapons?" interrupted Hersey.

Marla made a face and closed her eyes. "His fishing knife," she said softly.

"Did *you* use the fishing knife as a weapon? Tony's fishing knife, that is," asked De Groot in that same mild voice.

"No," said Marla acidly. "Of course not."

"Did you stab Royce?" His eyes bored maliciously into Marla's. "Did you shove him into the creek after you stabbed him?"

"No, no, no!" cried Marla, indignant and trembling. "Of course not."

"Okey-doke." Hersey shot a look at his partner that I didn't like. "We were just wondering."

De Groot pulled out a sheet from the bowels of his notebook, then smiled unpleasantly. "We were also pondering the fact that we have to answer to our boss, Ms. Korman. We know you want to get going to the doctor, and we need to get going, too. This is just a consent-to-search form, so we can look around your house. If you wouldn't mind signing it?"

I could no longer contain myself. "Don't do it, Marla!"

But to my dismay, Marla scanned the sheet, took the pen De Groot slipped her, and scrawled her signature. "Don't worry, Goldy, they're not going to find Tony. He's not here."

"It's a fishing expedition," I raged. "What is going on here? You know damn well that you can't be ransacking her house for anything that just might catch your eye!"

But De Groot plucked the consent form from Marla's hand and smirked as they sauntered out of the kitchen. Marla's defeated expression made my heart sink. "Just let them go, Goldy," she murmured. "They're not going to find a thing. They're certainly not going to find Tony. I swear to you, I honestly don't know where the *hell* he could be, and believe me, it's a question I've been asking myself ever since Saturday night."

I shook my head. The way Marla was handling these cops' treatment of her was scary, especially when I suspected they were carrying out some unknown agenda dictated by Captain Shockley. Her carelessness was mind-boggling. "You're going to need a lawyer, as soon as possible," I hissed. "You didn't even think of Tony's prescription up on your table!"

"That's nothing. What I need is a doctor and a *stronger* painkiller. I've heard Vicodin is pretty good . . . shh, here they come."

De Groot and Hersey slammed back into the kitchen. It wasn't difficult to see both were extremely unhappy.

"No skeletons in my closet," Marla toodled, and I repressed the urge to smirk at De Groot. He ignored me and pulled on the door of the closet, where he spent a few minutes groping about noisily. Then he opened the upper cabinets while Hersey peered in the bottom ones. Finally De Groot creaked open the door of the bathroom between the kitchen and the dark hall. He flipped on the light and peered inside. With a whoop of triumph, he emerged holding a piece of jewelry.

"What's this?" he crowed.

"It's Tony's watch," Marla said drily. "He forgets it here all the time."

De Groot examined the golden Rolex. "He usually leaves a twenty-thousand-dollar wristwatch in your bathroom cabinet?" he said scathingly.

Marla shrugged. "I think they're up to about twenty thousand five hundred, if you want to know the truth. He has his own closet here, too. So what?"

De Groot was staring at me, maybe because in surprise I'd inadvertently opened my mouth. "But your friend Goldy doesn't really believe Tony Royce would leave his valuable watch in his girlfriend's bathroom, now does she?"

Marla gaped at me.

Unwisely, I said, "If I knew *anything* about that watch, Deputy, I wouldn't tell you. And why aren't you wearing plastic gloves? Haven't you ever heard of tainting evidence?"

De Groot's face set in that familiar, enraging smirk. "Now that's what I call cooperating with law enforcement. We heard about this watch from our captain. He asked if we'd found the Rolex at the campsite, because it was Royce's most prized possession, and he never, *ever* was without it."

"Bull-*shit!*" Marla screeched. Her swings from passive behavior to rage were making me dizzy.

De Groot yelled right back at her, "Hey! Why don't you tell me the truth?"

"I *have* told you the truth!"

"Then you want to tell me what piece of clothing with whose blood all over it is in the trunk of your Mercedes?"

"I don't know what you're *talking* about!"

"Marla Korman," said De Groot, "you are under arrest for the murder of Anthony Royce."

Chapter 13

"No, no!" cried Marla. She rushed toward me and I clasped her tight.

"You *are* arresting her!" I protested. "Do you have Royce's body? What grounds can you possibly—"

Hersey shoved me toward the counter. I gasped and whirled back around. De Groot had seized Marla. Hersey reached a burly hand into the back pocket of his pants and pulled out handcuffs. Marla cried out in protest.

I leapt toward my friend. The cops were too fast. Hersey pushed my shoulder and I fell to the floor. De Groot pinned both of my friend's arms behind her back and clicked the cuffs into place. Marla cried out in pain, then fell silent.

"Mrs. Schulz." Hersey's little eyes were scornful as he stared down at me. I rubbed my shoulder and gave him a hateful look. "Get out of our way and keep your mouth *shut*. Otherwise we'll have to arrest you, too."

"But you can't, you just can't *do* this—"

"You are hurting me!" Marla yelled. She struggled against the cuffs for a minute, then added fiercely, "Officer, you are going to be so unhappy when my attorney gets through with you, you cannot even imagine—"

"Yeah, yeah, yeah," said De Groot, "the woman with the violent threats. We've heard all about you."

"Goldy!" Marla sobbed. "Help me! I need the pills in my purse! I need—" Hersey and De Groot pushed her toward the door.

"I'm following you," I called out. I scrambled to my feet and grabbed Marla's purse from the counter. "I'll be right behind you in my van! We're going to get this straightened out!"

"Goldy! Don't let them do this!" Marla's voice cried again. "Help me!"

"I will!" I called back as they tucked her into the sheriff's department sedan.

But I wasn't sure she heard me. My anxiety grew as the sedan pulled away into the fog. How in the world could they charge Marla with murder? Why wouldn't they tell me whether they'd found Tony Royce's corpse out there by the Grizzly Creek campsite? What words had Marla uttered that justified the homicide charge? Could they arrest her just because there was bloody clothing in her car trunk? *And why hadn't Tom called to warn me about all this?*

As I gunned the van down I-70 in the direction of the sheriff's department, I grew increasingly certain of one thing: Shockley was behind all this. Shockley the big investor, Shockley the paranoid cop, Shockley who knew all about Tony's gold watch and who had wanted to know where Marla had gotten the money for her expensive car. I braked abruptly as the van hit a patch of thick mist. Keeping Tom ignorant of a homicide investigation that implicated his wife's closest friend would probably give the boss-guy a keen sense of satisfaction. I'd bet anything that was why the captain had sent his two Rottweilers to interrogate Marla.

The fog thinned slightly as I drew up to the jail's garage entrance. The new ten-story building towered above the parking lot. There was enough visibility to make out a department car disappearing through the closing automatic door. I cursed silently and drew the van up to the video camera. The lens was trained on drivers wanting to go through the police entrance to the garage.

Static issued from the speaker under the lens. "State your business," a no-nonsense male voice demanded. Or at least I think that's what it said.

I exhaled in frustration. They'd never let me in now. I said, "Never mind. I'll just use the public entrance."

I don't know what I was expecting when I pushed through the entrance door to the jail. Despite my occasional involvement with investigating crime, I had never been to the place. Surprisingly, the reception area was similar to what one would expect in a small hotel, although more austere. Three pairs of plain beige couches were precisely placed on a spotless beige carpet. A free-form counter protruded from one of the beige walls like a concrete water lily. Breaking up the walls were vast expanses of wavy glass bricks held together with inch-thick white mortar. The thick glass was undoubtedly designed to allow sunlight to penetrate the lobby in a way that the eye— and bullets from avenging relatives, I imagined—could not. I hugged Marla's purse to my chest and pressed forward.

"I need help," I said haltingly to the short policewoman behind the forbidding counter. The deputy's dark green uniform stretched across her plump frame, and she wore her streaked blond hair in a French braid woven so tightly it would have given me a headache. "I'm here to see a friend, Marla . . . Marla Korman. She has . . . just been taken into the jail." I cleared my throat and willed control. "You see, there's been some terrible, terrible mistake," I said firmly, "because she would never—"

"Hold on," said the policewoman. She asked me to spell Marla's name as she typed on a computer keyboard. She puzzled over the screen for a minute, then turned to me, shaking her head. "I don't know what the charge is, and probably won't for a while—"

"Please," I begged, shameless now, "*please*. I'm Mrs. Schulz. Mrs. *Tom* Schulz. Couldn't you *please* call the officer on duty at the jail and find out what's going on with my friend? She's in poor health, and she's been badly beaten, and the cops who arrested her were hurting her. . . ."

The policewoman leaned forward. "There's *no one* to call, Mrs. Schulz. There won't *be* anyone until she's *processed*. I'm sorry to say this, but unless you're her attorney you're not going to be able to see your friend until *visiting* day Friday—"

"Friday! She could have a heart attack before Friday! She doesn't even have her medication!" I yanked Marla's purse up. "It's called Inderal. It's in here and they wouldn't let—" The policewoman relieved me of the purse in a smooth motion and stowed it under the desk.

"What you need to do," she scolded in a calm, even tone that indicated she had dealt with far more hysterics than she cared to, "is go *home*. Wait for your friend to *call*."

I was getting nowhere. I had to think of another way to help Marla. I ran back out to the parking lot and considered my options. I knew one thing: I was not going home to wait for Marla to call. Her plaintive cry to me as she was hauled away still echoed in my head. I trotted down the steps to the sheriff's department's main entrance.

"Tom Schulz, please," I told the duty deputy at the counter. His desk was a smaller version of the one in the jail lobby. The young deputy himself was so thin his uniform hung on him; he looked like a scarecrow. He couldn't have been a day over twenty. "Deputy . . . ?" I glanced at his nameplate. "Carlson? Would you please tell Tom Schulz his wife's here?"

Deputy Carlson picked up a phone and punched buttons, then spoke in low tones. I couldn't make out what he was saying and couldn't tell if he was calling Tom, the upstairs duty officer, or, heaven forbid, Captain Shockley. I vigorously shook off this last thought. My paranoia did not extend that far. After a moment the deputy hung up and said Tom would be right down.

Five minutes later, Tom strolled toward me with all his usual self-confidence. It felt like ages since I'd seen him last, although it had only been the previous night. His green eyes sought mine and he seemed to assess my mood instantly.

"Let's go up and get some coffee," he said pleasantly, as if I'd arrived to go over the grocery list.

He smiled and waved at the cop at the desk. *I'm in control here. Nothing to worry about.*

Sure.

"Come on," he said aloud in the tone that warned, *We're in public; act like nothing's happened.* "Let's go get some caffeine. There's an old friend of yours who wants to talk." When I gasped and brightened, he lowered his voice, but kept the same smile. "It's Armstrong. He's been up to the Grizzly Creek scene. He was in the vicinity checking a mountain lion report, and heard about the trucker's call on the radio."

I slipped my arm in his and walked by his side, as if I came down to the sheriff's department all the time to drink bitter vending machine coffee with my husband.

Three uniformed officers were leaving the break room just as we entered it. They nodded and said, "Schulz," but sent furtive glances in my direction. No doubt my wild eyes and splotched cheeks didn't play very well. *Poor guy,* I could imagine them thinking, *she's got some problem and expects him to solve it.*

"Does everyone know what's going on?" I murmured once Tom had brought me a steaming coffee with powdered creamer still dissolving on top. I stared into the brew with dismay.

"Tough to tell." Hardly had he spoken when Deputy Armstrong pushed into the room. I had known Armstrong—a pasty-faced man with thin brown hair—for a couple of years. He gave me a sympathetic look and joined us.

"They're putting her into jail pending formal announcement of charges," he began without cushioning the blow.

"When can I see her?" I asked. I sounded absurdly calm. "Is there anything I can do?"

Armstrong frowned. "They have visiting days. And no, there's nothing you can do to help. She'll call the lawyer she wants. They arrested her today because they found out she was planning on leaving the country."

Marla's calendar. I nodded, heavy-hearted. "But listen. She needs the medication I gave to the jail receptionist. That won't get lost in red tape, will it? Plus, she needs to see a doctor."

Tom touched my shoulder. "The jail nurse will see her. She'll get her pills. The last thing they want is a wrongful death lawsuit, believe me. Is she hurt? Or are you just worried about her heart?"

"Someone beat her up at the campsite and left her to die.

And whoever it was did the same to Macguire, I'm sure. Tom, Tony Royce is *missing,* and those two cops are saying she *killed* him. It's utterly absurd. Marla couldn't hurt anyone." Except the Jerk, and he'd asked for it.

"Do they think they fought, and she killed him in self-defense?" Tom asked.

"I don't know! Those cops tricked her," I told him ferociously. "That horrid De Groot Mirandized her when she hadn't the faintest idea what was going on. Had her sign a document saying they could search her home. *She* thought they were looking for *Tony.* I tried to stop them, but no one would listen to me. De Groot kept telling me to shut up. They shoved me, Tom. But they hurt her. . . ." I fell silent.

"She told them she was in a fight, right?" Tom asked gently. When I nodded, he added, "That's when she became a suspect in their eyes."

"But is Tony Royce dead? Do they have his body? How did he die? And what about his missing partner, Lipscomb? Marla *said* a bald guy was beating her up! Do you have *any* idea where he is? Why isn't *he* under suspicion?"

"Miss G., for what? Do you think Lipscomb was camping at the site and they surprised him?" Tom's eyes questioned me. I shrugged, and he went on: "Maybe a bald guy attacked her. But my bet is that the missing partner is long gone. He took that money and skipped. The one Shockley theory I've heard is that Albert Lipscomb, Tony Royce, and Marla were in on a scam together. When it went bad, she murdered Royce."

"Oh yes," I said impatiently. "They tried that one out on us. Then what bald guy attacked Marla?"

Tom tapped the table with his coffee cup and shook his head. "Who knows? If Lipscomb running off with all that money means the end of Prospect Financial, we might want to look at those investors. Seems to me they'd be pretty angry at the remaining partner, don't you think?"

Deputy Armstrong shrugged. "Seems like a long shot to me," he said softly.

I sipped the bitter coffee and pondered an even more bitter scenario: Marla in prison for murdering Tony Royce *and* for stealing three and a half million dollars.

Deputy Armstrong gave me a doleful look. "We don't have Royce's body, and we're not going to be able to search the creek for a long time to recover it."

I put my cup down. Suddenly I longed to be back in my own kitchen, where homicide, arrests, and missing partners who had embezzled enormous sums of other people's money couldn't touch me. "Let's start over. What *is* the status of the Royce investigation?"

"Okay," Armstrong said grimly. He knew he was giving me terrible news. "De Groot and Hersey were up at the site first. Shockley sent them because the report we'd gotten said the two people who might be hurt were involved somehow with Prospect Financial. It's getting to be a joke around here, how hysterical the captain is about his retirement account. Anyway, the trucker had driven some beat-up kid to the hospital, name of Perkins. Apparently you know him, too?"

I nodded. "Macguire's my assistant. He wants to be a cop, so that's why he started following Marla and Tony around after Tony's partner disappeared."

Armstrong raised an eyebrow, but didn't comment on Macguire's detecting ambitions. Beside me, I heard Tom sigh softly. "Anyway," Armstrong continued, "there was a report of a mountain lion mauling a dog by Bride's Creek, not too far from the Grizzly Creek campsites. Wildlife Service was already there, so when I heard the radio report on this possibly injured couple, I drove up to the campsite. De Groot and Hersey were already there." He pursed his lips. "I've never seen Grizzly Creek so high. *I* sure wouldn't want to camp there. If you fell in, lost your balance fishing, you'd never survive. And something was really wrong at the site. Firewood everywhere. Pots and pans. Clothing. Sleeping bags. In all that mud, it could have been two, three sets of footprints. Hard to tell. One set was from a man's boots." He looked at me. "The boots belonged to Royce, we know that. Expensive leather, hand-tooled. We found one boot by the creekbank. The other's missing."

I groaned. The trail led to the creek. So far, the evidence seemed to point to Tony Royce—alive or dead—having been dumped in the water. Not for the first time, I wondered if Marla was telling the whole truth. Maybe she *had* fought with Tony. Maybe she *had* pushed him into the water in self-defense. But what could they have been fighting about? I closed my eyes, then opened them and said resolutely, dreading the worst, "How can you charge somebody with murder when you don't have a corpse?"

"You can," Armstrong answered matter-of-factly.

Tom nodded. "People kill people and dispose of the body. If we've got enough circumstantial evidence, we can get a conviction, Miss G., even without a corpse. And as far as that high water goes—well, we get fishermen missing all the time in the springtime, don't pick up their bodies downstream for six weeks to three months, whenever the water recedes. . . ."

Assume Marla is telling the truth, I ordered myself. *Go from there.* "Marla said she was beaten up at night," I insisted. "I don't believe anyone was fishing. Also, Marla was and is physically wrecked. I doubt she'd have had the strength to push anyone into the water. Or to drag a body from the campsite to the creek."

Armstrong gave me that I've-seen-it-all cop look that always drives me crazy. "Maybe it was dusk. Point is, the water is high, and some people had a fight about *something*, and it *looks* as if Korman pushed Royce in. Where else could he be? We probably won't find him until his body catches on a rock in front of somebody's creekside house." He got up and bought a cup of hot chocolate from the vending machine.

"But that's just not possible," I maintained. "Think about it. Marla had her car. If they'd had a disagreement, why wouldn't she just drive away?"

Armstrong began a patient explanation. "Tom heard about the three-way scam theory. I'll tell you what I heard. Captain told the guy who sits by me that Tony Royce lost a lot of Korman's money over some investment. Captain even saw her arguing about it with Royce's partner Lipscomb only last week. And so another of our captain's theories is that maybe Royce didn't show enough interest in recouping Ms. Korman's big investment. She was furious. Fought with Royce at the campsite. But not before she took something of his. Maybe that's what they fought about. She wanted some payback and he wouldn't give it to her. Apparently, Royce had this gold watch he wore all the time. Not worth as much as what he owed her, but worth something. And then they found the watch at her house, right?"

"You mean, when they did their little search? Yes, they found a watch in the bathroom. But she says he left it there all the time."

Armstrong shrugged. He drained his cup and tossed it into the garbage pail.

I said, "A watch, a boot, and several sets of unidentified

footprints don't equal a murder arrest. I'm sorry. Shockley's theories are lame."

Armstrong crossed his arms. "Okay, then there's the bloody shirt. Did you ever see Tony Royce in a white shirt, initials monogrammed on the pocket? It was in the locked trunk of Korman's car." He glanced at Tom. "You know how Hersey is with those lock picks—"

"Wait, wait," I said. "They searched her *trunk* without a warrant? I just can't believe—"

"Exigent circumstances, Goldy," Tom told me. "The investigators have a messed-up campsite, a report of a teenager who's been beaten, two people missing, they're going to think, *There might be somebody in this trunk dying, we need to get him out.* When it's a matter of life or death, we can break into somebody's trunk. And before you ask, they can tell it's blood on the shirt with a chemical test. It'll take them at least a week with typing and matching to see if the blood belonged to Tony Royce."

"That's not all they found in the trunk," Armstrong added. "They found her keys, which would explain why she had to walk out and get a ride. So anyway, they're up there with all this stuff and they decide to call in and find out what's going on with this Marla Korman. And when they do, it turns out she's had a complaint lodged against her from a few years ago, from the guy she used to be married to. That was about money, too. Neighbor called it in as a domestic, and by the time the cops got there, this Doctor Korman had a dislocated shoulder. Get this—Shockley called up Korman this morning in Honolulu. The doc said, 'Yeah, my ex is as strong as an ox, has a bad temper, is always threatening violence when she doesn't get what she wants, and unlike a lot of women, has no fear about turning her violence on men.'"

I drank more of the coffee, shuddered, and tried to think. "I'm sorry, but I really cannot believe all this. I mean, I'm not saying you're lying, but this is such an incredible amount of baloney that it's ridiculous. Our ex-husband was physically abusive, and you have the photographs of *me* covered with bruises in your files to prove it."

"Do they have photos like that of Marla?" asked Armstrong.

"No," I replied, "she filed for divorce after the incident with the shoulder dislocation. She stood up to him a lot better than I managed to. And ended the marriage a lot quicker."

Armstrong sighed, and we were all quiet for a minute. Finally Tom asked, "Do you have a theory as to what happened, Miss G.?"

"Yes, I do." I tried to soften my indignation to earnestness. "I think the person you want is Albert Lipscomb. He disappeared after Marla accused him of using assays from a disreputable lab. The assays are crucial for a mine to be successful, because they are analyses of ore in the mine. They tell you how much gold is in your ore. If you don't have reliable assays, you're not going to have a gold-producing mine, it's that simple. When Marla found out what he was up to, Lipscomb panicked. He stole over three million dollars from the partnership account, and now he's killed Tony and set Marla up somehow. For heaven's sake, she *saw* him, or someone who looked just like him, up at the campsite."

Tom rubbed his forehead as he considered this. "Why would a fugitive, with a fortune in stolen money, risk taking on two people—make that three, including Macguire—at night, out in the middle of nowhere?"

"Revenge over a bad investment," I replied. "I don't know: Revenge for ruining a perfectly good venture capital firm?" I paused. "Maybe Tony had or *has* something else Albert wants. Maybe Albert had to get rid of Tony because he *knows* something, or Tony could figure out where his partner would go with the money. . . ."

Tom said gently, "I'm just telling you, it sounds more far-fetched than the stealing-the-Rolex theory."

"And I'm just telling *you,* there is no way on earth Marla would hurt anyone and throw him into the creek."

"There are big inconsistencies in her story, Goldy," Armstrong interjected. He counted off points on his fingers. "First, the times. The family that picked her up says she got into their car around nine, not seven, as she claims. And if Tony was missing and she'd been beaten up, why didn't she ask those people to call the police? Okay, her phone was out. But if she came home Sunday morning after a big fight with an unknown assailant, couldn't she have walked over to a neighbor's for help? Wouldn't you do that?"

"I don't know," I said miserably. He made it all sound so plausible. *Was Marla lying?*

"I'm not done," Armstrong went on. "What she says was in the trunk of the Mercedes and what was actually in there. Looks like whoever put the shirt in the trunk—and Shockley's thinking is that she did—dropped the keys in there by accident. That's why she had to walk out to the road. She locked herself out of her own car. And . . . there was a fishing knife in the trunk, too. Covered with blood."

I said, "Was there a gun in the car?"

Armstrong shook his head. "No gun."

I turned to my husband. "Tom, you *know* Marla. You know this can't be true. Please tell me you'll be able to help her. You can't imagine how rough those cops were with her."

He said earnestly, "Shockley won't let me touch this case.

Goldy, look. Tell me this. Do you really believe Marla's story?" His eyes challenged me. "Why wouldn't she ask that family to bring her to our place, where we could have taken care of her? She *always* wants *you* to get involved in her crises. What could possibly be her explanation for not coming to us that morning, if what she says is true?"

I stared at the grimy linoleum floor. Tom was right. Marla involved me in every aspect of her life. This had been true since her divorce from the Jerk, when we became best pals. But on Sunday, maybe she'd wanted privacy. She took great care with her appearance, and perhaps she'd been too humiliated by the way she looked. On the other hand, I'd visited her numerous times after the heart attack. She'd never looked great in the hospital, but she hadn't once shunned my company. I shook my head. There didn't seem to be an answer to Tom's questions.

"I hope she has a very good lawyer," Tom said quietly. He took my hand. "Because I will not be able to help her, and neither will you."

I looked at him for a long time, long enough for Armstrong to pad out of the room. Long enough for a quartet of loud detectives to come in and buy vending machine cinnamon rolls, which they heated in the microwave while they chatted about a ring of thieves stealing credit cards.

"I need to go," I announced stiffly. I pulled my hand from his.

"Goldy, I'm telling you," Tom warned in a low voice, "Shockley will put me on suspension if I muck up his investigation. If Lipscomb, or one of the investors, or some enemy of Royce's, framed Marla, we'll find him. Please be patient. Forensics is out at the site right now. Maybe they'll find something to clear her. I doubt any jury in this county would convict her on what we have at this point. There's just not enough evidence." He hesitated. "Can you talk to me about a motive she might have for fighting with Royce? Were they getting along?"

I chewed the inside of my cheek. "To be perfectly honest, I don't think they were. He told me he was going to ask her to marry him, but it certainly doesn't sound as if he proposed."

His face was unreadable. Finally he said, "I've seen a thousand nutty cases fall apart. Please. If you really care for Marla, if you really want to help her, don't land yourself in jail for obstruction of justice. Don't get in that kitchen and start cooking and think, Oo, oo, I'm gonna hatch something up. Please?"

I said evenly, "You have no idea how badly De Groot and Hersey treated her. She cried out to me to help her and I couldn't. Shockley is up to something, I'm telling you. This stolen-watch theory, for example. How lame can you get? He's out for her blood, and he's going to get it."

"She'll hire a good lawyer to get her out of this," he assured me.

Beg to differ. I stood. Something Tom had said about the Mercedes had sparked a glimmer of an idea: *a matter of life or death.* That's why the cops had broken into the trunk. And something Sam Perdue had related to me connected with it: *They have to do that when it's a matter of life and death.* What I was thinking was bizarre beyond words, but at least it represented a glimmer of hope. And I had to get Marla out of Shockley's clutches. "Would you do one thing for me? Actually, for Marla? Please?"

He looked dubious. "I can't imagine what *this* is going to be."

"You know how I worry about . . . what she eats. Her diet. Would you just bring up the jail menu for me on your computer? For lunch and dinner today? I'd feel better . . . knowing that she had some healthful options."

He raised one eyebrow, but nodded. I followed him to his desk, where he punched a keyboard and finally came up with the day's menu at the Furman County Jail.

For lunch at noon, the inmates were having tuna salad sandwiches, corn chips, and cookies. No help there.

For dinner at six, they were having chipped beef on noodles, green beans, rolls, and lime Jell-O for dessert.

Bingo.

Chapter 14

I told Tom I needed to visit Macguire, do a few errands, check on Arch, and try to call Marla. He said he might be home late. He was still working the soccer arrests. I squeezed his hand and left quickly. I tried to will away a pang of remorse. I wasn't deceiving him *yet*, I told myself. I just needed to help Marla.

I drove away from the sheriff's department in a thick mist. When I saw the orange and green lights of a convenience store, I parked. The day Marla had had her heart attack, I'd been away catering. I'd always felt guilty for my absence, as if her lonely physical ordeal, the Flight-For-Life helicopter ride, the surgery, were events where I should have been beside her. Now, almost a year later, she'd been savagely beaten, accused of murder, and jailed. No amount of lowfat cooking and cheery company were going to help her now.

I rummaged through my wallet, found the number I was searching for, then used the pay phone.

A crisp voice answered and I identified myself. I said, "I need to speak to General Bo Farquhar. ASAP."

The voice responded flatly: "The general's out in the field finishing trials on some equipment. You'll have to call back later. Say,"—I envisioned a bored glance at a blinking, state-of-the-art digital watch—"fourteen hundred hours?"

"Listen up," I retorted ominously, "don't give me that baloney. Bo won't want to know *you* were the one who prevented him from learning about a life-and-death situation affecting a family member. Because that's what I have to report to him *right now*—"

There was so much immediate static that I thought I'd gotten the Marconi version of *Go to hell.* then the line crackled.

"Farquhar here."

"It's Goldy," I began. The enormity of what I was about to tell him almost made me light-headed. I plunged ahead. "I have some bad news about Marla. She, I, we . . . need your help. We need to get her out of danger and clear her name." Then I quickly outlined, through the crackling static, what had happened. Or what I thought had happened. How Marla had gone on a fishing trip with her boyfriend. How she'd been attacked at night and had to hitch a ride home. How it looked as if the assailant had also attacked Marla's boyfriend, Tony Royce. Now Tony was missing, the police had found some bizarre evidence both in Marla's car and strewn around the campsite, and Marla had been charged with murdering Tony Royce. I told him about the high water at Grizzly Creek, about the signs of a scuffle, the knife and the bloody shirt in Marla's car. "Formal charges," I concluded, "are going to be filed within two days."

General Bo swiftly digested all this. "My dear," he said promptly, "what can we possibly do?"

"My idea is illegal," I said bluntly. "But I'm going to need you, a four-wheel-drive vehicle, camping equipment, and food for"—I counted mentally—"five people for two or three days, I think. And, uh, a good map of the back roads and the trails along Grizzly Creek."

"Can do," Bo Farquhar said.

I looked at my watch: eleven o'clock. "Can you be at my house with all that by five tonight?"

"You know," he observed wistfully, "I've always wanted to help my sister-in-law. I'm very fond of Marla."

"So you're willing to help?"

"We've just finished our equipment trials here. My ankle's healed up. I'll be at your house at seventeen hundred hours," he said crisply. His voice bristled with the authority that had become familiar when I was working for him. "I'll bring the supplies."

I hung up. My stomach growled fiercely. The mundane— in this case, no food all day—invariably intrudes when you least want to take care of it. I'd call Arch and then get over to the hospital. A place that made marvelous spring rolls was on the way. I'd take some to Macguire, too. Every time I'd been in the hospital, I'd spent a lot of time fantasizing about food.

I plunked in another coin to call home and heard Jake howling even before Arch could say, "*Goldilocks' Catering* . . . Jake! Be quiet! *Where everything*—"

"It's me. Listen, hon, there's something I need you to do."

"Jake, hush! Where are you, Mom?"

"Oh, honey, it's a long story, but Marla's having some problems." A mild understatement.

"She's not back in the hospital?"

"No." I took a deep breath. "She's in jail."

"In *jail*? For what?"

"She's charged with a murder she didn't do. But listen, I have to go over to Wheat Ridge to visit Macguire—"

"I like Macguire! May I visit him, too? What's he doing in Wheat Ridge?"

"Honey, he's in the hospital. He . . . got beaten up by the same person who got Marla into trouble."

"Can't I come with you? What's going on?"

"I promise I'll tell you when I get home, if you'll just do this one favor for me. Please call the main number for the sheriff's department and get connected with the women's side of the jail. Ask that Marla call you at home as soon as possible."

"Call the jail? Get Marla to call me from *jail*? What am I going to talk to her about? I'm going to feel really dumb."

"You just have to tell her one thing. It's very important, Arch. Tell her the message is from me, and that she has to eat as much Jell-O as possible at dinner tonight. Have you got that?"

He paused. "That is the *stupidest* message I ever heard. Besides, if you haven't checked—"

"Jell-O, Arch," I interrupted him, "you got it?"

His voice was resigned. "Oh-kay! Whatever! Can I be in on this, what you're planning?"

"Arch!" Then I relented. "Please just call the jail."

I hung up to Jake's melancholy howl.

I zipped the van down Interstate 70 to Saigon Carry-Out, ordered a batch of spring rolls, then crossed to Thirty-eighth Avenue and headed for Lutheran Hospital. *Help me, Goldy, help me!* That had been the pained cry from the best friend I'd ever had, as she was led away by two storm troopers. I tried not to think about her, tried not to imagine each situation she was going through down at the jail. Still, worries wormed into my mind. *Oh, Marla, what are they saying to you? Are they dressing your bruises and cuts? Are you taking your medications? Do you believe I'm trying to help you?*

Once I was on the right floor of the hospital, it didn't take long to find Macguire. A television advertisement for chain saws seemed to be emanating from a room with its door half open. But it was not the TV; Macguire's roommate was snoring. When I tiptoed into the room, Macguire raised his head from the pillow and squinted at me. His face lit up with such delight that I refused to gasp at the thick bandage around his head and the gash running across one of his acne-scarred cheeks.

I whispered, "Oh, Macguire! Look at you!" I glanced at his dozing roommate. "How can you sleep with that racket?"

Macguire wrinkled his nose. "I'm used to it now. Afraid I won't be able to sleep once I get back to Elk Park, it'll be so quiet. Listen, did you find Marla? How's she doing? How about Tony?" He sniffed. "Is that food? I'm starved. It feels as if all I eat here is oatmeal. Even if it's beef stew, it tastes like oatmeal."

I wheeled his bed tray over and opened up the bags of spring rolls. My appetite had mysteriously left me, but Macguire's was certainly healthy. When I scraped a metal chair over to his bedside, the snorer rumbled, stirred, and flopped over. "Things are pretty bad," I began, as Macguire dug into his second roll. I told him what had happened to Marla.

"*Murder?* Are you *kidding?*" Macguire exclaimed when I'd finished. He fell back on his pillow, then screeched, "Ouch!" He gaped at the ceiling. "That is just too far out. But Marla was beaten up? So . . . you think the same person hit me? But the cops think it was Marla? Marla wouldn't hurt me, I mean, she likes me! Man, I guess I'm lucky to be alive."

"Maybe so. Please, Macguire, you're going to have to *try* to remember if you saw *anything* else that night. Marla needs you."

Macguire pushed the food away and looked at the window, where fog nuzzled the glass like gray fur. His face crinkled in thought. "Okay," he said, "there are a few things I've been thinking about, stuff I didn't have time to tell you over the phone. It's all kind of disconnected, but maybe you or Tom can make some sense out of it. Could you hand me my backpack, from that closet?"

I hauled out the ragged maroon knapsack while he reached for a pad of paper on his nightstand. Then I glanced at my watch: just past noon. Time was going by too quickly. I wondered if Marla had reached her lawyer yet.

"Do you remember Albert Lipscomb from the party?" I asked Macguire. "Is there any way you could have seen him at the campsite?"

"Yeah, I remember him from the party. Bald guy," Macguire replied as he leafed through his wallet. "Naw, I didn't see him. All I saw were Marla and Royce. But I did take pictures before it got dark up there. I probably shouldn't have, it was sort of invading Marla's privacy, I guess. I mean, nobody's actually hired me to do surveillance. But I thought it would be such a great idea—"

"You took pictures?" I said sharply. "Where's the camera? Where's the film?"

"Well, you're not going to believe this." He hoisted himself back up and gingerly touched his swollen cheek. "But I'd taken pictures of Elk Park graduation on the first part of one roll. So I took a bunch of pictures to finish that roll. When I reloaded the camera I put the first roll in my backpack and locked it in my trunk. When I got hit, I lost the stupid camera! Anyway, I stumbled out onto the road with my backpack, and I was all hurt and bloody and everything, and that guy in the truck picked me up and drove me down here—"

I remembered De Groot's rapid-fire questions of Marla on this point. I demanded, "What guy? Do you remember his name? What kind of truck was he driving?"

Macguire furrowed the small part of his brow that was visible beneath the bandage. "Jeez, Goldy, chill! He told me his name was Wilbur Webster. Wilbur drove a red Toyota pickup. I told him I had to leave my film at the drop box down on Thirty-second and Youngfield. I even wrote *Rush* on the envelope. Wilbur thought I was some kind of nut. He asked if I was a spy." Macguire gave me a self-satisfied, goofy smile. "I said, 'Yeah, man, I gotta have pictures of this high school graduation wicked bad.' And Wilbur said, 'Well, you better try not to get too much blood on the envelope, or the photo people will call the cops.'" Macguire dug into his pack and handed me a wrinkled yellow chit. "Here's the receipt. The pictures might be ready by now. You can check that first roll out real closely, and see if, like, anyone else was at the campsite. Maybe I'm not such a bad investigator. Maybe Tom will want to hire me after all."

I took the receipt and carefully slipped it into my pocket. It was worth picking up the film, although I doubted there would be something on those photos. "But . . . you didn't see anybody else. Just Tony and Marla. And they weren't fighting."

"Yeah. No fighting. And they weren't doing anything weird." He blushed. "I mean, not that I would have watched, but I did hear a couple of things from Bitsy, including some kinky things about Tony Royce."

"Macguire, hush!" I hissed. Then: "What are you talking about? Did you hear about the Las Vegas stripper?"

He readjusted himself in bed to get comfortable. "I'll get to that part. You told me to ask Bitsy if there was anything else. Bitsy had lunch with Victoria Lear's secretary, and they talked some more about the Eurydice IPO. The secretary said Victoria was a real go–getter, highly organized, had a tickler file and all that. According to the secretary, somebody got on Victoria's case for jumping the gun on the initial public offering of stock for the Eurydice Gold Mine."

"Go on."

"Well. You know how Prospect made a lot of money on the Medigen IPO? Victoria explained to her secretary that Prospect claimed in the private placement prospectus for the Eurydice that they were going to take the mining venture public eventually. The implication was that *that* was how they would make their clients scads of money. So Victoria had just started on the paperwork, and then Victoria and some man had this real big fight. The two of them were yelling. Victoria Lear stormed out of her office, told her secretary she was going to tool around off-road so she could unwind. The secretary got a call to the front desk and didn't see the guy who left Lear's office. That was the last time anyone saw Victoria Lear alive."

"Oh, Macguire, did the secretary say what it was they argued about? Had Victoria discovered something? Was it anything to do with assay reports?"

Macguire shook his head. "All the secretary remembers is that she heard Victoria yell something about World War Two."

"Great." I listened to the roommate's violent snores, then sighed. "You said there was something else?"

Macguire blushed. "This part is more like rumor. Hearsay. I mean, it's pretty disgusting."

"I think I can handle it."

Macguire's cheeks reddened. "Well, one day around Easter Mr. Royce asked Bitsy out for coffee, but Bitsy's really into health food, so they went to get some tea at Alfalfa's—" He took one look at my impatient face and plunged on: "Anyway. Bitsy said Royce was kind of hitting on her, and she said it was a rush since he was like, the firm partner and all that. She was thinking maybe he'd give her a *raise* if they had sex. I mean, she *wanted* sexual harassment, if it would work for her. Do you believe that, in this day and age?"

"Macguire, in this day and age, I think I'd believe anything."

"So before long they got to talking about whether it was lonely at the top. Pretty soon he was taking her out for herb tea just about every other day. Bitsy kept thinking they were, like, two steps from the sack. But then Royce confessed that he was looking for a certain kind of girl. The kind of girl he was looking for, well, he wanted to go out with a nurse, and did Bitsy have any friends who were in nursing school?"

"And did she?"

Macguire eased himself up in the bedcovers. "Better than that, Bitsy found him a med student. A woman named Elissa who'd gone to Elk Park Prep and then C.U. It was Elissa's first year at C.U. Med School. Bitsy said that Elissa and Royce started to have this *very* kinky relationship."

"Bitsy told you all this?"

"Yeah. You know why she told me? Because she was so pissed that Tony never gave her anything, like a finder's fee, or something. I mean, she fixed them up in the first place, is the way she saw it."

I didn't ask Macguire why Bitsy didn't quit Prospect and just become a pimp, but I didn't want to distract him from his story again. "So Tony was two-timing Marla and going out with this med student. Marla knew he had other girlfriends." Did Eileen Tobey know? I wondered.

Macguire heaved out an exasperated sigh. "Well, if I knew about this, and I was his girlfriend, *I'd* have shoved him into that creek."

"Marla knew he was dating around for a while, Macguire. This is old news. I just don't understand why he wanted a nurse or med student."

He took a sip of water. "That's the weird part. She would do medical procedures on him before they . . . you know, did it."

I closed my eyes, then opened them. "What kind of medical procedures?" I asked, keeping my voice even.

"According to Elissa, Tony wanted his blood pressure taken, and his pulse, and his temperature—you know, vital signs. Then she would listen to his chest, test his reflexes—"

"Macguire, please. That's disgusting."

He touched his bandage. "They got together every Wednesday. Royce would have a room in his house all prepared. I mean, examination table, stethoscope, latex gloves, cotton balls, alcohol, sterile needles, blood pressure cuff, test tubes, thermometers, on and on. Bitsy was really disgusted when Elissa told her all this. Bitsy said *she* would have pretended to be a nurse for him, except he wanted the genuine article."

"So he had a medical fetish."

"The last thing the med student did before they had sex was to take his temperature. Tony wanted to know if he was really hot."

"Macguire, enough!"

"I told you it was kinky."

"I'll try to follow up on the IPO stuff, anyway."

We were both aware that a change had come over the room. It was like a siren stopping beside the car behind you. First the siren squeals in your ears, then you get used to it, then you wonder what happened to it. With one movement, Macguire and I turned our heads toward the roommate's bed.

A gray-haired man leaned up on one blue-pajamaed elbow in the bed. His eyes were wide and his mouth gaped. Perspiration beaded his forehead.

"Are you okay?" I asked anxiously.

He rasped, "Did she take his temperature orally or anally?"

✦

Ten minutes later I had said good-bye to Macguire and was heading toward a hospital pay phone. I had less than five hours before the general was due at the house. Less than five hours to figure out what was going on, less than five hours before I went outside the law and tried to help Marla. I would need as much information as possible before that time came. I sat down in one of the lobby phone booths and tried to think.

Except for the goat scheme a couple of years ago, everything at Prospect Financial had been going well. Going well, that is, until the firm decided to put money into the Eurydice. And why had the firm decided to put three and a half mil into a mine that had been closed for decades? Because Albert had inherited both the place and the fervent belief that it was chock-a-block with gold ore. His enthusiasm had been empirically borne out by the geology and assay reports that he and Tony had commissioned. It hadn't been difficult to be both promoter and investment company. With Medigen, Prospect

Financial Partners had already proven they had the Midas touch, and thirty-five clients had been more than eager to put up a hundred thousand each to make another killing.

But then Chief Investment Officer Victoria Lear had died suddenly while working on the Eurydice IPO. Marla had found a discrepancy in the assays. Albert had disappeared with the investors' money. Now Tony, too, was missing under suspicious circumstances. And Marla was being made the scapegoat.

Begin at the beginning, I thought. A month ago, Victoria Lear had been working on an initial public offering of stock for the mine venture. I punched the buttons for the Bank of Aspen Meadow and asked to speak with Eileen Tobey on a matter of great fiscal urgency.

"It's your caterer," I said breathlessly, when Eileen finally came on the line. "Just have a quick question, but it's really, really important. What do you know about initial public offerings? What do you have to do to make one happen?"

"Oh, for heaven's sake, Goldy, I'm busy!" Eileen snapped. Then her voice changed. "Look, I've got an important meeting in five minutes. But . . . I heard a nasty rumor about our mutual friend, Marla Korman."

"Really." My heart hardened; bad news sure traveled fast in the high country. No matter how busy you were, apparently, meetings couldn't proceed until people were up on their gossip.

Eileen's voice was like syrup. "I'll tell you what you want to know if you'll tell me it's true she knifed Tony Royce."

"It's not true," I said emphatically. "But she *is* in jail. Now listen," I plunged on before she could ask any more questions, "I don't want to keep you, Eileen. If I were a venture capital firm, and I'd done a private placement and raised a bunch of money to reopen a mine, what would I have to do to take the venture public?"

"Hmm. I don't suppose this has to do with a certain venture capital firm we all know and love?"

"Just tell me what I'd need for an IPO. Please," I added.

She took a deep breath and assumed an authoritative tone. "Very simply, the firm would hand the whole thing over to an investment banker, who would, among other things, hire an independent auditor to check all the facts presented in the prospectus."

"Like what kinds of facts?"

"Oh, that you were what you said you were. Say for a mine, you'd have to have the assays done by a reputable assay lab. You'd hire an independent mining consulting firm to go in and check your geology reports. Like that. It takes a long time and a lot of paperwork, Goldy. You have to spend *months* on an IPO. What are you getting at?"

"Oh, nothing," I said, dejected. "It was just a long shot."

I hung up and considered the narrow, smeared windows of the booth. I didn't have a copy of the prospectus, so I had no idea who the geologist of record was, or how trustworthy his or her reports were. *Then go to the next thing.* What had Victoria Lear discovered? If the assays could be proven to be fraudulent, as Marla had suspected, then finding out *who* had ordered and paid for those glowing analyses of the Eurydice's ore might offer something tangible. Maybe that was what Victoria had discovered. I certainly didn't have a complete set of the assays, and I didn't think anyone outside of the Prospect Financial offices did, either. But if I could find out who ordered them . . . it was a long shot, indeed. I dug out my credit calling card, phoned Nevada information, then the number for Kepler Assay Lab in Henderson.

"Ah, this is Kiki Belknap," I said when the lab receptionist answered. "I'm Tony Royce's secretary at Prospect Financial? Listen, Mr. Royce is out of the office at the moment? But I need to be connected to the first person he ever talked to down there—"

"Miss Belknap," the voice replied stiffly. "As you must be aware, discussion of assays is confidential. Information can only be released to the person originally requesting the assay."

"And for the Eurydice Gold Mine in Idaho Springs," I said breathlessly, "who exactly was that? We don't seem to have it in our files."

Kepler Assay Labs disconnected. I slammed down the phone. So much for long shots. The sheriff's department could get the information, but for that you needed a subpoena and all kinds of time. I glanced at my watch: 12:15. I didn't have all kinds of time. And then I remembered what Marla had said to me a week ago. *The mine was producing gold during the Second World War, and FDR had it closed down with that order of his, L-208. . . .* I turned this over in my mind. L-208. I thought about executive orders, pushing the idea back and forth and over again, the way I kneaded bread. Then I replayed what Macguire had learned about some man at Prospect and his last conversation with Victoria Lear: *They were arguing about World War II.*

Shouldn't there be public records about all this somewhere? Back to long shots.

I leafed through the phone book and called first the Colorado Department of Natural Resources, where I got switched to the Division of Minerals and Geology, which eventually transferred me to the Office of Active and Inactive Mines, where a very helpful person told me that I could find out a mine's history by getting it pulled—for a fee—from the state archives. Imagining a football stadium full of red tape, I called the state archives.

"Hi there," I said in a friendly voice when the archivist answered. "I'm wondering if I could get a quick look at the file on the Eurydice Mine in Clear Creek County. I need it this afternoon."

"Oh, is that you, Ms. Lear?" the archivist said with a laugh. "I recognize your voice. But the last time you wanted a quick look at that file, you were here for an hour!"

My skin chilled to the bone. Now I knew whose voice mine resembled so closely it had scared Albert's secretary. I replied, "I'll be there in forty-five minutes."

I sprinted out to the parking lot and gunned the van toward Macguire's photo place. While they were hunting for the roll of film, I put in a call to Tom.

"Have you found out anything?" I asked.

He sighed. "This guy Albert Lipscomb is bad. Want to know how bad? We just found the body of that bank teller he cozied up to last week. Dottie Quentin. She was supposed to be watching her neighbors' place. Neighbors had a hot tub. The teller was strangled and then her body was placed in the hot tub with the wooden top on. The neighbors found her when they came back from vacation."

"Oh, Lord." The man with the pictures had returned. I said into the phone, "So what does all this mean?"

"It means Marla is lucky Albert, if that's who it was, didn't kill *her*. So far though, only a few people here seem to think Lipscomb would come back to settle a score with Tony and Marla. Killing the teller, that they could see, Albert didn't want her to talk. But why come back?"

I said, "I don't know. Maybe Albert and Tony are in on something together and are trying—successfully, as it turns out—to throw law enforcement off their trail. Have you found out anything about *Marla*?"

"Only that you were right. Shockley's out for blood. Hers."

I said I wasn't surprised and signed off. I paid for the pictures and rushed back to my van, where I slid the envelope open.

Macguire's graduation pictures showed joyful, silly, mugging faces of teenagers atypically dressed in blouses above long chiffon skirts and pristinely white shirts and striped ties. The first picture after the graduation batch was of Macguire's scarred Subaru on a dirt road with pine trees in the background. I was willing to bet this was up by the Grizzly Creek campsite. Then Macguire had held the camera out to take a picture of himself swathed in a camouflage-cloth poncho. The rest of the photos were of Tony and Marla in the rain, busying themselves around the campsite. They'd pitched the tent on a mound. They'd lit the Sterno, heated and then eaten the soup I'd sent up. Then they'd hauled water out of the creek, cleaned up their dishes, and put the trash into the trunk of the Mercedes. This was all as Marla had reported.

I peered at the pictures of Tony. He wore an unzipped rainjacket, and under it, a sweatshirt with "University of—," but I couldn't see the rest. It didn't look as if he had the white monogrammed shirt on underneath the sweatshirt, but it was hard to tell with the fading light and the rain.

The next-to-last photo of the batch was a zoom-in on Marla and Tony's faces. Tony seemed to be laughing at something Marla had said. Marla, with a look of intense irritation, was staring straight at the camera. In the last picture, Tony had reached over to hug Marla, a movement that exposed his right forearm and wrist. A glimmer of light had caught the movement on film.

He was wearing a gold watch.

Chapter 15

As I exceeded the speed limits on my way to the state archives, I tried to convince myself that Tony was a rich enough dude to have two watches. But why would he have told Marla not to wear her own timepiece? Maybe it was just an issue of psychological control. He wanted to be the one telling time. Having been married to a doctor dedicated to psychological control, I knew the telltale signs.

Still, I thought as I accelerated the van toward downtown Denver, the fact that Tony was wearing a gold watch at the campsite made things look doubly bad for Marla. I was glad that I, and not the police, had Macguire's photographs.

I parked in front of the dull-looking government building, pushed through the vaultlike door to the basement archives, turned a corner, and arrived in a large, well-lit room with two desks, several long tables, a couple of rooms with microfilm machines, and row upon row of stacks. The smiling, frizzy-haired woman identified herself as the archivist. She asked me for three dollars for file retrieval of records for the Eurydice Gold Mine in Clear Creek County, then gave me a puzzled look.

"Goodness," she trilled, "you're not who I thought you were. You sounded just like someone else on the phone. So friendly! But so much in a hurry!"

"Victoria Lear's my friend," I lied. "I know she's very thorough, but always quite rushed. A good businesswoman, though, don't you think?"

"I suppose," the archivist replied noncommittally, as another patron had shown up at the desk. I knew questions concerning Victoria Lear's visits to the archives would be fruitless. Colorado librarians take patron confidentiality as seriously as priests do the seal of confession. The frizzy-haired librarian directed me to sit at one of the long tables, and I acquiesced. At least I had received a vital piece of information: Victoria had been here.

When the archivist brought me the legal-length file with its typed tab: EURYDICE—CLEAR CREEK, I felt a wave of panic. What was I looking for, and how would I know it when I found it? Could I see what Victoria had seen? A grandfather clock standing by a near wall said two o'clock. I ordered myself to get going.

Something related to World War II. That was what the argument between Victoria and someone at Prospect had been about. I flipped to the beginning of the file and perused an inspection report from 1915: *At present the work is confined to driving a crosscut to cut the Jack vein.* I read another from 1918: *I secured the samples you asked for and will bring them to Denver tomorrow.* In 1922, the mine produced 161.8 tons of gold ore, and employed ten people. In 1930 an inspector indicated the character of ore as *Gold, Silver, Lead, Zinc.* In 1931, a new inspector noted that there was *No fire protection* and that the mine was not producing: *Their objective is to sink the shaft deeper and get under the ore.* In 1937, the same inspector stated: *The gold and silver ore has played out. There is a large quantity of lead-zinc ore, and mining this on a small scale is their current objective.* But by 1944, production of lead at the Eurydice was in full swing, owing to the demand for bullets and resulting good prices for lead. Then in 1947, the mine was inspected and stated to be *Closed because of the falling price of lead, now that the war is over. There are no stockpiles. No ore has been sent to a mill or sold in the last year. No staff except a night watchman.*

Wait a minute. I flipped back to the beginning and read through the stack of inspection reports. In the twenties the mine had been producing gold at a good clip. Then the precious metal ore came to an end, and the mine produced lead. There was no mention of Executive Order L-208. *The mine had never closed during the Second World War, because the gold at the Eurydice had played out in the 1930's.*

Victoria Lear had been eager to get started on the initial public offering of stock in the Eurydice Mine. She'd started looking at documentation that someone wasn't prepared for her to see. The information in front of me had been her death warrant.

✦

A light rain misted the windshield as I coaxed my van up Interstate 70. Red sparks—brake lights of vehicles ahead—appeared and disappeared through the haze. It was like driving through a dream. I slowed the van and tried to get my racing mind to do the same.

After the gold was gone, the underlying ore, full of lead and zinc, had provided a bonanza for Albert Lipscomb's grandfather until the war was over. Whatever enthusiastic belief Albert's grandfather may have had that there was still gold in his mine was based on hope rather than reality. This hope, a common pipe dream in Colorado, had been fed by Albert, Tony, or both, in securing questionable assays and, I was now willing to bet, buying off a shady geologist. But the partners hadn't counted on Victoria Lear making a trip to the state archives.

Still—how did you get from there to Albert disappearing with all the money? And why had he felt he had to kill the teller? And what was Tony Royce's role in all this?

I sped up the van. Marla couldn't have murdered Tony, I told myself. She was impulsive, yes. She had a temper. But as far as I knew, she hadn't investigated the Eurydice beyond getting Macguire to show one of the Kepler assays to someone at the School of Mines. There was just no way she would fight with her boyfriend, knife him, steal his watch, throw him in the creek, then march over and assault the person who'd photographed their presence at the campsite. And to follow that up by hitchhiking back into town, then hiding out until she could claim she was assaulted by an unknown attacker? No way.

Now, it *was* possible that Marla had been extremely angry with Tony. She had ample reason to be, I countered as I braked hastily behind a grocery truck. Tony had been two-timing her. Make that three-timing, if you believed in the existence of the stripper. Or four-timing, if Eileen had lied about their breaking up. No matter what, Tony certainly had been involved with all manner of women until he'd made a pretense of loyalty to Marla. And if Marla knew of his playtime with the med student . . . I didn't want to think about it. Besides the infidelity, she could have been upset about Albert's absconding with her money. Tony hadn't warned her that his partner might be using a disreputable assay lab. And Tony might have suspected that Albert would steal money from the Prospect partnership account if one of their deals went bad.

So maybe Marla and Tony had had an argument. Maybe she had even hit him. But Marla wouldn't, couldn't hit Macguire. Of course, in the storm, and with him in the rain poncho, she may not have *known* it was Macguire. Then again, perhaps *Tony* had been the one to hit Marla and Macguire, plant the evidence, and take off with the gun. But *Tony* wasn't *bald*. And although he'd been wearing a watch, it was not his ultraexpensive one. The Rolex, I was willing to wager, was not a bauble you'd absentmindedly leave behind at your girlfriend's house if you were taking off for parts unknown.

"I just don't get it," I said aloud. At the exit to the upscale Genesee area, I wondered if the De Groot-Hersey investigative team was spending any time over at Tony Royce's house in Eagle Mountain Estates. His place was near Albert's. Perhaps the cops were still up at the campsite, or, for that matter, at Marla's house. Actually, I rather favored the idea of them being out in the rain.

Once I exited to Aspen Meadow, I passed a popular creekside picnic site that had been claimed by the overflowing Cottonwood. This was probably the place Sam Perdue and his sprained-ankle customer in the ambulance had encountered the near-drowned child. I shuddered. Water had boiled above the edges of the creekbed and now ran freely through a wide area of flattened grass. It gushed up the sides of a picnic table and bench. On the far side of the site, the grill stood just a few inches higher than what now looked like a fast-flowing river.

I wondered where Albert Lipscomb was at this very moment. I hoped that he, too, was soaking wet and suffering. Suffering *abysmally*.

I began driving down the new, recently widened highway that led to Aspen Meadow's Main Street, eight miles away. Mountain residents had bitterly fought the widening of this byway, formerly a tortuous two-way road. A broader route would bring more unwanted people, with their blight of problems, to our little burg, the protesters claimed. These invaders would drive away wildlife, wildlife that was viewed by a preponderance of Aspen Meadow residents as being a higher lifeform than humans. Now, with the clouds lifted just above the treetops, the tawny meadows on each side of the road looked deserted. Suddenly, though, the meadow seemed to shiver. I slowed and pulled the van onto the muddy shoulder. Moving deliberately across the sodden grass was a herd of elk, maybe forty head. Half a dozen calves trod haltingly next to their mothers on impossibly thin, delicate legs. Coming from the East Coast, Marla and I treasured this kind of sight. Lord, how I wanted her back.

I revved up the van and drove home. Without Marla to talk to and plan with, and without Tom to give me updates, I felt anchorless.

I'd been on the periphery of some of Tom's cases before. From time to time, I'd even become more involved than he would have liked. But with my friend under arrest, things didn't look promising for my taking merely a benign interest in the case. I sighed. My idea might not be feasible. It certainly wasn't legal. But what was the alternative? *Go home and wait for your friend to call.* It might as well have been, *Go home and wait for your friend to have a heart attack. Go home and wait for us to maltreat her. Go home and wait for our captain to convict her of murder.*

I ran toward my front door. I had to do something for Marla, because nobody else would.

"Gosh, Mom, where have you been?" Arch demanded as he came bounding down the stairs with Jake's long, nut-brown body at his heels.

"Did you get hold of Marla?" I demanded. Jake gave me his usual mournful, slobbery look.

"Yes, and I told her to eat Jell-O," Arch said. "She said you'd better bring her Epipen down to the jail. She said you'd know what that was." His face lengthened. "Mom, she said she was miserable."

My weight of guilt doubled. "Any other messages?"

"General Bo called. We had a nice talk. He asked all about how I was doing and about Jake." He paused to pat the hound reassuringly. "Anyway, Bo kept saying he wanted to talk to you *bad*. He's on his way over."

"Really?" It was just past three o'clock. I had lots to do, but I needed to talk to Arch. "Listen, hon, I want you to hear this from me instead of from your friends. Tony Royce is missing from the camping trip he took with Marla. The police think Marla hurt Tony. They arrested her this morning, and that's why she's in jail—"

"Yeah," he said, interrupting me, "Marla told me. I turned on the news, but there wasn't anything. Do you suppose the arrest will be in this week's copy of *The Mountain Journal*?"

I had no idea whether Marla was a big enough fish to warrant news coverage, even from our weekly excuse for a paper. I certainly hoped not.

"Probably not, hon. Arch, uh, may I borrow Jake?"

His face clouded. He clasped Jake's collar and the two of them awkwardly backed away from me. "Why?" His voice cracked. "For how long?"

"Well, he needs to be part of the thing I'm planning with

Marla. But I want you to stay home, because it might be dangerous."

"No," he said stiffly. His fingers held Jake's collar in a death grip. "You're not taking him. He's my dog and he trusts me. Jake was mistreated by his last handler. What do you want him to do? I'm his handler now. He won't perform well for anyone but me."

"Oh, *please*, Arch, I'm not going to mistreat him, and this is for Marla—"

Arch turned to go up the stairs. "C'mon Jake, let's go to my room."

"Wait, honey, wait." He stopped and gave me a hostile gaze. "Okay, Arch, you can come. But you have to promise to obey me if we get into a dicey situation."

"Dicey how?"

"I'm not quite sure yet. Please just go pack up clothes for an overnight. As if you were going camping," I added.

I ran up to Tom's and my room. The clock said three-fifteen. *Dicey how? Good question.* I packed some warm clothes. In the kitchen, I loaded paper bags with Jake's spare leash, kibble, homemade dog biscuits, and large plastic bags as well as small ones that zipped closed. I scribbled a note to Tom, telling him not to worry, no matter what happened. Then I glanced around the room—what could I have forgotten? Oh, yes.

"Arch!" I called up the stairs. "I need you to bring all your fake blood!"

While he was objecting, the front doorbell rang. Arch, Jake, and I arrived at the door simultaneously, and a quick glance through the peephole revealed General Bo Farquhar in a black sweat suit and heavy jacket. At least it wasn't camouflage gear. Arch turned off the alarm system and opened the door.

"Well," Bo boomed as he stepped inside, "long time no see! As in less than five days."

It might as well have been five months. Miraculously, General Bo's distracted air had vanished, as had his slumping posture and three-day growth of beard. He was freshly shaven, and I wondered how he could have become so tanned, given all the rain we'd been having. If his face seemed older for his prison ordeal and his bout with depression, he now had a firmness in his facial muscles that spoke of new resolve. Apparently the compound did have a barber. He'd had his pale blond hair cut so short he was almost bald. His pale blue eyes, cloudy and unfocused when I had visited him at the compound, now possessed the razor clarity and mesmerizing intensity I knew of old. He quietly closed the door behind him.

"Hello there, General. How's your ankle?"

He shrugged dismissively and held out his hands. "My dear Goldy. Arch, my buddy."

I shook his right hand, but Arch opened his arms and threw himself against the general's chest. Bo embraced him warmly.

"Wow! I can't believe it's really you!" Arch exclaimed as Jake gave a low, suspicious woof. My son pulled away. "This is my bloodhound, Jake. Jake, meet General Bo Farquhar."

I shook my head in disbelief as Bo stooped and put both his hands under Jake's chin. He said, "Jake, I'm very happy to meet you." The dog whined joyfully and wagged his entire body.

The general turned his ice blue gaze on me. "You want to tell me what your plan is?"

"What plan?" asked Arch. "What kind of Jell-O plan using Jake needs fake blood?"

Quickly, I outlined the essentials of how I thought we might be able to clear Marla.

"Gosh, Mom," Arch commented when I finished, "Tom is going to be *so* ticked off with you."

"That's something I'll just have to risk," I said. "First we need to make a stop at Marla's house."

It took longer than I expected to pack up the jet black Jeep Grand Cherokee General Bo Farquhar had borrowed from someone at the compound. I led the way in my van; Bo and Arch followed in the Jeep. By the time we reached Marla's house it was just after five o'clock. Fog still curled through her garden, and the house looked ominously deserted.

I hopped out of the van and approached General Bo, who had put on sunglasses despite the fog. His commando outfit, no doubt. I said, "Can you stay here with Arch? Explain to anyone who comes along that I'm just getting a few things to take to Marla?"

"Absolutely," he replied.

"What if somebody comes along and starts giving you a hard time?" I asked dubiously.

"No one's going to come along, Goldy." He lowered the sunglasses and gave me his spellbinding gaze. "But if they do, I have a nine millimeter semiautomatic Glock under my jacket. Want to see it?"

Arch said, "Yes."

I said, "No."

There were no police ribbons barring entry to *Chez Marla*. At least I wasn't breaking any laws. Yet. I grabbed the spare key and two large plastic bags I'd brought and walked purposefully up the front steps. Once inside, I retrieved the Epipen, an autoinjector containing epinephrine, from the upstairs bathroom. The label read: *For emergency intramuscular use. Cardiac patients may experience dangerous side effects. Use only under care of a physician.* I wrapped the injector in a hand towel, put it into the plastic bag, then stuffed a warm change of clothes for Marla on top. I looked around her still-messy bedroom and tried to remember what she'd said to the cops this morning. *He has his own closet here.*

I strode quickly into the green-yellow-and-white guest room and pulled open the two-doored closet. The first side yielded four plastic-covered hangers from the dry cleaner, each with slacks and suits. I yanked on the second door, where a single hanger held a pair of blue pants I knew to be Tony's. It looked as if he'd worn them once, wrinkled them slightly, then hung them neatly until Marla's maid could send them out to the cleaners.

"Hallelujah," I breathed. I put my hand into the remaining plastic bag and, touching the slacks only through the bag, carefully slipped them off their hanger. Then I clutched the bag upside down until the plastic fell like a shroud over the pants. I twisted the plastic hard and prayed that this would work.

Once we were out on Interstate 70, General Bo kept a two-car distance behind my van. Down through the gray mist we followed the road, until we passed the exit for the sheriff's department. Just after the highway reentry from that exit, I signaled and pulled onto a slice of shoulder. Following my instructions, Arch and Jake bounded out of the Jeep and stationed themselves twenty yards above us, where they had a good view of the interstate. Arch signaled us with a flashlight Bo had given him. It was nearly six o'clock. I prayed that this harebrained scheme would work.

Dinner was being served at the jail. I tried to picture Marla: She would have been fingerprinted and put in an orange prisoner suit. Right now she could be eating the Jell-O. Lime Jell-O: the gelled substance that contained artificial food coloring, specifically Yellow No. 5. Because Marla was allergic to that dye, it would close her throat, cause her to break out in hives, and make breathing difficult. The cops might disbelieve Marla if she feigned a heart attack, but there was no way a person could fake the physiological signs of an allergic reaction. And any nurse worth his or her salt would know that an extreme allergic reaction in a former cardiac patient was not something to fool around with.

The jail authorities would have to send her to the hospital. I was pinning all my hopes on Sam Perdue's report: *The parents flagged down the ambulance, and the EMT gave the kid mouth-to-mouth and CPR. They have to do that when it's a matter of life and death.* It was yet to be seen how convincing Bo and I could be in doing a life-and-death scene.

Six-fifteen came and went. With my face pressed against the van window, I watched for Arch's signal through the fog. Both Bo and I had left our car lights blinking; I fervently hoped that would be enough to keep people from pulling over to see if we needed help. Behind the wheel of the Jeep, General Bo looked serene. To him, this was probably routine covert operations.

At six-forty, I was about to give up. She hadn't eaten the Jell-O, she hadn't had a reaction, they weren't sending her to the hospital. And then an arc of light from my son, as well as the distant sound of sirens, said otherwise. I waved to the general and he revved his engine. I hopped out of the van, ran up past the Jeep, and watched as Bo signaled to get back on the road. No one was coming, thank God. Only the ambulance. With, I hoped, the department standard for a female prisoner: one paramedic driver, one female guard.

Bo accelerated rapidly. There was a crunch of metal and crash of breaking glass as he rammed my empty van into the road barrier. He leapt out of the Jeep and flung himself down on the pavement next to the rear of my crumpled vehicle. I trotted down to him, opened Arch's bottle of fake blood, and poured it out—first on Bo's face, chest, and legs, then on my face and hands.

And not a moment too soon. The ambulance slowed as it approached the scene of our 'accident.' I jumped up and waved my arms.

"Help!" I cried. "Help! My husband's been hit!" I motioned wildly and shrieked, "Stop, or he's going to die!"

The ambulance swerved and came to a stuttering halt on the shoulder. Bo murmured to me, "Just get out of the way when the paramedic arrives. Let me handle this."

A uniformed paramedic vaulted out of the ambulance and trotted toward us. "Okay, ma'am, can you make it down to the ambulance? Just move back and let me take a look at your husband."

I moved awkwardly to the shoulder as the ambulance driver knelt over General Bo Farquhar. I didn't even see how Bo managed to grasp the man's shirt and pull the Glock from the holster inside his jacket. But I did limp in front of them toward the ambulance so that the guard, still in the ambulance, wouldn't see them, either. When I came up to the driver-side window, I did what Bo had told me and got out of the way. Above us on the road, Arch and Jake climbed into the Jeep.

Wielding the Glock, Bo barked commands into the ambulance. I stationed myself behind the rear doors as the driver and the attendant police officer lined up by the emergency vehicle. The police officer was a woman I knew, but her name eluded me. She unlocked the ambulance doors. Marla, clad in an orange prisoner suit, emerged slowly. She hopped clumsily down onto the graveled shoulder. Her face was swollen with hives and she was gasping. Seeing me, her rasping breath turned instantly into wrenching sobs.

Bo demanded the guard's gun and got it. He threw it off the cliff that abutted the road. Down, down into the ravine the gun fell.

Holding the Glock high, Bo yanked something that I guessed to be the radio wire out of the ambulance. He ordered the ambulance driver back into the disabled vehicle. Then he ordered the female guard to do something to the driver. She leaned into the cab to follow Bo's orders.

"Marla! How sick are you?" I demanded anxiously. "Are you breathing okay?"

She wheezed, then said, "Well, I look a lot better than you, I can tell you that!"

"Blood's fake. Your epinephrine is on the passenger-side front seat of that Jeep up there. Go, take care of yourself!"

"Is that you, Goldy? Goldy Schulz?" the female guard called from the ambulance. "Are you nuts? Don't do this!"

I stared down at the policewoman. I still could not, for the life of me, recall her name. To my horror, General Bo raised his gun and brought it down on her skull. Her body crumpled to the pavement.

"Come on!" Bo yelled at me. The fake blood streaked on his face made him look ghoulish. "Bring that car down!"

My muscles felt as if they'd turned to sponge. "I don't believe he did that," I muttered as I jogged to the Jeep. I threw the car into gear and checked the rearview mirror for traffic. Beside me, Marla rasped a request to Arch that he avert his eyes so she could have privacy. Then she rolled down the waistband of the orange prisoner pants, took a shuddery breath, and stabbed herself in the hip with the Epipen. She rolled the pants back up and whispered an all-clear to Arch. My son stared,

openmouthed, at General Bo and the unconscious policewoman. He looked confused and scared, as if what we had just
done had finally penetrated his consciousness.

I veered onto the road and brought the Jeep to where Bo
stood. He holstered his gun and assumed a paternal tone.
"Please get into the back, Goldy."

As I hopped out of the car, a blue van traveling eastward
slowly passed us and stopped on the shoulder twenty feet below
the ambulance. The Front Range ambulance lights flashed in-
exorably: red and white, red and white. The guard's body did
not move. I couldn't see or hear the ambulance driver.

I opened the door to the back seat. Jake began to howl. On
the shoulder twenty feet from the ambulance, two women
emerged from the van. They were calling to us: *Need help?
Everything all right? Need . . . call on . . . cell phone?* Suddenly I felt Bo's hand grip my shoulder.

"Get back in the goddam car, Goldy. Climb back there
with your son, *now!*"

Arch was crying. His body was stiff with fear. I lost my
balance trying to sit and ended up both beside and partly on
top of Jake. The dog snuffled and whined. I was sorry to have
scared Arch. But seeing Marla so weak and frightened strength-
ened my resolve.

Bo checked the mirror, then zoomed the Jeep across three
lanes and careened up onto the bumpy median. The Jeep
rocked from side to side as it bounced, too fast, over the rocky,
unlandscaped strip dividing the interstate. Finally the car shot
up on the westbound side of the highway. Bo snapped the
steering wheel to straighten the shuddering car. The Jeep's
engine ground ominously as we sped back toward Aspen
Meadow.

Marla struggled to breathe. The rash on her chubby bruised

face made her look monstrous. Jake snuffled and licked my hand. General Bo was staring straight ahead, pushing the Jeep to high speed.

I looked back. Below the median, I could just make out the two women approaching the ambulance. The guard's body was still sprawled, limp, on the road.

We were fugitives.

Chapter 16

"Goldy . . . I'm sorry you had to . . ." Marla rasped. "I can't believe you and . . . Bo . . . what you did . . ."

"I need your wrist," I said matter-of-factly. "I've got to monitor your pulse. That epinephrine could zap your heart right into overtime."

"Great." She struggled to catch her breath. "So then what? Call an ambulance?" Finding this amusing, she wheezed with laughter.

"Look," I replied, "cool it. I can't do blood pressure or EKG, but you need to let me check you for extra heartbeats. We may end up at the hospital yet."

Marla cackled and gasped again. "Leave it to Goldy to break me out of jail using food. Marvelous—"

"Try to calm down," Bo ordered her gently.

Instead, to my dismay, she gulped for breath and started to

weep. She thrust her left hand in my direction. I clasped it, felt for a vein, and checked my watch. Normal. I knew enough about adrenal-type stimulation to expect bad side effects, if there were going to be any, within thirty minutes. On the other hand, the epinephrine should start alleviating her allergic reaction within a minute. *Let us pray.*

With her free hand, Marla opened the glove compartment. A cellular phone fell out. Sniffling, she slammed the compartment shut, groped in the storage compartment between the bucket seats, and pulled out a tissue. Awkwardly, she blew her nose. "Bo . . . I'm so . . . sorry I haven't been nicer to you . . ." She laughed between sobs. "Great time for remorse, huh?"

"Would you please stop talking and hold still?" I demanded. Still, the wheeze appeared to be fading from her voice. I concentrated on the vein in her wrist.

But Marla would not be quiet. "When I heard Bo's voice, saw the two of you, I . . . I didn't know what to think. What . . . what have you done? What's going to happen to us?"

Bo's smile beneath the fake blood streaks was small and guarded. He took a clean tissue Marla offered and dabbed at his face. "Is that allergic-reaction medication working? Do you need some ointment for your hives?"

She ignored his questions. "Why, Bo?" she insisted. Her pulse remained normal. The scratchiness definitely had cleared from her throat. "Aren't you violating your parole? Why are you here?"

He glanced over at her. "You're beginning to sound better." He frowned. "Why am I here? Because Goldy asked me to help. You know me, I'm a military-action kind of guy."

"Cut the crap," Marla snapped.

"All right, then," he snapped right back, "I did it because whatever's gone on between us, we're family."

"I don't know, guys," Arch interjected. His voice wavered. "This is all pretty . . . heavy." With my free hand, I patted his shoulder. He shook me off with a muttered, "Quit it."

Still clasping Marla's wrist, I twisted in the leather seat to check whether anyone was coming for the guard and the ambulance driver. But the roadside scene had long ago been swallowed in fog. I tried not to imagine how much trouble Tom would get into when news got out that his wife had held up an ambulance. I turned back and focused on Marla's pulse. Hunched over the wheel, General Bo sailed up the interstate. His prominent chin jutted out at a determined angle. The speedometer needle quivered just above seventy miles per hour.

"That guard's going to be fine," Bo reassured Arch. His grip tightened on the wheel. "She must have studied acting, that one. Or maybe she was truly passing out. When I want to kill or maim someone, I do it."

"So . . ." Marla groaned. "Where are we going? How is all this . . . going to end up?"

No one answered her. Bo glanced into the side mirror and changed lanes. I checked my watch: Ten minutes had passed.

"Getting back to cutting the crap," General Bo said mildly, "why don't *you*, Marla, dear, tell *us* what's going on. Goldy didn't have a lot of time to fill me in. She said you'd been accused of killing your boyfriend. Did you?"

Marla bit her bottom lip and said nothing.

"Self-defense?" Bo prompted. His eyes didn't move from the road. "Maybe you were just pissed off? God knows, I invested in that mine, too. *I'm* pissed off."

Marla shuddered. "I did not do *anything* to Tony. I know it *looks* bad, because I was the last one with him. . . ."

"Well, *next* to last, anyway," Arch added helpfully.

Marla went on: "Besides my hundred thousand in Prospect, he'd borrowed another eighty thou from me to put down on land in Steamboat Springs. He probably owes money all over the Denver metropolitan area. I *want* my money back. But I *didn't* kill him."

"Maybe he was cheating on you, and you just thought you'd hurt him," Bo offered, his eyes still fixed on the road. "Maybe he insulted you. Maybe you'd just had enough. Frankly, I don't care. But before we go farther, it would be best to know all we can."

Marla didn't bother to hide her hostility. "You're as bad as the cops. I haven't even *begun* to tell you how *they* treated me." She turned around. Even with the hives receding, her bruised face seemed hideous to me. "You should have heard them. 'What were you mad at Tony about? Did you hit him? How many times did you stab him?'"

The general groaned sympathetically, but glanced at her expectantly, as in, *Well? How many times* did *you stab him?*

Marla's tone was frosty and deliberate. "I don't know who hit me, I don't know why, I don't know who hit Macguire, I don't know who put the bloody shirt and knife in my car. I didn't take Tony's damn watch, and I certainly don't know where Tony is." She glared at us.

Another uncomfortable silence filled the Jeep.

"Jake could f-i-n-d Mr. Royce," Arch spelled out confidently.

"Dead or alive," the general whispered.

"So what are we going to do?" Marla asked angrily. "Go back to Goldy's house and wait for Tony to call?"

Twenty minutes had elapsed, and Marla's heartbeat, if not her humor, was in good shape. I took a deep breath. "Okay, look. You were attacked by a bald person. Maybe it was Albert. Maybe it was someone else. Tony's vanished. I think our only hope is to go back to the campsite. The Furman County Sheriff's Department has access to just one bloodhound these days—"

"Oh, yeah!" Arch interrupted. "The police in Aurora asked to borrow that dog a couple of weeks ago, and the handler's been involved down there, so they haven't been able to work that dog up in the mountains—"

"Are you kidding?" Marla exclaimed.

"Look, Marla," I protested, "it's our only hope."

"*What* is our only hope?" she squealed. "Going back to that damned campsite? In this weather? To look for what? Besides," she added sarcastically, "I thought Arch's dog was retired. Something about how he'd become untrustworthy. Please tell me I'm wrong."

Jake, sensing he was being discussed, began to whine. Perhaps the canine was smarter than I was giving him credit for.

Arch piped up, "Jake just had trouble with *three* trails last year! It was because the department got a new handler who didn't know what he was doing. Jake was mistreated and got all nervous. The department thought his smeller was off. But Tom and I know that isn't true."

"I think we should try to track Tony's movements," I said. I added mentally, *And rely on Jake's smeller* not *being off.*

"Mom's finally beginning to understand what Jake can do," Arch said with an eagerness that made me uneasy. "See, even with the trail going to the creek, we should be able to locate the body. In the water, I mean. All that stuff in movies about prisoners getting rid of their scent? You know, by wading in a stream or something? That is *completely* wrong. You leave your scent in the water just as much as you do on the ground. See, bloodhounds can follow the trail along the creek—"

To my astonishment, Marla burst into tears. "My life is hell," she wailed.

"Please stop," I murmured. "Please don't, you'll just—"

"*Who* is trying to ruin my life?" she bawled. "What did I *do*?"

"Don't try to talk," I told her gently. Bo pulled into the far right lane and slowed slightly until we came to a lighted green highway sign.

"All right, listen to me," the general began, as he peered through the mist. "Goldy's plan is good. We go to the site. We track Tony to the last place he was seen. Maybe he was kidnapped. We track him to where a car picked him up. Or say he was killed, thrown in a ditch. Ditto. Then whoever did it must be the one who planted the evidence implicating Marla. Arch, you said you and Tom have worked with Jake. You don't think the dog's unreliable, do you? We're all telling the truth here, young man."

"Okay, look. Jake had a couple of problems our first time out," Arch admitted. "He got confused by a pool scent. But he did better after that."

"My number-one priority on this trek is to keep everyone safe," General Bo announced fiercely. "With you first, Arch. I promised your mother. You take care of Jake. I'll take care of you. Okay?"

"All *right*," Arch replied angrily. "You don't need to baby me."

I said, "We're just looking for clues that De Groot and

Hersey might have missed. And to track Tony's last movements. Maybe with Marla gone, the sheriff's department will search a little harder for Albert."

I looked tentatively at Marla. Her face was set in deep doubt. No point in discussing any more until we got to the site. But to do that the fastest way, we had to go into Aspen Meadow and turn onto the state highway that led to Blue Spruce and the Grizzly Creek campsite.

We rounded the lake. I held my breath as we began the descent to the light on Aspen Meadow's Main Street.

"Christ," muttered General Farquhar. He pointed and I felt my heart clench. The law, it seemed, had already arrived on my street. Two patrol cars, lights whirling, were double-parked by the turnoff to our home.

The light at the intersection of Main Street and the highway leading to Blue Spruce and Grizzly Creek changed to red. With no place to turn around and the light against him, General Farquhar rocketed the Jeep through the intersection. He swerved wildly around a Volvo with a Kansas license plate, then barely missed a pickup truck as he plowed down the left lane. I guessed he was trying to find enough room to make a U-turn. He finally careened onto the sidewalk in front of the Aspen Meadow Café, plowed down a bush, and gunned the Jeep back up Main Street. Behind us, a siren sounded.

At the light, an enormous Safeway truck lumbered into the slow, tortuous turn toward the lake. The Jeep tires squealed as General Bo darted wide around the truck. The truck driver, confused by the Jeep's sudden appearance, braked. All traffic was suddenly blocked as we zipped through the narrow opening made by the truck. Bo veered left, heading west on the highway. Belatedly, the truck driver let loose with his horn. Drivers on three sides joined in the cacophony.

"What was that about keeping everybody safe?" I yelled. No one listened to me.

When we had gone less than a hundred yards, General Farquhar gunned the Jeep up the grass-covered hill next to the road. We slammed through a flimsy wire fence and careened across private property. For the next ten minutes, the general took us through two more yards and then across back roads until we came to the acreage of Furman County Open Space property. We met with some strange looks and barking dogs, but no police cars and no angry-tempered Coloradans wielding .357 Magnums. Thank heaven.

"Do you know where we're going?" I asked, once we were on a pathway that cut through a county-owned meadow. Bo did not answer. The overgrown, muddy path was sort of an off-road road. The Jeep wove around rocks and smashed back through someone else's fence before returning to a rural paved road that eventually intersected the highway leading northwest out of town. Maybe he did know where he was going.

We drove the next forty minutes in near silence. Carl's Trout Pond, High Country Auto Repair, and Blue Spruce all whizzed past. The road climbed until a sign swathed in tendrils of mist announced we were driving through national forest. At seven-thirty, we would have less than another hour of daylight. It was extremely unlikely that the police would still be at the campsite. When Tom had a team of investigators at the scene of a crime, they rarely stayed past a few hours, long enough to take photographs, make a videotape, and collect evidence.

At a dirt road where a collection of dilapidated signs stood propped like abandoned rakes, General Farquhar finally slowed. The rusty markers with their skewed arrows named a host of camps, picnic areas, and campsites that included Grizzly Creek. Grunting, Bo negotiated the razorback turn to get onto the dirt road. We jolted over a wooden bridge. Less than a foot below us, muddy, swollen Grizzly Creek teemed and foamed.

After crossing the creek, we wound swiftly upward through national forest. Occasionally, the fog cleared, revealing vistas of rock-strewn steppes and hillsides dense with evergreens. Stands of lovely white-skinned aspens randomly interrupted the green. We came into a narrow canyon where lodgepole and ponderosa pines stretched up bluffs on either side of the road. There were no cars, bicycles, or hikers. I dreaded the prospect of all the unknown territory out there—even more than I feared arriving at the campsite.

"You need to show me where you turned off," General Bo told Marla, and she pointed mutely to a still narrower, unmarked dirt road. We rocked through muddy ditches, turned and once again found ourselves next to Grizzly Creek, this time heading upstream. We paralleled the bloated waterway until it disappeared upward into a ravine. The water crashing over rocks roared so loudly we could hear it inside the car. We pulled up to a rough parking area lined with logs. Marla drew in a ragged breath. Arch leaned forward to peer outside.

Arch told General Bo to cut the engine immediately. My son said, "Carbon monoxide from the engine exhaust can destroy the scent at the site. All the rain will make Tony's scent stronger. A person drops individual bacteria and skin cells everywhere he goes," Arch added. "When there's little wind, no car exhaust, and a lot of moisture, the trail of a person's movement can be detected for a long time, even weeks." Even, as I had just learned, if he's gone into or through water.

My eyes skimmed the abandoned campsite. Because we had climbed from the main road, what had been a low-lying gray cloud just above us was now a mist drifting between the pines. A picnic table had been upended, either by campers or by the investigators. Bits of tissue, crusts of food, and torn paper plates spotted the mud. It looked as if the trash can had been emptied. My guess was that this had been done in search of evidence.

"Okay, I'm going to get out first," General Bo announced. He emerged stealthily from the Jeep and checked every corner of the campsite. His movements were hawklike, aggressive.

General Bo signaled to us to come. Jake began to snort excitedly. When Marla opened her door, I nodded to Arch, who hopped out with Jake in tow. I glanced at the cellular phone on the floor of the front seat. Call Tom now or later? I was going to call him, I was determined. I jumped out of the Jeep. Later.

Arch crouched next to Jake and murmured. Marla limped over to the creek and stood next to the raging water with her arms hugging her body. Arch reached into his backpack and pulled out his dog-handling gloves, then the working harness, which he snapped into place around Jake's powerful torso. My son's face was serious. I suspected he was beginning to understand the possible consequences of what we had done—or what we might find.

The general strode back to the Jeep and pulled out a large backpack on a frame. He hooked his arms through the metal support and fixed the straps around his waist. I took a deep breath of the cold, moist air and tried to think. Arch had told me that the record for a bloodhound tracking was one hundred forty miles in a day. Before darkness obliterated this fog, I doubted we'd go more than a tiny fraction of that distance.

At Arch's request, General Bo hauled out the bulging plastic bag that held Tony Royce's pants. Bo signaled to me to come, then handed Arch the bag and reached into his pocket for a tightly folded laminated map. In the gathering gloom we squinted at the map: Ragged red lines marked Grizzly Creek,

Bride's Creek, Clear Creek; blue lines indicated the back roads; a double yellow line showed Interstate 70. To the west lay Idaho Springs; to the east, Aspen Meadow. Bo looked up and scowled.

"You ready?" I asked him. He nodded.

In one fluid motion, Arch expertly opened the bag and clutched it from the bottom so that the open end was near Jake's nose. *Don't ever overwhelm a bloodhound with scent,* he'd told me. *You just give him a whiff, and that's enough.* Arch held up the bag and leaned toward his dog. Then I was startled to hear my son's mature command cut through the fog.

"Find!"

And off Jake went, glossy nose to the ground, long ears brushing the mud, long brown legs swaying from side to side. The hound cast around for a moment, then, tail curled up, ambled purposefully up the path away from the creek. Sensing that something was finally happening, Marla pulled away from her somber contemplation of the creek's edge. Thirty feet beyond, Jake made his way with determination up the hill. The dog tugged so hard on the leash that Arch's arms were straight and taut. Maybe I should have called Tom. But what would I have said to him? *Arch and I are trying to pick up on the trail of a guy who might be dead. With us are a) my friend who's been accused of murdering the maybe-dead guy, b) her brother-in-law who was so crazy the Pentagon dumped him and you sent him to prison, and c) a bloodhound the police retired for being unreliable. Wish you were here!* I sighed deeply and trotted toward the path. Marla called that she would follow at a slower pace.

Within moments the campsite was gone from view. I tried to recall the most Arch had tracked with Tom and Jake in a day. Two miles? Five miles? Far above the fog, the sun was beginning its decline to the west, and soon the light we did have would drain away. I wished I'd checked our exact location on the map.

My feet slipped on the dense, slick carpet of pine needles, and I stopped to wait for Marla. By the time she caught up with me, the mist was thickening to a light rain. Our scraggly company halted when Jake snuffled in an erratic circle. I hustled up in Arch's direction, then walked beside him as Jake scrambled over a cluster of rocks. Abruptly, the dog stopped by a pile of granite outcroppings.

"Pool scent," Arch muttered under his breath. "Maybe he or *they* sat down here."

Increasingly excited, Jake continued to wheel in a tight circle. I looked up into the pines. Every now and then the object of a search would climb a tree, as Arch's friend Todd had done on a trail only last week. The last thing I needed was to stare down the barrel of a gun aimed at me by Albert Lipscomb. But the lodgepoles and ponderosas were empty. The trees stood with perfect, eerie stillness in the swirling mist.

"Wait!" came General Farquhar's brusque command. He was peering at the ground. "Arch, pull Jake up." Arch obliged. "There's something here," the general insisted.

I walked carefully over the sodden ground to where Bo and Marla stood by the granite outcroppings. "Marla," I said as I stared at the ground, "would you reach into the pack and bring out the plastic bags?" Bo dropped down on his knees to make the backpack accessible, and Marla awkwardly unzipped the pack and dug around until she found the cardboard box of Ziplocs, which she handed to me. I impatiently opened the box, carefully removed one bag, and unfolded it over my hand. Then I reached down and snatched the object from the ground, folding the bag up and over, the way I had seen Tom do.

Jake started off again. General Bo stood quite still and looked at the plastic bag in my hand. Then he snared me in the spell of his eyes. In the fading light, I carefully maneuvered my hand around the article I'd picked up.

Marla stared at the bag in disbelief. I couldn't compute what was there. *Any graduate of Med Wives 101 knows that,* my inner voice reprimanded. What I held in my outstretched hand was a Vacutainer tube, the kind used in blood tests. The nurse sticks you with the hypodermic needle, draws out your blood, and it goes into a sterilized plastic tube. If you're in for a complete physical, first she fills one tube, then another. The tubes are labeled and capped: one to have your hemoglobin checked, another your thyroid, and so on.

But this was one plastic Vacutainer tube only, and it was broken. The shards were covered with dried blood.

Chapter 17

Marla spoke first. "So what does all this mean?" she demanded impatiently. "Is that Tony's blood? Albert's? Or somebody else's?"

"Here's my best guess," I said. "This tube?" I pointed. "This is where the blood came from that ended up spilled all over the shirt in your trunk."

"But whose blood *is* it?" she repeated impatiently.

Before any of us could answer, however, Jake darted off, away from the granite outcropping, up the hillside path. Tugged along by his dog, Arch yelled for us to follow. General Bo gave one quick shake of his head, leapt to his feet, and jogged up the path in pursuit. I held Marla's arm as the two of us struggled to follow.

The rain thickened to icy drops. Thunder rumbled overhead. The shaggy pine needles overhanging the path trembled as the chill rain pelted downward. I pulled up my jacket collar and looked anxiously up the trail for Arch.

"Safety alert," Bo called down to Marla and me. "We shouldn't be out in a forest, at this altitude, in a lightning storm." We mumbled assent, and Bo called for Arch to pull Jake up. Then Bo loudly summoned us to a retreat action. "Back to the Jeep, everybody! Time to get dry and look at the map!"

I made a U-turn on the path. No matter what you were doing, it seemed, the general wanted to be in charge. The rain leaked down my collar. My skin was chilling as fast as the thin membrane of ice that forms on Aspen Meadow Lake each November. Thunder boomed again, much closer this time.

I hustled up to Arch, who was unfastening the leash from Jake's working harness. Talking quietly to his dog, Arch then removed the harness itself. This was Jake's signal that the day's tracking was over. I held the working harness while Arch clipped on Jake's regular collar.

"You're done, boy, good boy," Arch murmured. "Dinner soon. I hope."

As we ran back toward the car, Jake's whines at being pulled off the trail almost rivaled the boom of the creek. Did I really want to find Tony? Yes, I said to myself as I gritted my teeth. I did. *Dead or alive.* I needed to know the truth.

"Lord," said Marla when we were all packed back into the car. "I'm an icicle in an orange prison suit."

I pointed to the storage area behind the back seat. "I brought a bag from your house. Extra sweaters, dry clothes." She mumbled a thanks but only hugged herself for warmth.

After snapping on both the overhead and dashboard lights, the general wiped the laminated map and offered it to me. He asked gruffly, "So what's the next part of the plan, Goldy? Now that both rain and night are falling?"

I tried to sound confident as I took the map. "Just give me a minute." On the seat between Arch and me, Jake shook himself and nudged closer.

Marla was immediately dubious. "What are we doing, a scavenger hunt? Or is this an off-road trip? How long do you think it's going to take the sheriff's department to swoop down on us?"

"Please relax," I said as I traced Grizzly Creek with my index finger.

Arch embraced Jake, who slobbered over his face in gratitude. General Bo turned on the engine and clicked on the heat.

"Do you think," Marla wondered aloud, "that the sheriff's department would take the investigation in a different direction, if we turned in that test tube?"

I snorted. "Do you want to risk the reactions of Hersey, De Groot, and Captain Shockley to what may or may not be evidence in your case? Especially now that you're an escaped suspect? It'll take them at least a week to run the tests to figure out whose blood is in your car. Matching with the stuff in the tube could take even longer. And then they'd have forty theories on what it proves."

She shook her head dolefully. I went back to the map. Rain pounded on the roof. The only other sounds were Jake's snuffles and the persistent roar of the creek.

I'm not great with maps, especially ones of the mountain areas that show elevations, streams, and roads. But this particular map was unusually complex. In addition to the main roads and towns, it depicted trails, campsites, four-wheel-drive roads, and historic landmarks. I had never heard of the Perdito Ghost Town or the Fallen Angel Mine. Making a mental note to check them out sometime, I searched for the Continental Divide. After a moment I made out Interstate 70, Clear Creek, Cottonwood Creek, and the Arapahoe National Forest.

"Jake's hungry," Arch announced to no one in particular.

"I've got food for him," I said, still bent over the map.

The general assumed a jovial tone. "Anyone for camping out?"

Marla groaned. "No, no, no. Not now. Not ever. In fact, there is nothing that would get me back into a tent at any point in my *lifetime. Especially* when it's raining. Besides, the last time I camped out on a night like this, bad things happened that I'm still paying for."

"Let me see the map," Arch offered helpfully. Jake awkwardly scrambled into the storage area behind the backseat. "Okay, here's Aspen Meadow." Arch's finger indicated our town's lake. Then he traced over to Interstate 70, eastward to the approximate point where we had taken Marla from the ambulance. "And here's where we've come." His stubby finger then indicated the road that ran northwestward out of Aspen Meadow, past the turnoff that led to the general's compound in Blue Spruce, toward the entrance to the national forest and Grizzly Creek. "That trail we were on goes over a lot of hills, and then just ends up back at I-Seventy, by Georgetown. Mom. Where do you suppose this guy or guys we're tracking are going? What do you think they're after?"

"Honey, that's what I'm trying to figure out. There are all kinds of roads back to these campsites."

"But," Arch objected, his concentration back on the map, "why would you go up that path instead of back toward the campsite road, where you could have a car?"

The general turned on the wipers. They swept thick ripples of rain off the windshield.

Arch chewed his bottom lip the way he did with a particularly odious math problem. "Okay, we're not going home or to the general's compound. And we're not going to camp out." He straightened his glasses. "I gotta tell ya, Mom, I don't think there's enough room for all of us to sleep in this car."

No one commented. Marla asked Bo to pop the trunk, which he did. She hopped into the rain. A moment later she ordered Jake to hold still as she clambered around behind us, looking for dry clothes.

"Okay everybody," I said solemnly, "*Bride's* Creek isn't too far away. Remember when we did that party at the Hardcastles' place, Arch? I think that's where we should go."

Arch said, "Some of the Prospect Financial people were there, weren't they? That's where I met Sam the soup guy."

I said glumly, "No one is supposed to be there now. Let's just hope the property isn't under water."

The general pressed the accelerator. The engine roared in response, and Bo snapped the car into reverse. Unanchored by a seatbelt, Marla squealed as she bounced across the storage area.

"Wait a minute!" she cried.

Bo braked and Marla yelped again. "I know where Bride's Creek is," he announced. "Adele's ashes are scattered there." At the mention of her dead sister, Marla groaned. Bo ignored her. "How do we get to this cabin?" he demanded.

I endeavored to keep the irritation out of my voice. What had I been thinking—getting us all into this mess? Tom was going to kill me. If the general didn't manage to do it first. "We need to be very careful," I said. "If I ever get back home, I'd like to have a business to go back to. We'll spend the night under a real roof and come back early tomorrow to pick up Tony's trail." *It shouldn't be so bad, if we don't break anything,* I consoled myself. Then I added mentally, *I'll give Edna and Whit a discount on their next party.*

If I have a next party.

Chapter 18

Marla scrambled back to the front seat, now clad in a sequined burgundy sweat suit. The general made an efficient three point turn. As we zipped along, I recalled the details of the roast pork luncheon Arch and I had done for the Hardcastles in the fall. It had been a lavish fund-raiser for historic lands preservation. I hadn't met Albert Lipscomb that day, but I knew he'd been a guest. Marla and Tony had been in attendance, too, as had Amanda Trotfield, although her husband had been flying a charter to Buenos Aires. Edna Hardcastle had hired Sam Perdue to make vichyssoise. She'd told me she was trying to spread her money around among Aspen Meadow food folks. At the time, I'd been miffed, but I'd been assured by Eileen Tobey, whose bank was a big sponsor of historic land preservation, that Sam's cold potato-leek soup couldn't touch mine. Now, I didn't give a hoot about the luncheon or what had been served. I concentrated on trying to remember where the Hardcastles kept the spare key to their cabin door.

With a screech and thud, the general catapulted the Jeep onto the state highway. To the east were his compound and Aspen Meadow; to the west, the Continental Divide and the high mountains. I half expected to see a dozen police cars lying in wait for us where the dirt met the gravel. But there was only the rain.

"May I see the map?" Marla asked meekly. I handed it to her. She turned the light on over her seat and bent over it.

Incredibly, undoubtedly from habit, I tried to decide what we were all going to have for dinner. I had no idea what foodstuffs General Bo had brought for us. The more I stared at the rain streaking our windows, the more unwelcome, catering-type worries crowded my mind. There was the problem of the Hardcastles' wood stove—would there be enough dry firewood to keep it going through the evening? And what would we have for breakfast? I almost laughed. Then my mind posed another question: Didn't the Hardcastles have a caretaker living near the cabin? Would he see us breaking in? If he did, wouldn't he call the police?

Within thirty minutes we turned onto the road paralleling Bride's Creek. After following the swollen, turbulent waterway for a few miles, we came to the split rail fence that announced the beginning of the Hardcastles' extensive property. Arch excitedly pointed to the driveway with its stone pillars. I held my breath as the Jeep rocked over the narrow wooden bridge that barely spanned the muddy wash of the usually idyllic stream.

Peering through the gloom for signs of life at the caretaker's white house, I quickly realized there wouldn't be any. Set in a low-lying area near the water's edge, the diminutive clapboard residence had been claimed by the creek's overflowing banks.

Water rippled around the house, which stood like a belea-
guered island.

"So much for the caretaker," muttered Marla. "It's just us
and the ghost of the bride."

"Excuse me?" said Bo, his eyes on the road. "When we
scattered Adele's ashes up here, it was because her Episcopal
church was still arguing about a columbarium. I never heard
any of the history."

Marla *tsk*ed. "They gave us the spiel on the reason for the
creek's name at the historic lands luncheon. There was a popular hotel downstream. Early in the century, the place was famous for luxurious honeymoon cabins." She sighed, as if
renting a honeymoon cabin was the stupidest thing she'd ever
heard of. "In the twenties, one newlywed couple came up in
their Rolls and took over the most spacious cabin. Under a full
moon, and presumably after the marriage had been consum-
mated, the bride stepped out for a stroll. She got too close to
the creek, slipped, and drowned. Now people say they see her
ghost by the water. Especially when there's a full moon."

"We probably won't be able to see the moon tonight,"
Arch commented pragmatically. "Too cloudy."

"Yeah, well," Marla said knowingly. "That doesn't mean
she's not still out there. They couldn't do autopsies back then,
the way they do them now. My guess is her new husband
pushed her into the creek and held her down. You'd have to be
pretty dumb to fall into the water. Pushing somebody, that's
altogether different. At least, that's what they kept telling me
down at the Furman County Jail."

"Tell me about the cabin," Bo demanded as we rounded a
stand of evergreens. The rain had once again turned to mist. "I
suppose it's historic, too?"

"Yes, we heard all about *it* last fall, too," I said wearily.

"Built around . . . oh, what did they say? 1860. It was a trap-per's cabin by the stream. The cabin became a stage stop and then a schoolhouse—the only one between here and Aspen Meadow. Then it morphed into a general store. Furman County came up about twenty years ago and claimed the cabin was on their right-of-way. They needed to pave the road along Bride's Creek, and they wanted to tear the cabin down. Mrs. Hardcastle's mother, Maureen Colbert, stepped in and waved a preservation flag, probably one of the first. Mrs. Colbert, who was also a big benefactor of the Denver Zoo, bought the cabin from the county, purchased this adjoining property, and had the cabin reassembled, log by log, on higher ground. When she died, she left it to her only daughter, Edna, who married Whitaker Hardcastle, a petroleum geologist. They've got a daughter, too, and she was supposed to get married up here this spring, but she reneged." I remembered how much my bank account and I had been looking forward to catering the Hardcastles' daughter's wedding reception. Now my bank ac-count seemed like the least of my problems.

"Yeah," Arch interjected, "but we did that lunch fund-raiser here last fall, after Julian left. It was one of the first times I helped Mom on my own."

We passed the toolshed, pump, and outdoor shower the Hardcastles had constructed near the cabin. Mrs. Hardcastle's mother had wanted the cabin not just to be moved but to be *restored,* so that when you came up to visit, you could stay there and imagine yourself a trapper.

Make that a very wealthy trapper. A real trapper wouldn't have built a fake well next to the pump. In her desire to make the cabin look authentically rustic, Edna Hardcastle had con-structed a cute little well superstructure—the round, roofed type the Disney folks might have put by a cabin in Frontierland. It was in the well bucket, I remembered suddenly as we pulled up, that the Hardcastles kept their spare key. I thanked heaven I'd remembered, and then silently requested forgiveness for felony trespassing.

We all jumped out. Jake immediately lifted his snout to the skies and howled; Arch shushed him. The well crank squeaked ominously as I hauled on the rope, but the bucket popped up, and I fished out the dark plastic container that held the key to the cabin's massive front door. As the general busily unloaded gear from the rear of the Jeep, Arch continued to reassure a nervous, barking Jake that he would eat soon. Marla stood apart, refusing to join us. Her arms were crossed, and she gazed into the distance. More than ever, I wanted to get her through this mess.

With a determined shrug—we were, after all, adding breaking and entering to our list of crimes—I put the key into the lock. Before turning it, I noticed deep, new grooves beside the doorjamb. It looked as if someone with a crowbar had preceded us.

Without touching the key, I pushed on the knob. The door creaked on its hinges and opened wide. Immediately a flood of damp, musty air washed out onto the stoop. I said weakly, "Somebody's broken in."

"All right, let me check this out," the general ordered. He assumed a straight-backed military bearing and pulled out his gun. In his free hand he brandished a high-powered flashlight that made the silver tube affairs I'd known from summer camp look like toys. Skimming silently across the floorboards with the Glock poised, he swept the interior space with the beam of his light. After a few minutes of probing, he seemed satisfied that the place was empty. He put the gun and the flashlight down on a table, fished out matches, and scraped one of the more sturdy-looking chairs into the center of the room. Then he lit the kerosene lamps hanging from the ceiling. Light filtered to the far edges of the cabin interior.

The small interior space—about four hundred square feet—was authentically without electricity or telephone. No sign of an intruder was evident. The antique furnishings that came into view were as lovely as I remembered: rocking chairs, a wooden love seat, two small beds, a fireplace that had been put in when the cabin had been reassembled, a spinning wheel, the black cookstove in one corner, an antique corner cupboard in another. There was even a chair that had a bucket underneath—a frontier toilet. But who had broken in? And when?

"Hold on," said the general as he scanned the room.

The glow from the lamp also illuminated the room's most unusual furnishing: an enormous tiger skin, complete with head. When Maureen Colbert had been a benefactor of the Denver Zoo, she had paid for a tiger to be brought from India. When the large female tiger—named Lady Maureen by the zoo director, to pay homage to Mrs. Colbert—had died some years later, the zoo had sent the animal to the taxidermist, then presented it to Mrs. Colbert. This way, she would forever have a reminder of her gift—albeit on the floor of her restored cabin. I didn't know what Jake would make of the Lady Maureen rug, and wasn't eager to find out. The general nodded to me, and I moved toward the tiger skin. When I'd heated up the pork on the cabin cookstove last fall, I'd spent quite a bit of time looking at Lady Maureen. Now something about the dead tiger didn't look right.

"Damn, it's cold," Bo muttered. "Looks like whoever broke in didn't leave much of a trace. I don't suppose the owners keep firewood inside. Or whoever's been here used it up."

"There should be plenty of wood under a plastic cover," I said quietly, "out by the toolshed."

When he reholstered the gun and nipped out the door, I knelt beside the tiger skin. Outside, I could hear Marla and Arch insistently telling Jake to hush up. I turned back and examined the rug from one side, then the other. After a moment, I figured out what looked strange. Someone—perhaps with a sense of humor—had wedged a flesh-colored balloon deep inside the tiger's mouth. The balloon was packed in so deeply that the plastic was barely visible between the tiger's teeth. I felt along the sharp incisors and touched the folds of the object. It was thicker than plastic, more like latex. Carefully, I pulled the rubbery thing out.

It was not a balloon. It looked like a flesh-colored covering of some kind. In the dim light, I could discern drops of dried liquid. I rubbed the pale bumps gently. Makeup came off on my fingers.

Check the trash, I could hear my mother's voice saying in my ear, her favorite means of getting to the source of the problem. I scanned the room and made for the stenciled trash can beside the wood stove. At its bottom was a small pile of crumpled sheets. I set the pink rubber thing aside and examined the sheets. They were pristinely dustless; they had not been in this trash can very long.

Five cellophane wrappers from Oriental noodle packages crinkled in my hands. I put these aside and reached for the rest: crumpled pages of type that appeared to have been photocopied from a book. The first was a sheet of instructions that included a diagram of an ear. Above the diagram in capital letters was the warning: "Be very careful when cutting around ears, that you cut only the cap." And at the bottom, a new section: "Applying Makeup."

I flipped through the pages until I came to one of photographs of men. The heading read: "Woochie Professional Quality Bald Cap." The introduction to the instructions began: "Woochie premium bald caps can sometimes be reused. . . ."

I stared at the pink balloon. A bald cap. Who'd put this thing in the tiger's mouth, and why?

I stuffed the papers and cap into the trash, replaced the can, and ran outside to check on Arch. My son was driving down on the water pump handle with all his strength. Water was not issuing from the spigot. Jake continued to howl. Marla yelled at the dog to hush as she showed Arch how to prime the pump with a full rain bucket. General Bo stood by the toolshed loading his arms with firewood. I ran over to him.

"Whoever hit Marla that night has been here," I told him. "I think. Been and gone, it looks like. The guy . . . left trash . . . a disguise that makes you bald."

General Bo shook his head. "Hold out your arms." I did so and he handed me the logs. He was already moving in Arch's direction. "We shouldn't have taken the working harness off the dog. He could have told us if what he's smelling up here is Tony. Maybe that's why he's barking so much."

"We could try him with the harness," I said as I hustled along behind him.

"No. It's too dark to get any tracking done. The dog needs to eat and rest. Start the fire. I'll get Arch, Marla, the dog, and the supplies inside." He pulled out the Glock. Suddenly Jake howled more fiercely than ever. The general called impatiently, "Come on, everybody inside! Carry as much as you can."

I stumbled with the wood to the cabin door. Jake yelped. If a person or persons was indeed nearby, they could be in no doubt of our presence now. Arch grabbed the bucket and Jake's leash. Marla limped toward us. I couldn't believe she was carrying a bag from the Jeep trunk. When the two of them were safely through the door, I brought it almost closed. A moment later, the general backed into the cabin, his non-gun-holding hand grasping a last bag of supplies. He bolted the door.

While I stuffed wood into the stove, my mind raced. Not believing he or she would be followed, this criminal had left evidence gleefully. *Catch me if you can.* But where was he going? Did he have Tony with him? And most important, would we sort out what had happened before the Furman County Sheriff's Department caught up with us?

Food, I told myself. We'll eat first and worry later. By the time Arch had poured Jake a bowl of water and Marla had dished out some kibble, I had the beginning of a fire going in the stove. Arch assured us that Jake would let us know if there was *anyone* in the vicinity of the cabin. I knew that to be true, as Jake had certainly alerted us to every rustle of movement on our street. We all agreed to relax. *If possible,* Marla said with a sigh.

The general built a fire in the main fireplace, and soon the cabin was lit with a cozy glow. I poked through the cabinets lining the cabin walls. The corner cupboard yielded an array of crockery and pewterware that looked authentically nineteenth-century. I thought with a pang that Tom, with his great love of antiques, would have admired the tankards and chargers. The Hardcastles had stocked two sets of plates: a collection of plain ironstone, and a lovely set of spatterware with a rose in the center of each plate. This, too, Tom had taught me the name for—Adam's Rose. Soon, I thought with a pang, he would return to an empty house, see my note, and wonder if we were still alive. Perhaps he was already home. As the rain beat down on the roof I was thankful, finally, for one thing. At least we weren't outside.

While Marla and Arch tried to figure how the four of us would make do with two small beds, Bo unpacked the bags of food. A large bundle of fresh asparagus lay next to a package of chicken breasts, a bag of rice, and several small jars of condiments. He had brought half a dozen eggs. Five of them were now broken.

"Thought you'd like to do a stir-fry," he announced solemnly. "Since I didn't know what our cooking situation would be."

Marla burst out laughing. Arch gave me a shy, *oh-well* sort of smile. I asked Bo to set us up on the small table while I hunted for, and found, a heavy cast-iron skillet that would do for a wok. In another pot, I started water for the rice and then turned my attention to the chicken. Anything to get away from thinking about the unknown lurking in the mist. And speaking of the unknown, why shouldn't I *call* Tom? That would at least put my mind at rest, if not his.

"Did you bring the cellular phone in from the car?" I asked General Bo.

He shook his head grimly. "No, and I don't want anyone going out until morning. Too risky."

Oh, great. I assessed the Oriental-style ingredients. I started the rice and sliced the chicken breasts. While the chicken marinated in egg white, sherry, soy sauce, and cornstarch—a tenderizing trick I'd learned from a television food show—I pressed a pungent garlic clove and sliced a pile of bright green asparagus and fragrant white onion. Soon the chicken, garlic, and onion were sizzling in the pan and a mouth-watering scent filled the cabin. I steamed the sliced asparagus and stirred in dark, tangy black bean sauce. At least I was making something for Marla that was lowfat, I thought grimly.

"Marla, I need to talk to you about something," I said when we dug into the heaps of steaming Chinese food. "I'd like you to take a good look at that map. You know the partners and the investors better than any of us. There could be a bank, an airstrip, somebody these guys know in a nearby town . . . anything that looks reasonable as a possibility of where one or both of them could have gone. We could skip going back to where we were tracking Tony, and try to assess his direction, pick up a fresher scent."

When we finished, Bo and Arch washed the dishes in water they'd brought in from the pump and heated on the cookstove. Marla and I spread out the map on Lady Maureen's striped back. We studied it and tried to peer into the mind of Albert Lipscomb. Or were we trying to psych out Tony Royce? Or both? Or someone else?

The campsite was a stopping point amid a network of trails that ran through the Arapahoe National Forest. The trail we'd been on with Jake was clearly marked. It followed Grizzly Creek and then crossed it, then came down to a four-wheel-drive road that led to Interstate 70 and Georgetown to the west, Idaho Springs to the east.

I pointed to the map. "Whoever we're tracking, whoever has Tony, has a two-day lead on us. So where would one or both of the Prospect partners, or one of their clients, be going?"

Marla nestled her large body into the tiger skin and stared down at the map. A scarlet-painted nail pointed. "If one of the clients is behind all this, then I have no idea. They could be at Denver International Airport, they could be in the Nevada desert." She paused. "But if it's Tony and/or Albert, we could look in one of two places, I'd say. The two of them shared a

Stir-Fry Chicken with Asparagus

4 chicken breast halves (approximately 1½ pounds), cut into ½-inch-thick, bite-size pieces
1 egg white
1 tablespoon cornstarch
1 tablespoon dry sherry
1 tablespoon soy sauce
1 small (6-ounce) onion, halved and thinly sliced
1 garlic clove, pressed
2 tablespoons canola oil
½ cup water
1 pound fresh asparagus, trimmed of woody stems and cut diagonally into 2-inch slices
½ cup canned water chestnuts, drained and sliced
½ cup black bean sauce (available in the Oriental food section of the grocery store)
Freshly ground black pepper
Approximately 4 cups of cooked, hot medium-grain rice

In a glass pie pan, thoroughly mix the egg white, cornstarch, sherry, soy sauce, onion, and garlic. Marinate the chicken pieces in this mixture for 30 minutes to no more than an hour.

In a large frying pan or wok, heat the oil over moderately high heat. Stir-fry the marinated chicken for several minutes, until it is just done. *Do not overcook the chicken.* Remove from the pan and set aside.

Reheat the pan over high heat and add the water. Quickly stir up the browned bits from the bottom of the pan, then add the asparagus, water chestnuts, and black bean sauce. Cover the pan and cook over medium heat for 2 to 5 minutes, until the asparagus is bright green but still crunchy. Add the chicken. Stir over medium-high heat until the mixture is heated through. Season to taste with pepper. Serve immediately over hot rice.

Serves 4.

If you cannot find black bean sauce in the Oriental section of your local grocery store, the grocery manager should be able to order it for you. The brand I use is Ka-Me. I ceased being frustrated by its frequent unavailability at my local store once I started ordering it by the case. Order forms are usually available at the customer service desk; the order generally takes about two weeks to a month to fill. Ordering by the case usually means you will receive a substantial discount.

house, sort of a mountain hideaway, in Estes Park. What's that, seventy miles from here? But you'd have to go east and then north from here. That's not the way Jake was leading us."

"Seventy miles," I repeated. I was suddenly so tired. My wet hair had dried, finally, but my muscles ached from the strain of the day. "What's your second idea?"

Marla said, "If Albert has three and a half million in cash from the Prospect account, he wouldn't want to carry it in this weather across a mountainous forest trail to find his partner, for whatever reason. So he'd have to stash it someplace." She tapped the map. "This is the direction we were heading. Northwest. Straight in the direction of the Eurydice Gold Mine." She looked at me. "Someone could have stashed the cash in one of those buildings by the mine. There's nobody up there, since they haven't hired a team to start exploration work. Plus, there's that safe deep in the Eurydice Mine, about a half-mile in. You know, that's where they keep those gold bars and samples."

I said, "And guess what I'd be willing to bet? They weren't samples from the Eurydice. But why wouldn't somebody, Captain Shockley especially, have gone inside the mine in the last week to check whether the samples were still there? I know he went up there when Albert was first missing, but the place was all locked up."

Marla shrugged. "Well, Albert knows the place well. I mean, he's the owner, but they didn't have him around to sign a consent-to-search. And what are the cops going to do, get a warrant to traipse through a mine? That string of lights doesn't go back very far. I can't believe someone from law enforcement would go deep into the Eurydice Mine just to look around." She paused. "On the other hand, Albert certainly wouldn't make a getaway without all that gold. It's worth a couple hundred thousand at least."

I said, "But still . . . if Albert's—or the disguised bald person's—point was to steal Prospect's assets, why wouldn't he or she have gone into the mine to get the gold samples sometime in the last week?" *Wait a minute.* I remembered back to the party, when Albert and Tony had both entered the mine to get the samples. Why wouldn't just one of them have gone, with a wheelbarrow? Why would they *both* go? "What do you know about the mine safe?" I quickly asked Marla. "How hard is it to get into?"

"Oh my gosh," Marla said suddenly. "Oh, Lord. This isn't generally known. I'll bet even Captain Shockley doesn't know. Opening that safe is like using nukes on a sub."

"Wow," Arch interrupted. "You mean when you have two guys with encoded messages? Then each guy uses his key to activate the weapons? It's so cool. You can't do it alone. That's to keep some crazy guy from like, blowing up the world."

I gave Marla a hard look.

She said, "It takes Albert and Tony *both* to open the mine safe."

Chapter 19

General Bo rubbed his hand over his mowed scalp. "So," he observed, "if our villain is after money—and so far he's proven that he is, if he's the same guy who hit the bank—then he's got to drag his partner up to that mine to get the gold out. Framing Marla was a brilliant way to get the authorities off his track, so he could have time to cash in and then get out."

"But why ruin the company?" I asked. "And why wait a week to do all this? There has to be some other explanation. Maybe this evidence points to some other person. Some other motivation."

Marla and I hashed it through. Eileen Tobey would know about theatrical disguises, the proximity of the cabin, the existence of the gold bars. Plus, she hated Tony and loved money. The clients closest to Tony and Albert were the Trotfields and the Hardcastles. They stood to lose a lot of money if the mine investment was a scam. Sam Perdue desperately needed capital for his soup restaurant chain. Victoria Lear, one of the primary rebuffers-of-Sam, had learned the lie of L-208. Had anyone else? Who besides Marla and the two partners knew of the two-lock safe deep inside the Eurydice? Maybe Tony had another girlfriend. Maybe Albert had told someone else, like the police captain in charge of security.

"Go to sleep," Bo chided after we'd spent a fruitless hour trying to figure out who knew what and when they knew it.

Marla and I lay down on the cold, musty-smelling beds. Arch and Jake claimed the back of Lady Maureen. The general extinguished the kerosene lamps, and stretched out on the floor. The fire's embers glowed, crackled, and waned, from time to time shooting up a flare of flame. I tried to sleep. Exhausted as I was, slumber eluded me. After a while I crept over to one of the windows and tried to send thoughts to Tom: *We're all right. We'll be home soon.*

Eleven o'clock. My son's measured breathing, a sound I would recognize even if he were thirty feet away, filled the darkened cabin. Midnight: The rain ceased, and Marla was snoring. By two, I thought I was the only one awake, although the general's breathing was as hushed and catlike as his movements. Out the window, the clouds had thinned to fast-moving wisps. When the moon emerged from behind a skein of haze, I glanced in the direction of the creek, half expecting to see the ghost of that tragic, long-buried bride. But there was only fog, wafting through the trees. *Tom,* I thought, *how are you?* But I heard no answer and saw nothing. The only spirit I felt was my own, and it was full of pain.

✦

I must have fallen asleep. I was startled awake with my forehead pressed against the frigid windowpane. I tensed and brought my head up abruptly. What was that sound? It was nearby: a door creaking open. Narrowing my eyes, I could make out Arch and General Bo Farquhar moving through pewter-colored predawn light. My son gripped the leash of a panting, nervous Jake. For a fleeting moment, I thought I must be trapped in a lost episode from *Little House on the Prairie*. Where was Michael Landon and his ever-hopeful little family? And why was I staring at the large head of a dead tiger?

I rubbed my eyes, surveyed the cabin interior, and tried to think. The chaotic events of the previous day welled up. I shivered and checked my watch. It was Tuesday, June 15, just after five in the morning. Outside, Bo, Arch, and Jake stopped beside the pump. The bloodhound was sniffing, his nose pressed to the soggy earth, his tail curled high. Ever wary, Bo held his deadly-looking gun at his side. Below the cabin, a milky fog poured between the trees. Usually a fast, low white cloud means a front is moving through. With any luck, the frigid vapor would soon burn off. Maybe we'd even have a clear day.

Marla roused herself to her knees, peered out, and grunted. "If we're going to have English weather, can't we at least have crumpets?"

Her eyes met mine across the cabin space. A lump formed in my throat. What a mess. My best friend had been arrested for murder and neither my policeman husband nor I had been able to help her. Now we were all outside the law, and the person who'd framed her for the crime was probably long gone.

I said, "How are you doing?"

Marla answered ruefully. "Wait until I have some caffeine, before you ask me that. I know, I know—I'm not supposed to drink the stuff, but I'm desperate. Is there any?"

"Is there what?" General Bo Farquhar's arrival startled me, as he always moved so silently. He entered with a load of firewood, Arch and Jake behind him. The dog looked crestfallen. "What do you girls want now, eggs Benedict?"

I pointed my finger at him. "Don't call me a girl, boy. Did you bring in that cell phone?"

He deposited the wood, spanked his hands together to rid them of mud and bark, and brought me the phone. "Try not to get the police onto us. Also, if you want breakfast, you'll have to improvise, since all the eggs are broken."

Breakfast could wait. Bo had activated the cellular; I punched in our home number and suppressed a worry of how cops traced cell calls. In any event, I seriously doubted the Furman County Sheriff's Department possessed such technology. The phone rang once.

"Schulz." His voice was scratchy with sleep.

"It's me."

I heard him sigh. "Where are you? Are you coming home? Is Arch all right?"

"He's fine, we all are. We're out in the wild trying to track Tony." He groaned. I went on: "Listen, I'm certain that Tony Royce didn't drown in that creek. And after I talked to you yesterday, I got information that Prospect Financial was lying about the mine being closed down during the 1940s. Also, we've found a bloody test tube and a disguise."

"A test tube and a *what?*"

"A bald disguise. Like a cap. That someone would wear to look bald. Say, if a person wanted to look like Albert Lipscomb. Think those two items would be enough to clear Marla of drowning her boyfriend? Talk fast, I don't want anyone to trace this."

"No way. Your skipping with Marla makes her look *more*

guilty. And I'm supposed to remind you to obey the law, wife."

"But what about that evidence?"

"I'd have to see it, Miss G. And with the current atmosphere down at the department, it'll take an act of God to clear Marla. Please—"

"I'll call you later. I miss you." I hung up abruptly. With the possibility of a trace, there was no time for extensive sentimentality. Unfortunately.

Poor Tom. I hadn't even asked what kind of fallout had rained on him from the ambulance incident.

I took a deep breath. Time to think of food. Cooking was low on my agenda. On the other hand, feeding everyone brought a sense of purpose, and might help me move beyond the guilt I felt for betraying Tom. While the general built up the cookstove fire and hauled in water, I scrounged through the Hardcastles' meager cupboard again. Flour, sugar, cinnamon, baking soda, buttermilk solids. No beef jerky, no dried fruit. I guess the Hardcastles thought trappers would feast on the fresh game they'd snared. After a few moments of grumbling, I came up with three stray teabags, an unopened jar of apple butter, shortening, cream of tartar—a find—and a griddle. A silly memory intruded—Arch's fourth-grade science fair question. What makes cookie batter puff up? The answer: an acid—cream of tartar—and a base—baking soda. Mixing the reconstituted buttermilk and dry ingredients to a soft batter made me stop fretting, if only temporarily. I kneaded the feathery dough, patted it into a circle on a wooden board, cut it into wedges, then dropped the scones into hot, bubbling shortening.

Ten minutes later, while Jake attacked his kibble, the four of us hunkered down on the striped back of Lady Maureen and

Cinnamon Griddle Scones

1 cup all-purpose flour
$^1/_2$ teaspoon cream of tartar
$^1/_4$ teaspoon salt
1 teaspoon sugar
$^1/_2$ teaspoon baking soda
$^1/_2$ teaspoon cinnamon
2 tablespoons dry buttermilk solids (available canned in the baking goods section of the grocery store)
$^1/_2$ cup water
2 tablespoons solid vegetable shortening such as Crisco

Preheat griddle over medium-high heat. Stir together flour, cream of tartar, salt, sugar, baking soda, cinnamon, and buttermilk solids. Add water and stir until well combined. Turn the batter out on a well-floured surface, knead a few turns, and pat into a circle about 6$^1/_2$ inches in diameter. With a sharp knife, cut the dough into 8 wedges. Melt the shortening on the griddle. When the shortening is *hot,* lower the heat to medium and place the scones on the griddle. Cook until the first side is golden brown, then turn and cook the other side. Test for doneness by splitting one scone. It should not be doughy, but should look like a biscuit. Remove the scones from the griddle and serve with butter and apple butter.

Makes 8 small scones.

proved the adage that hunger makes the best sauce. We slathered the hot scones with butter—the general had brought a stick with his supplies—and apple butter, courtesy of the Hardcastles. The butter and apple butter oozed comfortingly between the moist, tender, biscuitlike layers. A morning coffee devotee, I was surprised by the delicious taste of the English Breakfast tea I'd brewed. Any port in a storm.

"Time to pack up," the general announced. He wanted to get to Idaho Springs and the Eurydice Gold Mine as soon as possible.

We left the Hardcastles' cabin somewhat cleaner than we'd found it, and my only hope was that a new layer of dust would cover the interior before the Hardcastles took it upon themselves to visit their country property.

✦

When we drew up to the mine an hour later, it appeared utterly abandoned. The heavy grates across the menacing portal were wrapped shut by a thick chain. The sheds were tightly locked. How different the old site seemed now, with no tent, no portable ovens, no food, and no partygoers. Arch talked to Jake, who had howled on our way up High Creek Avenue. Jake scrambled over his lap, poked his nose out the window and let loose with a grandiose, ear-splitting wail.

"Not again," muttered Marla.

"Close the damn window," the general commanded.

"Okay," Arch said meekly, "but it's like up at the cabin. Bloodhounds remember a scent. When they smell it in the air, they howl. It's just the way they are. I think Tony's been here."

"Honey," I said mildly, "Jake always howls."

"Not true," Arch maintained, ever loyal.

"Well, then," I asked as we piled out of the Jeep, "what if whoever kidnapped Tony was here, and then went off? Or say the kidnapper got the gold, then came back down this dirt road? The dog certainly won't be able to distinguish between coming and going, will he?" And particularly not *this* dog, I thought somewhat peevishly.

"Bloodhounds always go after the freshest scent," my son replied earnestly, anxious to exhibit his beloved pet's unique skills. "At this point, the whole idea in Jake's mind, his whole purpose in life, is just to f-i-n-d Tony."

Arch coaxed the working harness, a leather and metal contraption attached to a thicker leather leash, back over Jake's head. Jake immediately lowered his nose to the train track leading into the mine. I turned and saw Marla staring at the portal. There was fear in her eyes. Jake cast along the area where the party tent had been, nose to the ground, paws taking him first here, then there. He sniffed out a ditch, then the entrance to a shed. My heart sank. This would never work. And even if it did, and if we did find Tony in the mine, what would we do? Suppose he really was dead? Would we call the sheriff's department? I couldn't imagine De Groot and Hersey driving up in a department vehicle with big smiles on their faces. *Hey, sorry everybody! Marla didn't kill Royce! Nobody got pushed into Grizzly Creek! Big mistake!*

Jake had a scent. He was pulling dementedly on his leash.

"Hold up," said the general. "There's a road around the side of the mountain. It goes down some rough terrain and ends up on a back road to Central City, not far from Orpheus Canyon Road. Maybe Tony and his abductor came for the gold samples, and they went out the other way. Be *very* sure to let the hound cast for the freshest scent, Arch."

But Jake was determined that there was only one scent to follow, and that led straight into the Eurydice Mine. He stopped at the closed grate, and howled.

"Wait," the general commanded briskly. He strode over to the corrugated metal shed on the right side of the mine, where the party tent had been pitched less than ten days earlier. He pushed hard on the door until the wood splintered and gave. A moment later, the string of lights leading into the mine lit up. I recalled that Marla had told me the lights had been specially hung for the investors' tour of the mine, and did not go in very far. But to me, the tiny lamps seemed to go down and in forever, like a vision out of Alice in Wonderland.

Bo poked his head out the shed door and signaled to us.

"I don't know this place at all," he said, almost apologetically. "And I have no idea what the scent will be like inside the mine. I don't even know where the safe is, but the tracks should take us to it. I'm hoping that's where we'll find Tony." He looked hard at Arch. "I really don't want you to be subjected to this, son. Please let me take Jake. You can stay here, in the car if you like, with your mother."

Arch pushed his glasses up his nose and squared his shoulders in unconscious imitation of Bo. "Wherever Jake goes, I go. That's the way it is. My dad's a doctor and Tom's a homicide guy. I know about life and death, and you know my mom's been involved with solving some crimes before."

Bo scowled. Then he nodded. Maybe he recognized that Arch could be as stubborn as he was.

"All right then," he said. "Here's the deal. Sorry to take over, Goldy, but with safety an issue, I'd feel better being in charge."

I nodded an assent.

The general went on: "I want Marla to stay at the portal

with my gun. Arch, Goldy, and I go in wearing mine safety equipment. We follow the rails with Jake to the safe. No matter what happens, we stay together. A lamp goes out, Jake starts to howl, we all come out and I go back in alone. Got it?"

Arch said yes. I nodded.

General Bo led us, catlike, through the shed. He handed Arch and me hard hats, then put one on himself. Arch clamped his foot over Jake's leash while he fastened the hard hat strap under his chin.

"Put these on, too," Bo advised. He held up bulky belts whose loops were crammed with equipment. When we had fastened the cumbersome leather straps around our waists, Bo grinned. "Before we take off, ladies and gentlemen, we'd like to demonstrate the safety features of your belt." He reached to one side of the belt and pulled on a round reflective device attached to a cord. "This is a cap lamp." He slid the light into a metal bracket in the front of his hardhat. "Used one of these once when I went into a VC tunnel in 'Nam." He flipped a switch on the lamp, and it came on. "Only use this if you have to." He touched the cord on the lamp. "It's attached to a wet cell battery back here." He grasped what looked like a minia-ture flask from the belt. "This is what's called a self-rescuer. If there's a fire in the tunnel, what you most need to worry about is carbon monoxide. You use this like diving equipment." He glanced around the shed, tucked his self-rescuer in his belt, and reached for another of the flasks. Unlike the ones on our belts, this flask was red.

"This is a training device. Nonfunctioning, that's why it's painted red. You pry up this lever to break the seal and discard the cover. Then you bite on this mouthpiece." When he pulled the cloth cover off the flask, underneath was a metal container with an attached nose clip. He held the mouthpiece of the training flask up to his mouth. "Then close your nostrils with this"—he pointed to the nose clip—"and breathe. The filter inside the self-rescuer turns carbon monoxide into carbon dioxide for about an hour, depending on the concentration of carbon monoxide. You probably won't need it." He nodded, his eyes sternly assessing us for signs of cowardice. "Okay? Ready?"

Arch said yes, eagerly, and scooped up Jake's leash. I bobbed my head inside the hard hat. It was tight on my head, and I wasn't sure I would be able to fit the cap lamp into the hat's bracket if I had to, much less use the respirator. All I wanted to do was find what we had come here for, and get home to Tom. If Tom wanted me back home.

General Bo carried a hammer out to the portal entrance, where he examined the chain and padlock. Loudly, he said, "Okay, here we go." A few swings of the hammer broke the padlock, and Bo unthreaded the chain.

"Don't worry, Mom," Arch told me as we neared the iron doors that Bo pulled open. Jake surged forward expectantly. "Mines are really safe these days. Not like they used to be."

"What a comforting thought."

Marla listened to Bo explain that the safety on the Glock was a small lever on its trigger. His ice blue gaze held her as he explained in a no-nonsense voice, "You aim and shoot. This is a nine-millimeter semiautomatic and you've got nine rounds. You see a guy. You see a jackrabbit. You see a bumblebee. You shoot. Got it?"

Marla nodded mutely and took the gun. I had my doubts about her ability to use it. General Bo lithely stepped out of the way so Jake, tugging Arch with all his canine might, could enter the mine first. I was the last one to step into the tunnel.

The dank air struck my nostrils like a blow. I don't know

what I was expecting, but it certainly wasn't cold, musty damp-ness blowing gently in my face. The moist breeze stank of metallic earth.

"Fifty-one degrees year-round," General Bo reported cheerfully. "No matter what the weather is outside, that's the temperature inside a mine or cave. Might get a tad warmer as we go in."

Jake tugged forward down the tunnel, then made a quick right into what General Bo informed us was a "drift" cut out of the rock. This was the way, I surmised, to the magazine that held the explosives I'd read about in the inspectors' reports. Once he was in the drift, however, Jake seemed to become confused. With his long ears flopping, he backtracked from the drift and sniffed energetically along the floor of the main tun-nel. He sniffed up the walls, around the tracks, started up the tunnel, then headed back to where Marla stood.

"What's going on?" I asked.

"Pool scent," Arch said as he tugged Jake back. He sounded discouraged. "Tony's been in here, Jake can tell that. But be-cause of the enclosed space, Jake thinks Tony's everywhere. In this kind of situation, it's very hard for a bloodhound to be able to tell exactly where the scent was, or how far back the person he's tracking went." He grimaced with dismay. "That's why they use German shepherds in places like this, like when some-one's trapped in a building. Shepherds don't get overwhelmed by so much scent."

"Just give him time," Bo advised. I felt less hopeful, but said nothing.

After more uncertain sniffing, Jake shuffled down the rail-road track. The general pointed to the shadowy tunnel ahead. We were to move into the mine. Just what I was dreading.

Step by echoing step, we moved deeper into the earth.

Twice I tripped on the old, rusted track. The damp breeze coming from inside the mine grew mustier and staler. Only three feet over our heads, the rough-hewn rock was occasionally covered with chain-link fencing.

"To sheath unstable rock," the general explained. "By the way, the top of the tunnel is called its back." He reached over to touch the stone walls. "These are called the mine's ribs."

The cold air was seeping through my outerwear and into my underclothes. Our footsteps echoed eerily. About fifty feet in, I looked back. Marla stood motionless in the entry, guarding the portal. I wished with all my heart that Arch and I were back there with her.

About seventy feet in, the tunnel and the track made a right-hand turn. Jake, still sniffing up the ribs, turned right also. But again he seemed confused. Water dripped from overhead. By the light of the lamps along the wall, I could just make out a crack in the rock above us.

"Fault," General Bo said matter-of-factly.

"Why does the air smell so bad?"

"That's one of the biggest problems, bringing ventilation to the miners. They ventilate the place with raises that go up the mountain. They're like shafts, only miners climb from level to level via ladders—"

We were diverted from discussing this by Jake scrabbling frantically up what looked like a timber wall built up on the left side of the tunnel. I glanced backward. Because of the turn we had made, I could no longer see Marla.

"What is it?" I said. "What's he found?"

"More pool scent, I think," Arch responded. He held out his hand to the wall. "Maybe this is the sump." He clambered up the side of the wall, put his hand over the side, and made a splashing sound. "Yep, it's water."

"The sump," the general explained, "is the reservoir of water that drains down from the mine. They use the water for the drilling, as I was saying—"

Jake was going nuts. He sniffed up the side of the sump wall, came back down, sniffed up again. He pulled furiously on his thick leash. It was all Arch could do to restrain him.

Tony, or Tony's scent, had spent some time by the sump.

General Bo reached back to get his cap lamp. Arch stepped firmly on Jake's leash but couldn't keep his balance to get up on the sump step without pulling too hard on his dog. I mimicked Bo's actions and groped along my belt for the cap lamp. Clumsily, I pulled the cord out, snapped the lamp into its bracket, and turned the knob. Given my current frame of mind, I was almost surprised when the light flashed on. My small thin beam swept over the ribs of the mine. While Arch struggled to secure Jake's leash, talking to and soothing the excited animal, the general and I climbed up the uneven steps leading to the sump. The hound whined as Bo and I shone our pale cones of light into the liquid depths.

The water was so still it was almost impossible to tell it was there. The pool seemed to go back about fifteen feet, and down about eight. We swept our lights along the murky surface of the water, and then down to the sump floor. I cried out in shock.

At the bottom of the pool, fully clothed, bald head shining, eyes wide with surprise even in death, was Albert Lipscomb.

Chapter 20

"Stay still, Arch," I commanded sternly as I turned away from the corpse to protect my son. "Just . . . wait until we get down."

"Why? What's there?" He was bent awkwardly over Jake. The leash had become tangled between his legs, and Jake was paying no heed as he pawed up and down and moaned deep in his throat. "Tony Royce must have sat down here or something," Arch said, frustrated. "The scent's really strong. That's why Jake's going ballistic. Is there something in the water, Mom?"

I turned back to the sump. If that fool dog was correct, we'd find Tony's body next. General Bo moved his light over the length of the dead man. I swallowed hard.

"It's Tony's partner," I murmured.

"I figured," Bo said. "This is the corpse we've been looking for, I'd wager."

I struggled to clear my mind. But yes, he was right. Victoria Lear had died because she had discovered the Eurydice was worthless. Albert had disappeared, ostensibly with all the money from the Prospect account. A bank teller who could have identified someone had been strangled. Marla had been accused of the murder of Tony Royce. But in discovering Albert Lipscomb, we'd found the main corpse, the key to unraveling the bizarre happenings of the last week.

His body did not float. This was Colorado, not Florida. As Tom had told me several times, it takes a month in forty-degree water for a corpse in a lake to come to the surface. Underwater, Lipscomb's narrow, surprised face had a waxy, bluish appearance. His skin was shriveled. His long fingers, splayed outward, looked like those of a person too long in the bath. I didn't remember him having age spots on the backs of his hands. I blinked and focused on the dark, round marks. They looked suspiciously like burns. As if someone had tortured him—

"No, no!" cried Arch. He'd unfastened the leather lead. "Jake, come back!" But even as Arch called frantically, Jake trotted away. Apparently his powerful nose was telling him to go back down the track in the direction we'd come. Or perhaps he was again confused by the pool scent. Or maybe, like me, he desperately wanted to get as far away as possible from the presence of death. Arch took off after his pet, but the general was faster, bounding off the sump steps and racing nimbly down the rails with the same stamina I'd come to expect from him. Arch tripped and made a spectacular spill in the mud. As I stumbled after my son, a gunshot cracked loudly down the close space of the tunnel.

"Arch!" I yelled. Sprawled on the earth, he didn't move. "Arch! Arch, tell me you're all right!" He did not appear to hear me. "Arch, please!"

Finally, he sat up and shook himself dazedly. "It's okay, Mom. I just fell. I have to go get Jake!" He scrambled to his feet, heedless of the danger behind us.

In the distance, Jake howled. The general was nowhere in sight. I heard Marla scream. "No! No! *Damn it! Damn you!*" And then another gunshot exploded. I grabbed Arch and shoved him against the rock wall, out of harm's way. After a breathless moment, we heard the general's voice bellow down the dark passageway:

"Arch! Goldy! Get down! Go back! Back where you—"

Light burst from the main tunnel like a blinding photo flash. A deafening boom flung us backward. In that instant, I somehow registered that all the light bulbs along the mine's ribs were shattering. Then it was like a flame suddenly snuffed in a blackout. Darkness abruptly engulfed us. My nostrils picked up the faintly acrid smell of smoke.

I don't know how long I lay, stunned, on the cold, moist stone before I tried to use my voice. "Arch," I said into the blackness. "Arch, please, please, where are you?"

The darkness was ominously silent. Then, to my immense relief, I heard a cough.

"Here," Arch called hoarsely. I struggled to my feet, but could see nothing: There was no light whatsoever. "Sorry, Mom." Arch's voice was close. "I don't know where *here* is. What *was* that? Do you know where Jake is?" As usual, his first concern was for his dog.

"I don't have a clue." *Get your bearings, get your bearings!* I ordered myself. *We've got to get out of here. It's not safe.* I held my arms out in both directions. But there was nothing to get bearings *from*. The dark was absolute, unyielding.

"Mom?"

I strained my eyes into the blackness. I squatted and felt

along the damp floor. No Arch. Then my fingers fumbled against a metal chain, and thick leather: Jake's leash. I crammed it into my jacket pocket.

"Arch? Where are you?"

"Here." Two feet away? My son drew in his breath sharply. "Jake, Mom! What happened to Jake? Is Jake okay? Oh, Mom!" he cried. In the dark, I heard him fumbling, then the scrape of his footsteps on the damp stone floor. "Hey! Jake! *Jake!*"

There was no response to his calls.

Suddenly, Arch pulled off a miracle. He switched on his cap lamp. Tucked in his belt, the bulb had somehow survived the explosion. I blinked in astonishment to see that he was only a few feet away from me. In the distance, I heard the general's voice calling to us. *Are you in there?* I fought off panic. Bo's voice was impossibly faint, as if he were miles away. *Goldy? Can you hear me? Are you all right? There was an explosion . . . Goldy?*

"Yes!" I called, but my voice, too, was swallowed by the impenetrable rock that surrounded us.

"Mom?" Arch wailed. "Oh, Mom, I have to get Jake."

"Arch," I said, forcing my voice to sound calm, "hold my hand." I reached for his gritty fingers, then clasped them tightly. Perhaps too tightly. *He's okay,* I told myself. *He's not hurt. We'll get out of this.*

Arch turned his head toward the sump, then swept his light across the rib of the mine. "That's the way out. Without the light bulbs along the sides, we're going to have to go carefully, Mom."

The smoke stung my eyes and made me cough. Was it getting thicker? Hard to tell. I called again to the general: "Yes! Yes! We're coming!"

"Do you have Jake?" Arch shouted.

But neither Bo nor Marla answered. Cautiously, holding hands, my son and I started back up the tracks. Arch kept his lamp beam down, focused on the rails. Had we heard one gunshot or two? Two. And then the general had shouted his warning, and the blast had rocked the mine. But why? Why a blast? I shook my head. My thoughts were whirling too fast.

I trod carefully, holding Arch's hand tightly in mine, determined to get us out of this claustrophobic hell. The smoke was indeed becoming thicker as we approached the bend. We made the turn. Arch lifted his beam toward the portal . . . or to where the portal should have been.

When he swept the light of his cap lamp down the tracks, all we could see was darkness and coils of smoke. My hopes plummeted. There were two explanations for our predicament: The blast had brought down massive quantities of rock, and a wall of heavy boulders now barred our way to safety. Or we were lost, and we weren't anywhere near the mine's entrance. I refused to contemplate that possibility. It also seemed to me that the smoke was not coming from the source of the explosion. Something was on fire—probably the timbers. Arch started to hack.

"Mom! Mom! Put on your respirator!"

"Okay, okay," I said, floundering along my belt. The more I tried to catch my breath, the more smoke I inhaled. In front of me, the tiny light on Arch's head began to wobble and fade. *Don't let me pass out,* I prayed. *I must get Arch out of here.*

I wrenched the self-rescuer out of the loop on my belt and tore off its cloth cover. To Arch, I said, "Do . . . you . . . have yours on?"

For a long moment he was silent, then, "Yes," came his nasal reply. "Need light?"

"No." I pulled up on the tether holding the nose clip, clamped my nostrils shut with it, and tentatively bit on the lug of the mouthpiece. I breathed. To my surprise, the carbon dioxide burned ravenously down my lungs. Disgusted, I let go of the lug. "I can't," I croaked into the increasingly smoky darkness. "The gas is too—"

"You have to, Mom!" Arch's voice was sharply adult. "Now breathe with that thing and let's find a raise back in the other direction! I have to find Jake!"

His gentle squeeze on the fingers of my free hand belied the harshness in his voice. I bit on the lug and breathed. It was like inhaling paint. Tears stung my cheeks as we turned and retraced our steps. Arch pulled on my hand just as Jake had tugged on the leash, up the tracks, back into the darkness.

After an eternity, we rounded the bend. Our footsteps grated over wet gravel as we passed the sump. Yes, there were shafts—technically called *raises*—for ventilation. This much I knew. But where were they? And what was at the top of them? A fan? Another locked grate? Wasn't there some law in Colorado about not having openings to mines, so people couldn't fall down them? And if we did somehow succeed in climbing the ladder of a raise, how on earth would we ever move a fan, if we encountered one?

Down, down the tracks we went, deeper into the dark bowels of the earth. I breathed smoke and cursed Tony Royce. And I cursed my own inability to see that he was the one who had caused the terrible problems which plagued us. Tony had somehow deceived his ever-hopeful partner, of that much I was now certain. And he had deceived us. Of course, the impact of Tony's wrongdoing had been compounded by the idiotic arrogance of Shockley's storm troopers, De Groot and Hersey. Their arrest of Marla had provoked our current disastrous situation. But most of all, I cursed my own stupidity for allowing Arch to track Tony on this ill-fated trip into the mine. With the pool scent that chronically baffled Jake, the hound had been utterly confused, scenting Tony Royce everywhere. In truth, it was my guess that Tony had been hiding out here since he'd left the Hardcastles' cabin after attacking Marla and Macguire and once again pointing the finger of guilt at Lipscomb. Perhaps he'd seen or heard us coming, quickly closed the gates, and hidden in the powder magazine. Then he'd only had to wait for us to get deep enough into the mine to seal it forever with God only knew how much dynamite. He had done all of this, so he could make it away with a fortune in stolen cash and gold. Poor Albert Lipscomb, like Marla, had only been a pawn in Royce's ruthless game.

We came to a fork in the mine passageway. The drift with the track went off to the left, into what seemed to me to be utter blackness. To the right, when Arch swept his cap lamp over it, the passageway narrowed sharply, and the rock surrounding the drift became much more rough-hewn. An unfinished corridor? Perhaps. Almost certainly another dead end. Arch's hand tugged me left.

One step at a time, one railroad tie after another. The rock was so rough, the darkness so total, and Arch's light so feeble, that I was afraid he would miss an escape route, if indeed there was one. When your eyes become accustomed to dark, I'd always believed, it is because your visual sensors learn to utilize the tiny amounts of light available to see. But when *no* outside light is available, then what? Then you watch your son flash his cap lamp, left to right, right to left. And breathe. Feel your lungs fight the smoking air. And breathe.

We're dying, I thought suddenly. I felt oddly light-headed.

Poor Arch. He should have had a better mother. Not someone who went tearing off at every opportunity to solve crimes. A mother who stayed in her kitchen where she belonged and left police work to the police . . . I bit hard onto the flaming-hot lug of the respirator. And kept walking into the fetid darkness with my son.

Suddenly, Arch clenched my hand and tugged me forward. His light had picked out a metal rod set in the wall. No—not a rod. His lamplight swung crazily over the stone. Not a rod—a metal chair. No.

Arch placed my palm around one of the rods. His nose-clipped voice rasped with triumph: "Ladder, Mom! It's a raise. Climb up!"

I pulled the respirator from my mouth. "No," I told him. "You first. Then if you fall, you'll fall on me instead of straight down. Use both hands. Clamp the self-rescuer in your mouth."

He groaned, but quickly acquiesced. I moved out of the way, listened to the weight of my son moving onto the metal ladder, and watched as his cap lamp lurched higher. He was ascending. I clamped my mouth back on the self-rescuer, and awkwardly started up behind him.

In the darkness, I had to grope for each new metal rung, tapping it like a blind person, moving my hand across its corrugated surface to assure myself it was really there. The one time I looked up, dust from Arch's sneakers fell into my eyes, and I resolved not to do that again. I breathed in and thought instead about Tony Royce. Up, up, I went, keeping myself sane by replaying all the incidents with Tony Royce that I could remember, vowing all sorts of nasty revenge. I even had a gratifying vision of testifying against him in court—*This man, Your Honor, is responsible for three murders, not to mention embezzling on a massive scale. And he duped my best friend. And framed her for his crimes.* I resolutely shoved that fantasy away. *Stick with what you know. What do you know?*

Arch was stamping on something. My fingers fumbled upward: a grate. No, it was a landing. I slid my body through the opening and felt around the edges of the landing with my hands and feet. Arch was already moving upward on another ladder, and I groped for the sides of these new metal steps, working hard to avoid the hole I'd just come through. Then I started upward again.

I breathed in the fiery carbon dioxide. *Think about Tony, I* ordered myself. *When you get out, what are you going to do to Tony?* But my lungs screamed with pain. The mouthpiece was so hot I could feel blisters forming. I would never get used to inhaling carbon dioxide, I thought. And how long did I think I would have to become accustomed to this gas, anyway? What had the general said? An hour? If the carbon monoxide in the smoke was not too concentrated—two hours? How far up did we still have to go? Yes—the mountain sloped back, and with any luck we would come out eventually on the grass and rocks of the steep hill, well above the mine. But how many feet would that be? Forty? A hundred? Two hundred? And how long would that take? Would our air supply last long enough for us to reach safety?

We arrived at what must have been our fourth landing. I wondered if Marla *had* shot Tony. Or vice versa. There had only been two shots. Albert's body, Jake scrambling away, the explosion, being trapped. It was all too much. I started up a fresh set of ladder rungs, hearing Arch's steps above my head. *We're not going to make it,* I thought as I breathed in the boiling-hot, acidic gas from the respirator. *Oh, Tom, I'm so sorry. I'm such an idiot. I didn't mean to get us buried alive.* Tears stung and I cursed them, too. *Damn it, Goldy. Think of Arch and go up a rung, then another, reflect back on what you really know about Royce. Why would he stay here for three days? Why wouldn't he have left the country right away? Because . . . because he was waiting. He was waiting for something or someone. Someone who could give him something. What? What did he need? Escape. Escape, the same as what you want now. . . .*

Arch paused. He was stamping around on one of the landings, but this one seemed to be bigger than the previous ones. And was some distant gray light seeping down, entering the landing, or was it a hallucination? Arch swept his light upward to a metal grate. On one side of the grate was a fan, but it was not revolving. The electricity which moved it had probably been knocked out by the blast.

"Let me try to open it," I said, since I was taller than Arch. I pulled off the nose clip. Oh, blessed, blessed air. It was smoky, but it contained sweet, sweet oxygen. I panted voraciously. I was a starved person, wolfing down air like the first food in a week.

"Move, move," I ordered the grate, and shoved hard at it. It didn't budge. "Could you point your lamp to the edge?" I asked Arch.

He did so, and I saw a lock like the type used on a fence gate. It appeared rusted shut. I heard—clear and close as a bell—Jake's mournful howl. Clenching my despised self-rescuer with all the force I had left, I swung at the lock. It made a hideous grinding sound before clanging away from the locked position. I stepped up two rungs of the ladder leading to the grate and desperately, with every ounce of strength I'd gained from hefting food trays, heaved my body against it. The grate screeched open. I wriggled through, onto a passageway that led horizontally to the side of the mountain. I held my hand out to Arch. His smiling face made my heart sing.

We ran down the sloping passageway. And then we were in the open, on grass, between rocks, looking out at the sky. The misty air smelled like heaven.

"Look, Mom!" Arch called excitedly. He was pointing down. There were the sheds, there was the Jeep, there were Marla and General Bo, puzzling over a map. And there, tethered to the general, with the spare leash, twirling awkwardly because he had caught the smell of his master on the breeze, lifting his nose to the air, and howling joyfully, was Jake.

Chapter 21

After we had scrambled down the mountain above the Eurydice, after we had all hugged and confirmed that we were okay, after we had marveled at the fall of huge rocks caused by the explosion, after Jake had licked the bloody scratches on Arch's face at least a hundred times—after all that, we got the bad news.

"He got away," the general reported, disconsolate. "Royce. I saw him. I was thirty feet away from him. . . ." He gestured with the hand that clasped Jake's spare leash, and sighed.

Marla's spangled sweat suit was smeared with mud. So was her face. "I tried to shoot him. The son of a bitch. I missed *twice*. Then he just pushed me down, into the mud." She shook her head, disgusted almost beyond speech. But Marla was never beyond speech. "I wish to *hell* I *had* killed him."

"But . . . where did he go?" I was incredulous, and felt a

whiff of fear. Who knew what more he was capable of? I scanned the sheds and the road below. But the shabby storehouses still looked deserted, as did the wide ribbon of mud that led away from the mine and down to Idaho Springs. "I'm still not clear on exactly what happened. How do you know he's not still around?"

Before they could answer, however, there was a sharp cracking sound. We jumped, thinking it was another gunshot. But this sound was thunder. Fat, chilly raindrops pelted out of the clouds. The general stuck out his chin. "I caught up with the dog and grabbed his collar. Then I saw the fuse. Smelled it first, actually. I saw Royce running, wearing a big backpack, holding a suitcase . . . or maybe it was a briefcase. Next thing, Marla was firing at him." He ran his fingers across his close-cropped head of pale hair. "I kept hold of the dog, but I ran like crazy after that guy. Only problem was, *he* knew where he was going, and I didn't. He escaped around there."

He pointed to the mountainside. There was a small garagelike hut on the far right side of the mine opening. I took a few steps in the thickening rain. Heading away from the garage was one set of muddy car tracks.

General Bo continued, "There's the four-wheel-drive road I told you about. Fifty feet down that hill—I checked the map. It goes to Central City, but first it crosses Highway Six heading back to Denver, so Royce could basically be anywhere." His keen blue eyes caught mine. "I called the authorities, Goldy, when the two of you were trapped inside there." He checked his watch. "At eleven hundred hours. That was thirty minutes ago."

The cold rain was turning the grime on my arms to a thin

sheen of mud. Half an hour, and not a single law enforcement or rescue vehicle had yet arrived? "Did you . . . call the Idaho Springs fire department?" I asked. "They should have been right up here."

The general glanced down the wet road. "No, I called your sheriff's department. Furman County. I said we had a dead man and two people trapped in a mine. Maybe they figured it was a hoax. But they could be here soon, if only to check it out. So, if you still want to protect Marla and keep running, we should be going—"

"We can go," I said, decisively. "But I want my son out of this mess. Now."

"We can't do both," said Marla sourly. "Come on, Arch." She put an arm around his thin shoulders. "I know where there's a shower in the shed over here. We'll get soap and water on those scrapes. We'll have a little while until the sheriff's department comes to bust me again."

Arch shot me a confused glance, but allowed himself and a damp, wriggling Jake to be led off by Marla without protest.

I asked Bo, "Did you tell the department who you were, and that you saw Tony Royce?"

"Yes, of course I did." His voice was flinty with anger. "I even said he drove off in a green Explorer, although God help me, my eyes aren't as good as they used to be, I couldn't catch the plate number."

So Tony had come up here in Albert's car. He'd thought of every detail. How long had it taken him to plan all this out? From the thinking I'd done ascending those interminable ladders in the mine, I had an idea that this faked-death scheme had been percolating in Tony's cranium for some time. He'd planned, he'd schemed, he'd set things up; he even had a backup strategy, in case anything went wrong. Marla's very public squabble with Albert at the party probably changed Tony's original time frame for his crimes, but that hadn't meant he'd abandoned his escape hatch.

"Look, Goldy," the general pleaded, "we could track him in less than a day—"

I held up a hand. "No."

I had had at least ten flights of metal rungs to think about what I was going to say to General Bo Farquhar, so I let him have it straight. "Here's my idea: I think Tony's trying to get out of the country, and for some reason he couldn't do that until this afternoon, possibly even tonight. You and I and hopefully the police can stop him, but I want Arch and Marla and the dog out of it."

He narrowed his eyes against the rain, gave a considered glance down the mountain road, then nodded. "Whatever you say. I just want this guy. I'm listening."

I shook my head. "We need to get out of here, because the Furman County Sheriff's Department probably still has it in for Marla. We need to take Marla, Arch, and the dog back to the Hardcastles' cabin. And then I'll tell you where I think Tony's headed."

The general gave me the full benefit of his commanding glare. "I hope for your sake, Goldy, that we'll have time."

"Either I've guessed his scheme or I haven't. You'll just have to trust me."

The general scowled. "Marla is the only family I have left. . . ."

"She's my oldest friend," I said quietly. "And I love her, too." In the distance, sirens sounded. "It's time to go. We've got a criminal to catch."

◆

An hour later, I watched Arch wave from the cabin stoop. Marla held up one hand in halfhearted farewell. With the other she gripped Arch's shoulder. Jake beamed with idiotic happiness as we climbed into the Jeep, probably delighted to see me go.

Then the general gunned the engine, and we catapulted back toward Bride's Creek. "Okay, what do you have in mind?" he asked, as if we were going out for dinner.

I glanced out the window at the thinning clouds. Then I asked, "Do you remember when I told you about Prospect's chief investment officer being killed in a car crash? Victoria Lear discovered that the gold ore at the Eurydice had played out. My guess is that she confronted Tony Royce with what she knew, and got killed for her pains. Then the party—that was when Marla and Albert Lipscomb had their terrible argument. They argued about an assay report from a disreputable lab. Albert didn't believe the ore was worthless, I'll bet, and he didn't know Tony was using an untrustworthy laboratory. Albert always trusted his grandfather's claims about the Eurydice still having gold in it. Whenever Marla heard about the mine, it was, 'Albert says.' Never, 'Tony says.' Never. But Tony was the person running the fraud, and in this state, gold scams are the oldest ones in the book.

"My theory is that after Marla confronted Albert about the rigged assay, Albert and *Tony* argued. Tony knew the ore he sent to the lab wasn't good. But he never thought anyone, least of all his girlfriend, would complain, after the splashy success the firm had had with Medigen."

The general turned the windshield wipers from constant to intermittent, but kept his eyes focused straight ahead. "Continue."

"So say they argue. Tony goes to Albert's house, says he

wants to talk. What do they talk about? These two men had tried to run a scam before, with their cashmere-yarn-and-goat-cheese enterprise. Maybe Albert thought they were going legit, once they'd scored with Medigen. But Tony, I now believe, wants with the mine to take their enterprises one level deeper, and he's in too far with the Eurydice to go back. Maybe Albert doesn't have time to disagree before Tony knocks him unconscious. I don't know what he used. Tom's told me even spraying someone with a can of engine starter fluid would do the trick. Anyway, once Albert is out cold, Tony works fast, packs up all Albert's stuff so it looks as if he's left town. Takes him up to the Eurydice, waits until he comes to, and then tortures him until he gets Albert's half of the combination to the safe containing the gold ore. Then Tony kills him. But Tony can't take the gold then. If he does, even Captain Shockley, who knows about the gold and the safe, could figure Tony's responsible for Albert's murder. But if, by some remote chance, Albert's body is discovered in that first week, Tony, who's still around, can say, Marla did it, she was mad at Albert, wasn't she? Everybody knows that."

The general muttered, "That guy is *such* a son of a bitch."

I went on: "Shockley did go up to the Eurydice after Albert disappeared, but without jurisdiction he didn't take the risk of going in. In any event, Tony always planned to have Marla take the fall for him. She knew too much about assays, and was too insistent on knowing the truth, to be easily shut up. But if she was busy defending herself, she wouldn't have time to try to reconstruct all that he had done. Especially if it looked as if she murdered *him* in a jealous rage, after she supposedly killed his partner. Royce figured on covering all his bases. It was a foolproof scheme.

"He gets his blood drawn by his girlfriend the med student. A Vacutainer tube has a blood preservative in it: You can keep it in the refrigerator for a week, sometimes two, and it won't coagulate. And he has ten days. He buys the bald cap. He fakes some of Albert's identification, which Tom is always telling me is fairly easy to do or get done. Then on Monday after the party, he tries to withdraw the cash from the partnership account. He can't get it that day, but he gets it on Tuesday, when he proceeds to charm the teller and then strangles her so she wouldn't identify him. Now he's got three and a half million in cash, plus two hundred-thousand in gold from the mine safe. After all, why leave it behind, when it's so easy to make someone else look responsible for the theft and murder?"

I took a deep breath. "He persuades Marla to move up the fishing trip they planned. He pretends to be interested in investing in restaurants, the new venture for Prospect Financial Partners. He leaves his fancy watch at Marla's so it'll look as if he didn't mean to be absconding permanently. And now we know how he staged his whole fake stabbing and drowning death. Unfortunately, he spotted Macguire Perkins, so he let him have it, too."

"Macguire's lucky Tony didn't kill him," the general observed grimly.

"Macguire's strong," I replied with a smile, "that's one of the reasons he's such a good catering assistant. He probably gave Tony a bit more muscle than he was expecting."

"Sounds like *you* were a bit more than Tony was expecting, too," Bo said with an answering smile.

"Yeah, I guess all of us might have been. Especially Jake. When Jake scented Tony up at the mine and howled, that was what let him know we'd really found him." I paused. "Tony always wanted something from me. And from other people, too, like his old girlfriend Eileen Tobey. He felt as if we owed it to him."

The general furrowed his brow. "Owed him what?"

"Oh, attention. Contacts." I could remember Tony's persuasive smile, the charming twinkle in his eyes. *Know any rich doctors? Guess not. Dentists? No. Plumbers? No. How about pilots?*

Pilots. Yes, I knew one. One unemployed ex-Braniff captain who had received a FedEx delivery last week of navigational maps. I had been the one who told Tony about Sandy Trotfield. I had told him, too, that Trotfield's wife—the one with the money—invested in art, but she might want to get into venture capital. Tony appeared to be interested in them as clients, but nothing more. Albert had even given them a cookbook. But I knew something else that I'd learned when the Trotfield's had booked me for last week's party: Sandy Trotfield was due in today from Rio de Janeiro. It was my guess that it was Sandy Trotfield whom Tony Royce had been waiting for. Sandy Trotfield who had acted so angry when the cops had invaded his kitchen. Sandy Trotfield who could fly Tony Royce out of the country without attracting attention, and be paid handsomely for his efforts.

All this I told the general. I looked out at the sky. The clouds were breaking up, offering a rare glimpse of a Wedgwood-blue expanse. The fast-moving front appeared to be passing through. Could this actually be happening? Could the sun truly be appearing, like Eurydice after a lengthy stint in the underworld?

The general groped under his seat for the cellular phone, found it, and punched in the numbers I told him.

"Yes," he said gruffly. "Mr. Alexander Trotfield? This is Investigator Beauregard Farquhar of the Furman County Sheriff's Department. We have a fugitive, a murder suspect, a man we believe has contracted you to fly him out of the country? Name of Anthony Royce. We need to know everything about your contact with Mr. Royce." He listened for several minutes, then gave me a thumbs up. "Furman County Airport? When? One-thirty. Your Citation. Which hangar?" Bo waited while Sandy talked. "Mr. Trotfield," Bo said urgently, "you may keep this appointment with Mr. Royce. But tell him there's been a delay. Do not act alarmed. When I arrive, please introduce me as your copilot. We will meet you at the hangar. Yes, the sheriff's department will reimburse you for all the expenses you incur. Thank you for your cooperation." He pressed a button to disconnect.

I said breathlessly, "Do you think he believed you?"

General Bo glanced at the clock on the dashboard and grimaced. "I've got an hour to buy a bomber jacket and find some dye to rub through my hair, just in case Royce got a glimpse of me at the mine, which I doubt." He reflected. "Did Trotfield believe me? I don't really care. The one I have to do a good acting job for is Royce."

I shivered. Sandy Trotfield wanted to be reimbursed for his time and effort. What a joke.

"Hey," said General Farquhar. "You better trust my acting ability, too. I'm going to need to talk my way close enough to Royce to snag him."

"Oh, yeah? And where am I going to be?"

The general's face was grim. "Nearby. Holding my gun."

Chapter 22

"No," I said quietly. "I'm not using a gun. I'm calling Tom."

Bo's glance was chilly. "You'd better not have him bring those two cops who arrested Marla."

"Don't worry."

I called; once again, Tom was not at his desk. I almost screamed with frustration, but instead left a two-sentence message on his voice mail: "The armed and dangerous person you seek is attempting to leave the country from the Furman County Airport this afternoon. We need help to catch him at Hangar C-9"

By twelve-thirty General Bo Farquhar and I had made two stops. The first was a sporting goods store in the foothills, where the general bought a leather bomber jacket and aviator sunglasses. His prominent chin held aloft, he scanned the outerwear racks as if he owned the place, and had just stopped in to pick up a new outfit in which to circumnavigate the globe. I saw him flash his thin-lipped, much-knowing smile at the female sales attendant, who predictably melted. How would he pay for his purchases, I wondered. There was probably a kidnapping charge outstanding against him, and any credit card use was sure to be traced. Well, if we were successful in trapping Tony Royce, we could worry about Marla's prison break and its consequences later.

"All I need now is a Navy pilot to give me grief," the general mumbled as we pulled up to our second stop. "They do get their noses so out of joint when a nonflyboy wears a bomber jacket."

I grinned. "I do believe Navy pilots are the least of our problems, sir."

General Bo grinned. He was loving this.

But I suddenly felt the weight of what we were about to do. The sheriff's department was twenty, perhaps twenty-five minutes from the airport. I judged we were a little less than half an hour away. This was all wrong. When I couldn't reach Tom, I should have called someone else at the sheriff's department and come clean. But thinking about Shockley made me shudder. *I just want to see Tom and Arch again,* I thought. *And maybe even Jake.*

We zipped along toward the airport. Since Furman County is mostly mountainous, the people who built the airport had been at some pains to find an area large and level enough for hangars and a runway. They'd eventually paid a rancher a staggering sum to move his herd of cattle to eastern Colorado. The starry-eyed airport builders had proceeded to divert a local brook, destroy two prairie dog villages, and pave over an elk migrating area while smoothing the rancher's fields. Then they'd failed to build hangars and purchase computers that were even close to within their budget range. The airport had not been profitable, and the resultant wrath of environmentalists and downgrading of the airport's municipal bonds had provided juicy material for *The Mountain Journal* for several years.

"Hangar C-Nine," the general muttered as we came down the incline to the south gate security fence. "Now if we can just . . . oh, for Pete's sake." He stopped the Jeep. Ahead of us a dozen cars stood motionless while a tow truck pulled a station wagon out of a large pool of rippling water. "What the hell—"

I craned my neck. "Flooding. No one's going in or out of the south gate for at least a quarter of an hour." I pointed. "That's the brook that used to go through the ranch."

"*What* ranch?"

"The ranch that used to be where the airport is."

He wheeled us in a U-turn. "Is there a north entrance to this godforsaken place? We need to find another way to C-Nine."

At my direction we raced up the state highway until we came to a sign for the small northern entrance to the airport. Like its southern counterpart, the north entrance road also sloped downward to our right.

"Ha!" exclaimed the general, triumphant. He careened the Jeep onto the road and accelerated down the hill. Just as quickly, he braked and stared at the road ahead. "Holy Mother of God." Hangar C-9 was up a hill to the right, about a hundred feet away. But the security gate and fence were underwater, claimed by the fast-rushing, no-longer-diverted brook. On the far side of the fence, the roofs of two cars were barely visible above the swirling, muddy torrent. "*Damn* this rain. How are we ever going to get around that?"

I sighed. "Fly."

Of course, I didn't think he'd take me literally. But I should have remembered who I was talking to. Bo turned the wheel sharply and gunned the Jeep off the road. Up and down we rocked, with Bo keeping a sharp eye on the water. Finally the road took us past the perimeter of the airport property. Abutting the highway was a small cliff that rose above the original brook. Over the centuries, the water had cut through the stone, so that on the far side of the brook, perhaps fifteen feet away, was another cliff. Bo expertly piloted the Jeep off the road, then brought it to a stop at the bottom of the hill that led up the cliff.

"Ready?" he asked.

"No, I'm not," I replied. "Remember the last time you and I were together on a cliff over water? With all the moisture in the rock, we could easily precipitate another slide—"

"So you're just willing to let Marla go back to jail for killing this guy who's about to split forever?"

"There must be another way—"

"There isn't. I could take a tank over that cliff. We'll make it, Goldy."

What other choice did we have? "We'd better," I told General Bo.

His face set with determination, Bo pressed the accelerator. The speedometer needle soared upward. My breath seemed permanently caught in my throat. We raced to the edge of the cliff, and then suddenly, we were airborne. My heart beat out the seconds as we flew through the air. *Oh, Tom, I'll never, ever get involved in crime again. I'll—*

We landed with a thud on the opposite cliff.

But before I had a chance to express relief, there was a deafening roar behind us. I twisted around and experienced a sight that was familiar, but still terrifying: rocks and dirt disintegrating in a landslide. Where there had been two cliffs and a picturesque brook, there was now a landfill created by an avalanche of dirt.

"Damn," murmured the general as the Jeep hurtled through the only nonflooded gate into the airport. "I just got kicked out of the Sierra Club."

Hangar C-9 was a large, pale green building with no cars parked outside. The general scanned the area, then said, "I want you to drive over to C-Seven, leave the Jeep in back. Royce might have seen this car when he ran out of the mine." He paused, his face as serious as I had ever seen it. "Goldy, I'm going to take this guy out. I don't want you involved. Watch for him from outside. Call in the troops if things get rough. I don't mean Tom, I mean the whole damn sheriff's department. Trotfield said his plane's a small jet, a Citation with the numbers four-eight-two-six Golf. I'll go into the hangar at the front. You watch for Royce or Trotfield from out here, then come in after me only if you *don't* see or hear Royce. If you do see or hear him, call the cops as quickly as possible. Last resort. With any luck, though, we've got at least fifteen minutes before they arrive." He checked the Glock. "Got that?"

I protested feebly, "Isn't the hangar locked?"

"A numbered security lock, and I got the code from Trotfield. Don't worry. You just do your job, and I'll do mine. Okay?"

I nodded and drove the Jeep to C-7, where I parked in back. The weather was finally clearing; where were all the pilots? Probably waiting to come in through the south gate. I scanned the road to C-9 for a dark green Explorer, and saw none.

I could not let the general undertake this alone. There had to be something I could do. I hopped out and sidled along the back of C-8. I listened and waited. Not a sound. I knocked on the door to C-9 and felt dizzy when the handle turned.

The barrel of the gun was pointed straight at me. "Goldy, for crying out loud," the general said amiably. He quickly holstered his gun inside his new bomber jacket.

"I want to help."

He glared at me, then pointed. "Go stand in the office behind that Gulfstream. Stay where you can get a good look at the Citation without being seen. Don't turn the light on. Check for a phone. And please, don't get involved. . . ." His head turned sharply to a sound that hadn't reached my ears. "Here he comes. Move."

I scooted into the office and scanned the space quickly. In the corner of the office was a shovel. I picked it up just as I heard Tony's all-too-familiar voice. "Excuse me? Who are you?" he demanded of General Bo. "How did you get in here?"

"I'm Trotfield's copilot," Bo announced genially. "Came in by the north gate. Glad to meet you, Mr. Royce."

No time to close the office door; it would make too much noise. Through a crack in the blinds, I saw Tony stride in wearing chinos and an expensive red leather windbreaker. His hair was perfectly blown dry, his mustache was evenly clipped. He was carrying a metal briefcase. The general gave Tony a huge smile. I gripped the shovel.

"Now all we need is Sandy," General Bo persisted in a jocular voice. "He's got the approach plates for Ordaz International, and our flight plan is already filed in the county's airport computer. Are the cars coming through the south gate pretty smoothly now?" He really appeared to be enjoying this. He even made a mock salute, before he turned and trod smartly toward the plane.

"It's not too bad. Look, we have some bags," Tony announced in a voice that indicated he expected the copilot to fetch them. But when General Bo continued toward the Citation, Tony followed. He asked mildly, "You been Sandy's copilot before? How do you think he looks with that new beard?"

The involuntary, incredulous grimace on the general's face as he turned back to face Tony sent nervous ripples up my skin. But Bo instantly wiped the look off and assumed the same easy tone. "Oh, I thought he looked better—"

But it was too late. Royce had tested Bo and he'd failed. The metal briefcase sailed up toward the general's head and caught him offguard. Bo flailed backward awkwardly and went down with a thud. He grabbed for his gun, but Tony ran forward and kicked it out of his hand. The heavy gun skittered across the hangar floor.

Oh, God, help me, I prayed. I raised the shovel and leapt for the office door. Tony trotted toward the hangar entrance. When I called his name and started to run toward him, Tony hesitated, his mouth open, stunned to see me. The caterer, of all people. And armed. . . .

Behind us, there was a shot. The general had scooted over to his weapon, fired at Tony, and missed. Startled, Tony reached inside the red windbreaker and pulled out a small gun. He took aim at the general and fired: *pop, pop, pop.* Then he walked toward the general. Two more shots reverberated.

I didn't think. I ran toward Tony and brought the shovel down with all my might. He groaned and cried out. As his body buckled, his gun sailed from his hand and landed near the hangar door. I swung the shovel down on his head. This time, he went down and did not move. Relief and anxiety mixed in a wave through my bloodstream. I struggled to catch my breath.

"My tellers will really miss their muffins," said a calm, cold voice behind me. I turned.

At the hangar door Eileen Tobey stood, holding Tony's gun. Sunlight silhouetted her muscular frame. I dropped the shovel.

"Don't, Eileen," I said. "You can't . . . I thought you *hated* Tony."

"Shut up. I'm just a great actress."

She held the gun aimed at me, but to my surprise, she didn't pull the trigger. I couldn't see her eyes. I slid my hands in my pockets.

"Get your hands out where they're visible," she said.

"I'm just looking for my keys," I told her, fighting to keep despair from my voice. "Don't you need them to get away?" I kept my hands in my pockets and started walking toward her. "The sheriff's department is going to be looking for Albert's Explorer. They know Tony killed Albert. If you take my Jeep, you'll be able to get away, far from all this."

I was three feet away from her. I stopped, both hands in my pockets, as if awaiting her response. I assumed a puzzled look. She seemed to be struggling with what I was saying about the sheriff's department and Albert's Explorer.

"So do you want the Jeep or not? Let me get medical help for General Farquhar, and you go—"

"All right," she said impatiently. She held out her left hand, and as she did so, the gun in her right hand dropped slightly. "Give me the damn keys."

Do it, I thought. I appeared to fumble in my pocket, then whipped out Jake's leash, the leash I'd put in my pocket in the mine, and swung it at her hand holding the gun. The metal bit into her hand. Startled, she dropped the gun. I flung my whole body against her. We went down together, out the hangar door.

Fury gave me an edge. I pulled Eileen's hair and whaled away like a madwoman. As I pushed her face into the dirt I heard her curse. I pushed harder, grinding her face into the mud until she stopped flailing. If only Tom could see me now. . . .

Tom said, "It's over, Miss G." His voice was angry, disappointed, relieved. "I shouldn't believe this, but I do."

My husband stood ten feet away from me, his .45 raised. When I gasped in surprise, he lowered his gun and signaled to the cops behind him to come get the woman I was sitting on.

Painfully, I stood up and allowed two policemen to cuff Eileen. To Tom, I said, "I'm sorry."

"I swear, you always say that." Two uniformed policemen rushed past us. Tom pointed at Tony Royce, who was clutching his head and cursing. The policemen swiftly handcuffed him. Ignoring his howls of pain, they led him outside.

Tom said to me, avoiding my eyes, "First we get a call saying Albert Lipscomb has been murdered and is up at the Eurydice Mine. The paramedics get there and radio back there's been some kind of an explosion. Then I pick up your message. So we hightail it out here. Good thing." Tom scanned the hangar and groaned. "Oh, Christ."

The general lay motionless on the concrete floor. While Tom barked into his radio for an ambulance, I ran over and knelt at Bo's side. Blood stained the bomber jacket and spurted to the floor. Tony had shot him.

"You can't die," I heard myself order General Bo Farquhar. My voice rang in my ears. "You can't die. Oh, please—"

The pale, pale blue eyes that I had known so well these past few years opened. "Goldy," Bo murmured. "Schulz . . . Marla didn't . . ."

"You did a great job," Tom told him, kneeling beside me.

"Marla will be cleared. Just hold on, sir." I'd never heard such respect in Tom's voice.

With enormous effort, Bo turned toward me. "I'm going to be with Adele. . . ." He raised his head feebly, then let it sink back to my lap. "I . . . you all . . . very much. . . ."

And then he died.

✦

A rescue team from the Colorado School of Mines cleared the entrance to the Eurydice Gold Mine. They brought out the corpse of Albert Lipscomb. Tony Royce was charged with, among other things, the murders of his financial partner and the First of the Rockies teller. The investigation into the death of Victoria Lear was reopened. Eileen Tobey was charged with grand larceny and being an accessory to murder.

Once Marla was cleared of wrongdoing, she called her lawyer to sue the sheriff's department for false arrest, harassment, and anything else the two of them could think of. The case against De Groot and Hersey looked very bad. At that point, the Furman County Sheriff, the boss of bosses and certainly the boss of Captain Shockley, invoked a long-standing Colorado statute, called "at pleasure." Back in the old days, when a Colorado sheriff gathered a posse and went after a criminal, he would release the deputies from duty after they caught the perpetrator. The posse served at the sheriff's pleasure, period. If he fired them, there was no appeal. There was no review. Three days after Tom apprehended Tony Royce, the Furman County Sheriff fired Investigators De Groot and Hersey. Rather than face the same fate, Captain Shockley promptly withdrew his newly recovered money from Prospect Financial Partners and took an early retirement.

His face set grimly, Tom informed me that I probably

would be charged with complicity in aiding an escape. But the female guard had actually fainted before General Farquhar hit her, just as Bo had maintained. She was fine, she told me repeatedly, and so glad to be rid of Shockley she could kiss me. So at least I wouldn't be charged with assault.

Two days later, with obvious reluctance, the District Attorney held a press conference. Because Bo, Arch, and I had helped clear up Albert Lipscomb's murder and aided in the apprehension of Anthony Royce and Eileen Tobey, there would be no charges filed against us. Despite this vindication, Marla's blood pressure went through the roof. Tony Royce, the man she loved, had deceived her, stolen her money and her heart, and killed people. And her loving brother-in-law had died trying to help her. Her cardiologist ordered her to spend a week in the hospital for tests. For once, too weary to protest, she allowed herself to be admitted, but talked her way into an early discharge so she could come with us to Bo's memorial service.

✦

A week later, the five of us—Tom, Arch, Marla, Macguire, and I, took on the responsibility of scattering the general's ashes. As his wife's ashes were scattered by Bride's Creek, we decided that would be an appropriate place for Bo's. We would take a small picnic that would include Bo's favorite food—chocolate. The bad weather had come to an end and summer had finally arrived in the high country. On a brilliantly sunny day, we piled into the newly repaired van. Of course, we took Jake, whom I now cherished like a human friend. After all, without Jake's persistence, we would never have found Tony Royce and broken his chain of crimes. From the knowing, eager expression in the dog's liquid eyes whenever he looked at me, I knew that he knew I'd had a change of heart toward him.

By the creek, we ate liverwurst sandwiches and tomatoes vinaigrette and munched Chocoholic cookies, and talked about our wonderful and dangerous times with General Bo Farquhar.

"He loved us all very much," Marla said, raising her voice above the thunder of Bride's Creek, when we'd finished our recollections. Lifting the urn above the water, she emptied the ashes into the raging water.

I said a silent prayer. I'd never known anyone like Bo Farquhar. The world would seem an emptier, less colorful place without him. Even as I thought it, Tom's fingers closed around mine.

As we turned to go back to the van, Jake flung his head up and howled. Arch tugged on his leash, but the hound wouldn't budge. Instead, Jake pointed his body in the direction of the pines and howled again, heartbreakingly. Arch shook his head, then squinted at the trees.

"Mom," he said softly. "Everybody. Look."

We turned. Moving through the sunlit trees was a solitary wisp of vapor. It seemed to have a military bearing.

Index to the Recipes

AUTHOR'S NOTE: *Plantation Pilaf and Stir-Fry Chicken with Asparagus are lowfat recipes. Banana-Pecan Muffins can be made lowfat by omitting the pecans. Cinnamon Griddle Scones can be made lowfat by cooking on a nonstick griddle lightly sprayed with vegetable oil spray, and serving without butter.*